KEPT

Also by Jami Alden

CAUGHT

UNLEASHED

Published by Kensington Publishing Corp.

KEPT

JAMI ALDEN

BRAVA

KENSINGTON PUBLISHING CORP.
http://www.kensingtonbooks.com

BRAVA BOOKS are published by

Kensington Publishing Corp.
850 Third Avenue
New York, NY 10022

All Kensington titles, imprints, and distributed lines are available at special quantity discounts for bulk purchases for sales promotion, premiums, fund-raising, educational, or institutional use.

Special book excerpts or customized printings can also be created to fit specific needs. For details, write or phone the office of the Kensington Special Sales Manager: Kensington Publishing Corp., 850 Third Avenue, New York, NY 10022, Attn.: Special Sales Department. Phone: 1-800-221-2647.

Brava and the B logo Reg. U.S. Pat. & TM Off.

ISBN-13: 978-0-7582-2547-4
ISBN-10: 0-7582-2547-4

First Trade Paperback Printing: March 2009
10 9 8 7 6 5 4 3 2 1

Printed in the United States of America

To my parents, Patty and C. B.,
who always believe in me, no matter what.
And to Gajus, for everything.

Acknowledgments

As always, I have so many people to thank, people who offered everything from brainstorming and idea generating to emotional support as I cranked this book out under the wire. First, to Bella Andre and Monica McCarty, for the daily sanity checks, endless encouragement, and help getting me out of tight spots. To the SF lunch crew—Barbara Freethy, Candice Hern, Anne Mallory, Carol Grace, Tracy Grant, Penelope Williamson, Veronica Wolff, Bella and Monica again—for helping me hammer out the details at the beginning of the book. Special thanks to Veronica, who came up with the hook, and to Penny, who reminded me to keep the body count high! To Karin Tabke, who put up with my endless heavy sighs that weekend in Tahoe. To my editor, Hilary Sares, and for the invaluable afternoon we spent locked in a room at the Marriott. And finally, thanks to my agent, Kim Whalen—your enthusiasm and support mean the world to me.

CHAPTER 1

WHERE THE HELL does she think she's going? Derek Taggart watched the woman dart around a matron dressed in a heavily beaded ball gown and a thickset older man in a tux as she made her way to the back corner of the ballroom. Derek had been tracking her movements for the past twenty minutes or so from his vantage in the gallery above, ever since a bloated, self-important toad in a tux had run his fat finger up and down her bare arm and said something that had made her smile falter and the color leach from her carefully made-up face. Even from a distance, he'd seen the way the muscles in her slim bare arm had tensed, like she'd wanted to smack the guy.

Derek found himself hoping she'd do it and was a little disappointed when her smile came back double strength as she said something and walked away. Too bad. A little tussle between a hot woman and an old lech would provide a little excitement to an otherwise snooze-worthy Saturday evening spent working security. This high-society charity function benefiting some socialite's desire to save the wetlands was so boring, Derek resisted the urge to sink into a padded, upholstered chair and settle in for a nap.

Emma Bancroft had requested Gemini; he'd gotten stuck with the assignment. Remembering her strained smile when he'd showed up a few days earlier to go over the mansion's floor plan, he wondered if she regretted it yet.

Derek couldn't blend in if he tried. Too big, too muscular, too uncomfortable in the confines of his expensive suit. He wasn't good at polite smiles and idle chitchat. He was there to do a job—mainly to make sure none of the party goers went where they shouldn't. Especially given the Bancrofts' concerns after last year's event, when several pieces of jewelry had gone missing from Emma Bancroft's bedroom as well as from the necks of several guests.

Which brought him back to Miss Thing, winding her way through the crowd, offering a smile here, an arm squeeze there, but never pausing as she moved purposefully across the room. It wasn't hard to pick her out of the throng, her slender, red-clad form moving like a lick of flame. Unlike the stiff gowns of most of the female guests, her short, silky dress left a good portion of her arms and legs bare, coming up to her throat in the front, dipping almost to her waist in the back. Even from this distance she seemed to glow, her skin and hair catching the light cast from the gaudy crystal chandelier hanging high above the ballroom.

She cast a quick glance over one silky shoulder and then ducked through a door hidden in a dark corner of the ballroom. He knew damn well she wasn't headed for the bathroom. Not only was the guest bathroom on the other end of the ballroom, but there was a low velvet rope propped in front of the door. The most polite KEEP OUT sign he'd ever seen. Now she was in a hallway that led to David Bancroft's study and a back stairway that led to the second story.

Maybe she just needed a quiet moment. Maybe not. Derek wasn't about to give her the benefit of the doubt. The last time he'd let something slide based on gender, one of his informants had ended up dead, along with his wife and two kids.

Big surprise that Derek didn't fall for the damsel-in-distress thing anymore.

Not that Miss Thing had enough room for a bomb under that dress, but the way she'd looked over her shoulder to see if anyone was watching told him she was up to something she didn't want anyone to see.

He started to speak into his headset—to tell one of his guys on the floor to check it out—and then stopped himself. Something—curiosity—nudged at him. Curiosity that had nothing to do with the supple curve of her back or her lean, tanned legs, or the silky fall of light brown hair across her shoulders, Derek thought as he moved quickly down one side of the gallery to the back stairway. He spoke quietly into his mic, alerting Alex Novascelic, the Gemini specialist who was working the main floor, to move up to the gallery to keep an eye on the crowd.

A caterer in a white shirt and black vest gave him a wary look and a wide berth as he passed. Derek did nothing to soften the expression on his face as he jogged down the stairs in hot pursuit. He was a cold, hard motherfucker, and the quicker Miss Thing realized that, the quicker she'd abandon any illegal activities she might be entertaining.

He slowed his steps as he hit the dim hallway, his feet silent on the Persian runner. As a sniper for the Army Rangers, he'd perfected the art of moving silent and undetected through all kinds of terrain.

He cornered her in Bancroft's study, taking a moment to observe her before making her aware of his presence. So far, she wasn't doing much of anything, leaning her butt up against Bancroft's desk, her fingers tunneled in her thick, sun-streaked hair as she massaged her scalp and temples.

From a distance, she'd looked attractive. Up close, she was beautiful in a slight, delicate way that didn't usually do much for Derek. He tended toward taller, sturdier, more understated types. Women who looked like they had more on their mind than what color of lip gloss to wear, women who looked like they could take care of themselves, because Derek sure as hell didn't have the time or the interest to cater to anyone's needs but his own.

But she was small and slender, like she might break if he grabbed her too hard with one of his big, calloused hands. She was leaning against the desk, but he'd bet that even in those lethal-looking heels, the top of her head wouldn't come much past his shoulder. In profile, her nose was straight and small, her chin pointy.

Dainty. Or some other stupid word you use to describe china or glass or something he could snap with one flick of his wrist.

She let out a low sigh and grabbed her minuscule purse in a sudden movement. She rummaged around, and when she pulled her hand out he could see a small metal box. She popped it open, her hands shaking slightly, and drew out a couple pills.

His mouth tightened. He wondered why the bathroom wasn't private enough to pop her pharmaceuticals.

She placed a pill in her mouth and gulped at a glass of clear liquid. Vodka? Water? Hard to tell from here.

She was lifting the other pill to her mouth when he finally spoke. "Bartender not mixing them strong enough tonight?"

She jumped from the desk, wobbling a little on her spiky heels, and the pill went skittering across the floor. "Oh, my God, you scared me!" she gasped, her hand flattened against her chest. She whirled on him, eyes big and startled, a nervous smile pulling at her lips. The impact of seeing that face head-on hit him like a Mack truck. Big green eyes framed with heavy black lashes and made smoky with makeup. A full, plump mouth glossed in a way that made it impossible for any red-blooded man not to fantasize about how it would taste under his own. How it would feel wrapped around the tip of his cock.

He jerked his thoughts out of his pants. Yeah, she was hot, but Derek never let himself be distracted by a beautiful face and a hot body. Never.

"I hate to be rude," she said, pulling her mouth into a smile that showed flawless orthodontia but didn't come close to reaching her eyes, "I came here looking for a little privacy, so if you could just give me a moment." She nodded at the door as though expecting him to turn and trot away like a little lapdog.

Entitled brat. Ethan would know how to deal with this. He'd shoot her his ladykiller grin, say something charming, and end up with the woman's phone number, if not an out-and-out invitation to spend the night in her bed.

All Derek could offer was a smile more like a baring of teeth. "If you want privacy, the restroom is right off the foyer. The Bancrofts don't want anyone back here."

She was busy searching the floor for her lost pill but spared him another phony smile. "I'm sure they won't mind."

Spotting the pill, she knelt down to retrieve it. Derek couldn't help but admire the subtle ripple of lean muscle under the golden skin of her bare thigh. This time he couldn't stop his fingers from tugging at his collar.

His eyes drifted back to her face as she straightened. Her fake smile faded as those green eyes stared into his with a knowing look. She cocked her hip, deliberately taunting him. "Was there something else you wanted?"

His mind spun with a thousand different scenarios, each one more spine-meltingly hot than the last. What the fuck was wrong with him tonight, getting all jacked up and spun out from the taunts of a pampered society girl? "Listen, sweetheart, you need to find another place to pop your pills. The Bancrofts hired me to keep guests confined to the ballroom, and I'll do it if it means I have to carry you out over my shoulder."

Her lips parted in surprise, as though no one ever had the nerve to talk to her like that. Then her mouth tightened as she gave up any pretense of friendliness. "It's ibuprofen," she said, holding the pill up for his inspection. "And I was just drinking water, okay? The last thing I need is some rumor starting that I'm popping pills."

"It's not my business what you take—"

"It's everyone's business," she said, her voice sharper now. "Don't you know who I am?"

He rolled his eyes. "You know how many times I've heard that at parties like this? Now be a good girl and go duck into the bathroom for privacy like everyone else."

She swallowed her second ibuprofen before taking a few steps closer to him. She stared at him, an almost wondrous expression in her eyes. "You really don't know who I am?"

Her full, glossy mouth curled into a smile, a real one this time that made her eyes crinkle and tip up at the corners.

"Should I?" he said, in less of a hurry than he should have been to get her out of the off-limits study and back out to the crowd.

The pouty frustration disappeared from her face, giving way to a self-deprecating smile that worked its way into his chest and slid down to curl low in his belly. "No," she said with a throaty laugh. "No, you really shouldn't. I'm Alyssa Miles," she said, offering her hand.

It was small, fine boned, and slender as the rest of her, tipped with short, manicured nails and decorated with a canary-yellow diamond ring on her middle finger. He automatically reached out his own, swallowing her hand in his broad palm and long fingers. "Derek Taggart."

Her skin was hot, unnaturally so. Heat from her hand flowed into his, racing up his arm, pulsing thickly in his groin, fusing his skin to hers as he momentarily lost track of space and time. Desire like nothing he'd ever felt before grabbed hold of him as this slip of a girl threatened to make him lose his mind.

The realization was like a bucket of icy water dumped over his head. He jerked his hand away. "Nice to meet you, Miss Miles, but you really should be getting back to the party." He moved behind her, keeping careful distance as he ushered her out, grateful that his suit jacket hung down far enough to hide the telltale bulge behind his fly.

You need to get laid. He'd brushed aside Ethan's snide comment and Danny's nod of agreement last week, reminding them both that meaningless sex with a stranger wasn't everyone's solution to everything from boredom to the common cold. Derek had needs like any other healthy, heterosexual thirty-two-year-old male, but he didn't like to slake them with just anyone.

But, shit, his reaction to the touch of Alyssa's hand was enough to make him reconsider. It *had* been a while. He'd had a nice friends-with-benefits thing going for a long time with his friend Melissa, when the woman had up and done the unthinkable and fallen in love with some guy she was dating and promptly cut off Derek's supply to convenient no-strings sex.

That had been almost a year ago, and he still hadn't found a viable candidate to fill her place.

As he watched the subtle bounce and sway of Alyssa's ass under the crimson silk of her midthigh-length skirt, his body begged, pleaded, demanded that she be the one to break his dry spell.

The need churning in his body was unexpected and wholly unwelcome in its intensity.

He'd forced his body and emotions into submission a long time ago, settling into a state of distance, an alert numbness that suited him just fine.

Now one touch of this woman's abnormally warm hand,

and he felt like he'd been jerked kicking and screaming back into reality.

All the more reason to get the hell away from her, take another step back from her, and force his gaze from the smooth skin of the backs of her thighs up over her head, past her down the hall. But he could still smell her perfume, fresh and flowery, mingling with the scent of sweet woman skin.

She paused at the door leading to the ballroom. He reached around her to open it, taking a long, indulgent inhale before cutting himself off cold turkey. She stared out into the crowd and straightened her shoulders, bracing herself as though going into battle.

He remembered the sleazy guy with his fat fingers running along the pristine smoothness of her skin, and something else surged in his gut to twist and tangle with the desire that had taken hold and wouldn't let go. He fought the urge to put himself between her and the crowd, protect her from whatever dragons she might face.

"Have a nice evening, miss," he said, an unsubtle hint for her to get back to the party. And the hell away from him.

She gave him a last, almost wistful look over one bare, creamy shoulder. "It was nice to meet you, Derek."

As she turned back to the crowd, her expression changed. The megawatt smile was still there, but it was tight, strained, and about as genuine as Pam Anderson's boobs, but no one else seemed to notice as she started to work her way through the crowd.

His lips curled in a knowing smile. Despite her fragile appearance, Miss Thing could take care of herself. Good thing, too. Derek knew he was too much of a coldhearted bastard to slay any woman's dragons.

"Where have you been?" Alyssa's stepmother, Grace Van Weldt, hissed in Alyssa's ear. Her reaction to her stepmother was the same as to a snake. Her blood went cold, her lungs tightened until she couldn't take a breath, and a sick pit of anxiety knotted in her stomach. The headache that had tightened around the base of her skull shortly after they'd arrived at the Bancrofts' charity ball redoubled, pounding through her temples with a force that nearly brought her to her knees.

She closed her eyes and prayed for the ibuprofen to take effect. If only she could have stayed a little longer in the seclusion of David Bancroft's study, maybe she would have had a chance.

"You're supposed to be modeling our auction item," Grace said, taking Alyssa's arm in a painful grip. "People aren't going to bid on these"—she yanked Alyssa's arm up so the four-carat-yellow-diamond ring and matching bracelet caught the light—"if you're not working the crowd like you're supposed to."

Alyssa kept her mouth shut, refusing to explain to her stepmother that she'd been doing a damn good job working the crowd, dazzling everyone with her witty conversation and even more dazzling jewels, doing exactly what she had done for the past six months as the face of Van Weldt Jeweler's campaign "Diamonds for All." Using her notoriety as one of America's most famous party girls to sell diamond jewelry to the masses.

And everything had been going just fine until that sleazoid Mort Zimmer had sent his wife off to fetch him a drink so he could assault Alyssa with a come-on that was nearly as offensive as his breath.

"I love the latest ads," he'd wheezed, referring to the most recent photos featuring Alyssa, naked from the waist up, shot from behind with five strands of diamonds set in platinum chains draped down the length of her back. She'd thought the shot was beautiful, sexy, but tasteful and classy.

The way Mort was leering at her, it might as well have been a spread in *Penthouse*.

But it got worse from there. "Of course, my favorite shots of you are of the more . . . candid variety." His mouth had slackened with booze and lust, and he'd reached out a fat, maggoty finger to touch the bare skin of her arm.

She knew exactly what he was referring to. It had been over a year since her ex had posted those photos, and people— even supposedly sophisticated, filthy rich men like Mort Zimmer—still thought it was awesome fun to throw them in her face at every turn. Alyssa had wanted to punch him, to bury her small fist in his sweaty, piggy face, but of course she couldn't. After all the work she'd done to prove to her father that she'd cleaned up her act, that she was worthy of his attention and affection, worthy of being accepted into his real family, she wasn't about to risk it all by getting into a public brawl with one of San Francisco's most prominent real estate developers.

"Are you even listening to me?" Grace asked, her face right next to Alyssa's, the scent of vodka like a physical presence on the older woman's breath. People who claimed vodka didn't have an odor hadn't been around Grace Van Weldt after four martinis.

Alyssa resisted the urge to jerk her arm from her step-mother's grip. *No public scenes.* That had been her mantra for the past six months, and she was sticking to it. Her temples throbbed so hard her knees almost buckled. Even if it killed her. "I'm sorry, Grace," she said, softening her tone with an appropriate level of contrition. "I needed a breather from the crowd."

"Ha!" Grace barked, drawing a few stares. Despite Alyssa's father's efforts to maintain an appearance of happy family harmony—scandal-courting illegitimate daughter and all— it was no great secret that Grace despised Alyssa and what she represented: Oscar Van Weldt's brief affair with the model and actress Alexis Miles. Or, as the press liked to call her, "Sexy Lexy."

Grace would have been content to look the other way and go on as before, had Lexy not turned up pregnant, insisting Oscar support both her and her child in a style she knew he could more than afford. Grace's animosity was nothing new. The first time Alyssa had met her stepmother at the age of four at her father's insistence, Grace had waited until everyone had left the room and then pulled Alyssa aside. "If I had my way, you would have been a stain on some doctor's examining table." The most chilling part was the smile that had never left her face.

Grace wore the same smile now, though the vodka caused it to blur around the edges. She was a master at that—saying the most horrible things to a person, a cool, perfectly composed smile on her face the entire time.

Alyssa tried to follow her stepmother's lead, though the building headache made it almost impossible. "I still haven't been over by the buffet, Grace, so if you would excuse me—"

"Is everything okay?" Alyssa's half sister, Kimberly Van Weldt, put her hand over her mother's and gently but firmly removed it from Alyssa's wrist. "Mother, Chandler Tate-Wallace was asking about the ring. Why don't you freshen your drink, and I'll take Alyssa over to her."

Grace muttered something about having to take care of her own drink but started off in the direction of the bar.

"Where's Chandler?" Alyssa asked, scanning the ballroom for the woman.

Kimberly smiled conspiratorially and waved a slender, perfectly manicured hand. "Oh, that was just an excuse to get Mother to leave you alone."

"Thank you," Alyssa replied, feeling her headache ease infinitesimally, and gave her sister's arm a grateful squeeze. When her father had proposed his plan to shoehorn Alyssa into both the Van Weldt jewelry empire and the family business, Alyssa hadn't expected an ally in the half sister she'd met exactly twice in her life.

But Kimberly had been shocking in her welcome. Despite her cool reserve and ice-queen good looks, she'd welcomed Alyssa with relatively open arms. Sure, she was still a little reserved, but considering she'd been born with a silver spoon in her mouth and a stick up her butt, she'd turned out to be surprisingly cool as far as Alyssa could tell.

Tall and elegant in her silvery blue strapless taffeta gown, pale blond hair in a sleek knot, and Van Weldt diamonds glittering at her throat and ears, Kimberly was the polar opposite of Alyssa. Where Alyssa was constant, kinetic energy and impulsiveness, Kimberly was cool elegance and reserve. While Alyssa's antics had been splashed across the covers of every major tabloid in the US and Britain, Kimberly had never so much as received a parking ticket.

So when Kimberly had stepped willingly into the role of big sister, Alyssa had glommed on without hesitation, hoping some of Kimberly's composure and control would rub off enough to make her father proud of her.

Alyssa glanced around the massive ballroom and saw her father's stocky, tuxedoed form as he spoke to the party's host. Grace had caught up with him and clutched his arm, probably to steady herself because the woman wasn't prone to shows of public affection.

Oscar looked and caught Alyssa's gaze. His face creased in a smile, and he waved her over. Her stomach clenched in nervous anticipation as she worked her way through the crowd. She'd grown so accustomed to his disapproval it was still hard for her to believe she would receive anything other than a harsh lecture when she reached his side.

But Oscar reached for her hand and brushed a brief, dry kiss on her cheek. It was as much affection as he showed anyone, and Alyssa's soul sucked it up like a desert drinking rain.

"You look very lovely tonight," he said, "and you are doing a beautiful job displaying the jewels."

Alyssa ignored Grace's scoffing laugh and slurred comment about other things Alyssa had displayed. Her father had just given her the kind of praise she'd been craving every day of her twenty-four years. She wasn't about to let Grace ruin it. "Thank you, Daddy," she said with extra emphasis for Grace's benefit. Usually she tried to have empathy for the woman's position—it had to suck to have to deal with your husband's illegitimate child—but sometimes Alyssa couldn't resist getting in a dig of her own. She held up her right wrist, adorned with a platinum cuff encrusted with diamonds. "But I think a warthog could be wearing these pieces and still get a good price."

"You make them glow," Oscar said. "That is why the campaign is so successful."

Pleased heat rose in her cheeks. She knew damn well the campaign was successful because of her notoriety, but it felt pathetically good to hear her father say different.

"Speaking of the campaign," her father continued, "I would like you to come to the house for breakfast tomorrow. I have things I need to discuss with you."

The warmth fled, and anxiety took over at the sober tone of his voice. "Is something wrong?" She racked her brain, going over her every move in the last week, wondering if she'd done anything to embarrass herself or the family. "Have I—"

He cut her off with an absent pat to her hand. "You have done nothing, but we need to have a talk." His watery blue eyes got a sad, faraway look.

"Okay," Alyssa said, uneasy despite her father's assurance that she hadn't done anything—this time.

Another guest, a prominent venture capitalist, came up and shook Oscar's hand. Instantly the distracted look was gone as Oscar smiled and greeted the man and his wife.

Alyssa took that as her cue to work the room, pimping the Van Weldt diamonds like a good little girl.

She flitted around the room, her bright smile fixed, teeth

gritted as she made inane conversation, laughed at stupid jokes, pretended not to notice the stares, the whispers, the snide comments behind her back.

It's worth it, she reminded herself, holding her father's small bit of praise close to her heart.

But it didn't make it any easier. When she'd moved up here from Los Angeles, she'd hoped for a new beginning. A clean slate away from the crazy spectacle she'd let her life become. Unfortunately four hundred miles wasn't nearly enough distance to wipe away the stupid things she'd done in her past, especially when her stupidity was well documented by international media outlets.

Someday I will prove myself. Someday these people will stop thinking they're better than I am.

Her temples throbbed again, and she felt a wild churning in her chest—the rising need to do something wild, something silly, something that would really knock this staid crowd of muckety mucks on their asses. The urge that made her want to give the world the finger and say, "If you're going to stare, I may as well give you something to look at."

The same impulse that, at the age of eighteen, had made her strip down to her bra and thong and do a swan dive off her mother's boyfriend's yacht in full view of the paparazzi lurking around Miami. The same impulse that had made her switch costumes with an exotic dancer last year so she could show off her pole-dancing skills.

The same impulse that had convinced her it would be fun to let her boyfriend, Eddie, take racy pictures of her for his own private enjoyment.

Unfortunately Eddie's idea of "private" included his Face-Place page, where he had about eight bazillion "friends."

She'd learned the hard way to ignore the devil on her shoulder who liked to egg her on, screaming, "This will be so great!" Yeah, it usually was great, and fun, and funny, for an hour, a day, even weeks. Until the rest of the world weighed in and called her a vapid idiot. And that was one of the nicer articles.

So Alyssa had been ignoring the urge for wild rumpus of late, both to please her father and for her own well being. She was twenty-four now, and it was time to stop acting like a child in constant need of attention.

Don't I know it, she thought as she felt the eyes of the crowd boring into her skin.

Through it all, she felt another pair of eyes. Hard and so hot they burned her from the inside out.

Alyssa nodded at the elderly woman who said something about the size of the diamond on Alyssa's finger, but her gaze strayed once again to the gallery where he stood.

This time she caught him looking at her. Her lips curved in a smile when he looked away.

Derek Taggart. His name suited him. Hard and tough with plenty of sharp edges. He was beautiful in a way that reminded her of the harsh granite faces of the Grand Tetons. Rugged and chiseled, with great eyes, square jaw, and cheekbones that stood out beneath his skin.

One look at him, and she knew he wasn't a party guest. She would have noticed him immediately if he'd been in the crowd. His size alone would have drawn her attention. He wasn't merely tall, he was huge, towering over her, but from what she could tell it was all hard muscle. But it didn't take a psychic to see he wasn't part of this crowd, that he was here to work and he took his job very, very seriously.

She watched him, stationed up on the gallery like a sentry guarding a tower, his weight going from foot to foot as he surveyed the crowd, ready to spring into action at the slightest provocation. The jacket of his suit pulled tight as he folded his massive arms across his chest. His gaze slid back to her, and even from across the room and one story down, she could feel its heat. It unknotted the tension in her neck, slid down her spine, and sent a warm glow shimmering down her thighs.

This time he didn't break the stare, and it was she who reluctantly turned away. She continued to work the room, shilling for silent auction bids on the small fortune in diamonds that adorned her finger and wrist. Through it all she could feel him looking at her, his gaze like firm, warm fingers tracing over her skin.

Being stared at wasn't new. She'd lived in a fishbowl her entire life, first thanks to her mother's and then to her own publicity-attracting antics. Yes, sometimes it chafed, never more than recently, but Alyssa had grown so used to being looked at, watched, and judged she was almost immune to it.

". . . disgusting. Mindy is sixteen, and because of Alyssa Miles she thinks it's okay to go around dressed like a whore and sleeping with everyone in sight."

The snippet of conversation pierced Alyssa's warm glow. Almost immune.

Alyssa turned and gave the woman a guileless smile as if she hadn't heard a single barb.

She blocked out the woman's comments, instead focusing on him. His stare, sliding over her like a hot flame. He wanted her. She could feel it. That, too, was nothing new. Not because she was extraordinarily beautiful. But she knew she had her appeal and had played up her image as a sultry, playful sexpot in the press. Now it was all but guaranteed that men looked at her and thought of only one thing.

But this was different. Derek was different.

He had no idea who she was.

A delicious thrill had shot through her the moment realization had dawned in the study. When he walked into the room, all her senses had gone on high alert. Not only was he a strange man, he was an *attractive* strange man. No. Scratch that. A smoking-hot-set-the-skin-of-your-inner-thighs-on-fire man. The last thing she wanted was for him to notice her reaction to his dark, sun-streaked hair, chiseled jaw, and acres of muscles.

So when he'd tried to hustle her back to the party, she'd done what she always did in those situations. Put on her "don't you know who you're dealing with" act and tried to shoo him away like the insignificant insect she pretended to think he was.

But he wasn't having any of it. He didn't care who she was. Because he didn't know who she was.

He hadn't so much as quivered an eyelash when she'd told him her name. She couldn't remember the last time that had happened.

Derek, who was already a blatant ten, had shot up to fifteen on the hotness scale. When he shook her hand she'd felt scorched all the way down to her red toenails.

And he felt it, too. She could see the surge of awareness in his eyes, the blast of desire, quickly shuttered by his dark gaze. But he couldn't hide it. Not completely.

The thrill shot through her again, and it was all she could do to keep still as another socialite held Alyssa's arm so the woman's husband could admire the platinum cuff. Derek wanted her. And not like other men wanted her. He didn't want the crazy-sexy party girl or the notorious heiress.

He didn't want to fuck her so he could brag to his friends and the media about how he'd nailed Alyssa Miles and it really wasn't all that great after all.

He didn't want to fuck her so she could introduce him to a producer, a director, or a record-label executive.

Derek Taggart looked at her and saw a gorgeous girl he'd met at a fancy party and wanted to get with. As simple as that.

Sure, he probably saw her as a rich bitch—her initial response ensured that, much to her regret. But she could get past that. Her public persona was another beast entirely. It wasn't an image she cultivated, but once established she used it to her advantage and had thought she'd made peace with the fact that it would forever taint every interaction she had with another human being.

But she felt a gut-deep thrill from knowing a man like Derek wanted her. Not the image. She couldn't remember the last time anyone had wanted her for herself.

There was nothing to be done about it, though. As the night wore on, Alyssa didn't have another opportunity to speak to Derek, even though she knew he tracked her every move. She considered sneaking back to the study, just to see if he'd chase her down, but as the silent auction drew to a close she was surrounded by guests who all wanted one last look at Van Weldt Jeweler's exquisite designs.

"I'm going to walk Mother and Daddy out." Kimberly leaned down to speak quietly into Alyssa's ear.

"But they haven't even done the auction yet," Alyssa said, frowning. She knew her father would want to stay and find out how much his donated jewels had fetched.

"I know," Kimberly replied, her voice lowering so no one else could hear. "But I'm afraid Mother is about to lose it."

Alyssa looked across the ballroom, where Grace clung to Oscar's arm. As Alyssa watched, Grace weaved, barely noticeable to the untrained eye. Her social smile was gone, and her mouth was pursed tight.

"Oh, and I reminded Bryan to pick you up in the back by the servants' entrance so you won't have to deal with the photographers."

Alyssa nodded, grateful her sister had remembered. In the past six months, Alyssa had done a complete one-eighty with the press. Now, unless she was with her family or doing publicity on behalf of the company, she avoided reporters like the plague.

Which only served to make her a more tempting target. She knew that along with the hired photographer there were dozens of paparazzi outside the Bancrofts' mansion in Atherton, waiting for a glimpse of Alyssa, hoping she'd do something stupid like slip and fall and lose her top or show her underwear.

Finally the auction was over, and most of the guests were milling around the front door, waiting for their cars and limos to arrive.

Alyssa did another scan of the room, tamping down her disappointment when she didn't see Derek. *Stupid. What do you think is going to happen?*

She closed her eyes, memorizing his face, taking that memory of desire in his eyes and curling it close.

She retrieved her coat from the coat check and slipped out the back entrance, down the short driveway that led to the street on the side of the house opposite the front door.

And waited. She looked at her watch. It was still early, not even ten. But the crowd at these things always skewed older, and Alyssa figured they all needed to get home and tucked into bed before midnight.

Another ten minutes passed, and Bryan, the driver from the car service, still wasn't there. Annoyed, she flicked open her cell phone and called.

Bryan's town car had been clipped on the freeway. Another car was en route, but it would be at least a half hour before it arrived.

Alyssa bit back a curse.

"What's up with you going where you're not supposed to?"

The deep, gruff voice slid around her, grabbed her, and wouldn't let go. She couldn't have held back her smile if she'd wanted to.

His eyes were hidden in shadow, but his mouth curved

into a half smile, and a dimple creased the left corner of his mouth. His lips were firm and full, and she knew they'd be hot against her skin.

"Do I even want to know why you're hanging out at the servants' entrance looking like you're about to stick your thumb out?"

"I didn't want to have to deal with the crowd on my way out. And now my driver got into an accident, so it looks like I'm stranded for a while."

He was silent for several moments, and though his eyes were shadowed she could feel him studying her.

Ask me.

"Can I give you a ride home?" He almost looked shocked that he'd asked.

She didn't let that stop her. "Sure," she said without hesitation.

A slight frown creased his forehead, but he gave her a curt nod and left without another word to get his car.

As she waited she shifted on her sky-high heels, restless, alive with anticipation. After so many months on her best behavior, a reckless urge was pulsing through her. Uncontrollable, unstoppable. She needed to forget the consequences and do something outrageous.

But this time it wouldn't be for attention, publicity, or her father's censure. This time it would be all for herself. She'd been so good, watching her every move for so long. Surely she deserved a little treat?

A silver Audi rumbled up to the driveway, and Alyssa wasted no time sliding into the passenger seat. The leather was cool against her bare thighs, and the interior of the car was full of his cedar and soap scent.

He backed out of the driveway and turned the corner, passing the snarl of limos and guests crowding the circular driveway of the Bancrofts' estate.

"Where to?"

Nerves warring with desire, Alyssa rummaged in her bag and dug out her lip gloss, slicking on a coat to give herself something to do.

Derek stopped at a stop sign. "Where are we going?"

She swallowed hard, her throat suddenly bone dry. What she was about to do was crazy. Stupid.

Necessary.

"You know, it's so early," she said and turned to face him. She kept her eyes locked with his and placed her hand deliberately on his thigh. "And I'm not quite ready to go home."

He stared at her hard for what felt like an eternity. His thick, dark brows drew together in a harsh scowl.

Her stomach bottomed out as she realized he was about to turn her down.

"You want to get a drink somewhere?"

The moment of truth. She slid her hand farther up his thigh, delighting in the swells and ripples of rock-hard muscle hidden beneath wool gabardine. "I'm not much for crowds. Why don't you just take me back to your place?"

Outside Mbuji-Mayi, Democratic Republic of the Congo.

Martin Fish checked his watch again and peered around the corner of the abandoned shack. Fifteen minutes. Marie Laure was fifteen minutes late. Martin dug a bandanna from the pocket of his cargo shorts and wiped the sweat already beading his brow. Though it wasn't even seven AM, the equatorial sun was already brutally hot, shimmering on the tin roofs that sent rusty streaks down the brightly colored shacks they sheltered.

The smell of cooking fires and jungle rot permeated the air, mingling with the stench of human waste. Nausea boiled in his stomach, mingling with tension as he nervously fingered the silver oxide batteries in his pocket. He was down to the last two disks, and Marie Laure was supposed to meet him here at six thirty to take them in exchange for a one-pound bag of lentils Martin had stolen from the nearby Population Services United mess hall.

Another bead of sweat trickled down his cheek, itching its way through his scruffy beard growth. He wondered if this was the day Mekembe had turned his wrath on Marie Laure.

And God help them both if Mekembe found the hidden camera and microphone. Mekembe would torture her until she gave him Fish's name, and then he'd kill Fish and whomever was unlucky enough to be in the vicinity.

The sound of footsteps and low conversation approached, and he shrank farther back into the shadows. In this part of the world, it wasn't safe for anyone, much less a white man, to be off on his own, skulking around the makeshift living quarters surrounding an unsanctioned diamond mine.

Mekembe and his men were savages, less civilized than the animals that ruled the jungle around them. Hopped up on palm wine and cocaine, they'd hack him to death with rusty machetes for the pure fun of it.

The shanty village surrounding the mine was just coming awake, workers scraping together a meager breakfast to fuel another day of backbreaking labor. Sipping from their canteens, they looked uneasily over their shoulders as soldiers for the People's Freedom Movement—some of them no more than twelve years old—emerged from their shacks, brandishing Kalashnikov machine guns as casually as they would a coffee cup.

If she didn't show up soon, he'd have to bail. He needed to get back to the relative safety of the PSU before anyone got a bead on him.

Fuck. He needed to pass off the batteries and retrieve the latest footage from Marie Laure. In the past three weeks since he'd set her up with a pinhole camera hidden in an unremarkable bead pendant, she'd provided him with some amazing footage of life in the diamond mine controlled by Mekembe.

But it still wasn't enough to make people care about the horrors of life in this godforsaken part of the world. Not enough to make people care about Martin Fish and what he was doing hiding out in the civil-war-torn DRC, disguised as a caseworker with Population Services United, an NGO with operations all throughout the DRC. He was aiming to be the next Bob Woodward, and he wasn't going to get that from a few hours of footage showing men slaving in horrific working conditions and women and girls being abused by their captors.

Heartbreaking though it was, these days it didn't rate more than a single column buried in the back of the world news section.

Meanwhile, Bernstein, AKA Charlie Farris, had long since sold out. When he and Martin had met in journalism school a hundred years ago, they were going to revolutionize the media. Bring it back to real news; show the world the truth about what was happening in the world.

Unfortunately all the world cared about was bimbos like Alyssa Miles and whether they were going to flash a beaver shot as they exited a cab. Charlie had accepted that years ago and left Martin and their self-run hard-news Web site in the dust.

Now Charlie lived in a house in the Hollywood hills, thanks to an awesome money shot he'd scored three years ago. It was of Alyssa Miles at Cedars-Sinai Medical Center, IV in her arm and a tube down her throat as the doctors struggled to save her life after she'd done one too many lines and gone into cardiac arrest. Charlie had had the only pictures of her in the hospital, and every fucking news outlet in the country had wanted them. With one picture, good old Charlie was set for life.

At the time, Martin had been in Afghanistan, trying to

avoid land mines as he sent daily dispatches buried three layers down on *Newsweek*'s Web site.

Over the years, Charlie had kept prodding him to give up the hard news, take the easy way out, but Martin knew he wasn't cut out for that. Charlie could still turn on the charm, make nice with the brainless contingent that populated the entertainment elite. But after years observing and chronicling the most godforsaken people and places on earth, that kind of life had sunk into Martin's pores, never releasing its clutches on his consciousness even when he got back to the first world. When he was in some third world hellhole, he couldn't wait to get back to working sewers, running water, and good whiskey that wouldn't ruin your guts like the local brew. But when he was home, he couldn't squelch the disgust he felt with people, their bloated white, ignorant faces. Sitting on their fat Wal-Mart–clad asses watching Alyssa Miles make a fool of herself on TV, with no fucking clue what was really going on in the world.

They'd have a clue soon enough. Alyssa Miles was about to make his career, just as she'd once made Charlie's.

Martin knew that to make his name he had to tie this operation to something—or someone—big. Van Weldt Jeweler was definitely big. And so was Louis Abbassi. While the press went crazy talking about that famous-for-nothing Alyssa Miles and her latest campaign for Van Weldt, they ignored the fact that Van Weldt had entered a supply agreement with Abbassi, a man who had made his fortune in the late nineties and two years ago had purchased a diamond-cutting operation headquartered in South Africa.

But no one seemed to care where Abbassi's diamonds came from, including Oscar Van Weldt. Martin had interviewed the CEO of Van Weldt right before he'd left for the DRC, under the guise of doing a fluff piece about marketing fine jewelry to the youth market. When Martin had probed Oscar about the deal with Louis and suggested some of his rocks were sourced from unsanctioned mines, Van Weldt had clammed up quick, threatening Fish with a libel suit if he so much as hinted that Van Weldt diamonds were dirty.

Martin hadn't expected anything different, but it made it that much more entertaining to expose Van Weldt's dirty secret. His lip curled when he thought of the ad campaign featuring Alyssa Miles draped in nothing but sparkling stones. He wondered what she'd do when she found out she might as well have been covered in blood.

Alyssa Miles at the center of a blood diamond scandal. And Martin Fish would be front-page news for breaking the story.

But first he needed Marie Laure's help to get him the footage he needed to give the story that heartbreaking dose of reality.

"Monsieur Fish?"

He sighed in relief when he heard Marie Laure's soft greeting. She shot a furtive glance over her shoulder before emerging from the shadow. Her eyes were huge and dark in her thin face. Spindly arms poked from the sleeves of her dress, her legs covered by a colorful ankle-length skirt. She shuffled forward on bare feet. "I am sorry to be late," she said in her lilting English. "My husband was slower to go out this morning."

Husband. Now, that was a euphemism if he'd ever heard one. Mekembe had stolen Marie Laure during a raid on their village nearly a year ago. In the course of the raid, her parents and younger sister had been killed, her younger brother taken captive and impressed into service for the People's Freedom Movement.

Marie Laure, an uncommonly pretty sixteen-year-old with smooth, coffee-colored skin and fine sculpted features, had been chosen by Mekembe to be his "wife."

Which Martin knew was code for sex slave. But it meant she had only one rapist to endure.

And uncommon access to Mekembe and those who helped him move the diamonds over the border.

"Give me the necklace," he said, reaching for it even as she slipped it over her head, careful not to dislodge the blue and white scarf wrapped around her head. "It's late. I'll be lucky to make it back to the camp without anyone seeing me."

He ignored the stab of guilt in his chest as she lowered her gaze and hunched her shoulders and quickly replaced the battery in the pendant.

She slipped it back over her head and reached for the bag of lentils.

"Uh-uh," Martin said, holding it just out of reach. "Before I give you this, you need to promise you'll get me footage of the next shipment."

Her full lips tightened. "Monsieur, I do what I can, but he sends me out when they are meeting—"

"Peek in the window, hide under the bed, for all I care. But if you want to get you and your baby out, you'll get me the access I need."

Her thin, long-fingered hand curved protectively over the small bulge of her belly pushing insistently against the worn cotton of her dress. "I heard him talking to someone on his handphone. Someone important, someone they call the *Français,* is coming in next week."

Martin barely kept his jaw from falling open. He couldn't possibly be this lucky. "The Français? You're sure of that?" He tried not to get too excited. No doubt a lot of shady characters of the mixed French persuasion did business in this part of the world. How likely was it that he would come here in person? Still, his insides churned with anticipation. "You get me footage of him, and I promise I'll get you out on the next transport to Kinshasa."

"And my brother, too," she said, losing her timidity.

"I'll do what I can," he said, knowing her brother was a lost cause. Finagling a pregnant teenage girl a spot on the helicopter was difficult enough, if not impossible. He still wasn't sure he could live up to that promise.

But he shoved aside his guilt as he handed over the bag of lentils and watched Marie Laure disappear around the corner, her bare feet silent in the red dirt. Even if he couldn't save one pregnant girl, if he broke the story the way he wanted, it would bring the plight of thousands like Marie Laure and her brother to the world's attention. If she had to be sacrificed to save thousands, so be it.

Martin sipped at a mug of malafu as he reclined on his canvas cot. He took another slug, wincing at the taste of the bitter local brew, but he'd learned the best way to consume palm wine was to power through the first couple glasses. Then you barely tasted the rest of the bottle.

He fumbled under his cot for a refill, nearly upsetting the notebook computer on his lap as his fingers twisted in the netting surrounding his bed. As accommodations went, a canvas tent in the PRC encampment wasn't much, but at least he had a net to keep the bugs out, a modicum of privacy to do his work, and access to a generator to keep his batteries charged. Add his satellite modem into the mix for easy Internet access, and, really, what more did he need?

Sweat trickled down his neck, but he barely felt the itch as the malafu flowed thick and warm through his blood. He posted his latest article onto his news site, FishBait.org, and checked the traffic stats. *Fuck.* Only a thousand goddamn people had bothered to read his news in the last month. Might as well have been zero.

Why do you waste your time? The voice in his head started out as his own and then morphed as it echoed around his head, becoming his ex-wife's, his daughter's, his parents— All the people he'd disappointed in the past two decades, angry at him for not being there because he was too busy chasing a story. Pissed that he wouldn't give it up and settle for some desk job writing business news for some bullshit paper in podunk USA.

Then another, smug voice. *Why do you waste your time?* Charlie's. Arrogant fucker. Martin surfed over to Charlie's site, creatively titled Celebzone. The glow from his screen cast an eerie light against the dark canvas walls of his tent. Outside he heard scuffing footsteps in the dirt, snippets of muffled conversation as aid workers made their way to their tents after a long day of trying to save a part of the world beyond saving.

Little of it registered as Martin stared, transfixed at the images on the screen. Headlining Charlie's site was a non-story about Alyssa Miles attending a charity event up near San Francisco. The story itself was nothing—a single paragraph on what Alyssa wore and something about tension between her and her stepmother.

What mesmerized him were the pictures that ran alongside. Alyssa, long hair spilling down a back left bare by her flame-colored silk dress, the hard glitter of diamonds at her wrists and fingers.

Below that was a picture from the latest "Diamonds for All" campaign, featuring a nearly naked Alyssa with cold, hard stones trailing down the curve of her spine. Martin swallowed hard. Resentful as he was at Alyssa and the dumbed-down culture she represented, even he had to admit there was something about her. An appeal, an allure, a natural charisma that went beyond beauty to draw people's attention, even though she'd never done a single useful thing to deserve it.

He stared at the photo, her pale gold skin giving off a glow, her eyelashes a thick fringe as she kept her eyes downcast, fixed on a point to the right of her shoulder. Most people thought the glow of her skin was a trick of airbrushing, but Martin had seen her in person and knew for a fact it wasn't. She really was that pretty, that flawless.

A perfect, empty shell.

He traced his finger over the screen as if he could feel her skin. Feel the cold bite of the diamonds trailing down her back. Marie Laure's face popped into his brain, her dark eyes bottomless pits of despair as she hunched her body around the bump of her baby. He gulped down another cup of palm wine to wash the image away.

It did nothing to dampen his resentment for Alyssa, so busy posing in ad campaigns and pimping jewelry at fundraisers, with no clue in her walnut-sized brain of the kind of suffering those sparkly little stones represented.

He saved the photo of Alyssa's ad to his desktop and re-opened it in a graphic design program. In a different window, he opened another photo, a still from the video footage Marie Laure had captured just a week ago, after one of the miners had tried to smuggle a stone out of the camp. First Mekembe had hacked off the man's hands with a machete. Then Mekembe had gone to the man's tent and dragged his wife and ten-year-old daughter out into the road.

As the man watched, his wife and daughter were gang-raped by Mekembe's men before having their hands hacked off with a machete blade. In this frame the man sat dazed in shock next to the crumpled forms of his wife and daughter. Blood pooled around them, darkening the already red earth to a near black crimson.

Marie Laure told him the daughter had died several hours later.

Lips curling, Martin clicked on the sea of thick red, transferring the color to the photo of Alyssa. As he clicked his way down her back, the diamonds became drops of blood, oozing down her skin like scarlet tears.

CHAPTER 2

HE WAS BATSHIT. That was the only word that explained Derek's behavior.

Why else would he be unlocking his door to usher in a woman he'd just met—some random society brat, no less—into his house?

Okay, not merely batshit. Completely nuts. He had been from the moment he'd taken her hand, felt the sensual warmth of her skin. And when she'd leaned over in the car, laid that hot hand on his thigh, burning him through the fabric of his pants, his cock had gone titanium hard.

Every drop of blood had rushed down to pulse and throb between his legs, causing temporary insanity. Because there was no way in hell Derek would be doing this otherwise.

That said, he was mesmerized by the swing of her ass, the subtle flex of muscle under the smooth skin of her thighs as she preceded him up the stairs leading from the garage to the kitchen. He wanted to lean forward, bury his face against the curve of her butt, take a nip out of a firm cheek. Push her forward, lift her skirt, and shove his cock into her from behind.

He reached past her to flick on the light, catching the scent of her as he did so. Fresh, citrusy, with a warm, musky tone underneath. The aroma went straight to his balls, curling around and squeezing like a woman's soft hand.

Like Alyssa's hot hand, circling and stroking his cock, burning him alive.

"Nice place," she said, surveying the recently remodeled kitchen.

"Thanks," he said. "I just finished renovating the kitchen and bathrooms." This was weird, standing here, his dick hard enough to cut glass, talking about his kitchen remodel.

She walked slowly forward, her skinny heels *tap-tapping* on the tile before she leaned one hip against a bar stool next to the counter. She looked up at him with wide, grass-green eyes and caught her bottom lip between her teeth.

Was she really nervous? Or was it an act?

Derek didn't kid himself. She probably did this all the time. He was merely her chosen nightcap at the end of the evening.

Still, she looked uncertain, waiting for him to make a move. The silence thickened, verging on awkward.

This was such a fucking bad idea. If he were Ethan—his twin who would have done this gig under normal circumstances—Derek would have a steady stream of flirty banter at the ready, a smile designed to make a woman feel at ease as he was herding her to the bedroom.

But he wasn't the player Ethan had been before he'd met Toni Crawford, world's sexiest computer nerd. Derek didn't take random women home, didn't have the time or desire to make meaningless chitchat and talk them into bed for equally meaningless sex.

So what the fuck was he doing?

Alyssa gave him a tentative smile and absently twisted a strand of golden-brown hair. The smile shot heat to his groin, and he had his answer.

"How about a drink?" Alyssa said. She slipped her coat off her shoulders and placed it on the bar stool next to her, not noticing—or not caring—when it slid onto the floor.

"Good idea." He could use something to take the edge off as the rational side of his brain—the one he listened to without fail—argued with his cock over whether or not he should throw caution to the wind or throw Alyssa out on her delectable ass.

Right now, the jury was still out. "I've got Scotch," he said, retrieving a bottle of Lagavulin from the liquor cabinet. "And a bottle of this cabernet. I think it's decent. I got it as a gift."

Alyssa took the bottle and eyed the label. Her appreciative "Ooh" made him wonder what noises she'd make if he buried his tongue in her pussy.

Logic was losing out to lust, big-time.

He poured himself three fingers of the Lag and dug a wineglass from the back of a cabinet. He filled it half full and handed it to Alyssa, making sure not to touch her as he did so.

"Let's go outside," he said, motioning to the French doors that opened off the kitchen to a small deck overlooking his patch of grass that served as a backyard. Sipping her wine, Alyssa went over to the deck's railing and rested her knee on the built-in bench at the edge.

His eyes were glued to the skin of her back, left bare by her dress, glowing silver in the moonlight. His mouth watered with the urge to brush her long, thick hair aside and run his tongue along the shallow groove of her spine, up over her shoulders, and back down.

He moved closer, catching her scent. Like an animal. He'd never felt this, the craving to take a woman, to have her, over and over.

And he hadn't so much as kissed her yet.

She had to go.

The Lag was starting to do its job, mellowing him out, dulling the edges of everything, including his defenses against the unwarranted desire for this woman.

"Listen," he began, "I don't do this kind of thing very often—"

"What? Have a drink on your deck or take random women home with you?"

"The second," he said, an involuntary smile pulling at his mouth.

She turned to face him, the light spilling from his kitchen bouncing off the delicate lines of her face. "Me neither. Go home with random men, I mean."

He didn't bother to hide his disbelief.

"Believe what you want." She tossed her hair over her shoulder. "It's true."

Fine, he'd humor her. Then he'd let her finish her drink and offer her a ride home.

No matter how much his dick throbbed in protest.

"Oh, yeah? So why me?" He tossed back the last of his Scotch.

She gave him a wry smile. "There's something about you that's different from most men I meet. Something that makes me want to be with you."

He thought he heard something in her tone, but he couldn't quite put his finger on it through the soft haze of the Scotch and the sudden rush of heat that blew through him as she eased closer, close enough for him to feel heat radiating off her in waves.

Hands were tugging at his lapels. "Come down here," she whispered. "I can't kiss you all the way up there."

Oh, this was such a bad idea. But he sat down on the bench and pulled her between his parted thighs, spreading his palms on the hot skin of her back.

"That's better." Her hands cradled his face, and her wine-scented breath caressed his mouth as she leaned in for a kiss.

Heat exploded through him at the first touch, and his fingers tightened around her back as he pulled her close. She tasted like peaches, he thought as his tongue slid into her mouth—peaches and something dark and rich and spicy.

The curve of her hip pressed against his thigh, and the softness of her belly cradled the hard ridge of his erection. His mouth opened wider over hers, his tongue thrusting inside. Not the light, introductory, how-you-doing kiss she'd started.

He half expected her to pull away—little slip like her probably wasn't expecting an assault from a caveman when she'd invited herself over to play.

Too bad. She'd slipped right through his control, wound him tight as a bow. Now she had to face the consequences.

To his shock, she didn't back off at all, but gave as good as she got. Her mouth opened under his, her tongue swept through his mouth, exploring him as hungry little moans bubbled from the back of her throat.

She leaned into him, crushing herself against his chest. He took off his suit jacket in jerky, impatient motions, resenting the way the heavy fabric kept him from really feeling her. His hand covered her breast through her dress, swallowing the plump curve in his broad palm. Alyssa moaned and sucked on his tongue. His cock strained against his fly, begging for the same treatment.

He stood up and clamped his hands around her waist, lifting her easily and carrying her through the kitchen, down the hall to his bedroom. He deposited her on the bed and switched on the bedside lamp. His last lover had been a strictly lights-out girl, and Derek had never cared.

But one look at Alyssa, blinking up at him with blurry green eyes, the hem of her dress flipped up to reveal the crotch of cream silk panties, and he knew he had to watch every second.

He stripped off his shirt in jerky motions, ripped by dueling desires to fuck her hard and fast and get this the hell over with before he completely lost his mind, and the need to linger over every square inch of her, discover every secret spot, see how many times he could make her come before he finally let himself go.

She kicked off her shoes and rose into a seated position. She reached around to the back of her neck. With a flick of her fingers she undid the button holding up her dress. Red silk pooled at her waist as her gaze slid shyly from his.

Derek felt like he'd taken a roundhouse kick to the chest. She was perfect—silky golden skin, small but luscious breasts tipped with dark pink nipples. Something twisted inside him, dark and aching and needy, yearning for this small woman perched on his bed.

He had to get this over with, fast. If he was smart, he'd follow his initial instinct and cut this off now. But he'd left smart behind about thirty minutes ago when his cock had told his brain to offer her a ride home.

Not fucking her was not an option. Not anymore. Not with her sitting on his bed with her buttery soft skin and nipples that begged to be sucked and tongued. But he could do it quickly, get her out of here, mitigate the damage. No soft words, no lingering explorations. Get her off fast, get himself off immediately after.

Over and done with, and then he could put this whole crazy night and the irrational pull she had on him out of his mind.

His hands went to his fly as he simultaneously toed off his shoes. He shoved his pants and boxers down in one move and stripped his socks off in fast, efficient movements. His cock was rock hard, bobbing and straining between his legs.

Alyssa's mouth curved in another soft "ooh," and she let out a little gasp. He felt her gaze like a caress as she stared at his erection, her eyebrows raised. Blood surged, and he lifted one knee onto the bed.

Alyssa looked up at him with a tiny smile curving her pink mouth. "Impressive."

Derek wanted to return her smile but couldn't. He wanted to laugh this off, inject some lightness into a moment that had sped from flirtation to way too intense in lightning speed. His hands shook as he reached for her and pushed her back on the bed. She pulled him down over her, sliding her fingers through his hair and pulling his mouth to hers for another hungry kiss. Her skin was hot against his, hot and smooth. Her nipples were like bullets pressing against his chest.

He shoved her dress all the way off and pushed on his arms so he could see her, all of her, naked except for a wisp of silk covering her mound. She raised her hands, ran her hands down his chest and sides, traced the line of hair that bisected his abdomen.

"You're beautiful," she whispered and slid her hand down the last few torturous inches to his cock. He wanted to return the compliment, but his brain turned to mush as warm fingers wrapped around him, sending a jolt of fire straight to his belly. A thick drop of precome beaded on the tip as he pulsed in her hand. He looked down, groaning at the sight of her small, manicured fingers circling his cock, and for a brief, humiliating moment he was afraid he was going to come in her hand.

Then she closed her fist around him and started to stroke. He arched his head back, gritting his teeth against the unbearable pleasure, allowed himself to savor it for a few seconds before he grabbed her hand away. Christ, she was going to burn him alive.

He leaned down and took her mouth in a hard, hungry

kiss, came fully over her until they were breast to chest. One of his thighs hitched between hers, and he could feel her damp heat against his skin. He pressed higher, reveling in her soft gasp, in the way she arched and rubbed herself against him.

His hands slid over her breasts, exploring, his thumb flicking over the firm beads of her nipples. He slid his mouth from hers, trailed hot, openmouthed kisses down her neck and chest before closing his mouth over one hard tip. He'd meant to be gentle, easing into it with teasing flicks of his tongue before sucking it between his lips.

Instead he sucked her, hard, like he wanted to devour her. And she seemed to love it, digging her fingers into his hair, holding him close.

"Derek," she whispered, "that feels so good."

Her breathy voice exploded through him, making his dick throb to get inside her even as he wanted to show her all the ways he could touch her and give her pleasure.

He buried his head between her breasts, pressing hard kisses against her skin as an unfamiliar tangle of desire and emotion roiled inside him. Derek had always considered himself a decent lover. Courteous, anyway. He always got his partner off, lingering as long as he needed to, doing whatever she needed done before getting onto his own satisfaction.

But he'd never felt this primitive need to give pleasure, the need to stroke her higher and higher. He'd never anticipated a woman's orgasm like he did Alyssa's, wanting to experience it almost as much as he wanted his own.

He circled her nipple with his tongue and pulled away to look at her. Her green eyes were narrowed into slits; her lips were puffy and red from his kisses. Red splotches showed on her delicate skin where his day's growth of stubble had rasped. She was so beautiful it made his throat tight to look at her.

He wanted to spend hours, days, touching her, tasting her, finding out all her secrets.

He wanted to steal her away to one of Gemini's safe houses, keep her there for about a month until he knew her as well as he knew himself.

Derek's brain, which had gone on a coffee break up until that moment, surged back into action.

What the fuck are you thinking? She's nothing but a rich girl who picked you up at a party for the purposes of a fast fuck. She's hot. You want her. She wants you. You know all you need to know. Now get it over with before you really lose it.

Right. So what if he wanted her more than he could remember wanting any other woman, ever? So what if she made him lose touch with his normal, levelheaded, logical self?

They were two strangers who had met and wanted to have sex. Nothing special about that. No deeper meaning beyond mutual lust.

Yet every instinct for self-preservation urged him to get this over with as quickly as possible before Alyssa Miles wreaked more havoc on his mental state.

Rolling to the side, he stripped off her panties with one hand, determined to regain some semblance of control. Then he almost lost it again at the first glimpse of her pussy. A tidy patch of bronze curls topped her otherwise smooth flesh. Her legs were slightly parted, offering him a mouthwatering view of glistening pink folds and the plump bud of her clitoris begging to be stroked. It was all the invitation he needed.

Derek took her mouth as he slid his hand between her legs, pushing one finger up inside her. Liquid heat enveloped his finger, pulsing around him, drawing him deeper as she moaned and squirmed underneath him.

Fuck, she was tight. And wet, soaking his fingers with her silky, slippery juice.

But tight. So tight he knew he couldn't take her hard and fast, not without hurting her. He pumped his thick finger inside her, flicked her clit with his thumb. Tiny muscles clenched around him, and another surge of moisture bathed his hand.

She arched under his touch, her legs shifting, teasing his cock with inadvertent brushes of her thigh. Derek knew he wouldn't be able to make it much longer. He slid another finger up into her, stroking, stretching, softening her for the much thicker invasion of his cock.

"Oh, God," she whispered. "That feels . . . mmm . . ." She bucked up against his hand, fucking his fingers as his thumb circled her clit with firmer strokes. Suddenly she convulsed, her muscles tightening like a fist around his fingers, her eyes flying open as though startled at the strength and swiftness of her own orgasm.

"Oh, my God," she whispered. A vein pulsed in her neck, and Derek leaned down to suck the spot. A shiver coursed through her, and he could feel her clench around his finger, still buried deep inside her. "I don't think I've ever come that hard."

"Let's see if you can do it with me inside you," he said. It took an act of will, but he coaxed his fingers from the slick warmth of her body, rolled onto his back, and reached blindly for the drawer of his bedside table. He vaguely remembered throwing some condoms in there a while back. A few seconds of fumbling, and his fingers closed over the foil packet.

His hands shook as he unwrapped the packet, and he swore as he fumbled with the latex. Jesus Christ, he was so far gone he could barely get the condom on. His fingers felt like they'd tripled in thickness, big and clumsy and incapable of fitting the ring of latex around the engorged head of his cock.

"Let me," Alyssa said, pushing him onto his back as she knelt beside him. He leaned forward and took a nipple in his mouth, sucking and tonguing her. She took the condom from him and smoothed it down the length of his cock, her fingers burning him, making him arch and thrust against her touch. He pulled her down to him and settled her thighs on either side of his hips, realizing vaguely that he had less of a chance of hurting her if she was the one to control his penetration.

But she rolled off him, onto her back, pulling him down over her. "I want you on top," she whispered.

"You're small," he protested. "I'm way too heavy—"

"I want to feel your weight over me," she said, pulling his hips to hers as she bent her knees and parted her legs. Gripping his cock in one small hand, she guided him to her, slicking the plump head up and down, around her clit, drenching him with liquid fire.

"Put me in," he demanded, needing to be inside her before he went off like a rocket.

Still holding him, she fit him against the entrance to her sex, taking a sharp inhale as he squeezed inside. "God, you're big."

"And you're so fucking tight." He drove slowly forward, sliding in another inch. Jesus, not even two inches in her, and his orgasm was already looming, tingling in his balls, urging him to drive home and pound away.

He paused, took several deep breaths, reaching for the ironclad control that had disappeared at the first touch from this confounding woman. He pushed forward, pausing again when he saw her lips tighten.

"I'm hurting you," he panted.

She tossed her head against the pillow. "No. I mean, it's okay. It's just been a long time."

"How long?" He panted out the question before he could stop himself. There was no reason he should care.

"A little over a year," she said, lifting her hips, killing

him with shallow little thrusts as she struggled to accommodate him.

He froze, his sex-fuzzed brain chewing over that piece of intel. It had been nearly as long for himself, and they'd picked each other from the crowd to end a mutual dry spell.

It doesn't mean anything. But his whole body tensed, hesitating, afraid if he went any further it would mean a whole lot more than he'd ever bargained for.

She lifted her knees higher and ran her hands up and down his back. "I want you, want to feel you." Her back arched, her pretty pink nipples pointing to the sky.

It was back again, the burst of something hot and fierce and scary in his chest. Derek shoved it aside and turned his focus wholly on Alyssa, on her pleasure. He rose up on his knees to give himself better access and slid his fingers between her lush pussy lips, stroking her clit as he thrust and withdrew, going a little deeper each time. His breath knotted in his chest as he fought his climax. The sight of his cock sinking inside her and pulling out, shiny wet with her juice, was almost enough to send him over the edge.

She arched against him and moaned, her body seeming to suck him deeper like a greedy mouth. "Deeper," she murmured. "Please come all the way inside."

Derek filled her with one long, thick thrust, squeezing his eyes shut as she took him all the way. He held himself there, circling against her as sweet, hot sounds bubbled between her lips. Every detail came into sharp focus. The molten grip of her body around him, the scent of her mingling with the scent of him. The wet, sucking sounds of sex as he sank into her, over and over.

God, she was so hot, so beautiful. Her skin was like cream and satin, and he wanted to wrap himself up in her. Her pussy was hotter, tighter, than anything he'd ever felt. She made his cock so hard he was afraid when he came it was going to kill him.

"I'll be surprised if either of us make it out alive," she moaned.

Derek's eyes flew open as he realized he'd said at least that last part out loud. He hooked Alyssa's leg up over his hip and went as deep as he could go, pumping, circling, grinding as he covered her mouth with his. He wanted to taste every breath, every noise as he drove her over the edge.

He could feel her pleasure building with his, her pussy tightening around his cock as his balls drew in tight against his body. The muscles in his thighs bunched, every sinew tightening, readying for release.

Her moans rose in volume, a series of short, high, "ah's" mingling with his deeper groans before she froze, convulsing against him with a force that shook the bed. His climax hit him with devastating force, ripping through him, making him shake and moan as his cock pulsed and jerked inside her.

Derek rolled off her hours or seconds later, feeling as drained as if he'd run a marathon. The last ripples of his orgasm sizzled through him like electric currents, aftershocks of physical devastation.

She curved against him, and he ran his hand up and down the delicate curve of her spine. His brain grappled for something to say. Something cool, casual, flattering without implying any promises. Something that would show her he brought women home with him all the time and this was no big deal.

"I need to take care of the condom." *Real smooth.* Fuck it. The intrusion of reality in the form of birth control was a good thing, he thought as he pulled away, ignoring the chill that enveloped him as he pulled away from her warmth.

When he emerged a few minutes later she was waiting by

the door, her dress, purse, and panties clenched against her front like armor. "Do you mind if I freshen up?" she said and darted past him.

Derek pulled on a T-shirt and a pair of jeans and went out into the living room. He found his Scotch where he'd left it and tossed it back in one gulp. The smoky bite washed the taste of her from his mouth, as his brain started asking him all kinds of questions about what the fuck he thought he was doing.

"I called my driver to pick me up."

Derek turned to face her. She stood just inside the living room, back in her red silk dress. With her shoes off, she was even shorter than he'd originally thought, topping out at about five foot two, five three, max. She'd washed her face and wiped away the heavy layers of mascara, powder, and lip gloss. Now he could see the freckles across her small nose, see that her thick, full lashes were the same golden brown as her hair.

With her small stature and delicate features, she could have passed for a teenager. Thank God she wasn't.

Her lips curled in a knowing smile. "Don't worry. I'm twenty-four. I'll show you my driver's license if you're really worried."

Twenty-four. Still too young for his own thirty-two. Not that it mattered, as this wasn't going anywhere. Derek held up his hand. "I'm not." She might look young, but she fucked with the confidence of a woman. His cock thickened behind his fly, more than ready to test that confidence again, but she was slipping on her shoes, ready to make her escape.

He bit back a wave of disappointment and fought the urge to talk her into round two. He should be grateful she was leaving on her own, as eager to get out of there as he was to have her gone. Okay, maybe he wasn't as eager as he should be, taking one last, regretful look at her slim, silky legs and heart-breaker face.

He had about a thousand different things he'd still like to do to her, he'd barely scratched the surface. But she was dangerous to him, to his peace of mind, to his carefully constructed detachment. Even a guy who didn't spend too much time on self-reflection could see that.

Best to get her out of there, end this whole crazy night now.

"Do you mind giving me a ride to the Four Seasons? I asked my driver to pick me up there."

His brow knit. "Why not just have him pick you up here? Or, better yet, I can give you a ride home."

She shook her head and gave him a smile he couldn't quite read. "I like to keep things mysterious. Let's keep this our secret."

He shrugged and grabbed his keys and wallet. It wasn't his job to decipher the whims of a woman he barely knew.

Within ten minutes they were at the hotel.

"Pull into the parking lot and park over there," she said, indicating a row of spaces a good fifty yards from the main entrance. He could see a town car idling in the circular driveway.

"So, should I call you or something?" He mentally punched himself as the question slid past his lips. He needed to let this go right here, right now. He had no intention of calling her and no business giving her the idea he meant to.

She turned to him, and in the darkness he could just make out her soft smile. "How about I look for you at the next charity auction, and we'll leave it at that?"

A sharp stab hit him, something that felt way too close to regret for his comfort. "I'll keep an eye out for you."

She leaned over the gearshift and kissed him, sweet, soft, and hot, sliding her tongue in his mouth for a last, lingering taste. "It was really nice meeting you, Derek. Thank you for a lovely evening."

She was out of the car and halfway across the parking lot before he could formulate a reply.

Lovely.

He sat there, watching her disappear into the night, feeling like a grenade had gone off in his chest. And she said it was "lovely."

He'd count himself lucky if he never laid eyes on Alyssa Miles again.

CHAPTER 3

THE ONLY DOWNSIDE to acting on her impulses was the inevitable crash back into reality. Alyssa closed her eyes and sank into the leather seat of the town car. Pleasure still sizzled through her in tiny bursts, faint echoes of the most mind-blowing orgasms she'd ever had in her entire life.

"You'll have to remind me exactly where you live, Miss Miles!" Aaron, the driver, called from the front.

She looked at her watch and made a split-second decision. "I'm going to stay at my father's tonight." It was already after one AM, and breakfast for Oscar Van Weldt started at eight on the dot. Alyssa had been chastised often enough for her tendency for tardiness. She kept a spare change of clothes in the guest room she regularly used, so it would be easy enough to roll out of bed and into the dining room right in the nick of time.

Grace wouldn't like it, but as far as Alyssa was concerned right now, Grace could suck it.

She shoved thoughts of her stepmother aside, not wanting the stress of her sour relationship with Grace to ruin the lingering glow from the last few hours. She closed her eyes and focused on Derek, on the intense heat in his gaze, on the way his big hands shook with need as they touched her. On the way he moved his body over her, in her, so huge and strong but gentle despite his size. She licked her lips, savored the taste of that last, hungry kiss, the way his eyes had moved over her and his hands had clenched around the steering wheel like he was struggling not to grab her and pull her back into his Audi.

For now, she wouldn't worry about what he would think when he realized who she was. She didn't kid herself that he wouldn't find out sooner rather than later. A Google search would bring up thousands of hits, hundreds of pictures.

She swallowed past the knot in her throat, wondering what Derek would think when he read the articles and saw the pictures.

No. She shoved the negativity aside. She wasn't going to think about that tonight. Tonight she was just another girl who'd had incredible, amazing sex with a gorgeous man, a man who saw nothing but a girl he wanted. Not a celebrity to sell out to the tabloids or use as means to an end.

Pretty sad state of affairs when a man wanting you only for sex is the biggest boost to your self-esteem in recent memory.

Alyssa squeezed out the thought with one of Derek, braced over her, his face a mask of barely checked need as he sank into her with ever-deepening strokes. She ran every second of her evening with him through her head, frame by frame, lingering and savoring every second as the town car pulled off the highway and navigated the narrow streets of her father's wealthy neighborhood. The few street lamps cast their yellow glow on the rain-damp pavement and illuminated the high fences and gates that concealed some of the priciest homes in the San Francisco Bay area.

As Aaron pulled up to the driveway, fears and doubts came rushing in, chipping away at the lingering pleasure. What if Derek decided to tell the press how Alyssa Miles had practically begged him, a stranger, to take her home with him and have sex? She could only imagine the headlines.

The tabloids would pay him a fortune. His place was nice, but not that nice. Definitely not nice enough to guarantee he'd turn down a six-figure payment to tell his story.

Her headache was back in full, brutal force. She was such an idiot. Her father's words rang in her head. *Do you ever consider the consequences of your actions before you make a fool of yourself and this family?*

Her stomach churned with shame. She'd been trying so hard, doing so well keeping a low profile, and was beginning to have the kind of relationship with her father she'd always wanted. One where he didn't look at her like he was waiting for her to fuck up sometime in the next five minutes.

Alyssa and Oscar had made great progress, but their relationship was by no means stable. She had no illusions about his love and approval. It was purely conditional, ready to be withdrawn—along with her generous salary—if she made a single misstep.

And now she'd risked it all, and for what? For one hot night of sex with a gorgeous man who would probably tell the tabloids within an hour.

God, why was she so stupid, so impulsive? Just when everything was starting to go well, she had to fuck it up over a hot guy she barely knew. No sex, no matter how amazing, was worth the interrogation she'd face in the morning.

Hands, hot and rough, skimming over her hips. A deep, raspy voice whispering how hot and tight and good her pussy felt around him. Full, firm lips closing over her nipples.

A burst of warmth chipped away at the building dread. Okay, maybe sex with Derek Taggart would be worth it.

The car pulled up in front of the Van Weldt estate, and the driver paused to key in the security code.

Aaron opened the door, and Alyssa thanked him as he assisted her out of the car. She looked up, stomach sinking when she saw the lights were on upstairs. *Oh, crap.*

She hadn't even considered that anyone would still be

awake. She'd hoped to greet them in the morning with a vague story about being tired and not wanting to miss breakfast and tell them she'd arrived shortly after the auction ended. If Grace or her father caught her she would have to explain why she was still out this late and come up with a plausible accounting of her whereabouts.

There you go again, Alyssa, thinking things through.

She should just go home. She turned just in time to see Aaron driving away. She winced as the gate clanged shut and considered calling him back. But that would mean more noise and make it more likely that her father or Grace would hear and come to investigate.

She sucked it up and went inside, praying Grace was far enough gone from the martinis she'd chugged at the fundraiser and that her father wouldn't hear her from the master suite in the back of the house.

She paused and took several deep breaths, stalling before keying in the security code.

Alyssa slipped off her heels and tiptoed across the marble tiled foyer. She just needed to make it past the curving staircase to the door that led to the guest wing of the house, and she'd be home free.

Her fingers closed over the door latch, and her heart accelerated. She was going to make it, free and clear, at least for tonight—

A loud, popping sound erupted from upstairs, and she froze. Then another. And another, like two firecrackers going off in rapid succession.

"Dad?" she called, moving automatically to the foot of the staircase. "Grace? Is everything okay?"

Her heart thudded against her ribs, and cold dread settled in her stomach. She raced up the stairs as though propelled by an unseen force, fear tightening her rib cage with every step. Heedless of the danger, she hurried down the hallway, calling her father and stepmother's names.

She skidded to a halt outside the door to their suite and pounded on the closed door. No answer. She opened the door, her mouth opening wide in a silent scream at the sight that greeted her.

The huge master suite was lit by only a single lamp on top of an end table, but it was enough for Alyssa to make out her father, lying sideways across the king-size bed. A crimson stain bloomed on his chest; another rapidly spread on the cream silk comforter under him.

Hand over her mouth, one arm wrapped around her stomach as if it could contain the horror rising in her gorge, Alyssa took a tentative step into the room, looking frantically around for her stepmother.

She rounded the bed and saw Grace Van Weldt crumpled in a heap on the floor, blood burbling from a wound in her head. Loosely clasped in her limp right hand was a handgun.

The French doors that opened onto a small deck stood open. A cool breeze blew in, stirring the silk hem of Grace's nightgown and whipping a strand of hair across Alyssa's face. But the breeze couldn't mask the smells in the room. The acrid smell of gun powder and something else she didn't recognize. The sweet metallic smell of blood. And death. A scent so thick she could taste it on her tongue.

The two sips of wine she'd had at Derek's erupted in her throat, and she barely made it out onto the balcony before heaving up the contents of her stomach. As she straightened she saw a shadow out of the corner of her eye. The killer? Panic made her knees weak.

Don't be stupid. It's just a raccoon or a shadow of a tree branch. It's obvious what happened here tonight.

Alyssa walked back into the bedroom, averting her gaze from the gory scene of her father and stepmother. Her hands shook, and stars hazed her vision. *Hold it together.* She couldn't fall apart yet. She ran out of the room, unable to

stand it for a second more, and crossed the hall to her stepmother's private office. She picked up the phone and dialed
the police.

"Nine-one-one. What's your emergency?"

"I think my stepmother just shot my father."

As the words fell from her mouth, Alyssa felt like she'd
taken leave of her body, like she was listening to herself
from several feet above as she gave the dispatcher the address and additional details about the scene.

Still, she managed to hang up the phone and dial Kimberly. Kimberly would know what to do, how to handle the
situation.

It was only when Kimberly answered that it hit Alyssa.
She was about to tell Kimberly that her parents were dead,
and that Kimberly's own mother was the cause.

"Kimberly," was all Alyssa could force out before she
started to sob. It took her several tries before she could finally choke it out.

"Oh, my God." Kimberly's voice was small, quiet, quivering with barely contained emotions. After several seconds
of silence, she said, "Were they fighting? Did you hear anything?"

"No." Alyssa sniffled, trying to channel some of her sister's composure, even in these horrific circumstances. "I just
got here. I was going to my room, and I heard the shots—"

"Why are you even there? What are you doing there so
late?" Kimberly's question snapped across the phone line.
"You left hours ago."

"I . . . met someone," Alyssa said, her encounter with Derek
feeling sleazy and tawdry as she admitted what she'd done.
"I'm supposed to meet Daddy for breakfast, and it was so
late I decided to stay here."

"Oh, Alyssa." Kimberly sighed in the tone of disappointment universally dreaded by all children. "Listen, when the
police get there, don't tell them where you were. Tell them

you were with me before you went to Mother and Daddy's. I'll be there as soon as I can."

"Okay, but why?"

"Really, Alyssa. It will be bad enough to have Mother and Daddy's private lives torn apart in the press. Do you really want them talking about you and your one-night stand on top of it?"

Alyssa couldn't believe her sister could care about what the press would think when her father had been murdered and her mother lay dead of a self-inflicted gunshot wound. Then she felt horrible as Kimberly's soft sobs echoed across the phone lines.

"I know it shouldn't matter," Kimberly said. "But Daddy loved you, and I know he wouldn't want to see you crucified all over again for something so foolish. So do it for him as well as yourself."

Alyssa nodded, unable to speak as tears stung her eyes and sobs clawed at her throat. Sirens approached, rising to a crescendo as several police cars pulled up to the house. The intercom beeped insistently. "The police are here. I have to go," Alyssa said and hung up the phone.

She answered the intercom and let the police in through the security gate, and then she opened the front door to let them in. Alyssa spent the next several hours answering their questions, going over again when she had arrived, what she heard, if she could remember the exact time she heard the gunshots.

Kimberly arrived soon after Alyssa had called. Her blond hair was pulled back into a tight knot, and she was dressed in jeans and a turtleneck sweater. The knife-sharp creases in her pants and five-hundred-dollar designer flats kept her from looking anything but coolly elegant. But dark circles framing her eyes and the redness around her nose and eyes showed faint cracks in her composure.

Richard Blaylock, Van Weldt Jeweler's vice president of legal affairs, had arrived shortly after Kimberly. In his early forties with a lanky build, blue eyes, and blond hair, Blaylock's clean-cut good looks made him, along with Kimberly, a natural spokesperson for the Van Weldts' business affairs. More than that, after nearly two decades of working closely with the Van Weldts, he had become a close family friend.

Alyssa didn't know him very well but had gratefully accepted his comforting hug when he'd arrived. After he released Alyssa, he'd pulled Kimberly close. "This is horrible. How are you two holding up?"

Alyssa shrugged. "I feel so awful. I can't help thinking, what if I had been here?" Her voice cracked, and she choked back a sob. "Maybe I could have stopped her—"

Kimberly shook her head, grief and resignation closing over her face. "We all knew Mother was getting worse. If you'd been here"—she paused, squeezing her eyes shut against tears as her shoulders heaved once, twice, before she regained control—"if you'd been here, who's to say you wouldn't have been killed, too? We all know Mother didn't want you here."

Guilt coiled like a snake around the pit of Alyssa's stomach. She'd wanted her father to accept her into his life, into his family, more than anything. But not at this price.

"Stop it," Kimberly said, taking her by the shoulders and giving her a light shake. "This is not your fault. If anything, it's mine." She held up a hand when Alyssa opened her mouth to protest. "I knew how unstable Mother was, how out of control her drinking had become. I knew I needed to speak to Daddy about getting her into a treatment program, but I kept putting it off. I didn't want to have that discussion with him, didn't want to have to deal with the public fallout of Mother being carted off to rehab."

She sank down on the sofa and buried her face in her hands.

"I was afraid of how the family's reputation would suffer, especially after you moved up here and we launched your campaign."

Alyssa tried not to take the comment personally.

"It's no one's fault," Richard said soothingly. "Your mother made the choice to put a gun in her hand. No one forced her."

"You don't have any reason to believe a third party is involved?" Detective Thomson, who had arrived within minutes of the police, entered the living room, having obviously eavesdropped on their conversation.

Kimberly shook her head. "As much as I never thought my mother would be capable of this kind of violence, I knew she was depressed, maybe even suicidal." She wiped away a tear with slender fingers. "I never imagined she'd hurt Daddy, too."

The detective nodded. "We won't finish the investigation for several days, but I'm sorry to say I think you're right."

He spent another half hour questioning Alyssa before letting her leave. "I need a number where you can be reached," he said.

Alyssa gave him her assistant's number. "Andy will always know how to reach me." She stood up, feeling dazed as she looked around her father's living room. "I suppose I should call Aaron or a cab to take me home." She started to pull out her cell phone.

"Not on your life," Kimberly said and slid her arm around Alyssa's shoulders. "You shouldn't be alone tonight, and God knows I don't want to be. I'm taking you home with me." Through the horror and grief, Alyssa felt a little spurt of warmth. This was new, having someone she could lean on, someone who needed to lean on her, when things got really bad.

She quickly packed a bag of essentials from the collection

of odds and ends she kept in the guest room and followed Kimberly out to her car. She ducked into the backseat of Kimberly's Mercedes. Kimberly slid into the passenger seat as Richard climbed behind the wheel. As they pulled out of the front gate, their path was blocked by at least four news vans. Flashbulbs popped, and reporters banged on the windows, their barked questions muffled through the glass. Alyssa slumped down nearly to the floor and pulled her bag up over her head, feeling the lights and noise like physical blows.

Richard gunned the engine and laid on the horn; a squad car gave a warning burst of its siren and flashed its lights. Several neighbors lined the usually serene street, staring, speculating over what was going on behind the massive iron gate.

Once again, the Van Weldts were prime tabloid fodder. But for once, Alyssa thought, she wasn't to blame. Tears streamed down Alyssa's face. Right now she'd give anything to have the scandal be about her.

Three weeks later . . .

"What have we got?" Derek sat down at the oval mahogany table that dominated Gemini Securities' conference room. He joined his older brother, Danny, who sat at the head of the table, his younger-by-six-minutes twin, Ethan, and Ethan's girlfriend, Toni, who also happened to be the latest addition to Gemini's team. Rounding out the group were Ben Moreno and Alex Novascelic, both former Army Rangers like Danny and Derek, who now worked as security specialists at Gemini.

Danny, Derek, and Ethan had started the private security and investigation firm four years ago after they'd all gotten out of the military, and had built up a respectable list of corporate and private clients.

"We've got a personal detail on the CEO of GeneCor.

He's nervous now that animal rights activists have turned their attention to him. Alex, you up for that?" Novascelic nodded and took the file from Danny.

"Moreno, I want you to do the site evaluation in Sacramento. It will probably take you a week or so. Plan to stay over."

Moreno groaned. "Come on, man, I have two dates this week."

Danny pinned him with a steel-gray stare. "Cancel."

"I can't cancel on Angela. Do you have any idea how long I've waited to get with her—"

"If Angela and her superpussy are so special—"

"Hello, HR violation!" Toni said.

Danny shot her a glare, but said, "Okay, forget I said that. If your lady friend"—Danny looked at Toni, who nodded and smiled in approval—"is so important to you, then commute. I don't give a shit. But you be at LogicCorp's facility in Sacramento at eight thirty sharp every morning until five o'clock every day, got it?"

Derek met Toni's grin with one of his own. That was just one thing he liked about her, the way she didn't take shit. No small order, dealing with three six-foot-plus ex-military types who ran roughshod over most women they came in contact with.

A chick needed attitude in spades if she wanted to keep a handle on any of the Taggart brothers. Toni had it, all right, and she'd wrapped his brother Ethan handily around her slender finger.

"Derek, you finished the risk assessment at AtlaCorp, right?"

Derek nodded. "Submitted my analysis to the COO on Friday."

"Good." Danny's face lit with an almost savage grin. "Because we've got a new client, a big fish who's going to need a lot of personal attention. And if we play this one right, it could mean beaucoup bucks for a long time."

Everyone perked up at that. They'd kept business steady since the whole Kara Kramer story had hit the news but hadn't landed any significant new clients. Under normal circumstances, the high-profile, muckety-muck jobs went to Ethan, who had the ability to deliver a certain amount of ass kissing while maintaining complete control over the situation.

But after the public interest generated by the Kara Kramer case, Ethan was on an enforced sabbatical from any high-profile public jobs for the next six weeks. On the one hand, Ethan was being lauded as a hero for saving Kara and bringing down an elusive international criminal.

On the other hand, the fact that information Ethan uncovered in the course of his investigation was used to put Kara's father—and their client—Jerry Kramer, in jail, didn't sit well with some of Gemini's existing and potential clients. Derek, Ethan, and Danny agreed that while publicity was good for their security and investigation business, notoriety wasn't. So Ethan was keeping a low profile these days, working mainly from the office or doing legwork from home. Not that the bastard minded, seeing as it gave him time to indulge in his latest obsession: Toni Crawford.

With Ethan still effectively benched back here in the office and Danny in charge of an ongoing corporate job, Derek knew it was up to him to impress whomever their new client was with the services Gemini provided. "So, who is it?" Derek prodded.

"Harold Van Weldt. Chairman and CEO of Van Weldt Jeweler. He wants us to find out who's leaking company information to the press and to provide personal security to select family members, namely his niece, Alyssa Miles."

"You've got to be fucking kidding me." The words were

out of Derek's mouth before the internal editor could call
them back. All eyes locked on him, everyone in the room
surprised by his outburst. Ethan studied him closely, and
Derek felt the uncomfortable prickle of his twin trying to
probe his brain.

"Is there a problem?" Danny's voice was low, controlled,
lined with cold steel.

Derek focused his attention on his older brother. Most of
the time he didn't believe in any of that twin-bond bullcrap,
but every once in a while something happened between him
and Ethan, a transfer of knowledge that couldn't be explained any other way. Maybe if he avoided Ethan's curious
stare, Derek could drop the equivalent of a mental invisibility
cloak over his brain. He hadn't told anyone about the night
he'd spent with Alyssa Miles, and the last thing he wanted
was for his twin to somehow ferret out what had gone on.

"No, no problem," Derek replied, covering his earlier outburst with a flat, emotionless tone. "But are they really the
type of client Gemini wants to cultivate?"

"Do you have any clue who these people are?" Danny
asked.

"It would be hard not to," Derek said. The night he'd
met Alyssa he'd had no idea who she was, no idea she was
anything more than another trust-fund baby, flitting from
one society event to another.

But that had changed the second he'd turned on CNN the
following morning. He'd already had the argument with
himself about whether or not he was going to dig up any
more information on the heiress Alyssa Miles. In the end
he'd come down definitely in the "not" column. What purpose would it serve? Even if she did want to see him again,
she wasn't his type, and he doubted he was hers. They had
nothing in common other than incredible physical chemistry, and until three weeks ago, Derek hadn't used that as a

compelling reason for a relationship since he'd been too young and horny to know any better.

All the more reason to relegate Alyssa Miles and their one hot night to the memory banks, never to be repeated. He already knew everything he needed or wanted to know about her. There was no point cyberstalking a woman just because she made his dick hard.

That morning he had flipped on the TV in his kitchen, having no clue he was in for the shock of his life. There on the screen was a picture of Alyssa, with the caption CELEBRITY HEIRESS'S FATHER DIES IN APPARENT MURDER-SUICIDE.

The anchor had given a quick recap of the life and death of Oscar Van Weldt but spent the majority of the time talking about Alyssa Miles and her escapades. Hard-core partying when she was barely out of diapers? Check. Nude photos of her "accidentally" leaked to the press by a boyfriend? Check. A stint in rehab for a coke and pill problem that nearly killed her? Check. Alyssa Miles had hit all the highlights of a young Hollywood starlet.

The last woman in the world Derek wanted to get messed up with.

For the first few days after the murder, he'd existed in a state of heightened agitation, ready at any moment to be contacted by the police or the press to talk about the hours he'd spent with Alyssa Miles. Every time his phone rang he'd braced himself, tried to figure out how he was going to explain to the world how he'd unwittingly ended up in bed with one of America's most famous.

But apparently she didn't want anyone to know about their tryst any more than he did, because no phone call came, and no uniforms showed up at his house or his office. Alyssa's public statement was that she'd been with her sister up until she'd gone to her father's house, and Derek was happy to let her stick to that story.

"You know what kind of publicity they could bring to Gemini," Danny said.

"I don't know that we want to be associated with family scandal and party girls," Derek snapped. Three weeks later he still had the punched-in-the-face feeling he'd gotten when he'd learned the truth about her. He felt stupid and strangely betrayed, though logically he had no good reason to feel that way. It wasn't like she'd tried to hide her identity from him. She'd told him flat out who she was, even given him the "don't you know who I am" treatment.

He couldn't blame her for his cluelessness.

But that didn't stop him from feeling angry every time he saw another newscast or picture of her in the paper. Whereas before he hadn't had a clue, seeing as Alyssa didn't show up much in *The Economist* or in *The Wall Street Journal,* now everywhere he turned there was something about her or the Van Weldt family, which always included a mention of her. There'd even been a line drawing of her in the *Marketplace* section of last week's *Journal.*

"Since when did you get to be such a tight ass?" Ethan asked.

"Not wanting our firm to be associated with the queen of tabloids isn't being tight-ass."

"She's not that bad," Toni interjected. "She's totally turned over a new leaf since she got involved with the family business."

"That explains the picture of her falling out of a limo last week," Derek said.

"She's grieving for her father. Which you should know because you read the story in the *Us Weekly* you stole," Toni said, pointing her finger at him.

"You left it in the break room for anyone to pick up," Derek said. He hoped no one noticed the heat rising in his face as he remembered how he'd snatched up the magazine when he saw Alyssa's picture on the cover. "Point is, after all the chaos the Kramer case caused, we don't need to be known as the company who guards a train wreck waiting to happen."

He felt a little guilty for that. The beautiful woman he'd met at the party had been funny and sexy, not afraid to go after what she wanted. Hard to reconcile with the human mess who'd been plastered all over the media accompanying lurid tales of Oscar Van Weldt's final hours.

"Will you excuse us?" Danny looked pointedly at Ben, Alex, and Toni. "We need to have a partner meeting, get a few things clear."

Alex and Ben looked relieved to escape. Toni looked put out but didn't argue. They left the room.

"What do you care about our clients' personal lives?" Danny asked.

"I care if they impact the image of this company, something you should maybe be more concerned with after the last couple months."

"Exactly why we need a client like the Van Weldts. They're one of the largest jewelers in the United States, with offices all over the world. The business opportunity is huge."

Derek's mouth tightened. He couldn't deny Danny's point.

"Besides," Ethan said, "you get to work with Alyssa Miles. She may be a train wreck waiting to happen, but she's still hot." His gaze flicked uneasily to the door, as though he expected Toni to bust him. "Not that I notice that anymore." Ethan, once king of the stick and move, was on a crusade to prove to Toni he could be happy and satisfied as a one-woman man.

Danny made a whip-crack sound, followed by a high-pitched meow.

"Say whatever you want," Ethan said. "I'm the only one in this room who's gotten any in the last month."

Not entirely true, but Derek wasn't about to correct his twin. He didn't even need to close his eyes to remember how her hot, smooth skin had felt against his hands, the salty sweet taste of her nipples in his mouth. The gripping wet heat of her pussy milking him to climax.

Christ. All the more reason to make sure he never got within ten feet of Alyssa ever again.

"What do they need us for? Doesn't the company have its own security personnel?"

"Since Oscar Van Weldt was killed, the company has been having internal issues that have somehow made their way to the press. His brother, Harold, has taken over as CEO and wants us to find the leak."

"Clients like this need a lot of ass kissing and hand-holding. You know I'm not the right guy for this," Derek said, grasping at straws. "Put Alex on it. He's better at making nice with clients, and you know it."

Danny shook his head. "They want a partner on it. Because loverboy here"—he gestured at Ethan—"is still benched for the time being, that means you. Besides"—he held up his hand when Derek would have protested—"I get the feeling Harold Van Weldt is a real hard-ass. He cuts to the chase, doesn't put up with a lot of bullshit, and wants someone who won't be impressed with the fame of certain family members." He cocked his dark eyebrow. "Something tells me you'll be perfect."

CHAPTER 4

ALYSSA WALKED INTO the boardroom of Van Weldt Jeweler's San Francisco headquarters, chin up, shoulders thrown back in her best approximation of a confident, in-control woman. She'd chosen her outfit carefully this morning. Nothing said professional like black tailored slacks and a crisp white shirt. Five-inch black boots added height and confidence, and she'd styled her hair in a sleek chignon with a deep side part. She had no idea why her uncle Harold wanted to meet her this morning but hoped it was to discuss the holiday marketing campaign about to hit. If that was the case, she wanted to make sure she dressed the part of savvy executive.

She felt her hopes dwindle as soon as she met Harold's icy blue glare, his disapproval a near tangible force. Then again, Harold always looked like he smelled something rancid when he looked at her, so why should this morning be any different.

Kimberly, seated at Harold's left, offered her an encouraging smile. Alyssa locked on that smile as she slipped her hand inside her oversize shoulder bag and made sure her folder of notes and ideas for the campaign was still there. She placed her bag in a seat across from them, next to Richard Blaylock, who was already seated and drinking coffee out of a heavy mug emblazoned with the silver and blue Van Weldt logo.

She got herself a cup of coffee from the silver service on the mahogany side table, stirring until every last granule of sugar dissolved. Anything to stave off confrontation with Uncle Harold, if only for a few more seconds. As she turned to take a seat, her gaze snagged on a portrait on the wall above the head of the table. Rendered in oil and surrounded by an ornate gold frame, Oscar Van Weldt looked upon them, a benevolent smile in his pale blue eyes. Coffee sloshed over the rim of her cup as her step faltered.

She risked a glance around the room to see if anyone had noticed, but everyone was busy shuffling papers and going over notes. Oscar had been dead only three weeks, yet everyone seemed back to business as usual.

Maybe she should take a tip from them. Now wasn't the time to wallow in her painful relationship with her father. Nothing could come of dwelling on the fact that just as she had started to have a real relationship with him, just when he'd finally found something in her to be proud of, he'd been taken from the family in the most horrific manner possible.

"How is everyone this morning?" she asked brightly.

"We're fine, considering it's been three weeks since your father's death and we're still surrounded by this media circus," Harold said in his clipped Dutch accent. Unlike her father, with his stout build and ruddy cheeks, Harold was thinner, almost slight in his handtailored navy suit. But he radiated leadership despite his small stature, and Alyssa admonished herself not to shrink away from his flinty blue gaze.

Her cheeks burned with heat. In the past few weeks, everyone from the *San Francisco Tribune* to *Star Magazine* had dug into Oscar Van Weldt's life, including of course his infamous illegitimate daughter. Every story about Alyssa's wild partying and unwise choices in men had been rehashed until it seemed like Alyssa couldn't turn on the TV or open up a Web page without seeing a caricature of herself flashed up on the screen.

The old stories she could block out. She'd dealt with the sting of being called "rich white trash" by venom-spewing bloggers like Charlie Farris. She'd survived the humiliating betrayal of having her former fiancé post private, naked photos of her all over the Web.

But nothing prepared her for the implication that she was responsible for her father's death. That her growing relationship with her father had pushed her stepmother over the edge into psychosis. That asshole Farris from Celebzone.com had even posted pictures of Alyssa and Grace from the Bancroft gala. It didn't take an expert in body language to read the tension between herself and Grace, but just in case, Farris had included his own helpful commentary. *It was no secret Alyssa Miles's involvement in the Van Weldt business put added strain on the Van Weldt marriage. Did Alyssa's wild ways and intrusion into the family push her stepmother over the edge?*

The insinuation wouldn't have stung had it not perfectly echoed Alyssa's own fears.

"I'm sorry about everything that's being said," Alyssa said, her lips suddenly dry despite their generous coating of gloss.

"Yes, well, in addition to the unwanted attention you've brought us, we also have the problem of confidential company information somehow getting out to the press."

Alyssa sat up straighter in her chair. "You can't think I have anything—"

Harold held up his hand. "Who knows what you're capable of? In any case, it's become clear to me that you are incapable of controlling yourself and your behavior, so I've hired someone to do it for you." He buzzed the intercom. "Susan, you can send Mr. Taggart in now."

Panic squeezed Alyssa's stomach and brought a film of cold sweat to her hands.

It's a coincidence. It has to be. There have to be hundreds, maybe thousands of Taggarts in the state of California.

The door opened, and Alyssa felt like all the air in the room was sucked out into the hallway. Heat rushed through her as every cell reacted to his presence. Her gaze devoured his face, eagerly taking in every detail of the face that had lingered in her dreams and nightmares for the past three weeks.

For the first few days she'd braced herself, forced herself to imagine the worst-case scenario, the most insulting thing he could say about her to the media, as if that would soften the blow when it hit.

Then, to her absolute shock, he said nothing. Not a single peep. Which somehow made him and their night even more special as it became clear he wasn't going to exploit it for money or his own fifteen minutes of fame.

What was on the surface a meaningless one-night stand had taken on far greater significance, a special secret Alyssa held close, using it to reassure herself that no matter what anyone in her family or the press said about her, somewhere out there was a man who saw the real her, wanted her, maybe even cared for her a little.

Never let it be said she didn't have a vivid imagination.

"I would like you all to meet Derek Taggart of Gemini Securities."

Now all she could do was panic again as her special secret collided violently with her real life. Alyssa sat frozen as Derek shook Richard and Kimberly's hands, both of whom exchanged questioning looks. They hadn't known about Harold hiring him either.

"And I'm sure you know Alyssa Miles, Oscar's other daughter."

Derek gave her a bland smile and regarded her with flat,

unreadable eyes as he took her hand in his. "Is it possible to live in America and not know who Alyssa Miles is?" Though his tone was pleasant, a hard edge appeared in his eyes, and the corners of his mouth pulled down.

Any silly fantasy she'd harbored that Derek Taggart might care about her after the night they'd shared died a swift and painful death. Her blood ran cold, and she slipped her hand from his, unable to stand touching him when he looked at her like that. Gone was the heat, the need that had permeated his expression that night.

In its place were all kinds of judgments and assumptions. He'd read everything about her, seen all the stories, probably the pictures, too.

She didn't even have to ask whether or not he believed them.

"It's nice to meet you, Miss Miles," he said, his voice so cold she was surprised ice chips didn't fall from his mouth. Tears threatened again as she locked eyes with him. Anger lurked behind the judgment.

"You can call me Alyssa," she said, smiling tentatively as she searched his eyes for any softness, a grain of affection.

Nothing.

"I prefer to keep things formal, Miss Miles."

Ouch.

She pulled her attention away from Derek and struggled to maintain her composure as she turned back to her uncle. "I don't understand exactly why you've hired Mr. Taggart's firm," Alyssa said to her uncle. "We already have plenty of security on staff."

"I have to agree with Alyssa," Richard, who had remained silent until then, said. "There are legal matters to consider in bringing in an outside firm—"

"All of which you're more than capable of dealing with, I'm sure," Harold said and leveled Alyssa with a cool, almost reptilian stare. "Though your appeal is beyond me, you've managed to charm most of the security staff into indulging your every whim. I've decided we need someone from the outside to come in and take a more objective look at things. Mr. Taggart, won't you sit down."

Richard looked like he was about to protest but was interrupted by his cell phone ringing. He frowned down at the display. "Will you all excuse me?" he said, already on his way out the door. "I need to take this."

Alyssa kept her gaze trained forward as Derek sat down in the seat beside her. She didn't spare him so much as a sideways glance, but that didn't stop the screaming awareness of every nerve in her body. His scent drifted over her, pine-scented soap and his own male smell. Her mouth flooded with the memory of his taste, warm and salty on her tongue. She focused all her energy on making herself as small as possible, sure that if she brushed against his jacket-clad shoulder she'd go spinning off like a top.

"I'll focus on finding the leak and put one of our security specialists on Miss Miles's personal detail."

The sound of Derek biting out her name snapped her back into focus.

"No, I want you looking after my niece. I hired you because I expect the highest level of service."

"Mr. Van Weldt, I assure you that all our security specialists at Gemini are very qualified to handle Miss Miles—"

"What do you mean, 'handle me'?" Alyssa broke in.

"I want to be assured you will behave in a manner that does not bring further disgrace on this family or this business," Harold replied.

Alyssa drew back as if from a blow. "You don't need to hire him to keep me in line. I've more than proven I can behave myself in public—"

"Oh, really?" Harold threw something on the table—a magazine, opened to a picture of her. Taken last week at a benefit for AIDS research, it showed Alyssa slumped in a corner of a velvet sofa, eyes nothing but blurry slits in her flushed, shiny face. She looked like hell, like someone messed up to the point of passing out.

"I had the flu," she sputtered, barely remembering the night, she'd felt so awful. The nausea had hit her without warning. One minute she'd been sipping a glass of champagne and chatting with the lead singer of an up-and-coming local band, and the next thing she knew, she'd been tossing her cookies in the bathroom. Andy, her assistant, had helped her to a quiet corner of the club, but of course someone had seen her and helpfully documented the moment with his or her camera phone.

"The flu? That's the best excuse you can come up with for acting like a drunken slut when you're out representing the Van Weldt name?"

"I wasn't drunk!" Anger boiled to the surface. She struggled to keep her composure as she looked around the room and realized no one believed her. Least of all Derek.

Even Kimberly believed the worst. "I know you've been having a hard time with Daddy's death. We all have." She delicately wiped under her eyes and sniffed. "But if Mother taught us anything, drinking and drugs aren't the way to cope."

"I wasn't drunk, and I've been clean for over three years," Alyssa said. "And I don't need some meathead dogging my every move!" Seeing her uncle's glare narrow, she brought her temper back under control. "If I'm such a blight on the family," she said, her tone measured, "why don't you just let me move back to Los Angeles? Then you can wash your hands of me and go back to pretending I don't exist."

It was a question that had plagued her since her father's death. Despite Harold's obvious dislike of her, he'd expected her to keep all her engagements that related to Van Weldt business and had signed off on the budget for the new advertising campaign starring Alyssa.

And while Kimberly had welcomed her and worked to build a relationship with her, Alyssa knew her half sister wasn't comfortable with the notoriety Alyssa's past brought to the company and family. She was just too polite to ever say anything.

For the first time during the meeting Harold looked uncomfortable. "As much as it pains me to admit, since you've been directly associated with the company, revenues have increased by fifty percent. Because of the public's inexplicable fascination with your every move, Van Weldt has become a household name. As much as I detest everything you represent, I'm too smart of a businessman to get rid of you while you still prove useful."

She felt Derek shift next to her. Alyssa straightened in her chair, determined to not let him see her be so easily cowed. "I'm an adult, Uncle Harold. If I decide to move, there's nothing you can do to stop me."

"That is true," he replied, lowering his gaze to a stack of papers in front of him. "However, you may miss the generous salary you receive as a spokesmodel for Van Weldt."

"Uncle Harold," Kimberly said in a scolding whisper, but he cut her off with his raised palm.

Alyssa knew when she was trumped. Though she got a generous stipend from her trust every month, it wasn't enough to cover her skyrocketing expenses over the past year. She needed the extra income, and Harold knew it, damn him.

She slumped back in her chair. If it were just her, she would have gone, no question, as the stipend from her trust was more than enough to cover her own expenses. Unfortunately these days it wasn't all about her.

"As you're well aware, your father didn't leave any provision for your mother's care. So if you want her to continue receiving treatment, you'll cooperate with me and Mr. Taggart."

Alyssa swallowed back bitterness and nodded. She hated

to be such a fucking doormat. But not only had her mother let her health insurance lapse before she was diagnosed with cancer, she also had to fly to France every few months for experimental treatments. It was possible Alyssa could earn more money through endorsements and appearances, but it would take a while for her manager to line things up. And she needed steady cash, guaranteed. There was nothing she could do but swallow her pride and prove to her uncle she could be the well-behaved daughter her father had always wanted.

"Now, if you'll excuse us, Kimberly and I need to discuss next quarter's marketing campaign. Kim, I sent you my comments on your budget. Did you get them?"

When their father was alive, he, with Kimberly's help, had been in charge of all sales, marketing, and publicity. Since his death Kim had completely taken over that aspect of the business.

Kim nodded and pulled her laptop out of her briefcase. "I haven't had a chance to read them in detail," she apologized.

Alyssa licked her lips nervously and reached into her bag. "Actually, I was hoping to sit in on this meeting. I have some ideas—"

Harold looked up, his gray-blond eyebrows raised in genuine surprise. "Ideas? You?"

She focused on her uncle, determined to block out the presence of the large, overbearing male presence next to her. "I've been hoping to get more involved on the business side, and now that I've starred in two campaigns, I thought I should be involved in the overall marketing strategy."

Harold barked a laugh. "You expect me to believe you think at all beyond your next party or next shopping trip? Did you think last weekend when you embarrassed us all by losing control at the AIDS benefit?"

Alyssa could feel Derek stiffen next to her and felt humiliation's icy grip curl around her insides. Constant press scrutiny had forced her to grow a thick skin, and for the most part her uncle's comments bounced off her. But having Derek there, listening to him berate her, made her want to curl up in a ball and hide under the conference table. "You may not care about my ideas," she said, hating how her voice shook with embarrassed rage, "but I'm still a significant stockholder in this company. That gives me a right to be involved with the business."

Bull's-eye. She took keen satisfaction in the way Harold flushed all the way to his thinning blond hairline. He was still furious that her father had changed his will, splitting his share of Van Weldt Jeweler evenly between herself and Kimberly. It had been a shock to everyone, Alyssa included, but Harold had taken it as a personal affront.

"Your shares are still in trust and therefore under my control. So for the time being, your only job is to look pretty for the camera and not embarrass us in front of the press. A task I hope Mr. Taggart will assist with." Harold's anger fled as quickly as it flared, and he bared his teeth in a smile that didn't reach his eyes. "Let's not pretend. We all know where your value to this company lies, and it's not between your ears. Your job is to smile for the cameras. And when you're not doing that, you do your best not to make an ass out of yourself."

Vapid. Stupid. Brainless. Every insult to her intelligence the media had ever doled out came back in a searing rush.

She looked to her sister for support, but Kimberly kept her gaze focused on the screen of her laptop, the tight lines of her mouth the only sign the tension in the room was getting to her.

Alyssa's stomach churned with embarrassment, made all the more acute because Derek was there to witness it. She shoved it aside and pasted on her famous, toothy, party-girl smile as an alarm went off deep inside her leather bag.

"Well, speaking of smiling and looking pretty, I'm about to be late for a spa appointment."

She stood up, trying not to shiver when Derek's shoulder brushed against hers as he stood, too. She turned on her spiked heel, striving for a dignified exit though she felt about a tenth as confident as she had when she'd entered the conference room.

"Mr. Taggart will accompany you, of course," Harold said.

Alyssa froze, her megawatt smile pulling down at the corners. "I'm perfectly capable of going to get a pedicure and a bikini wax on my own. Besides, Andy will be with me." Andrea, the assistant she'd hired right after she moved to San Francisco, was waiting for her in the lobby. *God, I hope she remembered my ibuprofen,* Alyssa thought as her temples began to pound.

But Derek reacted as if she hadn't even spoken and used his powerful body to herd her toward the door. "After you," he said, gesturing her to precede him.

She stepped out in the empty hallway and turned to face him. Even in five-inch heels, she barely came to his chin, and she had to tilt her head back to meet his eyes. At the hard, closed expression on his face she was reminded of her first impression. That he was like a craggy peak of a mountain. Stone cold and just as forbidding.

"Listen," she began but found she was tongue-tied under that flat, emotionless stare. Was this really the man who had touched her with such eagerness his hands shook? The man who had whispered hot, dirty things in her ears, moaned against her neck as he'd thrust deep inside her?

"Yes, Miss Miles?" he prodded after several seconds of her silence. His voice was blank, all business.

"This is incredibly awkward for both of us. Given the circumstances, don't you think it's best you tell my uncle you can't work for him?" She couldn't stand this. Bad enough her uncle had sicced a keeper on her, but she couldn't bear having Derek follow her around, watching her every move.

His answer was a short, quick shake of his head. "No can do. The Van Weldts are one of our biggest clients. I can't quit because of personal reasons."

She stamped her foot and clenched her fists. "Then put someone else on the job. I saw you working with other people that night. Can't one of them play prison warden?"

"Sorry, princess. I'm afraid I'm it. Your uncle wants me to keep tabs on you and report back anything he might not like, and that's exactly what I'm going to do. Like it or not, we're stuck with each other until your uncle says different."

Andy Ingram took the bottle of pills Richard Blaylock handed to her and slipped them into her purse. "When do you want me to use these?"

Richard consulted his calendar. "Wait a couple days. The press is still getting a lot of mileage out of last week's pictures. There's the WhiteLight benefit coming up next weekend. Dose her at the beginning of cocktail hour so it kicks in right around the time she goes up to accept the award."

Andy smiled and nodded as if Richard had asked her to pick up his dry cleaning. But she couldn't help anticipating the sight of Alyssa stumbling on the stage as she went up to accept the award the WhiteLight Foundation was going to present her with for all her "activism." As far as Andy could tell, Alyssa's philanthropy consisted of showing up, baking some cupcakes, and posing for photos. She didn't care about those girls, Andy knew. It was all a big ploy to help clean up her image, to distance herself from the party-girl persona that had gotten her on the cover of magazines.

It made Andy sick to the tips of her toes. Andy had graduated magna cum laude from Brown with a degree in English literature, but when she moved to San Francisco, she'd been told she was lucky to get an entry-level job at a local magazine. The accompanying entry-level salary didn't even cover her rent, much less her massive school loans.

When she'd heard through a friend that Alyssa Miles was in the market for a new San Francisco–based assistant—and, more importantly, what the position would pay—Andy had swallowed her pride and gone for an interview. It hadn't been hard to convince Alyssa she would be the perfect assistant. Efficient, organized, hardworking, and, most importantly, she had no interest in using Alyssa's show-business connections to further her career.

At least, that's what Alyssa thought. Andy was, in fact, building up quite a Rolodex of press contacts she planned to use once she'd paid off her debts and left Alyssa Miles far behind. After all, they would owe her after all the tips she'd given them over the last six months.

Still, she felt a little sick to her stomach when she woke up every morning and braced herself for another day of performing useless, meaningless tasks for a useless, meaningless celebrity like Alyssa. It was so unfair. Andy had clawed her way out of her working-class Massachusetts neighborhood, gotten an Ivy League education, yet she was reduced to babysitting a famous-for-nothing celebutante.

Fortunately, Richard Blaylock had recently approached her with a little side project. Andy was only too happy to participate because the extra money she earned meant her loans were nearly paid off. Plus, it had the added bonus of ruining Alyssa's public image, right when she was on the verge of proving to the public she'd left her wild, hard partying days behind her.

Andy loved to watch Alyssa unwittingly reap what she'd sown.

"You're sure she doesn't suspect anything?" Richard asked, glancing surreptitiously over his shoulder to make sure no one was coming.

Andy shook her head. One thing she'd learned very quickly

about Alyssa was that while she knew she needed to be careful of people, she so badly *wanted* to trust people, it was rather easy to get into her confidence. All it had taken were a few late-night conversations, shared secrets, and a few careful compliments, and Andy was in. Alyssa had given Andy almost unlimited access to her life; it didn't occur to Alyssa that Andy might try to screw her over. "I just tell her they're ibuprofen, and she takes them without looking."

"Well, watch the dosage next time," Richard warned. "Last time was too close. We don't want to have to explain an overdose."

"Of course," Andy said. She didn't know why Richard and whomever he was working with wanted to make it look like Alyssa was relapsing. All Andy was concerned with was keeping the prescriptions to the various pharmaceuticals filled and receiving those extra deposits in her online checking account every month.

"Andy? Where are you?" Andy's shoulders tensed as she heard Alyssa's voice from down the hall. "I have to be at LaBelle by eleven. I managed to squeeze in a facial for you, too, so we can't be late."

"One more thing," Richard said when Andy started to go. "Harold hired some bodyguard to keep an eye on Alyssa. You'll need to be really careful, make sure he doesn't suspect anything."

"Don't worry," she said reassuringly. "As long as the money keeps showing up in my bank account, no one will have any idea Alyssa's not a relapsing junkie headed for a meltdown."

CHAPTER 5

DEREK WOULD HAVE thought following one celebutante around San Francisco would be child's play in comparison to his previous life as a sniper. Once during a mission in Afghanistan, he'd lain motionless for nine straight hours in a shallow trough dug into a rocky mountainside. He hadn't moved so much as a nostril, not even when a group of goat herders walked within six inches of his stand, so close they could have brushed the cold metal of his muzzle. Watching, still as death, waiting for them to pass and for his military targets to come into focus, waiting for the moment when he could pick them all off like ducks in a carnival game.

After two days on Alyssa Miles's tail, Derek was ready to shoot anything. Starting with himself.

Yesterday was bad enough. He'd dutifully accompanied Alyssa and her mousy assistant, Andy, to a spa so pink and feminine he worried he was going to have to hand over his balls at the reception desk. The woman at the reception desk had assured her there was no one else in the spa, and, when pressed by Andy, that all cell phones and cameras had been confiscated.

"You clear out the whole spa?" Derek asked. He found it hard to swallow that he could be so attracted to the kind of woman who needed a whole goddamn spa to herself.

"You would, too, if someone took cell-phone pictures of you getting a Brazilian wax," Alyssa snapped.

He didn't think he'd seen that one. But the mention of Alyssa's wax job was enough to make his hands sweat and his mouth go dry.

The receptionist flushed red and murmured an apology. "We've banned her from the premises, Miss Miles. And we'd like to thank you with a complementary honey wrap for being so understanding."

"Thank you, Gina," Alyssa said and flashed the woman a dazzling smile. Then she handed Derek their purses, and she and Andy followed Gina back to the treatment rooms and left Derek to cool his heels with a back issue of *Vogue.*

A honey wrap. He wondered what the hell that entailed. Imagined a woman trickling honey over Alyssa's bare, smooth skin. He remembered in vivid detail exactly what Alyssa looked like naked. Especially the sweet, juicy fruit nestled between her legs, almost completely denuded of hair save for a dark bronze tuft of the sweetest, softest curls he'd ever touched.

Cold. Calm. Professional. This is just another job. He ripped his thoughts away from Alyssa and reminded himself what he was doing. He had a job to do. That was it. He'd never gotten emotionally involved with any of his clients, and he wasn't about to start now.

Besides, the Alyssa he met the night of the charity auction and the woman he was assigned to keep tabs on were not the same person. Sure, she was still quick with a smile and tried to be friendly, but from the moment he sat down beside her in Van Weldt's office, he'd felt cold standoffishness emanating from her in waves. Even her hand was icy when he'd taken it.

So different from the sultry, flirtatious sex kitten who'd run her hot little hands all over his body. If he closed his eyes he could still feel her fingers wrapping around his cock, sending him up in flames.

Now she wanted absolutely nothing to do with him.

So he kept his eyes wide open, reminding himself sharply that the woman he'd taken home that night was an illusion. She was only having a little fun at the expense of the one guy in the world too clueless to know who she was. The girl who had her fake, toothy smile always at the ready as she met her adoring public—that was the real Alyssa Miles.

But that didn't stop his thoughts from wandering after a couple hours. What the hell were they doing to her that was taking so long? Sweat beaded under his collar as he imagined her, lying on a table, covered in honey.

Was she getting waxed again? Was she at that moment lying with her legs parted as another woman reached down. . . .

He shifted in his seat, crossing his legs to hide his burgeoning erection. Shit. His thoughts were taking on the tone of a bad porno.

He was jolted momentarily out of his daydreams by the trill of a cell phone coming from Alyssa's purse. He ignored it. But when it rang three more times in quick succession, he figured it might be something important.

Maybe he should bring her phone to her.

Or maybe you're looking for an excuse to go find out what the hell's going on behind the pink doors.

He pushed through the doors into a dimly lit hallway. The sweet, sultry scent was stronger back here, and wind-chimey new-agey music piped through invisible speakers. The hall was lined with closed doors. He listened at each one until he heard the low murmur of voices.

He opened the door and felt all the blood in his brain make a beeline for his cock at the sight that greeted him. Alyssa was half reclined in a padded, upholstered chair. A fluffy white robe fell open at her knees as she propped her feet on a stool. The woman kneeling at her feet poured oil into the palm of her hand before rubbing it into Alyssa's foot and then working her way up Alyssa's calf and midway up her thigh. Another woman sat at Alyssa's right, working oil into Alyssa's hand and arm with sure, firm strokes.

Alyssa's eyes were closed, her expression one of relaxed bliss. Her cheeks were flushed, her mouth soft, her body languid. He swallowed hard, feeling like he'd stepped through a time warp into a secret harem, where Alyssa was being stroked and oiled, ready to be delivered for his pleasure.

He watched, mesmerized as the woman at her feet moved to the other leg. His palms itched at the remembered feel of her skin under his hands. Smooth, hot, silky soft. He wanted to banish the women from the room and put himself in their place. Kneel at her feet. Stroke his way up her thighs and part her legs wider. Dip his head down. He licked his lips. He'd been so wild that night, so focused on getting inside her before he lost control, he hadn't had a chance to taste her pussy. Now his mouth watered for it, his body throbbed with the need to do all the things he hadn't had a chance to do in their one brief, mind-blowing encounter.

"You really shouldn't be back here."

Derek whipped his head around at the scolding voice and started at the sight that greeted him. Andy stood at his left shoulder, dressed in a thick, white spa robe. Her dark hair was skinned back from her face by a headband, and her mouth was pursed in a scowl. At least, he thought it was a scowl, but it was hard to tell with her face covered by a coating of thick green goop.

He blinked, but the creature from the black lagoon was still standing there, waiting for an explanation. "Her phone was ringing." He gestured lamely with Alyssa's purse. "Thought it might be important."

"Who was it?"

Derek looked over to see Alyssa watching him with heavy-lidded green eyes, a lazy little cat woken from her nap in the sun.

Andy rummaged around in Alyssa's bag and looked at the display. "It was Marianne. Probably about the fund-raiser. I'll call her back and see what she wants."

Andy ducked out of the treatment room, leaving Derek standing there like an idiot, heat rushing into his face as Alyssa and the two women working her over pinned him with inquisitive stares. He mumbled something about meeting her in the waiting room and backed out, praying none of them noticed the raging hard-on tenting the front of his pants.

After the torturous trip to the spa, Derek was relieved to learn that today Alyssa was keeping her clothes on, for the time being anyway. She had an interview with a reporter from *Bella Magazine,* and he assumed there would be no reason to remove her close-fitting jeans and striped sweater. Later she had a photo shoot scheduled and, having seen some of Alyssa's past layouts, Derek didn't even want to think about what he was in for.

He followed Andy and Alyssa into the restaurant where they were first scheduled to meet the reporter. The restaurant hadn't yet opened for lunch, but the manager had opened it up so Alyssa and the reporter could talk privately.

As they walked into the dimly lit bistro, an athletic-looking brunette dressed in black pants and a dark green sweater stood and waved them over. She held out her hand to Alyssa. "Meredith Winslow, *Bella Magazine.*"

Alyssa shook her hand and smiled. "Alyssa Miles. This is my assistant, Andy." Andy stepped up to shake Meredith's hand.

Alyssa took a seat at the table while Andy sat down a few tables away and pulled out her BlackBerry.

"And who's this?" Meredith asked, eying Derek with speculation and unmistakable interest.

Alyssa's careful smile pulled tight at the corners. "This is Derek. He's . . ." A tiny frown line appeared between her brows as she struggled to decide how to describe him.

"I'm her personal security detail," he clarified.

Meredith's brows pulled into a frown. "Does the heightened security have anything to do with your father's death?"

Derek felt the hairs rise on the back of his neck. Despite her look of concern, Derek sensed something predatory in the reporter's manner.

"Not exactly," Alyssa said, her smile strained.

"How have you been holding up since his death?" Meredith's face was all sad eyes and sympathy as she switched on the tape recorder.

"It's been difficult," Alyssa replied. Her fingers twisted nervously on the table in front of her.

"I can only imagine. Finding your father like that, it must have been awful for you."

Alyssa nodded. "I have pretty bad nightmares."

"Really, like what?"

Alyssa got a faraway look in her green eyes. "I dream about that night, about finding them. Sometimes I dream there's someone else there, waiting to kill me, too." She shook her head, as though jolting herself back to reality.

Meredith looked down at her pile of notes. "Interesting." Derek didn't like the way her eyes lit with morbid curiosity. "I read that in the initial police report you said you thought you saw a shadow running across the lawn."

Alyssa nodded.

"So do you think the police were too quick to pin the blame on your stepmother? Maybe someone else was involved?"

Alyssa's smile was long gone. Now her face was a stressed mask, her lips pressed into a tight line, her mouth pulled down at the corners. She was silent for several seconds, lost deep in thought. Finally she shook her head. "It was all so scary and overwhelming," she said, the horror evident in her voice.

Derek felt an unwilling tug of sympathy as he watched Alyssa try to compose herself. The gory crime scene had been well documented in lurid detail. He'd seen his share of blood and death, and even *he* couldn't say he ever got used to it. He could only imagine how someone like Alyssa, sheltered from any of life's harsh realities, would react to such a scene.

An unfamiliar urge washed over him—the need to comfort her, hold her close, reassure her that everything was going to be okay.

"It's hard to know exactly what I saw," Alyssa continued, "but I'm sure the police knew what they were doing."

Meredith nodded. "And how do you respond to the people who say your presence in your father's life and your involvement with the business drove your stepmother over the edge?"

Alyssa flinched as if she'd been hit, and Derek forced himself to stay seated in his straight-backed chair. He looked over at Andy, wondering why she didn't say anything. She continued to poke at her BlackBerry, oblivious.

"My stepmother was troubled," Alyssa said carefully. "I deeply regret any pain I caused her, but I'm not sorry for trying to have a relationship with my father."

There was a tight, pinching sensation in Derek's chest that he tried to ignore. He didn't want to feel sympathy for Alyssa, didn't want to be touched by her vulnerability. He wanted her to be the vapid trust-fund baby he'd read about, not this big-eyed, sad girl who sat there and took it while this reporter aimed repeated jabs.

He was just about to say screw it, end the interview, and hustle her out of there, when Alyssa seemed to gather herself up. She sat up straight in her chair, pasted the toothpaste smile back on her face, and cleared all emotion from her wide green eyes. "Do you mind if we talk about something else? I'd really rather not dwell on tragedy."

"Of course. I apologize," Meredith said, her smile as sincere as Alyssa's. "Let's talk about fun stuff. Are you seeing anyone these days?"

Alyssa's cheeks blushed hot pink. "N—no, not really." She lowered her eyes.

The damn woman couldn't lie to save her life. He wondered if the reporter noticed.

Meredith gave her one of those conspiratorial, "hey, it's just us girls here" smiles. "Please. You can't convince me you don't have tons of guys knocking down your door."

Derek was locked on her face, waiting for her to give him a look, to betray some sign to the shark of a reporter that their relationship wasn't strictly personal.

Then another thought hit him. Maybe the stammering and blushing wasn't all about him. He'd seen the articles linking her to everyone from a skinny, eyeliner-wearing rock star to the French-Lebanese dude who supplied the Van Weldts with the majority of their diamonds.

Who knew what—or who—Alyssa had been doing since Derek had seen her last?

"I'm single right now," Alyssa said, and this time the conviction rang true. "My relationship track record hasn't been so hot lately." She gave the reporter a sheepish smile, and Derek fought the urge to warn her not to let her guard down.

"You're referring to your relationship with Eddie Bennett?"

The dusting of freckles across Alyssa's nose stood out in stark contrast to skin gone pale as marble. "That's one example, yes."

Meredith cocked a dark eyebrow at her. "Do you regret your relationship with Eddie Bennett?"

He could see the moment Alyssa finally went over the edge, when her fragile hold on her composure snapped.

"Considering he told me he loved me and then put naked pictures of me on the Internet for the entire world to see and then told everyone I was the worst lay he's ever had, yeah, I'd say I regret it."

Even Andy was startled out of her BlackBerry coma by Alyssa's mini tirade.

Derek bit back a smile. Even though the reporter's expression spelled doom for Alyssa, he couldn't help but admire her for standing up for herself.

Alyssa stood up from her chair and stuck out her hand. "I'm really sorry to cut this short," she said as she pumped a surprised Meredith's hand, "but I have a photo shoot in about half an hour."

"It's not—" Andy started to say, only to be shut down by Alyssa's stony look.

It was the first evidence Derek had seen of Alyssa's supposedly divalike behavior.

She straightened her spine, threw back her shoulders, and sashayed out of the restaurant, never faltering on her four-inch stilettos. She motioned for him and Andy to follow, a princess summoning her lackeys.

Her poise crumbled the second they hit the sidewalk. "I am so screwed," she moaned, burying her face in her hands.

"It's not that bad," Derek said, compelled to console her even though she was probably right.

"It's not good," Andy said, shaking her head and tsking like a schoolmarm.

Derek shot her a glare over Alyssa's bent head.

"I'm not trying to be negative," Andy said defensively. "But this is the first time Alyssa's commented publicly about the pictures. Everyone's going to pick up on it."

"Andy, why don't you go get the car," Alyssa said, rubbing at her temples like she was in pain.

Andy nodded and hurried off.

"Why can't I just keep my mouth shut?" Alyssa asked. "I know better than this. They're always asking, and then the next thing I know I'm saying things I know I shouldn't." She shook her head and broke off.

"She was pushing your buttons," he said, shoving his hand in his pockets so he wouldn't slide his arms around her in a reassuring hug.

"Still, I shouldn't have talked about Eddie. I don't know what's wrong with me lately. It's like my brain totally loses control over my mouth."

"Did he really say you were the worst lay he'd ever had?" The question was out of his mouth before he could call it back.

"What, you didn't read all about it when you did your research?" Her face was pale except for two streaks of red on her cheekbones, and she wouldn't meet his gaze.

"I must have missed that article." Truth was, other than reading the headlines, he'd avoided the articles about her relationship, because it made him unreasonably, illogically angry to think of her with another man.

"Well, you're the only one."

"If it's any consolation, it's not true," he said. "The part about you being the worst lay, I mean." Now his cheeks were red with embarrassment as she looked up at him. "Maybe he didn't know what he was doing or something, but the problem couldn't have been you." He told himself to shut up, but he couldn't stop the words from stumbling out. For the first time in his life his need for detachment was outweighed by the need to make a woman feel better. "As far as I'm concerned, you're the best—that I've ever had, anyway." His head was so hot he was surprised flames weren't shooting out of his ears.

"Oh," Alyssa said, astonished, and in her eyes he could

see her remembering, like a movie trailer, every touch, every kiss. "Uh, likewise."

Her lips were pink, shiny, soft, daring him to bend his head and trace them with his tongue. He might have done exactly that had Andy not pulled up to the curb in Alyssa's gold Mercedes at that exact moment.

Two hours later Derek sat in a photo studio while Alyssa posed for a series of photos for an ad campaign that would launch in the new year.

Derek had figured they'd put Alyssa in a dress, throw a necklace on her, snap a few photos, and that would be it.

He wondered what he'd done that God felt the need to create Derek's own personal hell on earth.

"Alyssa, tilt your head this way. No. Back more. And arch your back. Bring your right knee up just a hair. Perfect."

Derek tried not to look but couldn't stop himself. Alyssa was on a platform made to look like a satin-draped bed, reclined back on her elbows with her head back, throat arching up to the ceiling. One slim leg was bent.

Oh, and she was practically naked. She wore a flesh-colored bikini bottom decorated with diamonds at the crotch and a pair of pasties over her nipples. A diamond choker circled her throat, and thick cuffs sparkled at her wrists and ankles. A bra thing that looked like it was made out of fishing line and diamond studs was draped over her small, firm breasts.

Dozens of black-clad people buzzed around, touching, primping, tweaking. A makeup woman went at Alyssa's face and body with a tool chest full of cosmetics until every inch of her was covered in powder and glitter. A lanky, goth-looking guy interrupted after every shot to move the swath of gold fabric one nanometer to the left or to instruct another assistant to change the angle of the lights by a degree.

Then there was the beefy-looking guy with a black goatee who was in charge of "wardrobe." Meaning he was abnormally focused on Alyssa's tits and crotch and the way the diamonds were positioned over those parts of her body. The guy ran his fingers under the fishing-line diamond contraption covering Alyssa's breasts after nearly every shot, claiming he wanted to catch the light at precisely the right angle.

It was just an excuse to feel her up, and they both knew it. After about the hundredth time, Derek stood from his chair, ready to fuck protocol and pop the guy in the face. But as he moved toward the dais, Derek caught the guy's attention. And it didn't take world-class gaydar for him to see that Alyssa wasn't this guy's primary target.

He sat back down, rubbing his neck as sweat itched under the collar of his shirt. Derek had already ditched his sport jacket. With the lights blazing from every direction, it was about a thousand degrees in the studio, and the constant motion and noise was starting to give him a headache.

But Alyssa didn't complain once, suffering through the touching, the tweaking, the groping, holding the same uncomfortable pose for as long as it took for the photographer to get the right shot.

Long enough for Derek to wonder if he had the self-restraint it was going to take to keep his hands off Alyssa. Lying there, her honey-colored skin sparkling with diamonds, her soft, perfect tits arching up at the ceiling, Alyssa made him want to throw everyone out of the studio, join her on that satin-covered bed, and peel off those barely there bikini bottoms so he could check out her Brazilian up close.

He stared hard and saw a tiny bead of sweat trickle down her rib cage. It was all he could do not to run up there and catch it with his tongue—to hell with their audience.

"Now let's change it up," said the photographer, a skinny Asian guy whose purple pants matched the streaks in his hair. "I want you facing forward, on your knees."

Yeah, that sounded about right to Derek, too.

He watched as Alyssa rose to her feet in one sleek move.

"Hold on a sec," she said and raised her arms above her head. "I have a knot I need to work out."

A shot of heat went straight to his groin as she arched her back, making her tits jut out behind the jewel-encrusted mesh that functioned as her top. Derek didn't need to see her bare nipples to remember what they looked like. Their soft pink color that darkened as he sucked was burned into his brain.

Then Alyssa almost killed him by bending at the waist and flattening her palms against the floor, raising up first on one heel and then the other to stretch out her hamstrings. "Sorry," she said, her voice muffled by her heavy hair. "That last pose made my butt go numb."

He shifted in the metal folding chair and crossed his leg over his knee, hoping no one noticed the growing bulge in his crotch. Jesus Christ. First the woman tempted him into an uncharacteristic one-night stand. Now she had him popping wood like a thirteen-year-old in gym class.

Derek had learned to master his breathing, slow his heartbeat, trained himself not to react to anything during his missions when the slightest move might give away his position. Now his ironclad control was unraveling like a cheap sweater, thanks to about a buck-ten worth of light brown hair and silky skin.

Even worse, he was starting to like her. Really like her. Admire her even, for her professionalism, her attempt—however failed—to keep her composure when she'd been poked and prodded by the reporter. Liked her enough to breach bounds of professionalism and tell her she was the best lay he'd ever had—a boneheaded move if there ever was one.

He would be the last to ever admit it, but despite all evidence to the contrary, he was starting to think maybe she wasn't the wild, overprivileged mess the press made her out to be. Derek certainly hadn't seen any signs of her supposed drug use since he'd been with her. Maybe she was misunderstood, victimized by a media machine that wanted her to be the wild and crazy diva whose face and antics sold magazines.

"Is there anything we can get for you?" asked the photographer's assistant, a rail-thin girl with dyed black hair and a tattoo, creeping up the back of her neck.

"You know what I'd love?" Alyssa said, her voice muffled as she bent and stretched. "That grilled wild salmon from Farallon and some mixed wild greens."

Never mind that it was three in the afternoon, well before the dinner hour, and the restaurant—one of San Francisco's finest—didn't do takeout.

When Derek pointed that out, Alyssa stood back up, flipping her hair back over her head in a motion straight out of a shampoo commercial. "Just tell them it's for me."

So maybe her diva rep wasn't totally unfounded.

The assistant called to order the food as Alyssa moved to kneel on the fake bed. She shifted into the pose, and as she turned to the camera, her gaze caught Derek's. Heat pulsed through him, arcing between them in an electrical charge so fierce he was surprised the lights didn't explode under the force.

"That is exactly the look I want," said the photographer, scrambling for his camera. "Sexy, knowing, like you've got a secret you're dying to tell. Whatever you're thinking, go with it."

Derek had a good idea what she was thinking. He was thinking the same damn thing. About them in a sweaty naked tangle on his bed, hair-roughened skin meeting silky smoothness. His rock-hard cock sliding into her slick heat.

Her sultry green gaze sucked him in, pulled him under. It was there again, that tight ache in his chest that tried to sneak up on him whenever he looked at her.

He couldn't look away, her steady stare holding him like a tractor beam. Her glossy pink mouth curved in a slight smile. A remembered taste of peaches flooded his mouth. "See something you like?" She pursed her lips at him in a little air kiss.

You have no idea. But he schooled his face into a hard mask, unwilling to let anyone—least of all her—see how powerfully she affected him. He had no business flirting back, no business treating her like anything other than a client.

His phone rang, and he seized the excuse to leave the room as he took Danny's call. "What's up?" he asked.

"Just checking in. Have you been running?"

"No? Why?"

"You're breathing hard."

You would be, too, if you were trapped in a furnace-hot room with a nearly naked woman you want more than any woman you've ever seen. "I'm at a photo shoot. It's hot in here."

"How's it going with the train wreck?"

Everything in Derek bristled at Danny's word choice. "Don't call her that. She's not as bad as they say."

"Wow. You must really like her for me to hit a nerve. Don't tell me you're contemplating going where so many have boldly gone before?"

His shoulders bunched in irritation at Danny's crassness, but it was a good reminder of how the rest of the world saw her. Yeah, the press could exaggerate things, but most stories had a kernel of truth. She'd had a hand in creating her public image, no matter how bad she wanted to change it now.

"Not in this lifetime," Derek replied.

"You gotta admit she's cute. A little on the small side, but that's not always a bad thing—"

"Did you call me for a reason? Because if all you want to

do is talk about Alyssa and her dubious appeal, you're welcome to come check her out for yourself. In fact, you could take over this assignment completely—"

"Dude, don't get so riled up," Danny said with a chuckle. "Try to see the bright side. After the Kramer cluster fuck, this is a cakewalk. All you have to do is follow a beautiful girl and keep her out of trouble. Enjoy it."

Right. He was enjoying it about as much as he enjoyed a root canal. He went back into the studio, grateful to find Alyssa off her knees and sitting in a makeup chair.

"We're almost finished," she said. "Sorry it's so hot in here. I know you must be uncomfortable."

"I'm fine," he replied, careful not to look at her as the photographer's assistant carefully removed the jewelry from her wrists and ankles, along with the fishing-wire-and-diamond bra.

He heard a faint ripping sound, followed by Alyssa's pained gasp, and spun around. And wished he hadn't when he saw Alyssa cupping her own breasts, wincing as she gave them a gentle massage.

Even under her heavy makeup, he could see the pink bloom in her cheeks when she caught him staring. "The pasties always hurt when they come off," she said with a little laugh that hit him straight in the gut. "It's not all glamor, even when you're dealing in diamonds."

Martin sat in the bar of the Grand Hotel, edging deeper into the dark corner he'd found. Even in midafternoon, the dim room was noisy with the din of French, Lingala, and the occasional English conversation as he edged deeper in his corner. A lazy ceiling fan stirred the hot, smoke-filled air as he darted his gaze around the room. Unlike the semicivilized city Kinshasa, Mbuji-Mayi was an isolated wasteland. The only people who came here on purpose were misguided aid workers who thought they could save the savages from themselves, businessmen looking to join in on the rape and pillage of the DRC's vast mineral resources, and guys like him. Journalists working an angle, trying to sniff out a big story to sell.

Or not sell, if the price was right.

For the first time in weeks, the faintest tingle of optimism fired in Martin's belly. His story was pulling together, details falling into place even better than he could have imagined.

First, there was the murder-suicide of Oscar Van Weldt and his wife. Or was it, as Martin suspected, a double murder? Sure, Grace Van Weldt was a boozer and a pill popper and on her way off her rocker, but the timing was a little too close for Martin's comfort. What were the odds Grace would lose her shit and off Oscar and herself only a few days after Martin had put a bug in Van Weldt's ear about Abbassi?

Van Weldt's death had made Martin's story a lot more interesting. And potentially a lot more dangerous.

And now this. Martin sat transfixed in front of his computer monitor. He took another gulp of malafu, his attention riveted to the scene unfolding on screen. When he'd enlisted Marie Laure's help, he'd dreamed of capturing footage like this.

Again he checked his video recording program, ensuring the feed was being recorded even as he watched it live. He pulled the laptop closer, even though the privacy filter he'd put over the screen ensured no one would be able to see from the side.

Though the camera Marie Laure wore had its view slightly obscured by the edge of a tent flap, Martin had a clear shot of all the players surrounding the army truck that had pulled into the center of the mine's encampment earlier that afternoon. Mekembe and three of his men flipped up the heavy canvas that hid the truck's cargo. Even in the grainy shot,

Martin could see that the back of the truck was bristling with weapons. Kalashnikovs, AK-47s, and Uzis were unloaded from the truck. There were even two rocket-propelled grenade launchers with enough firepower to take down a helicopter or a small plane.

Then a tall, lean man with dark, Mediterranean features came into view. Louis Abbassi. Marie Laure had referred to him as "the Français," though he was actually a Lebanese national who had dual French citizenship, thanks to his French socialite mother. His father was a wealthy shipping magnate. When Mohammed Abbassi died, Louis stood to inherit millions. But the promise of wealth hadn't stopped Louis from making his own fortune in everything from diamonds to aviation. He'd painted himself as a benevolent philanthropist, allowing aid organizations and NGOs to use his fleet of South African–based aircraft to transport goods all over the continent.

But Martin knew those planes didn't transport just rice and bandages.

Abbassi was a ubiquitous figure in the international press, flaunting his wealth and always photographed with at least one beautiful woman on his arm. He'd dated actresses and models from all over the world.

Including, according to various sources, Alyssa Miles, whom he reportedly met when he signed a deal with the Van Weldts to supply diamonds through his South African–based diamond-cutting facility.

Though Abbassi claimed all his rough came from certified mines in conflict-free South Africa, Martin knew enough about the man's other business dealings to smell a rat. So he'd done a little digging and discovered ties to at least three illegal mines, including this one in the DRC. Once he was finished here, Martin planned to go public with the story despite the lack of real hard proof, willing to settle for implication and innuendo and let the public decide for itself.

This—this was like a gift from God.

He watched, a smirk pulling at his mouth as he saw Mekembe hand Abbassi an innocuous canvas bag. Though he couldn't hear the audio, it was clear from the handshakes and brief conversation the men were making a deal.

He couldn't believe Abbassi's arrogance, the sheer stupidity, of making the delivery himself. Before, if Martin had gone public with his story, it was unlikely Abbassi would face prosecution. He could easily claim ignorance. After all, he had certificates of authenticity for his diamonds. How was he to know they were forged? And all his planes' flight plans were registered. No one could ever prove he'd been in the DRC.

But transporting weapons—weapons liberated from a former Soviet stockpile, if he wasn't missing his guess—for diamonds so the rebels could continue their reign of terror? No way the Lebanese bastard could talk his way out of that.

Suddenly the view jerked forward. Martin's stomach bottomed out as Mekembe whipped his head toward Marie Laure, shouting something Martin couldn't hear. Shit. She'd been found out. He watched, helpless, as the ground rushed up to her. Then he got a view of Mekembe's angry face blocking the sky. His screen filled with nothing but green shirt as Marie Laure was pulled up. Then he got a view of the inside of a tent. Brown arms struggled in front of the camera.

Then the camera was buried under a pile of shifting fabric, and he couldn't see anything.

Martin switched off the monitor and swallowed back his nausea, trying not to imagine what was happening to Marie Laure as he sat in the relative comfort and security of the hotel lounge. He looked at the flash drive curled in his hand and signaled for another cup of malafu. He had the footage he needed, and that was what mattered.

The server left his drink, and he drained it in two gulps.

But it wasn't enough to get images of Marie Laure out of his head, her slender body bloated with a kid. Lying under that animal, Mekembe, as he rutted over her. Martin wiped his face. This place was getting to him, sinking its claws into his brain, overrunning his head with nightmarish visions that no amount of palm wine or whiskey could obliterate.

He couldn't worry about her. He had to focus, keep his eyes on the prize. Even if he did manage to get Marie Laure out of this shit hole, there were thousands more like her. Girls who would be raped, tortured, killed, as these backwater savages destroyed themselves.

He focused instead on Alyssa, her golden beauty reeking of wealth and pampering. Too ignorant to realize she was dating a diamond smuggler and arms trader. Unaware that the diamonds sparkling on her body were drenched in the blood of girls like Marie Laure.

Four days. Four days, and he would be out of this shit hole, and he would never look back. He smiled, imagining the look on Alyssa's face when he burst her privileged little bubble and brought reality crashing down over her.

CHAPTER 6

"SORRY I'M LATE," Alyssa said, running down the hallway from her bedroom as fast as her high heels would allow.

Derek sat sprawled on the cream-colored sofa in the sitting room, his muscular bulk taking up most of the space.

"That's what you're wearing?"

"Yeah, you like it?" She did a little twirl. One look at his face told her she'd hit the jackpot with her midnight-blue sequined minidress.

"I just don't understand how you can spend all that time getting ready and come out in your underwear."

She rolled her eyes but couldn't suppress a smile. She'd seen the heat that had flared in his eyes before he'd squelched it. She'd had fun teasing him in the week he'd been acting as her shadow.

You're the best—that I've ever had, anyway. The words spun through her mind on an endless loop, combined with the image of his cheeks flushing red as his eyes flared with desire he couldn't hide. Big, tough, stone-cold Derek, blushing. It was adorable.

He'd almost kissed her.

From that moment, she'd been doing her damnedest to find a crack in his seemingly emotionless facade. Tried to get a rise out of him to see if she could get him to drop his iron-clad control and let loose with the heat she knew bubbled just under the surface.

So far, no luck. Despite the awareness he couldn't hide 100 percent of the time, he was determined to ignore the chemistry arcing between them like an electric current.

She wished she could do the same. Since Derek Taggart had reappeared in her life, she'd been wound tight as a spring. Bouncing around, buzzing with the kind of energy that came from being around someone she was wildly attracted to.

And that she knew exactly how good he looked naked and exactly how he felt sliding hot and thick inside her only made it worse.

"Don't you have a coat or something you could wear?" he asked. "Like this one." He pulled a floor-length trench coat from her hall closet and went to wrap it around her.

"That's not even my coat," she said, swatting him away. "Besides, I have my matching wrap." She gestured at the scrap of midnight silk hanging from her arms.

"That's a handkerchief. On top of a slip."

"It's not that bad. The skirt almost hits my knees."

"Halfway down your thigh is not almost your knees," he muttered. "Whatever happened to floor-length gowns? With sleeves?"

She couldn't hold back a laugh. "God, you sound like an old geezer. 'Back in my day, if a woman showed an ankle she'd be stoned.' "

Warmth curled in her stomach at his reluctant smile, complete with dimples that made her bare knees weak. How was it that making one man smile make her feel like she'd conquered the known world?

Derek looked pointedly at his watch, breaking the spell. "We need to get moving."

He drove his own car to the Fairmont, where the party

for the WhiteLight Foundation was being held, leaving Alyssa to ride with Andy in the limo.

"He makes me nervous," Andy said. She watched Derek's Audi pull away and climbed in the limo after Alyssa. "The way he watches us." She gave a little shudder.

"He's supposed to keep an eye on me," Alyssa answered.

"He's watching me, too," Andy pointed out. "It's disconcerting, the way he lurks around like some big, angry thug."

"He's not the most personable guy in the world, but he's not that bad. Besides, I kind of like having him around." Understatement of the century. And not for the obvious reason that she could stare at his gorgeous face and body for hours on end, thinking of things she wanted to do to him.

But because, for all that he had been hired by her uncle, he made her feel safe. She liked the way he stayed close, watching her but also watching everyone else. He had a knack for picking up on when she wanted someone to keep his or her distance, and he placed himself between her and the world.

As soon as they got to the Fairmont, Derek took up his position a few feet away from Alyssa. She moved through the crowd and greeted Marianne Caruso, the director of White-Light and the organizer of the evening's event. "My, that's quite a dress," the older woman remarked, and Alyssa wondered if she'd miscalculated and crossed the line from tastefully sexy to inappropriate.

She thanked Marianne as though she'd been complimented and scanned the crowd, breathing a sigh of relief when she saw Kimberly. Kimberly looked elegant and sophisticated in a simple black sheath, and Alyssa noted that most other female guests were dressed similarly. Suddenly Alyssa felt like a flashy peacock in her blue sequins and lethally high heels.

"You look amazing," Kimberly gushed as she rushed over to greet her.

"I don't think Uncle Harold approves."

"He's been under so much stress lately, since Daddy . . ." Kimberly's voice trailed off, and Alyssa placed a comforting hand on Kimberly's shoulder.

Alyssa felt her own throat tighten. It had been almost a month, and that night was never far from her mind. She dreamed about it almost every night, saw herself stumbling into the room, all the blood, her ears ringing with screams and the wail of the police sirens.

Dreams haunted her, dreams that the shadow she saw running across the lawn was a man, a murderer fleeing the scene.

She always woke up in a cold sweat, terror mingling with guilt over the fact that she hadn't come home that night until it was too late. Despite Kimberly's reassurances, Alyssa knew that if she'd arrived a few minutes earlier, she might have been able to stop her stepmother from going over the edge.

Kimberly blinked back tears, and Alyssa gave her arm a comforting squeeze. "I know. I miss him, too." At least Kimberly had had an actual father to miss, Alyssa thought, unable to completely curb her jealousy. All Alyssa had had was the idea of what she'd hoped their relationship could be.

She'd been close, but not quite there. Not before he died.

Now she wanted to make it up to his memory, prove to him—hell, prove to herself—that she was worthy of being part of this family, no matter what stupid, immature things she'd done in the past.

Accepting tonight's award was a good start, though Alyssa wasn't completely comfortable taking on the role of family spokesperson. "I still think you should be the one accepting the award," Alyssa said, steering herself and her sister away from the subject of their father.

"It makes sense for you to do it," Kimberly said. "You've done much more work with the foundation than I have. Besides, your involvement will generate more press coverage."

As if on cue, a photographer appeared in front of them.

"Ken Hayes, *San Francisco Magazine*," he said. Alyssa barely managed to paste a smile on her face before the flash blinded her. Several others from different publications followed suit, and a correspondent for an entertainment program asked her to comment on the cause.

"It's an amazing organization," she said, choosing her words very carefully. She'd learned the hard way that if she didn't think through everything she said, statements could be edited to make her sound like she had an IQ of about fifty. "WhiteLight provides a great opportunity for underprivileged girls to explore professional careers, and I'm very honored to be a part of it."

Alyssa took a grateful sip of the sparkling water Andy handed her. The crowd pressed in, too close. Her gaze darted around, and she saw her uncle staring, always watching, waiting for her to mess up.

"Smile," her sister admonished softly. "Remember, you're the guest of honor. You're happy to be here, raising awareness."

Alyssa nodded, shamed by her sister's reminder. Of course she was happy to be there, accepting an award on behalf of the Van Weldt family and their generous support of the White-Light Foundation. She'd initially gotten involved at her father's behest, agreeing it would be a good way to boost her public image, make her seem "a bit less self-centered," to quote her father.

But after several months working with Marianne and the girls, she found she genuinely enjoyed using her celebrity for something useful. Though she did find it ironic that she, who had never technically held down a day job, was supposed to give the girls career advice. Still, she could talk to them about overcoming feelings of inadequacy and had used her connections to arrange internships in fashion, publishing, even in software companies.

She looked around the room for some of them, glad a

few of the girls had come tonight and that the crowd wasn't solely made up of uptight donors.

She felt Derek stiffen beside her as a body burst past the reporter. A petite girl with waist-length dark hair and a caramel-colored complexion froze, dark eyes wide as Derek stepped in front of Alyssa and pinned the girl with a cold, forbidding stare.

"It's okay," Alyssa said hastily, reaching around Derek to grab Maya's arm. Maya gave Derek a wary look as she returned Alyssa's hug.

"He's not going to throw me out for touching you or anything, is he?"

Alyssa shook her head and shot Derek a dirty look. "Derek, this is Maya Castillo, one of the recipients of WhiteLight's scholarship this year. She'll be starting at UCLA this fall. Maya, this is Derek. He's my bodyguard, so you'll have to forgive him for being a little overprotective."

"Nice to meet you, Maya," Derek said, flashing a dimpled smile that made color rise on Maya's cheekbones.

Maya turned back to Alyssa. "I wanted to tell you—I got the internship at *Ravage*! I can get school credit for it and everything."

Alyssa squealed and gave Maya another hug, ignoring the popping of flashes. After learning about Maya's interest in recording and producing music, she'd set Maya up with an executive at a record label in Los Angeles. "I knew they'd love you."

Maya pulled back and shot her a knowing look. "I never would have had a shot at something like that without you, and you know it."

She was probably right. A foster kid, moved around all her life, Maya was lucky she'd found WhiteLight and the scholarship program. But even that wouldn't have helped her land a job in an industry where networking and connections got you in the door. "Anything I can do to help, let me know," Alyssa said. "I still have lots of friends in LA." She made sure Maya had her cell-phone number before the girl went back to join her friends.

After Maya left, the anxious, suffocated feeling that had overcome her the moment she'd entered the party returned. She was the guest of honor, the most famous person at the party—she should expect to be the center of attention.

Still, her skin crawled with the feel of hundreds of eyes on her. As she greeted people and walked away, she heard the whispers, the speculation. No one cared about the fundraiser; no one cared about the cause they were there to celebrate. Everyone was talking about her father and stepmother, rehashing the whole sick tale. She could sense them speculating whether she'd make a spectacle of herself again tonight like she had at the AIDS fund-raiser two weeks ago.

Usually she could take it, but lately she felt like she needed to escape, to get away someplace where she could be anonymous, not have her every move tracked.

She needed to disappear. It was difficult, but not impossible. She had the perfect place to go and had pulled it off in the past, but not since before she'd moved up to San Francisco. Maybe . . .

Alyssa scanned the room and saw her uncle watching her, his watery blue eyes narrowed, and felt her shoulders slump. No way she could get away with it without her uncle going totally ape shit.

"Are you okay?" Derek's deep voice washed over her, instantly calming.

"Just a little nervous," she said. "I'm not really looking forward to getting up and speaking to everyone."

He cocked a skeptical brow.

"Yeah, I know," she said with a laugh. "Me, shy in front of a crowd?" She shook her head. "You ever have that dream where you have to speak in front of a group, and you realize in the middle of your speech you're not wearing any clothes?"

He nodded, his lips quirking with the hint of a smile.

"Now imagine that thanks to your ex-boyfriend, everyone in the room *has* seen you naked."

Derek nodded in understanding.

"I hate speaking at things like this, knowing no one will take anything I say seriously, that they're just waiting for me to do or say something stupid."

Before he could reply, a waiter appeared at her side with a glass of champagne. Alyssa accepted it with a heartfelt "thank you" and drained it in two gulps.

Derek grabbed the glass from her hand, his thick brows pulling into a frown. "Better knock that off, or you *will* be in trouble."

Alyssa rolled her eyes. "Just one glass to take the edge off isn't going to do me in."

He glared down at her. "Yeah, well, if you make a fool of yourself on my watch, my ass is on the line, too."

"Right," she said, hating the little stab of hurt. "I'll do my best not to contaminate you with my sullied reputation."

Something like regret flashed in his eyes, gone in an instant behind his usual expressionless mask.

Despite Derek's protective presence, she felt the crowd start to close in on her. "I need to go to the restroom," she said, turning quickly on her heel and making a beeline for the ladies' room. She gave a weak smile to the other patrons and escaped into a stall. Her breath was coming too quickly, and her heart pounded. She knew if she didn't get ahold of herself, she'd melt down in a full-out panic attack.

That's all she needed, she thought as she bit back a hysterical laugh. She could see the headlines now: PARTY GIRL ALYSSA MILES HAS NERVOUS BREAKDOWN AT CHARITY EVENT.

She closed her eyes and took several deep breaths, practicing the relaxation exercises her therapist had taught her to combat her frequent headaches and occasional anxiety attacks. The exercises hadn't done much good in the weeks since her father had died, but Alyssa refused to take the next step and go on antianxiety meds. She knew the press would get wind in a heartbeat and made sure she was never seen consuming more than one drink at a party.

It still didn't stop them from speculating about her drug use, but Alyssa could control only so much.

With that thought in mind, she slowed her heartbeat to a manageable pace and pulled her breathing back under control. When she stood up to exit the stall, she still felt a little dizzy but no longer on the verge of a heart attack.

"There you are," Kimberly called out as Alyssa entered the ballroom.

Alyssa pasted a smile on her face as she recognized the man at her sister's side. In his early forties, Louis Abbassi was good-looking with his liquid dark eyes and olive complexion, his body lean and muscular under his tailored designer suit. A neatly trimmed black goatee framed a full mouth and gave him a slightly disreputable air despite his tailored designer suit.

Louis smiled, his eyes lighting up in awareness as they raked down Alyssa's body. "*Chérie,* it is wonderful to see you."

"You, too, Louis," she said, wishing again she'd worn a dress that offered a little more coverage. She automatically tilted her face so he could kiss each cheek, forcing herself not to cringe as his lips lingered too long on each side. Louis was a close associate of the Van Weldts, a critical factor in the success of the "Diamonds for All" campaign. A certain amount of ass kissing on her part was required, but Alyssa made sure to keep a certain distance. She hadn't always proven herself to be the best judge of character, but something in Louis's cold lizardlike gaze put every instinct on high alert.

Still, the press had speculated about their supposed romance, after they'd been photographed together over the past several months. It didn't take a rocket scientist to see that Louis would love to add some truth to those rumors.

"We missed you in Saint-Tropez this year," said Louis, his deep voice laced with a French accent. His smile vanished, and his eyes took on a somber cast. "But I understand you could not get away. I am very sorry to have missed your father's funeral. He was a good friend."

Alyssa nodded and tried to pull her hand back, but he tightened his grip and brought her hand to his lips.

"Next time you will join me, won't you? We can do a photo shoot on the yacht. I can see it now, you draped in jewels as the sun sets behind you."

"You'll have to work that out with Kimberly," she said.

"In the meantime," Louis continued, his grip still firm on her hand, "perhaps I may treat you to dinner soon. Cheer you from your sadness." Though his words and tone were innocent enough, there was a hard, speculative light in Louis's eyes that made Alyssa's blood run cold.

"I'm sure that would be lovely," Alyssa replied. He lifted her hand to his lips, and she swallowed a wave of nausea at the feel of them on her skin.

"I will call you this week," Louis said, as if it were a given. "Before I leave again for Europe."

"I—" Alyssa looked helplessly at Kimberly, whose look said she expected Alyssa to jump at the invitation.

"I think Marianne is looking for you." Alyssa almost fell to her knees in gratitude as Derek's interruption saved her from having to make an awkward excuse.

Louis's smile dimmed as he locked eyes on the man who would dare interrupt him. She could feel Derek stiffen next to her as he wrapped his hand around her bare arm. The touch of his fingers sent a jolt of warmth through her but still wasn't enough to extinguish the chill that had suffused her at Louis's touch.

"Surely you can spare a few more moments," Louis said to her, but his eyes were locked on Derek. "We have not seen each other in many weeks."

Alyssa's eyes darted nervously between the two men. Though not as tall as Derek, physically Louis was hard and lean, and she got the feeling that if it ever came down to it, Louis wouldn't hesitate to fight dirty.

Derek's fingers tightened ever so slightly around her arm, and she felt his weight shift next to her. She risked a glance at him, saw that his eyes were locked with Louis's in a death stare, and knew that if they were dogs their hackles would be up.

"I'm so sorry, Louis," Alyssa said and laid a friendly hand on Louis's arm. "But I really should get ready for the presentation."

"I will call you," Louis said. "We will make a date."

Alyssa smiled weakly and allowed Derek to pull her away.

"Stay away from that guy," Derek said as he led her over to the podium where Alyssa would receive the award.

"I'll do my best, but he's a business associate, so I can't avoid him completely."

"I don't like him," Derek said bluntly. "Don't go out alone with him."

Another wave of dizziness hit her, almost making Alyssa stumble in her heels, but she managed to correct herself before she fell. "What, are you, like, jealous or something?" Her teasing lost some of its impact as her tongue slurred the S in something.

"Not jealous, just careful. It's my job to keep you out of trouble. If you have to see him socially, make sure I'm there."

Alyssa nodded and then swayed as the small action caused her head to swim and her vision to blur around the edges.

"Are you okay?" Derek asked. His voice sounded like it was coming from the end of a tunnel.

"I'm fine," she said. Or thought she said, because it seemed to take about a year for the words to travel from her brain to her lips.

"You're freezing," Derek said. Through her haze, she could feel him chafing her arms.

"I'm fine, just a little dizzy," Alyssa said. But panic pierced through her suddenly blurry senses. What was wrong with her? This was just like the other time. One minute she was fine, the next she was so sick she could barely walk.

She took a deep breath, felt cold sweat film her legs and arms and struggled to keep from shivering. Marianne approached, her smile melting into a look of concern when she saw Alyssa. "Is everything all right?"

Alyssa's vision swam, her stomach sinking as she focused on the other woman's face. Alyssa knew that look. Shock, mingled with disgust, with a dash of "what kind of disaster is this girl going to cause me now."

"I'm fine, it's fine," she said, willing it to be so. "I must be coming down with something." *Just make it through the speech. Then you can leave.* She forced her face into what she hoped was a reassuring smile. "But maybe we should move along with the presentation."

"We should leave," Derek said. "This is going to be bad."

Kimberly rushed over, looking worried. Her uncle Harold was close behind, his face an angry mask. Alyssa's vision closed in until all she could see was his face, his features taking on an exaggeratedly evil cast.

The Devil.

"What is wrong with you?" Kimberly said, her voice laced with shock, and Alyssa realized she'd said it aloud.

She could hear a voice echoing in the background. Marianne was at the podium introducing Alyssa.

"I'm fine," Alyssa said, feeling like she was chewing through cotton to get the words out. "Just a little dizzy. I don't know what's wrong with me."

"I think we all know," Harold bit out in a low whisper.

"How badly you must want to humiliate us to do this to yourself tonight."

"I didn't do anything," she protested weakly. Even in her haze, she knew what he meant. He thought she was on something, that she'd chosen tonight to get high in public. "I don't feel well. I think I'm sick." She looked at her sister for support but could see from Kimberly's ashamed, almost pitying look that she didn't believe her.

"And now I'm pleased to introduce Alyssa Miles to accept this award to thank her for all the support she and her family have shown the WhiteLight Foundation."

She turned to mount the stage, felt her heels give way under her feet.

"Don't." Derek's warm grip and low voice cut through the fog. She wanted to turn into his chest and beg him to take her away, somewhere away. Somewhere safe.

But she had to get through this. If she fell apart, the whole world would use it as proof that she was nothing but a vapid idiot who didn't have enough sense not to get wasted at a charity event benefiting troubled young girls.

The tabloids would have a field day.

She turned away from her uncle's judgmental glare and her sister's disappointed frown. Alyssa took each step with exquisite care, placing her feet squarely in the middle of each step as she fought for balance in her too-high shoes. She murmured a thanks to Marianne, her own voice muffled in her head.

She tried to remember her prepared speech, but her brain was working at quarter speed. She opened her mouth, tried to speak, but her tongue lay like a bloated slug in her mouth. Faces in the crowd tilted, people started to whisper, the hissing growing louder in volume until Alyssa's brain echoed with white static.

What's wrong with me?

The spotlight was hot, burning its white light into her

eyes. Her knees started to buckle as a wave of vertigo smacked her to the ground.

Strong arms grabbed her before she hit.

She knew that touch, knew that smell. Derek. She let him help her offstage, clinging to him like a lifeline as her uncle's angry voice cut through the hiss of voices buzzing in her head.

"Get her out of here before she makes an even bigger spectacle of herself."

"Help me," she whispered and felt Derek's arm close around her waist as he half dragged, half carried her through one of the doors behind the stage. Her eyelids drooped, and she struggled to stay conscious as he walked her down a long hallway.

By some miracle, there was no one in this hallway, but even in her half-conscious state Alyssa knew the press would be all over her in an instant. Her vision started to go dark.

"Stay with me," Derek said. "Stay with me till we get to the car."

She shook her head to clear it and had the vague impression of being in an elevator. Then cold air hit her skin, making her shiver even harder as Derek carried her to his car.

"You're okay. I'm going to get you home."

Tires squealed as he whipped out of the parking space and slammed the car into gear. "No," Alyssa said, swallowing back her nausea as he screamed down the ramp of the parking garage. Black fog suffused her mind. She was going to pass out. She hoped she passed out before she threw up all over Derek's leather upholstery. "Too many press," she managed to slur out. "Not home."

CHAPTER 7

DEREK BALANCED ALYSSA'S inert form against his leg, supporting her weight with one arm as he unlocked the door that led from his garage to his house. Even though she was dead weight, he didn't have much trouble carrying her. How much of what had she taken to get herself in such a state?

Anger pulsed in his veins. At her, for being so goddamn stupid to do this to herself. At himself, for all the messed-up, protective instincts she inspired, even when her stupidity could cost Gemini a valuable client.

He carried her into his bedroom and laid her across the bed, trying really hard not to think about the last time he'd had Alyssa Miles in his house, in his bed. "Why do I bring you home with me when it's nothing but a guaranteed disaster?" he asked. Not that he expected her to answer. She was out cold, having drifted in and out of consciousness on the drive to his house. He wondered again if he should have brought her to the hospital. But he could still rouse her, even if it took some doing, and he knew that was a good sign. And he knew that as soon as she was admitted, some nurse or orderly would be on the phone, alerting the world that Alyssa had shown up in a drugged-out mess, accompanied only by her bodyguard.

He shook her again, just to be sure. Her eyelids fluttered open. "Derek," she whispered, and the sweetest goddamn smile spread across her pale face, kicking him square in the gut, before she turned on her side and snuggled into his pillow with a soft snore.

Anger rose up again. How could she be so reckless? She'd almost OD'd in the past—she should fucking well know better. She was so small, it wouldn't have taken much of anything to mess her up. How much more would it have taken to kill her? He wanted to punch his fist through a wall at the thought of her stupidity. He seized the anger, nurtured it, because anger was easier to deal with than the terror he felt at the thought of her accidentally overdosing.

When he'd felt her go ice cold, seen her start to waver, he'd been overcome with a storm of unfamiliar urges. The need to protect her had overshadowed everything, and all he'd wanted to do was get her away from the crowd to someplace safe. Her whispered plea for help, the way her fingers clung with a desperate grip, had just about brought him to his knees.

Now cold reality smacked him in the face. He was no knight in shining armor, and she was no damsel in distress. What she was was an out-of-control starlet who was so beyond common sense she couldn't keep from getting high, even at a high-profile public function.

He was such an idiot. This whole week, he'd been thinking that maybe she wasn't as bad as the press made her out to be. Deluded himself into thinking she was misunderstood, misrepresented. Despite his resolve to keep his distance, he'd thought maybe there was a chance he'd met the real Alyssa the night of the charity auction. Maybe his instincts weren't completely haywire, and maybe he'd recognized a funny, intelligent, surprisingly innocent woman the rest of the world couldn't see behind the party-girl front.

He shook his head, his lips pulling tight in disgust. He

was just seeing what he wanted to see. More to the point, what his dick wanted him to see. Jesus Christ, of all the women to threaten his unflappable control, why did it have to be her?

Even now he couldn't quite squash the tender emotions. She looked small and vulnerable lying in his big bed. And pretty. So damn pretty it made his chest hurt.

She shifted in her sleep, raising her leg up so her knee almost touched her chest. The short skirt of her slip dress rode up her hip, giving him a mouthwatering view of one ass cheek, left bare by her thong underwear.

Fuck him. First the spa, then the photo shoot, and now this. If he'd known this job entailed seeing Alyssa in various states of undress on a daily basis, he would have told Danny to go fuck himself.

Derek's mouth went dry as blood rushed to his groin. She shifted again, and the heel of her silver stiletto sandal snagged on his bedspread. He unbuckled one shoe, and then the other, slipping them off her small feet. He held her foot in his hand, absently stroking the arch with his calloused thumb. Her skin no longer had that terrifying chill, but she was still cold.

He yawned as a wave of exhaustion washed through him. The mattress of his king-size bed called to him, tempting him to lie down and rest.

Alyssa shifted in her sleep, gathering a pillow close as she curved her arm around it, cuddling up to it as if it were a lover.

Bad idea. Do not get in bed with her.

He yawned, a jaw cracker that made his eyes tear. Sleep had never been easy for him. Too many faces in his scope. Too many heads exploding as he pulled the trigger. And the one who tormented him most, the one who got away.

He'd been seeing her in his dreams lately. Walking across the courtyard, sandaled feet kicking up dust as she walked up the walkway to Massoud's house. The view through the scope of his M21 so clear he could see individual pebbles, a stray thread hanging from her veil, even from a distance of eight hundred meters. The feel of the trigger against his finger so familiar it was like part of his hand. His hesitation to kill a civilian, a woman, even if his instructions had been to kill anyone approaching. Then the explosion, all hell breaking loose. In his dream sometimes she reappeared, walking away from the burning building. Even though Derek couldn't see her face through the burka, he knew she was smiling. Mocking him and his moment of weakness.

Two nights ago, he'd had the dream. When the woman had walked out of the burning house, black smoke billowing behind her, she'd done something she'd never done before: she removed her veil.

Alyssa's face greeted him, smiling, mocking him, daring him to let down his guard one more time.

Derek wasn't big on psychobabble, but he didn't need Dr. Freud to help him figure out what that one meant.

He blinked hard, almost asleep on his feet. He thought of the lumpy double bed in the guest room. Too small for his frame. His feet would dangle off the end, and he wouldn't get comfortable. Besides, he wanted to stay close to Alyssa in case anything happened. He still didn't know what she'd taken or how much. What if she had a seizure? Threw up in her sleep and aspirated?

He left her long enough to change into a T-shirt and gym shorts. The bed was big enough that even with her sprawled, there was still plenty of room for him to sleep without even brushing up against her. Ignoring the voice that asked him what kind of idiot he was to get back in bed with Alyssa Miles—no matter how noble his intentions—Derek lay down on the bed. Careful to keep a good two feet of distance between them, he closed his eyes, asleep in seconds.

* * *

Martin Fish paced the trash-strewn alleyway, compulsively checking his watch for the fifth time. Oppressive heat drew a toxic sweat to slick his skin. The numbers on the digital readout and his head throbbed as he struggled to focus. Marie Laure still had four minutes before she was officially late. To his relief, she'd shown up for their meeting two days ago. After what he'd witnessed on the video, he'd resigned himself to the fact he'd never see her again.

Still, he went to the meeting, swallowing back bile as the malafu he'd consumed threatened to blow back up on him. And shoved aside the relief he'd felt when she finally appeared.

He couldn't afford to have a soft spot for the beautiful, softspoken girl-woman who had agreed to help him. But that didn't stop him from hoping everything worked out. Because if it did, today was the first day of the rest of Marie Laure's life. Now that he had proof of Abbassi's link to the PFM, he could get out of this godforsaken hellhole. And he was taking Marie Laure with him—to Kinshasa anyway. He'd secured her a spot in the UN refugee camp outside the city. If he got her there, she'd be guaranteed food, shelter, and help caring for her baby. The camp was no paradise, not by a long shot, but it was a hell of a lot better than what Marie Laure had dealt with for the past year.

His own daughter would be fourteen on her next birthday, only two years younger than Marie Laure. Katie's world was all about malls and boys. Or at least it had been the last time he'd seen her over a year ago. That's the kind of life a beautiful young girl should live. Going to school, chasing boys. Not kidnapped, raped, impregnated with her enemy's child.

He paced up and down the alley, his brain racing with the pieces and parts of this story, which was getting crazier by the day. Just last night another odd bit had appeared, an interview with Alyssa Miles in some women's rag his friend

Charlie had sent in a link. Everyone was quoting the story because it contained Alyssa's first public commentary about the beaver shots that had shown up on the Web a while ago.

But Martin didn't give a shit about it. Another subhead caught his eye. Alyssa had said she thought she may have seen someone that night. Was it possible? Could she have seen something that night and not realized it, something that would prove his hunch that Van Weldt's death wasn't the result of a wife pushed too far?

Maybe he needed to rethink his strategy. Instead of taking Alyssa down as collateral damage in this story, she could help him fill in the missing pieces. She was an outsider in her family, but she still had access. He'd felt it before, but now he was certain. She was the key. The link that tied together this godforsaken place and her glittering, meaningless life of luxury.

He was still trying to wrap his throbbing brain around everything when Marie Laure appeared. Martin tried not to wince when he took in her condition. Her left eye was still swollen nearly shut, and her right arm was suspended in a ragged sling. Her right forearm and hand were swollen to nearly twice their normal size. From the way she moved carefully, taking shallow breaths, he knew she had a couple broken ribs.

In her left hand she carried a small satchel. All her worldly possessions fit inside.

"We have to hurry," he said, ignoring her wince when he grabbed her left arm and steered her down the alley. Two blocks away a jeep waited. The UN driver would take them to the meeting point where the helicopter would pick them up, along with twenty-five others lucky enough to make the list this time around.

"Monsieur—my brother, you have a spot for him, too?" Marie Laure's breathing was labored, both from the pain in her side and the fast pace he forced her to keep.

"Sorry, kid, I couldn't swing it."

She tripped. Martin's grip on her arm kept her from going down. "I promised him. I cannot go without my brother—"

He yanked her to a halt and gave her a little shake, ignoring her cry of pain. "I didn't promise shit. I told you I'd try. Your brother is a soldier for Mekembe. You knew it was impossible."

He took off again, dragging her behind him. The jeep idled half a block away. He shoved her in and climbed in next to her. Though hardly anyone was about this early in the morning, he had a tight, anxious feeling in his gut telling him to get the hell out of Dodge before his luck ran out.

He put his hand over the zipper pocket in his cargo pants, and his finger traced the outline of the computer flash drive. The proof he needed, the risk Marie Laure took, was right there on that small piece of hardware.

The jeep bounced along the rutted excuse for a road, and Martin swallowed back vomit. Fuck, he needed a drink. He felt the anxiety ease a degree when he saw the helicopter waiting.

Soon. He'd be in Kinshasa, in a hotel that stocked a full bar, and then on a plane enjoying all the complimentary booze he could handle.

A line of people waited to board, refugees anxiously checking in, ensuring their names were still on the list. Poor souls who actually believed they were going somewhere better. A crowd formed around them, yelling, shoving, trying to convince the aid workers to take them, too. They were held at bay by heavily armed guards keeping a tenuous hold on the crowd.

Martin grabbed his backpack and duffel from the back of the jeep and motioned Marie Laure to walk in front of him. They were among the last to arrive. Most of the other passengers had already boarded the helicopter. The rotors started a lazy spin, kicking up red dust. Martin held up his hand to protect his eyes.

Suddenly a vehicle came screeching around the corner—a rusted-out Hummer Mekembe had converted into a makeshift tank, complete with a machine gun mounted at the top.

Martin's blood went glacial when he saw Mekembe himself in the driver's seat.

Seated next to him was Marie Laure's brother, Charles.

"Marie Laure!" Mekembe shouted.

"Don't stop. We have to go."

"Shoot her!" Mekembe shouted. "You wanted us to stop her, so shoot her yourself."

Martin tried to hurry Marie Laure to the helicopter, but she wouldn't move.

"Charles!"

Charles held his AK-47 loosely in his hand, aimed to the side, his eyes wide as Mekembe held his own gun to the boy's head.

"Kill her," Mekembe said. "You wanted me to keep her from escaping. Now show me you are loyal, or I'll kill you and her next."

"I didn't mean for you to kill her," the boy said, starting to cry. "I don't want you to go, Marie Laure." His body heaved with sobs; mucus ran from his nose. Despite the lethal weapon in his hand, in that moment he was nothing but a boy who wanted to stay with the sister he loved.

Marie Laure lurched toward the vehicle, but Martin kept a tight grip on her uninjured arm. "We have to go, or you're both going to die."

Mekembe was screaming at Charles as he sobbed, "No, no," over and over again.

The soldiers guarding the helicopter hefted their weapons, warning Mekembe to lower his weapon, or they would open fire.

The helicopter rotors sped up as the pilots, anxious to flee the quickly unraveling situation, prepared to take off.

Martin yanked Marie Laure's arm, dragging her, screaming, to the helicopter.

Gunfire erupted, barely audible over the helicopter blades.

Marie Laure's screams turned to wails as her brother's
body crumpled.

The crowd scattered as the soldiers opened fire on
Mekembe's vehicle. Bullets pinged off the sides as he whipped
the Hummer into reverse and sped back in the direction of
the mine. Charles was shoved from the moving vehicle, his
lifeless body rolling several feet before it came to a stop in a
heap in the middle of the mud road.

Martin wrapped his arm around Marie Laure's waist, dragging her the last few feet to the helicopter. The rotors drowned
out any noise, but he could hear Marie Laure's screams
echoing in his head. He shoved her into the helicopter and
climbed in after her just as the runners left the ground.

Marie Laure curled herself around the ball of her belly,
silent now as tears flowed down her face. Martin strapped
himself in several feet away, shutting out the voice that told
him he should have tried harder to get a spot for Charles on
the helicopter. It didn't matter. He was just a boy. It didn't
matter that he'd been no more willing to kill for Mekembe
than Marie Laure had been to share Mekembe's bed.

He'd been a soldier. Way down on the totem poll when it
was decided who got a spot on the evacuation flight. Martin
had kept his promise to Marie Laure and gotten her out.
She had no right to expect anything more.

As the helicopter climbed, Martin focused on the thrum
of the rotors, the pain in his head, trying to block out Marie
Laure's wails as she sobbed beside him.

Alyssa forced her grainy eyes open. The room was almost
completely dark, and her heart jumped to her throat as she
realized she didn't recognize any of the dim features. She
shivered, her bare arms and legs breaking out in goose bumps,

both from fear and from the near-arctic temperature of the room.

Where was she? How had she gotten here?

The mattress shifted next to her, and she froze as she sensed a presence next to her. Holy crap! Had she had too much to drink and ended up in some strange guy's bed?

Panic gripped her chest as the evening's events pieced back together like disjointed frames of a movie. The benefit. Feeling suddenly so dizzy and sick. Going up onstage to make her speech. The bright lights.

Her angry uncle Harold. Kimberly's look of disappointed disgust as Alyssa made a public spectacle of herself.

Then strong arms carrying her. A deep voice telling her to stay with him, that everything was going to be okay.

A muscled arm slid around her waist, pulling her against a solid-rock wall of a chest.

Alyssa's fear evaporated like mist as she snuggled eagerly into the warm body against her back.

Derek.

Now that she realized where she was, she could pick out familiar features of the dim room. The gooseneck lamp mounted to the wall above one side of the headboard. A tall chest of drawers across from the foot of the bed. The shadowy lump of an armchair piled high with laundry.

Overcome with the need to pee, she slid from the bed, careful not to disturb Derek. Her head swam when she stood, and she steadied herself on the bedside table. She carefully padded to the bathroom and took care of business. Her head was still fuzzy, but nothing like before. She had a headache and felt a little urpy, like she had a slight hangover. And her mouth felt like someone had sucked out every last drop of moisture from her tongue. She drank two glasses of water and brushed her teeth with her finger and wondered how she could go from being so sick, so fast, to on her way to recovery. Unease snaked around her spine. Maybe there was something really wrong with her.

She made her way unsteadily back to the bed and lay down a few inches from Derek. His big body took up more than half the bed, his broad chest expanding and contracting with his deep, even breaths. Alyssa moved as close as she dared, not wanting to wake him.

She closed her eyes in bliss when he reached for her again and pulled her back against him, his warmth settling over her like a down comforter.

She didn't remember drifting off, but when she woke up again light filtered through the beige curtains. Her headache was gone, and her gaze wandered around the room, taking in details she'd been too distracted to notice last time she was there. Her impression was . . . beige.

With an occasional splash of brown for color.

Derek's room was simply, tastefully decorated but had no personality whatsoever. With its putty-colored, pictureless walls and heavy wood and leather furniture, it might as well have been an above-average hotel room.

There was no art, no decoration, save for a black-and-white photograph on the dresser that she couldn't make out from this distance.

Oh, and the two-foot pile of magazines on the bedside table. Looked like Derek was a heavy reader of *The Economist* and *Information Week*.

No wonder he'd had no idea who she was when he first met her.

Derek's arm was still an iron-hard band around her middle, and sometime in their sleep he'd hitched his thigh up so its hair-roughened hardness rested between her legs.

Warmth, chased by the first tickle of desire, settled in her belly as memories of the last time she was in this bed bubbled into her consciousness. In the past week since he'd bulldozed back into her life, she'd tried to shove all the memories of that night back into the vault, never to be revisited. But each day it became more difficult. After the interview for *Bella,* she'd felt his sympathy. He was loosening up, millimeter by millimeter, almost as though he liked her.

And the way he'd come to her rescue when she was sick . . . Okay, so he was being paid to keep tabs on her, but still. He didn't have to bring her to his house and tuck her into his own bed.

Maybe he was starting to care a little.

She tilted her ass back to snuggle more firmly into the cradle of his hips. His hand tightened on her waist, sending a pulse of heat between her legs. What was wrong with her, getting so turned on by a guy who didn't even seem to like her much?

But unlike Derek, Alyssa wasn't the best at controlling her impulses, and she couldn't control the primitive reaction of her body whenever he got close. Heat shimmied through her, tightening her nipples into hard points. As if sensing it, Derek slid his hand to her stomach, flattening his palm against her abdomen as he drew her more fully back against him.

His breath was a hot sigh on the back of her neck. Her skirt had hitched up, leaving her behind bare in her thong panties. She wiggled closer and felt the unmistakable bulge of his erection against her butt, the stretchy fabric of his gym shorts doing nothing to hide the heat and dimension. Anticipation shot through her. In the weeks after she'd been with him, she'd tried to convince herself she'd embellished his size, his skill, her body's devastating response to him. Now, with his long, thick cock rising urgently against her, she had to admit she hadn't embellished a bit. And her memory didn't come close to doing him justice.

She turned slightly and looked at him over her shoulder. In sleep, his chiseled features lost their harsh edges, giving him an almost boyish look. She looked ruefully at his dark lashes resting against his cheekbones. They had a length and thickness it took her three coats of very expensive mascara to achieve. His full lips were soft and slightly parted, and dark stubble dusted his jaw. But there was a faint tightness in his forehead, a thin line forming between his brows. Even in sleep Derek Taggart couldn't completely let down his guard.

She reached down and covered the hand he'd flattened against her stomach, tracing the veins and tendons and the strong length of his fingers. His fingers twitched under her stroking, and she held her breath as his hand slid up over her rib cage. The heat of his skin burned through the thin silk of her dress, and heat pooled between her thighs. She sucked in her breath as his hand slid another few inches, his fingers dipping into the deep vee neckline of her dress.

The knot of arousal tightened between her legs, sharp and hot and almost painfully intense. His hand cupped her breast, his thumb brushing over and around her nipple. Her breath hitched, and she arched into him, craving a firmer touch. She ground her ass more firmly against his surging cock, hitched her leg higher over his so the hard muscle of his thigh pressed against her mound.

She felt his breathing change. His hand stilled on her breast, and she knew he was awake. Heart pounding, she turned her head to look at him. His eyes were dark slits as he stared down at her. She tilted her head, parted her lips in invitation.

His hand tightened on her breast, and he licked his lips. Alyssa tipped her chin higher, bringing her lips to within a millimeter of his.

With a groan he bent his head and covered her mouth with his, his tongue sliding between her lips to rub against her own. He was hot and musky, tasted even better than she remembered. She turned in his arms, shivering with need as he pulled her down on top of him. Her knees rested on either side of his hips. One of his hands slid up her bare thigh, up her skirt to rest on one bare cheek.

Alyssa wanted him so much she shook with it, every nerve ending firing on all circuits as she cupped his face in her hands and kissed him like she was starving, sucking, biting, pulling at his lips. "Derek," she whispered.

He stiffened under her, and his hand froze on her butt. His eyes popped open, and he shoved her off him, sending her sprawling on her back, his move so swift and sudden it took her a few seconds to get her bearings.

She sat up and shoved her hair out of her face. He was already up and off the bed, breathing hard as he paced and raked his fingers through his hair.

"What the fuck is wrong with me," he muttered almost to himself. Then he focused on her, eyes dark with torment. "I'm sorry, Alyssa. That was totally unprofessional and inappropriate."

She felt her jaw drop toward the floor. She was a ball of unfulfilled arousal, one hip twitch away from orgasm, and he was worried about professionalism? "Derek, it's fine. Really. I didn't mind—don't mind."

Her stomach got tight as his face lost all traces of tenderness or arousal, and his usual closed expression took over like a garage door dropping into place.

"I can't believe I even touched you, with the shape you were in." Disgust laced his voice. For her? For himself?

"But I'm fine now," she protested, pitifully close to begging but unable to help herself. Her body had gone cold at the absence of his touch, and she needed that warmth back, needed it like she needed air. "Whatever was wrong seems to have passed, just one of those twenty-four-hour things." She still couldn't shake the fear that something was seriously wrong with her, but she didn't want to dwell on that. Right now she wanted Derek, back on the bed, his hands all over her. And despite his self-recriminations, judging from the huge erection tenting out the front of his shorts, he still wanted it, too.

His mouth pulled in a tight line, and his eyes narrowed. "A bug? Why don't you cut the crap, Alyssa?"

She sat back on the bed and crossed her arms over her chest, suddenly feeling very naked in her flimsy cocktail dress. "I don't know what you're talking about." But of course she did. He thought she was a drugged-out mess, just like everyone else.

"What are you on?"

"Nothing," she said curtly and slid off the bed, as eager now to get away from him as she'd been for him to touch her. "Where are my shoes? I want to go home."

"Tell me what you're on," he said, grabbing her arm in a grip that stopped just short of pain.

"Nothing," she repeated through clenched teeth. "Why is it so hard for everyone to believe that I was sick? That maybe I had a virus?"

"Right," he scoffed. "A virus that totally fucks you up but you feel fine in the morning."

"It happens," she said, hands on her hips, chin thrust out. She felt small and insignificant, like a little kid standing up to his bulk.

"Twice in the same month?"

"Maybe there's something really wrong with me," she said, an edge of fear creeping into her voice as she shrugged off his hold.

"When you can't control your addiction enough to keep from getting high in public and making an ass of yourself, yeah, I'd say there's something really wrong with you."

"I don't do drugs."

He cocked a disbelieving eyebrow. "I did a lot of research when I took this job."

Heat flamed in her cheeks. "Yes, I went to rehab, but I've been clean for over three years."

"You nearly OD'd on pills and coke," Derek bit out.

Alyssa bit her lip. It was a dark time, one she didn't want to revisit. She'd been dating a musician, a heavy drug user. At the beginning, she'd loved the feeling of invincibility the coke gave her, the sense of peace she could find with pills. Then she'd received a wake-up call in the form of a trip to the emergency room to have her stomach pumped. "I dealt with the problem before it got out of control." She went to rehab and ditched the boyfriend and found that once she was away from that life, the drugs weren't nearly as attractive. "People like to make it more of a problem than it was."

"Don't give me that 'poor me, persecuted by the press' shit, Alyssa. We both know the truth."

His words hit her like a blow, hurting more than they should. She was used to the rest of the world seeing her as a fuckup, and on most days her skin was pretty thick.

But it killed her a little to see that Derek was just like everyone else, ready to make assumptions and judgments based on the stupid choices she'd made in her past.

"Come on," he said, his voice softening a little. "Tell me the truth. Let me help you."

He sounded almost like he cared. Which would have been awesome if he also didn't believe she was a pill-popping junkie. "I told you. I'm clean."

His look of mingled disgust and disbelief made the rage boil in her throat. "Fine. I'll prove it to you. Our family has a personal physician on call. I'll pee in a cup and take a blood test right now to show you I don't have any drugs in my system."

"That's impossible," Alyssa said, staring at the toxicology report Dr. Patel had handed her.

"I can run the tests again, Miss Miles," Dr. Patel said in his lilting Indian accent.

Alyssa blinked, praying that when she opened her eyes the

notes on the paper would miraculously change. But there they were in black and white. Opiates. Ketamine. Both found in the drug test Dr. Patel had expedited through the lab.

This was crazy. She looked at Dr. Patel, a slightly built man in his late fifties. He'd acted as the Van Weldt family physician for years, but Alyssa had met him only recently. The doctor's liquid brown eyes were carefully blank.

"This is impossible," Alyssa repeated. She huddled in her chair, wanting to disappear inside the oversize sweatshirt she'd borrowed from Derek. She couldn't bear to look at him sitting rigidly silent beside her.

"He can stay," she'd said with such bravado when Dr. Patel had suggested Derek leave the room when he gave her the lab results. She'd been so smug, anticipating the moment she would rub his face in the truth.

Now fear clawed at her insides as the truth hit her like a brick wall. Someone had drugged her. More than once.

"Someone must have slipped it in my drink," she said, fear making her voice small.

Derek made a scoffing sound in his throat.

"I don't care what you believe," she said, exploding out of the chair. "I didn't take any of that stuff. Even when I was using, I never did heroin or methadone, or special K."

Derek stood, too, towering over her as his brows pulled in a frown. "How can you deny it when it's there on the lab tests? Jesus, Alyssa, I've heard of denial, but this is fucking ridiculous."

"Please," Dr. Patel said, "keep your voices down." He turned to Alyssa. "There are several facilities where you can get help—"

"I don't need help," Alyssa said, hating the way her voice shook. But she couldn't shove the fear down. She did need help, but not the kind he was talking about. Someone was drugging her, making sure she made a complete fool of herself in public.

She looked at Derek, immovable as a mountain with his face carved in stone. So strong, so capable. And no more inclined to believe her than the rest of the world.

Alyssa grabbed her bag and stalked to the door. "Just take me home. Take me home and leave me alone."

CHAPTER 8

"THIS IS INDEED upsetting, but hardly a surprise."
Harold Van Weldt sat across from Derek, his fingers
steepled against his chin as his eyebrows pulled into a thought-
ful frown.

"I just want her to get the help she needs," Derek said, ignoring the uneasy feeling in his gut that he was selling Alyssa
out. After the fiasco at the doctor's office, he'd dropped Alyssa
at her apartment and left her in Andy's calm, capable hands.

He went home and spent a sleepless night in sheets that
still held her musky peach scent and wrestled with what he
was about to do. In the end he'd called this meeting with
Harold. What choice did he have? He owed it to Harold,
his client, to tell him the truth, and he owed it to Alyssa to
make sure she got the help she needed.

He had no illusions she'd see it that way. She would be
hurt and pissed and would probably never forgive him. He
knew he shouldn't give a flying fuck how Alyssa Miles felt
about him. Hell, he shouldn't care whether or not she went
off the deep end in a drug-induced stupor.

But like it or not, he cared. A lot. So much he couldn't get the
image of her fear-soaked eyes out of his mind as she'd claimed
she'd been drugged. Couldn't get out of his mind the feel of
her slender fingers digging into his arm as she'd begged him

to help her. No matter how he tried to keep himself locked up tight, he hurt for her; whatever weird reality she'd concocted in her head, she believed it 100 percent.

Whatever was going on, Alyssa was seriously messed up, and she needed help. Derek had stood by and watched his mother fall apart all those years ago and hadn't done anything. Until finally it was too late, and Anne Taggart had disappeared without a trace, leaving them all to pick up the pieces. But Derek had been a kid then, unwilling to confront his mother about her problems or to lay out to his father just how bad things had gotten.

But he didn't have that excuse anymore. It might hurt Alyssa in the short term, but until she admitted she was relapsing into addiction, she was a danger to herself.

"Thank you for coming to me first," Harold said, "and with such discretion. I don't want this getting out to the press."

Derek's fingers curled into a fist at Harold's callousness. "The more important issue is that Alyssa has a problem and that she needs help," Derek said tightly.

A tight bark of a laugh burst through Harold's lips. "The important issue is that her string of public fuckups does not hurt our sales or our reputation."

Derek bit back an angry retort and tried to ignore the pinching sensation in his chest. Jesus Christ. If Alyssa was as messed up as he feared, she was going to need a lot more support than her so-called family seemed ready to give.

Harold's fingers formed a triangle against pursed lips as he regarded Derek steadily, daring him to protest. "Our official statement is that she fell ill, but no one is buying it. I trust you will keep what you have learned to yourself."

Derek nodded, agreeing not out of loyalty to Harold but because Alyssa had enough bad shit being said about her, and he didn't want to add fuel to the fire. "I think the best option is to get her into some sort of program—"

Harold shook his head and raised his hand to cut Derek

off. "If she goes to rehab, that's all anyone will talk about. We will keep a closer watch on her for the next few weeks and then decide what to do from there." He spent the next several minutes outlining what he meant by "a closer eye" on Alyssa.

Fuck. House arrest, was more like it. If Alyssa thought he was like a prison guard before, she was in for a rude awakening.

Derek shook Van Weldt's hand when he offered, stifling the urge to wipe his hand on his pants. Danny was determined that the Van Weldts were the kind of clients Gemini should cultivate and keep, but Derek wasn't sold. What kind of person referred to the recent murder of his brother as an "unfortunate passing"? And what kind of man prevented a young woman from getting the help she needed?

What kind of hornet's nest had he stumbled into? And why was Alyssa so determined to take her place among them?

He rounded the corner into the lobby, his steps slowing as he saw Alyssa and Andy. Andy sat on a couch dressed in jeans, boots, and a blazer, her dark brown hair pulled into a tidy ponytail at her nape. Her thumbs flew across the keypad of her BlackBerry. Alyssa stood by the window overlooking bustling Union Square traffic. Her phone was pressed to her ear, and she was pinching the bridge of her nose as though in pain.

Her hair spilled down her back, damp from the rain that had been falling in a steady downpour since last night. She looked bedraggled, fragile, and weary, and Derek was blindsided by the urge to scoop her up in his arms and carry her away to someplace safe. His mouth tightened in self-derision. He seriously needed to get over this protective thing he had for her.

"I don't know if I can do that for you."

Despite his resolve, Derek couldn't suppress the stab of concern he felt at the audible strain in her voice.

"I know," Alyssa said to whomever was on the other line. "I know I promised." Alyssa's thin shoulders hunched inside her blue sweater as she seemed to curl up into herself. "Of course I care. I know you're right, Mom."

Right, her mother. Derek's brows pulled together when he remembered Alyssa's mention of her mother's cancer. From what he gathered, Alyssa was paying for her care. Derek felt an unwanted stab of sympathy at the look of strained resignation on Alyssa's face.

He lingered out of her view, shamelessly eavesdropping on her conversation until Susan, the secretary, nodded at Andy, who in turn went over to Alyssa and motioned to her with a thumb over her shoulder. Alyssa nodded and finished up her conversation with a soft, "Hey, Mom, I love you."

She flipped her phone closed, and in that moment all traces of the fun-loving party girl were gone. Alyssa looked weary and sad and older than her twenty-four years.

He took a step toward her, not sure what he wanted to say. Sorry? He wasn't sorry for telling the truth.

Just then, Kimberly Van Weldt walked into the lobby and called a good morning to Alyssa. Slim and elegant in her business suit, she was everything Alyssa was not: cool, elegant, untouchable.

But even subdued, tired, and still working out the aftereffects of all the shit she'd taken, Alyssa gave off a glow of energy that grabbed Derek by the nuts and wouldn't let go.

Kimberly wasn't alone, Derek noticed with distaste. Louis Abbassi walked beside her, his lean frame draped in a two-thousand-dollar suit. Despite the expensive suit and refined airs, there was no hiding the thug lurking underneath. Derek knew it like he knew his own name.

Kimberly would have walked through the lobby with no more than a quick greeting, but Abbassi made a point of stopping to say hello to Alyssa. Derek's eyes narrowed, and he took another involuntary step forward, his stomach curl-

ing as he watched Abbassi lift Alyssa's hand to kiss it as he
had the night before. Abbassi ran his dark eyes over Alyssa's
form like he wanted to devour her and spit out the bones
when he was finished.

Derek's skin crawled at the sight of him touching her. He
told himself he was just looking out for her.

But there was something else there, something primitive
and territorial that made him want to snarl like a wolf defending what was his. When he'd taken this case, he'd come
across several reports linking Alyssa and Louis romanti-
cally. The thought of him touching her, kissing her, made
him physically ill.

Alyssa returned Abbassi's greeting with what Derek had
quickly learned to recognize as her "I'm supposed to smile
even though I want to get the hell away from you" smile.
He was irritated at how relieved he was to see that whatever
Abbassi's agenda, the attraction wasn't mutual.

"I didn't expect to see you again so soon," Alyssa said,
trying and failing to retrieve her hand.

"Yes, I have a meeting with your sister and later your uncle.
But running into you is a very good surprise," he said. "We
must have dinner," he added, abruptly. "Tonight."

"I need to check my calendar," Alyssa said, her gaze flicking in his direction as she tried to catch Andy's eye over
Louis's shoulder.

Derek knew the second she spotted him. Her entire body
stiffened, and her soft mouth thinned to a narrow pink line
before she turned to Abbassi, cranking up the wattage of
her smile another thousand volts. "Call me later," she said,
suddenly the coquette, and then excused herself to go meet
with her uncle.

Derek wanted to bum-rush her out of there and warn her
not to fuck around with guys like Abbassi. He didn't know
the specifics—yet—but he'd run into guys like Abbassi before.
He recognized that predatory, reptilian air, a core of vicious-

ness no amount of money could hide. Derek knew Abbassi thought that money would let him get whatever he wanted at any cost—even a woman like Alyssa.

But for the moment, Derek let her pass. He didn't try to speak to her as she brushed by him without a word, her face pinched, her green eyes staring at a point past his shoulder.

But he would be waiting when she came out, and he'd make damn sure Abbassi didn't have another chance to get to her again.

Alyssa didn't bother asking Derek what he was doing at her uncle's office that morning. She had a pretty damned good idea, suspicions fueled by the grim yet self-satisfied smirk on Uncle Harold's face.

"Andy, would you do me a huge favor and run and grab me a Starbucks?" Alyssa said before Andy even had a chance to sit down. Alyssa knew this meeting was going to suck, and she didn't want anyone, even her assistant, to witness her bending over and taking it from her uncle.

Andy smiled, but her eyes were dark with sympathy. "Of course. Venti black coffee with two sugars?"

Alyssa nodded, and Andy gave her a reassuring squeeze on her shoulder. "I'll get some of that pumpkin bread you like, if they have it."

Alyssa offered a wan smile. It would take a little more than pumpkin bread to improve her morning, but she had to give Andy credit for trying.

"Mr. Taggart informed me of the drugs in your system," Uncle Harold said bluntly.

Though Alyssa knew as much, she felt like she'd been punched in the stomach. Rationally she knew Derek worked for her uncle, not for her, and it was his job to tell Harold what he'd discovered.

But it felt like a betrayal. And it didn't help that she'd lain in his arms earlier that morning, practically begging him to have sex with her, only to have him shoot her down because he believed she was a druggie. Going to the doctor had seemed like such a brilliant plan.

Now it had all backfired brilliantly in her face.

The real kicker was, she still wanted Derek. Her whole body had thrilled at the sight of him, even as her stomach sank at the knowledge that he'd just sold her out to her uncle. And when she'd brushed past him in the hall, she'd wanted to fling herself into his arms and bury her face against his thickly muscled chest and lose herself in the safety of his embrace.

But there had been no safety in his dark, emotionless gaze. He'd thrown her to the wolves. Not that she had any right to expect any better.

". . . so you will understand you leave me no choice."

Alyssa blinked hard, focusing on what Uncle Harold was saying. "What was that? I'm sorry?"

His fleshy mouth pursed like a cat's ass. "I was going over the terms of your employment here. I warned you last week that if you couldn't control your behavior, there would be consequences."

She swallowed hard, anxiety knotting in her stomach, humiliation pouring through her at being chastised like a five-year-old.

"I'm cutting back your salary by fifty percent," Harold began.

"I need that money," she protested.

Harold cut her off. "Your stipend from the trust is more than ample. You should have no trouble living on that."

Alyssa's eyes widened. "After I pay Andy's salary and send my mother money for her medical bills, I'll have barely enough to cover household expenses." Especially since she'd just gotten off the phone with Alexis. Her mother had her eye on a three-bedroom town house in Beverly Hills, claiming her current two-bedroom penthouse was "no longer suitable for entertaining."

Alyssa's challenge that Alexis didn't do much entertaining between chemo treatments hadn't been well received. There was no way she could afford her mother's new mortgage on what her uncle was proposing.

"Mr. Taggart will search your house and remove any drugs he finds. I've also instructed him to search you and Andy, as well as any packages you receive." He turned back to his computer screen.

She swallowed back a surge of nausea. Derek would be watching her even more closely than before, treating her like a criminal in her own house. "Harold," she began, biting back her anger, knowing it wouldn't buy her any points. "I know how bad this looks, but none of this is necessary. And please, don't cut my salary right now—"

He looked up from his screen as if surprised to still see her there. "We're finished, Alyssa. Now, I suggest you go home and stay there until your presence becomes necessary elsewhere."

She walked out of her uncle's office and found Andy waiting for her in the lobby with her coffee. Abbassi was thankfully nowhere to be found, but Derek was still there, all six-foot-plus of him sprawled like an angry mountain in one of the lobby armchairs.

She ignored him, using the tried-and-true "if I pretend not to see him maybe he won't see me" strategy.

"Is everything okay?" Andy asked.

Alyssa nodded, not having the heart right now to tell Andy she might not be able to afford to employ her for much longer.

"Alyssa." Derek rose from his seat when she would have breezed past.

She didn't respond, just stomped past him to the elevator as fast as her Christian Louboutins would take her. Andy followed her in, and Alyssa punched the "door close" button several times.

Of course he slid in before the doors closed.

He seemed to suck up all the air in the tiny compartment, and Alyssa felt her chest constrict as she struggled to get enough oxygen.

"How could you?" she said, unable to hold back any longer.

"I'm trying to help you, Alyssa," he said, so matter of fact, like she was an idiot for not realizing it.

"Help me? Help me?" she said, hating the way her voice rose with hysteria. "You think ratting me out to my uncle is helping me? If you really wanted to help me, you would help me find out who's slipping me drugs."

"Jesus Christ, Alyssa, will you let it go already?" he snapped. "I only told your uncle so maybe you'd face reality—"

"Yeah, I faced reality, all right. The reality of having my salary cut in half, so now I have barely enough to cover my mother's medical expenses—"

She snapped her mouth shut, remembering his "poor little rich girl" comment. She wasn't going to pour out her stupid, sad tale. She didn't need his help or his sympathy. She'd figure out who was drugging her on her own. She'd get her manager to line up more work. Someone would pay her for something, no matter how trashed her public image. She'd take care of herself. "Forget it. Just leave me alone. But I'm not taking drugs." She turned to Andy, who stared straight ahead, pretending not to hang on every word. "Andy, you're always with me—you live with me, for Christ's sake. Tell him I'm not using again."

Andy's eyes got wide behind her glasses, and she pressed her lips together. "I haven't seen you taking anything," she said. But Alyssa's triumph was short-lived when Andy continued, "But I'm not with you twenty-four hours a day, and I know from experience that addicts become very good at hiding their behavior."

Alyssa looked at her supposedly loyal assistant, gasping like a dying fish as she struggled for words. Was everyone determined to believe the worst about her?

"It's going to be okay, Alyssa," Andy said. "I'll help you get through this."

Good old Andy. Always there for me, Alyssa thought snidely.

The elevator doors slid open, and Alyssa stepped into the parking garage, feeling like she'd stepped into some bizarro world where nothing worked right. Her life had been messed up before, but ever since she'd moved up to San Francisco, life had been one bizarre blow after another.

First her father was killed. Now someone was slipping her drugs, trying to make her look like an addict.

Fear curled in her gut, and a chill snaked up her spine. What if the two were somehow related. What if she—

Alyssa didn't have time to finish the thought as shouts of "There she is!" echoed through the garage. Suddenly she was surrounded, flashes popping in her face, hands grabbing her as she struggled to get to her car.

"Alyssa, is it true you spent last night in the emergency room?"

"Alyssa, is there any truth to the pregnancy rumors?"

"Alyssa, with this latest relapse, will you be going back to rehab?"

The questions, the snapping cameras bounced off the concrete walls, creating a cacophony in her head, disorienting, dizzying. Her vision was clogged by bodies pressing in. Her lungs seized as panic set in. She couldn't get enough air. She was going to pass out, and everyone would chalk it up as more evidence that she was out of control.

A strong arm wrapped around her shoulder. She didn't need to look up to know it was Derek. She knew him from the way her body immediately relaxed, the way her panic eased so she could breathe again, no longer on the verge of losing consciousness.

Angry at him or not, Alyssa clung to him like a lifeline, using him as a human barrier as he cut through the throng of reporters like a hot knife through butter before shoving her into the passenger seat of his car and told Andy to take her car. Alyssa flashed back to last night, a vague impression of Derek executing similar driving skill as he'd extracted her from the party.

He had her home in minutes. But instead of driving into her garage, which was blocked with reporters, he parked around the block and brought her in through a side entrance only accessible from the narrow alley that separated her house from her neighbor's. Because the reporters didn't recognize Derek's car, they had no idea Alyssa was even in the vicinity.

Alyssa's hands shook so much she could barely unlock the door. Derek tried to take the keys, but she hit him with a sharp jab of her elbow, feeling grim satisfaction at his grunt of pain.

She walked through the entryway, her heels thumping on the wood floors as she marched down the hall to her bedroom. She flung the door open. "Go ahead, do your search."

Andy hovered nervously behind Derek. "Is this really necessary?"

Derek's mouth was a tight, grim line. "I'm afraid so." He addressed Andy, but his dark eyes remained on Alyssa's face. "I need to search the whole house."

Andy hurried off, muttering something about tidying up. Alyssa couldn't imagine what she had to do. Andy's neatness bordered on OCD. Even her bras were color coordinated.

Alyssa stomped back into the living room and flopped on the couch. Anger bubbled and hissed until she thought steam was coming from her ears. She turned on the TV, struggling to block out images of Derek pawing through her clothes, searching through her bathroom, seeing private, girlie things women didn't want men to see.

Finally he emerged, a flush riding his high cheekbones. She wondered if her lingerie drawer had done him in. Served him right.

"Find anything?"

He shook his head and wordlessly searched the rest of the house. Alyssa retreated to her room. Though he hadn't moved or disturbed anything—the mess was all hers—she could feel his presence in the room. He'd looked through every drawer, run his hands over every surface.

She paced, feeling the walls of the spacious master bedroom close in over her. She twitched back the curtain of the bay window facing the street. Reporters swarmed like ants.

She could hear Derek and Andy moving through the rest of the house, catch muffled bits of their conversation. Her stomach rumbled.

No way she was going back out there. She'd eat her own hand first.

She couldn't stand this. The need to escape that had reared its head the night before came back, even stronger. She had to get away. Her uncle's face flashed in her mind. There would be consequences. But right now she couldn't think that far ahead as the panicked claustrophobia threatened to drown her.

A plan formed in her mind. Not foolproof, but if she was careful, she could pull it off.

She flipped open her cell phone and sent a quick text. **Need 2 get awy. Cn use beach plc?**

Almost immediately, her phone buzzed with a reply. **Of crse. U OK? U call if u need nythng. Nythng!**

Alyssa smiled. At least someone out there had her back.

She forced herself to go to the kitchen for a snack, knowing that if she stayed locked in her room, Andy would come in after her. Or, worse, Derek, thinking she'd pulled some pills from some unmentionable place and was sitting in her room getting high.

As soon as it got dark she made a big production about going to bed and left Derek and Andy sitting in uneasy silence in front of the flat screen.

She dressed in jeans, running shoes, and a sweater, throwing a water-resistant shell on top to keep out the worst of the rain. She dug a backpack out of her closet and filled it with enough to get her by for a couple days. She didn't plan to be gone long, just enough for a breather. She gave thanks for the blaring TV as she eased open the window. Like most of the old San Francisco Victorians, hers had a fire escape that crawled down the side. Lucky for her, it was accessible from the master bedroom.

She dropped the bag onto the metal deck of the fire escape and slipped out after it. Heart pounding, she lowered herself to the ground, praying no one would look up and take notice. Her feet hit the ground, and she breathed deeply of the cold, rain-soaked night.

The bedroom of the hotel suite echoed with Louis's grunts as sweat dripped on the woman beneath him. His hand tightened around her throat, his lips pulling back in pleasure as her blue eyes widened. Her face flushed red, and a vein pulsed in her forehead as she struggled underneath him.

He pumped hard with his hips, slamming her into the mattress as her fingers clawed at the hand around her throat. In the dim light, if he let his vision lose focus, he could almost believe it was Alyssa.

Savage pleasure surged through him at the thought of having her underneath him. Her small body pinned under his as he fucked her. His huge hand wrapped around her delicate throat. Her very life in his hands.

The girl struggled, thrusting her hips frantically to buck his weight off her. Louis heard the harsh trill of his phone but didn't stop the brutal thrust of his hips. He was almost there. He kept his gaze locked on the girl's face, imagined it was Alyssa's pink mouth parted in a silent scream as he choked out her breath.

One last thrust, and he came with a bellow. He collapsed on top of the girl and released his grip on her throat. She sucked in a desperate breath, sobbing and heaving as tears streaked down her face.

"Careful, lover. I like it as rough as the next girl, but that got a little scary," she said and tried to regain her composure.

Louis's mouth curled in distaste at the harsh sound of the woman's voice, the too firm press of her fake tits against his chest. He'd picked her up the night before, another club slut lured by a wad of cash and a taste of high-grade nose candy.

Another nameless, faceless distraction for him while he waited for his prey to come into range.

Alyssa.

He'd wanted her from the moment he first met her two years ago on some rap star's rented yacht off Saint-Tropez, but she'd barely given him the time of day. At the time she was infatuated with the same stupid nobody who would later post naked photos of her all over the Internet for the entire world to see.

She'd made the deal with the Van Weldts all the sweeter. Soon he'd have same control over her as he did the rest of her family's business.

His phone rang again, and he rolled off the bed and walked naked across the bedroom to answer it, his brows pulling into a frown when he saw the number on the display.

"What kind of an idiot are you to call me at this number?" he asked as he walked into the sitting room of his hotel suite. His head of security, Marius, looked up from the magazine he was thumbing through. The big Boer didn't raise an eyebrow at Louis's nudity.

"Alyssa's gone." Richard Blaylock's voice vibrated with tension.

"What do you mean, gone?" Louis snapped his fingers and motioned Marius into the bedroom. No time for a second round with the girl, he thought with passing disappointment.

"Andy called me two hours ago. I've been trying to reach you since last night. I didn't know what to do."

The woman came stumbling out of the bedroom, clad in the skintight dress she'd arrived in. She'd brushed her hair and wiped away some of her makeup. But there was no hiding the angry red marks ringing her throat. Louis's lips curled in a smile at the sight.

"I thought the bodyguard was watching her. How can one of the most recognizable women in the world disappear?" Louis asked impatiently.

"I don't know," Richard said testily. "But it wouldn't be a problem if you'd let us finish her off and get it over with."

Louis's grip tightened around his phone. "I would watch my tone if I were you." He was growing tired of Richard, his jumpiness, his insolence, his questioning of Louis's decisions.

"All I'm saying is she's becoming a problem. First the comments in that article, and now this. We need her taken care of before this whole thing blows up—"

"You will leave her alone until I decide different," Louis replied. Richard worried needlessly. No matter what she said about her nightmares, Alyssa had seen nothing that night. His men were professionals, and the police had seen exactly what Louis had wanted them to see.

They wanted Alyssa out of the way, for reasons that had

nothing to do with what she may or may not have seen the night of her father's death, but Blaylock and the others knew better than to cross him.

Louis had his own plans for Alyssa, and he wanted her very much alive.

Some might call what he felt for her obsession, his need to possess her, body and soul. From the moment he'd met her, he'd sensed the heat, the vibrancy of her, known it would translate into explosive energy in bed. He wanted to be master of that energy, hold her life in his hands as he showed her the true pleasure that comes only when you taste death.

"This can't be good," Richard protested. "She knows something. Why else would she take off?"

"Do not deviate from the plan," Louis said, his voice brooking no argument.

Richard was silent for several seconds, and Louis could feel his hesitation through the phone. "You fuck me, and I will fuck you harder than you can imagine," Louis said, breaking the silence. "If the truth of Oscar's death gets out, I will not be taking the fall."

Not to mention, due to gross mismanagement, Blaylock and the Van Weldts desperately needed Louis's influx of capital and steady supply of stones to keep the company afloat. Just as Louis needed them to move large volumes of stones without too much scrutiny.

A stab of satisfaction fired Louis's belly as Richard's wet swallow echoed over the line. "Of course," Richard said. Then, "Harold has sent Taggart after her. What if she tells him something? Are we going to kill him, too?" Louis could practically smell the odor of fear-laced sweat coming from Richard's pores.

His mouth tightened. Taggart could be a problem, but not for the reasons Richard thought. Louis saw the way Taggart looked at Alyssa, the proprietary stance even as the man tried to keep his distance. Yet despite his fuckup in letting

Alyssa slip away, Taggart and his brothers were purported experts at finding missing persons. "Let him bring her back." The woman eyed him uneasily as she lingered by the door. "I will deal with her as I see fit."

"But—"

Louis hung up the phone, rage and frustration humming through his veins. How hard was it to keep tabs on one small woman, especially when her family and the press tracked her every move?

She'd be back soon enough, and he could use her disappearance and drug addiction to his advantage. Once he had her to himself and controlled every aspect of her life, she would do anything for her next fix. He merely had to bide his time, wait for the right moment to take her, willing or not.

In the meantime . . . "Come here," he said to the girl with a feral smile. He slipped the sash from his robe and looped it around her neck. His cock hardened as he imagined it was Alyssa's eyes pleading with him to let her live.

CHAPTER 9

DEREK ALMOST DIDN'T recognize the small figure exiting the diner, one of three buildings that constituted main street for the tiny coastal town about a hundred miles north of San Francisco.

Dressed in jeans, a bulky fisherman's sweater, and a maroon Gore-Tex shell to ward off the icy, biting rain, Alyssa was so far from her usual dressed-to-the-nines glamorpuss self it was no wonder she'd managed to make it this far without anyone catching on.

He watched her from his car across the street, eyes narrowed on her as she made her way to her car. She wasn't driving the gold Mercedes. Sometime after she'd slipped through the window—the fucking window, for Christ's sake!—she'd gotten her hands on a navy-blue Ford Mustang.

As he watched her point the keys and unlock the car, the anger he'd been nursing for the last day and a half surged to a boil, hissing and seething and threatening to bubble over. He'd been operating on fury and adrenaline ever since Andy had shaken him awake on the couch to inform him Alyssa had flown the coop.

She'd slid down the fire escape while he'd watched *Nightline*. To say he felt like a fucking idiot was the understatement of the century.

And Harold Van Weldt hadn't been any more pleased, earning Derek a major ass chewing not only from Van Weldt but also from Danny. Derek knew if he didn't find Alyssa, like, yesterday, his ass was grass, and so was Gemini's reputation.

Fortunately Alyssa's feeble attempts to cover her tracks had been no match for modern technology. Yesterday he'd managed to slip a tracking device into Alyssa's phone, so now pinpointing her exact location by a matter of yards was as easy as logging on to a Web site.

Yet something kept him from letting Harold in on that bit of intel. For reasons he still couldn't decipher, he hadn't followed her right away, curious what the little Alyssa dot was doing in a beach house outside of a town that was little more than a pin dot on a map.

The house, he'd learned, was the property of one Raj Gupta, a multimillionaire software mogul. Derek would have been jealous to see Alyssa running away to his house, had Gupta not also been very openly gay. Still, he wondered, since when was Alyssa friends with genius software developers?

Whatever she was doing there, she didn't seem inclined to stray far, and after giving her a day to do whatever she needed to do, Derek knew he couldn't put off going after her. She'd made him look like an ass long enough. Now it was time to pack up her bags and go on home like a good little girl.

Alyssa clicked the seatbelt and glanced warily in the rearview mirror as she backed out of the diner's gravel parking area. Under the thick turtleneck collar of her sweater, her hair prickled on her neck, and she got that strange pulling sensation along her shoulders that told her she was being watched.

She couldn't see anything out of the ordinary, and the few residents braving blustering coastal weather didn't give her a second glance.

She flicked on the wipers and pulled out onto the rain-slicked highway, kicking herself for venturing into town. She didn't think anyone in the diner had recognized her. The broad-shouldered, flannel-clad woman who had waited on her had dismissed her as a crazy tourist right off the bat.

"Not the best time of year to visit," she'd said, tilting her chin to the rain as she'd handed Alyssa a to-go cup of thick, black coffee. "Most people come in summer or spring."

"I like it now," Alyssa had replied. "It's quieter."

A couple loggers had given her a once-over as she'd moved to the door, looking not at her but through her. But as soon as she'd stepped out into the downpour, she couldn't shake the uneasy feeling she was being watched.

She gradually increased her speed, and the tires of the borrowed Mustang hugged the slick pavement as she took a sharp curve. No one was behind her, she assured herself as she glanced in the rearview and saw nothing. Still, she shifted the car into fourth and increased her pressure on the gas, eager to get back to the house and behind a heavy-locked door.

She smoothly guided the car up over a rise and around another curve. Headlights appeared in the rearview mirror, and her heart leaped to her throat. Big, silver, like an un-marked police car, it loomed behind her.

It's nothing. Lots of people drive on this road.

She pushed the Mustang harder, gripping the wheel with one hand as she downshifted with the other to navigate a sharp turn. The lights disappeared, and her heart rate slowed. She gave another glance in the mirror to make sure the big silver car was nowhere in sight as she turned into the cypress-lined lane that led to Raj's beach house.

She parked under the wood-shingled carport and pulled the hood of her shell up over her head. As she swung her legs out of the car, she could hear the roar of an engine over the steady drum of the rain.

It was the big silver car, headed straight for her. And she

didn't feel an ounce of relief when she saw Derek's angry face behind the wheel.

Derek pulled the Marauder up beside the Mustang, skidding to a stop in the gravel and mud. He jumped out of the car, impervious to the rain as he grabbed Alyssa's arm.

"Watch it!" she yelled as coffee spurted through the lid on her coffee.

"What the fuck are you thinking, driving like that in weather like this? You trying to kill yourself?" Truth be told, if it had been anyone but Alyssa, he would have admired the way she'd put the Mustang through its paces and negotiated the twisty coastal highway.

She glared at him through the sheets of rain. "I wouldn't have had to drive so fast if you hadn't been riding my ass." She ducked around him to look at his car. "That's not your car. What, did you rip off a cop?"

"I like the Marauder for long drives. More leg room." Plus, other drivers tended, like Alyssa, to mistake it for an unmarked police car, and hence got the fuck out of his way. "What the fuck were you thinking, taking off like that?"

"I don't owe you an explanation," she said, shoulders squared, chin tilted up stubbornly. The effect was ruined by her nearly blue lips and the subtle quaking under her jacket.

He shook his head and steered her toward the wooden staircase that led up to the front door. "Let's get inside. You look like a drowned rat."

She gave an offended huff but let him guide her to the door of the rambling wood shingle house that sat perched on a bluff overlooking the churning Pacific.

She unlocked the door and shucked off her jacket. She dropped it in a pile on the floor before toeing off her shoes. Derek grabbed it off the floor and hung it on a hook to dry before following her into the house. "So, tell me, what the hell were you thinking?"

"I'm going crazy, okay? I needed to get away."

"Go to a spa like everyone else," he said flatly. "Or, better yet, go to rehab."

"I don't need rehab," Alyssa said through clenched teeth as she tossed the house keys on the coffee table. "You have no idea what it's like. Constantly being watched. Having the press report your every move, printing stories that you're a drugged-out skank."

Derek felt his anger soften at the slight trembling in her voice and tried to restore his anger's edge, reminding himself of how she'd made him look like a fool.

She padded across the carpeted floor of the great room to a set of sliding glass doors. She pulled back the curtains, filling the room with feeble gray light. Derek did a quick scan of the house. It was not the kind of place he would have expected Alyssa to choose as a retreat. Though large, with a spectacular view of the waves crashing through the sliders, the furniture and fixtures were dated. It was comfortable but far from the luxury digs he would have expected.

"Not to mention someone is slipping me drugs and making sure I make an ass of myself in public." She shot him a glare. "Not that anyone believes me, of course."

His jaw tightened, wishing she would do them all a favor and admit the truth. As cover stories went, someone slipping her drugs without her knowledge was about as lame as you could get.

Alyssa tossed her cell phone on the kitchen counter and turned to face him, her arms folded across her chest. "I just needed a few days to breathe, you know? Get away from being watched and monitored and commented on. Try to figure out why someone would want to drug me," she said with a pointed look. "Can you understand that?"

Her eyes were wide and pleading. Derek had to admit to himself, however begrudgingly, that he could see what she was talking about. Still, she'd brought this on herself. "You

can't spend your adult life courting attention and expect it
to turn off whenever you want," he said bluntly.

Her full mouth pulled into a tight line. "How did you
find me so fast?"

Derek nodded at her phone. "GPS locater. I slipped it in
yesterday. Kinda like I knew you'd try something like this."

Her eyes flashed with annoyance. "Isn't that illegal?"

Derek shrugged. "Your uncle demanded I keep close tabs
on you. I do whatever's necessary to get the job done."

As quick as it had appeared, her annoyance was gone.
She sat down heavily on one of the kitchen chairs, her entire
body slumping with defeat. "I suppose you called him as
soon as you figured out where I went."

"I haven't told him yet." And he had yet to come up with
an answer why.

She looked up at him, hope glimmering in her face. "I
don't suppose there's any way you could not tell him. Just
for a couple more days." She folded her hands and brought
them to her chest, almost as if in prayer. "Please," she said.
"Just for a couple days. After everything that's happened, I
need some time to get my head together."

He swallowed uncomfortably, stunned at how tempted
he was to give in. When he didn't answer, she stood up from
her chair and stood in front of him. "Please," she said softly
and took one of his hands in both of hers. The heat of her
palms jolted through him. His skin warmed under her touch,
the heat spreading through him as he looked down into her
face. "Hold my uncle off for a little longer, and I swear I'll
come home day after tomorrow."

He was struck by how vulnerable she looked, her eyes
old and tired in her otherwise youthful face, pleading with
him to give her a reprieve.

He was sinking. Sucked into the vortex of those big green
eyes. He knew what he needed to do. She was a job. A task
to perform. A person he was hired to keep out of trouble,

even if it meant going against her wishes. He'd already compromised himself and his company by waiting this long to come after her.

Yet he couldn't bring himself to say no.

"Okay, but just until day after tomorrow." He couldn't believe the words actually passed his lips, even when her eyes lit up with delight and relief.

She grabbed him in an enthusiastic hug. "Thank you! Thank you! I can even meet up with you on my way home so it really looks like you caught me."

Derek tried not to notice how good her rain-damp hair smelled when it brushed against his face or the softness of her tits pressing through the thick knit of her sweater. Fuck, what had he gotten himself into? "I'm not going anywhere."

Alyssa stiffened, released her hold on his shoulders, and took a step back. "Why would you want to stay?"

"Want has nothing to do with it," he said. "But I'll be damned if I'm going to let you sneak off again."

"I won't! I promise I'll be back on Thursday, but you can't expect me to relax with you here."

"It's a big house. Ignore me." But he could feel the warmth of her small, tense body, even from several feet away. Even in a house this size, he wouldn't be able to ignore her.

She arched a light brown eyebrow at him. "You really think that's possible?" Her gaze slid down his body. Sexual heat poured from it like a caress, and he felt it the same as if she'd reached out and stroked his cock. "Suit yourself," she said, straightening to her full height and turning away. He watched, mesmerized, as the dim gray light from the window haloed her. He couldn't see a single curve of her small body through her bulky outfit. But wool and canvas had never looked so sexy.

The reality of what he'd agreed to started to sink in. Two days alone with Alyssa. Alone in an isolated beach house, with no one around to see what they were up to. Alone with a spoiled woman child who twisted him up in knots.

Fucking idiot. Screw the deal. He should load her in the car and haul her ass back home, no matter what he'd agreed to.

But he was a man of his word. He'd given her two days reprieve. Surely he could control himself for that long, no matter how bad she got to him.

She wasn't there. Martin Fish stood on the corner across the street from Alyssa's house, glaring as the door closed behind a mousy brunette. Even though he couldn't make out her features, he knew the jean-clad butt was about two sizes too wide to belong to Alyssa.

His head pounded, and his vision blurred. Fuck, he needed a bed. And a drink. A woman in a trench coat tapped by on high heels, giving him a wary look and a wide berth as she passed.

He didn't give a fuck that he looked like a degenerate, having come straight from the airport to Alyssa's house. He didn't care about his wrinkled clothes or the jungle stink that still clung to him. He just wanted to get to Alyssa.

But she wasn't fucking there. He'd heard the photographers lining the sidewalk outside her house say they hadn't seen her since yesterday, not even a glimpse of her moving around the apartment. Disappointment had flooded through him, combining with fatigue to make him slump to the sidewalk. Just in case, Martin had hung around for hours, waiting for her to appear so he could seize an opportunity to talk to her. But the only person he'd seen going in or out was the fat ass.

He rubbed at his tired, gritty eyes, and as he turned, he caught his reflection in a window. Lean and gaunt in his jeans and canvas jacket. Hair lank and flattened to his head with rain. He looked dirty and disreputable, like a homeless person.

He realized, in a jolt of clarity, how close he'd been to fucking this all up. Did he really think he could get past her entourage and security to get to her? There was an article this morning about her uncle hiring some bodyguard to watch her. Martin wasn't thinking right. No way anyone would let him get close.

There was a better way. Play this right, and Alyssa would come to him.

Blood. It was everywhere. Down the stairs like a torrent. Slicking the floor of the marble entryway. Alyssa struggled up the stairs, pulling herself along the banister as it rushed past her, threatening to sweep her away in a thick red flood. The gamey metallic odor filled her nostrils as she continued down the hall. The blood was up around her knees now as she waded down the hall. The door to the master bedroom pulsed, haloed in white light.

She didn't want to open it. She wanted to run away, but when she tried to turn, her feet were bogged down, sucked into thick, blood-black mud.

She opened the door, and the blood hit her like a wave, washing over her, soaking her, receding like the tide.

They were on the floor, the wound in her father's chest still gushing, pumping like a geyser. And her stepmother across from him, her face stretched in a deathly grimace as blood poured from the wound in her head.

Alyssa's mouth opened in a scream, but the sound strangled in her throat, hissing, high-pitched. She stumbled to the French doors onto the balcony. A man was there, big, hulking, his features indistinguishable. But there was no mistaking the gun in his hand as he turned it on her.

"No. Stop!" But her words were garbled, and the cold barrel of the gun pressed into her chest. "Stop it."

"You can't expect it to stop now." The words, the voice, were Derek's.

She sat up with a cry, heart pounding, body shaking in the aftermath of the nightmare. The dark was absolute, smothering as Alyssa struggled to get air into her lungs. She fumbled for the bedside lamp and switched it on.

The dim light seared her eyeballs as sharp pain stabbed her head, and nausea roiled in her stomach. The dreams about her father's death were growing more violent, and now when she woke she always had a piercing headache. Like something was stabbing, probing at her brain, digging around as it tried to get her to remember something.

She put her head in her hands and rubbed at her temples. Despite what she'd said to the reporter, she'd been able to brush off the dreams as nightmares. Horrible, violent, but ultimately meaningless.

Then yesterday she'd received the mysterious text message from someone claiming to know the truth about her father's death. Probably just a malicious prank, but it unnerved her just the same.

And to top it all off, Derek had shown up, blowing apart her tenuous peace. Denying her even a few days of quiet before she was forced to return home to the storm.

Ignore him. Her head throbbed. As if. Even asleep two doors down, she could feel his presence. He'd barely spoken to her all afternoon, ignoring her in favor of the books he'd found in her friend Raj's bookshelves and, later, a movie he'd found on cable. She, in contrast, had been on high alert, every cell aware of his presence on the other end of the couch.

They were completely alone. If anything happened between them, no one would ever have to know. The thought tormented, tantalized her until she had to excuse herself before she did something really dumb like throw herself at him. Again.

The words he spoke in her dream, echoing what he'd said in the coffee place, played through her head, bringing on a fresh wave of pain. She walked on shaky legs to the bathroom, unable to shake the creepy, unsettled feel that lingered from her dream.

She rummaged through her toiletry bag, squinting and cursing as she tried to locate her bottle of ibuprofen. Finally she laid her hands on it and popped the top.

"Everything okay?"

She jumped and shrieked, sending little red pills skittering across the tile counter. She bent to retrieve them, her balance wavering as blinding pain shot through her head. As she stood up her elbow knocked into the glass next to the sink. She made a fumbling grab, watching helplessly as it tumbled, end over end, slamming against the toilet and exploding into millions of shards.

Muzzy-headed from her nightmare and stabbing headache, Alyssa stepped forward, even as Derek shouted for her to look out.

Too late. A sharp pain pierced the sole of her foot, and she started to stumble. Derek cursed and grabbed her under the arms, snatched her off her feet, and carried her into the kitchen.

He snapped on the light and set her down in a kitchen chair. "Don't move," he said, his face set in stern lines. "Do you know if this place has a first-aid kit?"

"Raj keeps one under the sink of the bathroom," she called to his already retreating back. "Be careful not to cut yourself!" The overhead kitchen light did nothing to help her headache, and she squeezed her eyes shut. "Can you see if you can salvage any of my Advil while you're in there?"

He returned a few moments later, first-aid kit in one hand and her mostly empty bottle of ibuprofen in the other. She grabbed the bottle from him and shook out two pills, so eager for the relief they'd provide she swallowed them without water. Probably just a placebo effect, but the minute the pills hit her tongue she felt the pain in her head ease.

She opened her eyes and saw him watching her. His gaze slid meaningfully to the pill bottle in her hand.

"If you need something stronger, you don't need to fake it with Advil on my account." He pulled up a chair across from her, sat down, and lifted her bare foot up onto his lap. He was wearing only a pair of flannel pajama bottoms, his thickly muscled chest bare. Even through her headachy haze she was struck by how gorgeous he was. She'd been with some really good-looking men, actors, performers—men who kept their bodies in perfect condition because their careers depended on it.

He lifted her foot to the light, his muscles rippling under tight, tan skin. A few scars, light streaks against his sun-darkened skin, showed through a dusting of hair that arrowed down his eight-pack abs. An arrow that led to one of the most impressive pieces of equipment she'd ever had the pleasure to encounter; Derek made the hottest men in Hollywood look like a bunch of metrosexual wusses.

So mesmerized was she that it took a few seconds for his words to sink in. "I'm not faking it with Advil. Even if I wanted something stronger for my headache, I don't have anything in the house."

He glanced up from her foot, the look in his eyes one of patent disbelief.

"It's true," she said, trying to snatch her foot back. He tightened his grip on her ankle, not enough to hurt, but enough to let her know she wasn't going anywhere until he let her. A shiver of warmth snaked up her leg, penetrating through the pain of her headache. "Go look for yourself. I don't have any OxyContin or horse tranquilizer or whatever else you all seem to think I'm on."

"I was there when you got the lab results," he said, extracting a pair of tweezers from the first-aid kit.

"And I told you I don't know how they got in my system!" She winced as he probed with the tweezers. "Ouch! Are you trying to cripple me?"

"Chill out. It's just a little glass shard, but it slid in deep." He probed again, and she gripped the seat of her chair at the needlelike pain. On the plus side, the sharp sting in her foot distracted her from her headache.

"There. It's out." He held up the glass for her inspection, a tiny shard no wider than a needle. He went back to the first-aid kit and pulled out a white foil packet and a Band-Aid. He ripped open the packet, and the sharp smell of alcohol filled the air. She hissed as he pressed the damp pad against the sole of her foot. "You really expect anyone with two brain cells to rub together to believe you're being drugged?"

"I don't care what you believe. I didn't knowingly take any drugs." It scared the shit out of her to know someone could get close enough to her to dose her without her knowledge.

"You know it's impossible for anyone to believe you." He peeled the backing off the Band-Aid and stuck it to her foot. But he didn't release her ankle. His other hand rested on the top of her foot, his thumb stroking absently over the smooth skin.

The brush of his calloused thumb was so arousing he could have been touching her breast instead of her foot. But even her arousal wasn't enough to ward off the hurt. "What is that supposed to mean? Because the press likes to bring up problems I had in the past? Because making me look like a mess helps them sell magazines?" She looked at him, her stare unwavering as she willed him to believe her.

He stared right back, disbelief evident in the hardness of his dark eyes, in the arch of his thick brows. "Everything the press writes about you is false?" The skepticism was so thick she could have cut it with a knife.

"Was everything the press wrote about your mother true?"

His thumb stilled on her foot, and his fingers tightened around her ankle hard enough to make her wince.

It was a low blow, and she knew it. After weeks of resisting, she'd finally given into curiosity and Googled Derek Taggart shortly after she'd arrived at Raj's house yesterday. She hadn't known what to expect, but certainly not what she'd found. His bio from the Gemini Securities Web site had popped up first. He was ex-military, graduated from West Point before becoming an Army Ranger. That hadn't surprised her. With his hard edges and serious take-no-prisoners attitude, his military background was like an extra layer of skin.

But she'd been shocked to learn he'd been involved in one of the most notorious missing persons cases to ever hit the San Francisco Bay area. She'd been young—only seven at the time—but she vaguely remembered the story of a wealthy housewife gone missing penetrating the celebrity-heavy news in Los Angeles where she'd lived with her mother.

Plagued by morbid curiosity, Alyssa had spent several hours yesterday following the links that led to stories of a beautiful but troubled woman who had apparently decided to pick up and leave her husband and teenage sons without a backward glance. Many of the articles speculated on her motives, ranging from struggles with drugs and alcohol to extramarital affairs.

Something flashed in Derek's eyes, a nanosecond glimpse of vulnerability, and Alyssa felt about an inch tall for lashing out. Then his face closed up like a door had slammed, and his eyes went dark and expressionless.

He dropped her foot and began packing up the first-aid kit.

Alyssa watched him, her mind flashing to one of the few photos that had accompanied the stories. It showed Derek and his brothers, Ethan and Danny, along with their father, Joe, as Joe spoke to a reporter. Danny stood beside his father, arms folded, face hard, a teenager trying to be a man.

Ethan smiled for the camera, charming, sunny, all-American. Derek had been off to the side, half of his body cut off from the frame, his face in profile as he stood apart from the rest of his family.

She wanted to sink into her chair and disappear.

"I'm sorry," she said. "I shouldn't have said that."

"No big deal," he said as he zipped closed the nylon case containing the first-aid supplies. "It happened a long time ago. I'm over it."

She doubted that. She got up and limped after him as he retreated down the hall. "Still, it was a shitty thing to say, and I'm sorry." She laid her hand on his arm, her fingers closing over the tight cords of muscle.

"It's okay," he said with a half smile that didn't quite reach his eyes. "But you're right. Not all of it was true. At least, not that we know of."

"So you know how things can be exaggerated, even made up." He nodded, studying her, and she could see his conviction crack. She could feel him giving her the tiniest benefit of the doubt.

It wasn't a declaration of faith, but, hey, she'd take what she could get.

She was standing so close, she could feel the heat radiating off his bare skin and could smell his woodsy, musky scent. Her fingers tightened around his forearm as desire hit her like a physical force. She knew the second he felt it, too, could sense it in the subtle tightening of his muscles, the slight hitch in his breath.

Derek bent his head, and Alyssa stood on tiptoe to meet him, her lips parting eagerly to accept the invasion of his tongue. She whimpered into his mouth and pressed against him, wrapped her arms around his neck and tried to climb up his body. He lifted her, backing her up against the wall and pinning her there with his hips.

He was rock hard, his cock nudging at her stomach through

his pajama bottoms, and an answering heat bloomed and pulsed between her legs. All he had to do was kiss her, and she wanted him, slick and wet with a need so fierce it scared her. She'd never felt anything like this, the desperation to have a man—*this man*—on her, inside her, making her come until she couldn't see straight.

With a groan, Derek ripped his mouth from hers and backed away so quickly she slid down the wall and landed with a thump.

"I can't do this," he muttered almost to himself. "Not with you."

"Why not?" she asked, not sure if she should be insulted. "I want you," she said, knowing she sounded needy and desperate but not caring right now. Why couldn't she stop throwing herself at him? What was it about him that made her lose every shred of self-preservation?

She reached out and boldly stroked him through the soft flannel of his pants. He sucked in a breath, quivering under her touch like a barely tamed animal. "And I know you want me."

"That doesn't matter," he said and inhaled on a hiss as she flattened her palm against his shaft and shamelessly stroked him. "You're a client—"

"I'm not your client," she whispered and leaned close enough to flick her tongue across his flat, copper-colored nipple. His cock jerked in her hand.

"You know what I mean," he huffed, sounding like he was having trouble remembering what he was talking about.

Alyssa opened her mouth against his chest, sucking and licking his salty skin with teasing swipes of her tongue. "Do you remember the night we met? The first time you took me home?"

"Christ, yes." His breath was coming in harsh pants now, his hands fisting at his sides as though he wasn't sure whether to hold her close or shove her away.

She was more than happy to help him decide. She dipped her hand inside his waistband and closed her fingers around his rigid erection. He was so thick her fingers barely met as she slid her hand up and down, stroking, sliding, squeezing as her sex throbbed in anticipation of having his whole thick length shoved deep inside.

"You had no idea who I was," she reminded him as her thumb swirled around the plump head, wet and slick with thick beads of precome. She skimmed his chest with open-mouthed kisses, bent her head to trace the ridges of his abs with her tongue. "All you saw was a woman. A woman you wanted to be with."

He gave a low groan as he thrust his hips against her grip. "It's different now, now that I know."

"It doesn't have to be," she whispered, tilting her head back so she could look into his face. She saw a man at war with himself, his mouth tight, strained, his eyes stormy as need threatened his rigid control. "Pretend I'm nobody. Like any other woman you've ever been with. Like I was that night."

"Trouble is, the real world's always waiting for us," he said as his hands came up to close over her shoulders.

"Not for another two days," she said with another swirl of her thumb around his cock. "No one knows we're here. No one knows what we're doing. For the next two days, I'm a nobody. I'm just like any other girl you've ever met."

CHAPTER 10

JUST ANOTHER WOMAN? Was she fucking kidding? There was no way Derek could act like Alyssa was like any other woman he'd ever been with.

No other woman made him feel like this, insane with lust from the slightest touch of her hand. Rock hard and ready to go from the sweet smell of her skin.

And absolutely, completely incapable of turning her down.

He bent to kiss her, moaning as her grip tightened around his cock. What he felt for her went beyond want, beyond desire. Dark and primitive, going against every instinct that demanded rationality and self-preservation, leaving him needing, wanting, powerless to control it. He knew he should push her away but couldn't make himself stop touching her, kissing her, licking her.

Just one more taste. One more touch. Memories of their one night roared through his head until he knew he couldn't stop himself from indulging one more time.

He tugged her stretchy tank top up over her head and slid his hands over the silky skin of her back. Warmth radiated off her like rays of the sun, bathing him in her heat. Her hand slid up and down his dick, stroking him into oblivion. He reached down and grabbed her wrist, knowing if he didn't stop her he was going to blow in her hand.

"I knew the minute I laid eyes on you, you were going to be nothing but trouble," he muttered, sinking to his knees in front of her. Tight, pink nipples stared him dead in the face, and he sucked one into his mouth. Salty, sweet, she tasted even better than he remembered. "God, you have the sweetest tits," he murmured, taking each into his mouth in turn, sucking and licking the bullet-hard tips.

"Thanks." She laughed breathlessly. "My mom was always trying to convince me to get implants because they're so small."

"Crazy," he said, his hand closing over the giving softness. "You're perfect, sweet, soft." He didn't know where the words were coming from. He didn't say stuff like this, didn't talk during sex or compliment his lovers' bodies. He made sure they got off before he did, made sure they were happy, but he didn't lose control or get all swept up in the moment. He sucked her nipple between his lips. Maybe with his mouth full he'd shut the fuck up.

She cried out and arched against him, and the sound made his balls tighten and his cock harden another inch. His hand slid down the curve of her waist and closed over her hip. His mouth released her nipple and skimmed the soft plane of her belly. He dipped his tongue into her navel, smiling a little at the way her muscles jumped and twitched. She was like a live wire under his mouth and hands, switched on.

He shoved her pajama bottoms off her hips and down her legs to pool around her ankles. His mouth watered at the sight of her pussy, sleek and bare except for that damp patch of curls at the top. All he'd done was suck her tits, and she was already dripping wet, her clit a moist little berry poking through, begging for attention.

He pressed his mouth to her in an openmouthed kiss, his tongue delving into her folds, sliding up and down her clit as he lapped up every last drop of juice. His name exploded from her lips as her hands fisted in his hair. She was silky hot and salty sweet, the taste and scent of her flooding his senses, pushing him to the brink.

Her body tightened; pain pricked his scalp as her fingers pulled his hair. Her hips arched against his face. She shifted her legs, trying to part them wider, only to be hampered by the pajama bottoms tangled around her ankles.

Derek didn't help her. He liked her like this. Vibrating like a tuning fork as her orgasm hovered just out of her reach. Wanting him so much she shook with it.

Like any other woman. Christ, it couldn't be further from the truth. He didn't tease women, stroke them to see how high he could take them before he made them come. Didn't ease up and tease their pussies with featherlight strokes of his tongue until they arched and moaned and begged him pleasepleaseplease don't stop. Didn't hold his lovers on that razor-sharp edge for as long as he could just because it made him feel like king of the fucking world that he could bring a woman to such a state.

Another surge of wetness bathed his tongue as her clit pulsed under his lips. One more suck, one more stroke.

Derek's cock pulsed, insistent, greedy. Selfish. He wanted to be inside her the first time she came, feel the ripple of sleek, tight muscles around his aching cock. He backed off and stood up, ignoring her cry of protest as he scooped her up into his arms and carried her into the bedroom.

He left her long enough to get a condom from the giant box under the bathroom sink. He wondered in passing what the hell Raj had going on up here that necessitated that many rubbers. The sight of Alyssa naked, on her back, knees parted to reveal the shiny wet folds of her sex, rendered him incapable of wondering anything other than how fast he could get inside her and how fast he could make her come so he could follow her headlong into oblivion.

* * *

As Derek approached the bed, he reminded Alyssa of a battle-hardened jungle cat. With his big, heavily muscled body and tracing of scars, he was all barely leashed strength, barely controlled fury. A shiver ran through her, and she remembered the first time they'd had sex. The same fascination tinged with fear had swept through her then. He was so powerful, so big. He could so easily overpower her if he wanted, do anything he wanted to her, and she would be powerless to stop him.

Call her sick, but that made her even hotter for him because she knew, with every fiber of her being, that he would never hurt her. Not physically anyway.

Her gaze caught on the huge erection jutting between his thighs. He was big everywhere, she thought with a small smile. And as gorgeous there as he was everywhere else. Long and thick with a tracery of bulging veins, the plump head so engorged it looked as if it were going to burst from his skin.

"Oh, yeah, nothing but trouble." She looked up. He was watching her look at him, a long dimple creasing his cheek as his mouth crooked into a smile. She heard the rip of foil and watched him smooth the latex down the length of his cock. Her legs shifted, her hips arching off the bed as her body pulsed in anticipation. He knelt between her legs and hooked her knees in his hands, spreading her wide.

Alyssa grabbed him with shaking fingers and guided him in, her back arching as he slid home. He lifted her knees, pressing them back against her chest as his cock stretched and squeezed its way inside her body. She was so keyed up that was all it took to send her over the edge, her orgasm hitting her with stunning speed and intensity.

She pulsed and shook around him, clutching his hips as he thrust hard and fast, riding her through her peak until she didn't know if she was having multiple orgasms or one long, endless wave.

She didn't really care as long as Derek kept the thrusting, swirling rhythm, pounding into her with his granite-hard cock until she was shuddering and shaking, molten at her center like a chocolate lava cake. She loved looking at him braced above her. Every muscle stood out in sharp relief against his sweat-slick skin.

She'd never been with anyone like him. So quiet and controlled but like a barely tamed animal in bed. But still he held something back, kept his lust in check as he measured his thrusts, controlled the motion, didn't quite let himself go at her with total abandon. His dark eyes glittered through his thick lashes as he watched her, taking in every detail of her response, adjusting the pressure, the depth, the angle accordingly until she felt like every nerve ending was on fire. His thumb flicked her clit, and her body convulsed again, the pleasure so keen tears stung her eyes.

She rocked her hips against him, wanting to pull him even deeper, helpless to fight this thing building and building inside her that made her want to grab on to Derek and cling tight. His hips jerked against her, and his thrusts picked up speed. His face pulled tight with pleasure, and harsh groans pulsed from his throat. She loved watching him come, knowing she had, even for a second, broken through his ironclad control.

Derek collapsed beside her, breathing hard, and she wound her arms and legs around him. Through the haze of pleasure she felt a niggle of fear. What had she gotten herself into? She'd meant for this to be playful, fun, to steal a few days of pleasure with a man she found insanely attractive. This was dangerous, the pull he had on her. She'd been a complete idiot for a hell of a lot less.

* * *

Derek stretched as he padded into the living room the following morning at a little after nine. He paused in the kitchen to pour himself some coffee, frowning when he looked around and didn't see Alyssa. The door to her bedroom had been open when he'd passed it, and he'd poked his head in to find the bed empty.

A suspicious thought tightened his stomach. Had she fucked him into complacency so she could sneak off again? He took a sip of coffee to wash away the bitterness of the thought. Surely he wasn't that stupid.

He moved into the living room and started to call out for her when he caught a glimpse of pink outside the sliding glass doors that led to the house's massive redwood deck. He moved in for a closer look, his mouth going bone-dry at the sight that greeted him.

Alyssa's lusciously rounded ass was pointed up at the sky as she executed a downward dog position worthy of a professional yogi. Her legs, clad in stretchy pink pants, were slightly parted, her palms flat on the damp wood of the deck in front of her so her body formed a perfect vee. The rain had finally stopped. The sky was bullet gray, the air swirling with fog off the Pacific, but she didn't seem to notice the cold as she jumped her feet forward, straightened halfway, and then lowered herself into a half push-up, arched her chest forward, and then pushed back into the inverted vee.

He watched, enthralled, as she repeated the sequence three more times, wondering how he could be so turned on watching Alyssa do yoga when he'd fucked her six ways to Sunday less than eight hours ago. But watching her bend, stretch, twist made him think of a thousand other ways he wanted to fuck her. From behind, with that surprisingly round ass of hers bouncing against his hips. Her on top, her strong, flexible legs spread wide as she rode his cock to oblivion.

Derek grimaced as his cock thickened behind his flannel

pajamas. What the fuck was wrong with him? He'd scratched
the itch that had been nagging him since Alyssa Miles had
been thrown back into his life. Finally confirmed that, yes,
sex with her was as good as—no, better than—his fevered
memories had insisted.

But now the itch was scratched. Case closed. She'd gotten
what she wanted—another tumble with a guy who wouldn't
sell her out. And he'd gotten what he needed—a good lay to
hold him over for the next several weeks.

So there was no reason in hell he should be popping
wood all over the place and calculating how long it would
take him to retrieve a condom from the bathroom, strip off
those pink pants, and have her spread-eagled on the nearest
flat surface.

Derek struggled to wipe his face of expression as Alyssa
straightened and turned to come into the house. If she had
any inkling that he'd been watching her like a dirty old man
at a peep show, it didn't show in the wide smile that encom-
passed the entire bottom half of her face. She stepped through
the sliding glass door, the mist floating in behind. Her long
hair was caught back in a ponytail. Derek tightened his hand
around his coffee mug as he fought the urge to smooth his
fingers over a damp tendril that had escaped to curl next to
her ear.

Her cheeks were flushed from exertion and the damp,
cold fall morning, and she smelled like fresh rain.

"Good morning," she said brightly as she breezed past
him into the kitchen. "You found the coffee—I hope it's
okay. I don't make it a whole lot, so I sometimes make it too
strong."

"It's fine," he said, studying, watching her for any signs
of discomfort or morning-after awkwardness. He was surprised when he saw none, especially after he had basically
rolled off her and beat feet to the guest room for the rest of

the night. When she'd asked him sleepily where he was going, he'd muttered something about sleeping better on his own.

The truth was he'd needed to get out of there, away from her soft skin, tight body, and insane pull she seemed to have on him. Needed to breathe and convince himself she was, as she'd put it, just another woman he'd taken to bed.

She seemed to have taken it all in stride, judging from the way she bopped around the kitchen, putting a few dishes in the dishwasher in between bites of a banana. Then again, he thought as the pit in his stomach made another unwelcome appearance, maybe she was used to fucking guys like it meant nothing and didn't care one way or the other if they spent the night or not.

The thought stuck in his throat, choking him with a knot of things he had no business feeling.

"I'll be back in forty-five minutes," she said and tossed her banana peel in the garbage.

Her pronouncement jolted him from his jealous musings. "Where the hell do you think you're going?"

Her eyebrows shot up at his harsh tone. "I'm going for my morning run."

"Alone?"

"Is that a problem?" She was already lacing up her shoes.

He put down his coffee cup as it became evident she was going whether he liked it or not. "Hang on, I'll go with you."

"You don't need to," she protested. "It's totally safe up here, and no one knows who I am anyway."

Her voice trailed him down the hall as he quickly pulled on the workout clothes and running shoes he always carried with him. She was right. He didn't need to go with her, not for safety reasons anyway.

"It's not like I'm going to try to escape on foot," she said testily when he emerged from the guest room.

"I'll feel better if I keep an eye on you." Watching her little pink butt bouncing down the road wasn't going to do anything to quell his libido, but at least he couldn't do anything about it for the next five miles or so. Besides, despite her protestations, he still didn't trust her not to try to ditch him again.

They ran in silence for ten minutes or so. She was surprisingly swift, her strides long and even. He didn't have a problem keeping up with her, but the pace was fast enough to get him breathing hard. The road they ran along paralleled the beach, offering glimpses of crashing waves and craggy rocks through the thick coastal fog. The houses dotting the coast were similar to the one where Alyssa was staying, sprawling, wood-shingle structures designed to make the most of the dramatic views. Nice, but not the kind of five-star resorts where Alyssa was known to frolic.

"So, how do you know Raj Gupta?"

Her stride stuttered, and she shot him a surprised look. "How did you—"

"Once I knew where you were, it wasn't that hard to track down the owner. So, tell me, how does someone like you hook up with one of the greatest technology innovators of the last decade?"

Her eyes narrowed slightly. "Haven't you ever seen that show *Beauty and the Geek*? Every nerd in the world wants a piece of airhead arm candy like me." She tried to surge ahead, but Derek was right beside her in a single stride.

"That's not what I meant. And, anyway, Gupta's gay, so I know it's not about trying to nail you. But you have to admit it's an unlikely friendship."

Her ponytail swished across her shoulder as she gave a little shrug. "I met Raj in rehab, and we hit it off. He's been there for me ever since. So now when I need a place to escape, he lets me use his place."

The only sounds were feet hitting the dirt trail and waves crashing in the distance as Derek let that digest. "This place doesn't seem your speed."

She slowed her pace to a walk, stretching her arms above her head as she looked out to sea. "I can breathe up here," she said, taking a deep inhale. "No one has any reason to think I'd be up here. No one recognizes me. No photographers waiting behind the bushes to catch me doing something stupid." She started jogging back the way they came. "No one slipping me drugs and trying to make me look like I'm a mess."

He could hear the tension in her voice, mixed with something else. Fear? "Alyssa," he began but didn't know what else to say, didn't know which way was up. Something in him—instinct? Gut feel?—told him she wasn't lying. She had a terrible poker face. He'd seen that already. If she were lying, he'd know it.

But he also knew what addicts were like. Remembered what his mother was like before she'd taken off. The secretiveness. The manipulation. Hiding liquor and pills all over the house, making it look like she was in complete control.

It hit him in the chest like a bullet. Was he following in his father's footsteps? Falling for an emotional wreck of a woman? An addict who would wring him dry and leave him empty? Even now, nearly two decades after his mother's disappearance, Derek's father was still obsessed with her, desperately following any lead that might explain her abrupt and complete disappearance from their lives.

"I know you don't believe me," she said tightly. "You can search my stuff when you get home. I don't care. I have nothing to hide."

He didn't tell her he already had. And, just like in her apartment, he'd found nothing stronger than a half bottle of red wine and the ibuprofen tablets scattered all over the bathroom floor.

Her shoulders stiffened and she picked up her pace as if running away from old demons. "I won't lie. Several years ago, I went through a really bad time. I started dating a guy who used a lot. It just seemed a way to escape."

"So you blame the boyfriend?" Derek asked.

"Not at all," she said, staring straight ahead as she ran down the path, her stride steady and sure. "I did it because it made me feel good. When I was high, I felt invincible. I didn't care what anyone thought about me, what anyone wrote about me, what anyone said about me. But then it got out of control, and it wasn't so much fun anymore." She sprinted the last few yards up the path to Raj's house.

"And then you almost died," he said, telling himself the tight feeling in his lungs was from that last sprint. Not because the thought of her hurt or dying left a giant sinkhole in his chest.

"Yeah," she said, slightly breathless as her chest rose and fell. "I was lucky." She regarded him, her gaze steady and grave. "I didn't die. And my dad got me into one of the best rehab centers in the world. I spent three months dealing with my drug problem, and I've never relapsed."

He listened to her words, stared hard into her eyes. He was trained in interrogation, was able to pick up a lie before it was uttered. Everything about Alyssa reeked of truth and conviction.

Was it possible she was telling the truth? Or was he so far gone he was seeing only what he wanted to see? He followed her up the stairs and into the house, wondering which fucking end was up.

"Aren't you tempted?" He'd go with this, keep her talking, seize on the first sign of a lie.

She went to the kitchen and poured herself a glass of water. "Not really."

"Never?"

"I'm not around it anymore, which helps a lot. And three

therapy sessions a week really helped. I had a therapist I loved in LA," she rambled on almost as though to herself, "but I never found anyone after I moved. Have you ever been?"

"To LA?"

She laughed like it was his fault for not following her curving line of conversation. "No, to therapy. Like after your mom disappeared." She stared at him expectantly.

"No," he said.

"Seriously? I can't believe your dad didn't throw you and your brothers into counseling after something like that."

"He had other things on his mind." Derek turned his back on her to retrieve a water glass from a cabinet.

"You should go," she said, not taking the hint. "I mean, I have trust issues with my mother and abandonment issues with my father, but I can't imagine what it must be like for you."

No wonder she got in trouble with the press. After everything, she was still so open, so willing to talk about her personal problems to anyone who would listen.

He avoided women like Alyssa like the plague. Women who wasted time analyzing their feelings inevitably wanted to analyze his. The mere thought made his skin crawl. "I don't have any issues." She could only choke out a scoffing sound before he cut her off, needing to nip this conversation in the bud. "Back to what's important. Say you're right. Someone is slipping you drugs. Why would someone want to do that?" He pulled back, tried to cast an impartial eye on the situation. She'd been publicly intoxicated twice in the past several weeks. In the week he'd spent with her, he hadn't seen any evidence of drug use, other than the night of the benefit. There were no drugs here in the house. If she'd planned to be alone, would she have worried about hiding her stash?

Uneasiness clenched at his gut. As crazy as her story sounded, he had to entertain the possibility that she might not be lying.

"I have no idea." That helpless look was back, the one that made him want to pull her into his arms and tell her everything was going to be okay. "But if I don't find out soon, Uncle Harold's going to cut my salary completely, and then I'll really be screwed."

"And so will all the shops on Union Square."

"Don't treat me like I'm a spoiled little brat," she snapped and slammed her water glass on the counter. "I have bigger things to worry about than my shopping budget."

"Right, the chemo," Derek said, feeling like an asshole. He pinched the bridge of his nose. "Who would be out to get you like this? Any ex-boyfriends? Ex-employees you've pissed off?"

She shook her head and tugged the fleece pullover off. Derek tried not to notice how the T-shirt underneath rode up and bared a creamy swath of skin. "Andy is my only employee other than the cleaning lady, and she'd never do anything like that. And I told you I haven't dated anyone for over a year."

"What about Abbassi?" He immediately wanted to call back the words and the naked jealousy that dripped from them.

Alyssa rolled her eyes. "I never dated Louis."

"Press says differently." Why was he pushing her? He shouldn't give a flying crap who she slept with.

"I've met him a couple of times, and now that he's involved in the business, we end up at a lot of the same events. The press likes to photograph us together and insinuate that we're sleeping together. It's not true."

"He wants it to be." His lips curled into an involuntary sneer, thinking of the way Abbassi's dark, covetous eyes ran over Alyssa's body.

Alyssa didn't deny it as she shot Derek a knowing smile. "That's his problem. Right now I've got my hands full."

Her phone rang, preventing him from digging any deeper, and she turned away with a sassy twitch of her hips. Her smile faded as she stared at the display. Her shoulders tensed, and her fingers tightened around the small red phone, but she didn't answer it.

"Who was that?"

"Can you trace anonymous phone calls?"

He walked over to her, hand held out. She handed it over without a word, and he thumbed through the call list. "Is someone threatening you?"

"No. I never answer anyway, and the person always hangs up. But I did get this weird text message." She took the phone from him and clicked open a message.

If u want to no the truth ansr ur fon.

The message had come in the day before.

"Truth about what?"

She shrugged. "It's probably just a prank, but I'd rather find out who it is and make them stop. I've had to change my number, like, four times in the past year."

"I'll take a look at your phone records and see what I can find."

Another ring pierced the air, this time from his phone.

He let it ring a few times as he watched Alyssa walk through the sliding glass doors onto the redwood deck.

Might as well get this over with. He flipped his phone open, and Danny's voice ripped through the static. "What the fuck is going on with you?"

"Everything's fine."

"Your locater shows you in the same place for over twenty-four hours. Have you found her or what?" Ever since they'd started Gemini, Derek, Danny, and Ethan kept track of each other with tiny GPS locaters implanted in their watches. No surprise, Danny had been keeping tabs on Derek while he searched for Alyssa.

"Yeah, she's fine." He didn't tell Danny he'd spent the last twenty-four hours with her in a billionaire's beach house, knowing he'd never hear the end of it.

"I just got off the phone with Harold Van Weldt, and he ripped me a new one about you not returning his calls. I assured him you have the situation well in hand. Tell me I wasn't lying."

"You weren't." Alyssa was squatting next to the sunken hot tub, sitting back on her heels as she struggled to remove the padded cover.

"Then why haven't you updated Van Weldt yourself? Why isn't her ass on its way to San Francisco as we speak?"

"She needed a couple days to chill out," Derek said. "I told her I'd keep quiet for a little longer." He knew how stupid he sounded even before the words left his mouth.

He was met with dead silence on the other end of the line. He could picture Danny holding the phone away from his ear, staring at it in puzzlement. "What the hell is going on between you two?"

"Nothing," Derek replied, trying to keep the defensive note out of his voice. "She's under a lot of stress and needed a little time away. No big deal."

"Since when do you care so much about her mental state?"

"I don't." Steam billowed up from the uncovered hot tub, mingling with the salty ocean mist until Alyssa was rendered nearly invisible.

"Yeah, well, I shouldn't have to remind you, Van Weldt is our client, not his mess of a niece."

Derek bit back an angry response, knowing it would only ratchet up his brother's suspicions another ten degrees. "We'll be on our way first thing tomorrow," he said evenly. "In the meantime, I need you to look at her cell records. She's been getting some anonymous messages." Before he could stop himself he said, "And find out everything you can about Louis Abbassi."

"Why do you give a shit about her boyfriends?"

"He's not her boyfriend," Derek snapped. "And something about him bugs me."

"You know why I put you on this case, right? Because you were the only one I could count on not to get starstruck by a whiff of celebrity pussy and start thinking with your dick."

Derek watched, his mouth going dry as Alyssa peeled off her long-sleeved shirt, followed by her jog bra. Yoga pants were next, landing in a puddle on the deck. "You have nothing to worry about." The bitter taste of the lie flooded his mouth as his cock thickened, tenting out the front of his running shorts. As he watched, Alyssa pulled her hair out of her ponytail, sending it tumbling down between her slender shoulders as she stepped down into the sunken hot tub.

Naked skin. Hot and silky wet.

Danny's voice faded into the background. Derek registered a fraction of it. ". . . too close . . . too personally . . . need to back off."

It all faded into the ether because right now all he could think about was Alyssa, naked and wet and waiting for him in that damn hot tub.

"You may be right," Derek admitted. But right now he really didn't give a shit as he throbbed insistently with the need to get inside Alyssa, feel her envelop him in her molten heat. "I gotta go." He cut Danny off midsentence and tossed his phone onto the coffee table, ignoring it when it immediately began to ring again.

He made a quick detour to the bathroom and the giant box of condoms, dumping a fistful on the table next to his phone, saving one to take with him.

She glanced back at him at the sound of the sliding glass door opening. Her pink mouth stretched in a knowing smile when she saw his cock straining the front of his shorts. She gazed at him from under her lashes, a siren inviting him to smash himself against the rocks of his own need.

CHAPTER 11

DESPITE THE HEAT of the water, a shiver ran through Alyssa's body as Derek toed off his shoes and stripped off his shorts, shirt, and pullover in quick, angry motions. His mouth was tight, his face set in harsh lines. She knew she was taking a tiger by the tail, messing with him while he was on the phone with his brother. But she hated how easy it was for him to turn on and off, to shut her out until trying to talk to him was like beating herself against a brick wall.

He was so big, so tough, impenetrable, but she needed to flex her power, meager as it was. Remind them both how easy it was for her to get under his skin.

Derek sank into the tub, seating himself on the bench next to her. Without a word he yanked her onto his lap, his mouth coming over hers with a passion and hunger that belied his carefully controlled exterior.

"You think you're pretty fuckin' cute, don't you?" he growled against her throat, his teeth closing over her earlobe in a nip. The slight sting sent bolts of heat to her already bullet-hard nipples and between her legs.

She squirmed in his lap, shifting until the ridge of his cock rode between her legs, velvety soft skin over steel sliding back and forth against her slit. She moaned as his hands slid down her rib cage and closed around her waist. He lifted her until her breasts cleared the water, lifting her to his mouth. The cold air washed over her skin, a delicious contrast to the heat of his lips and tongue sucking and nipping at her breasts.

"What the hell is it about you?" he murmured between firm pulls of his mouth. "This isn't me." His voice was harsh as she rocked against him. "I don't get mixed up with women like you."

She shoved aside a pang of hurt that threatened to invade, focusing instead on how his shaft glided against her clit, the hot water, and the sweet friction making the pulsing knot between her legs throb. "What's wrong with wanting me?" Alyssa whispered. She tunneled her fingers in his hair, cradling his head to her breasts as a wave of tenderness penetrated the haze of lust. She bent her head and nuzzled his damp hair, kissed his cheeks, licked a salty bead of sweat from his skin. "Especially when it's so good."

He didn't reply, groaning around her nipple as his lips sucked harder.

Call her crazy, call her naive, but she felt something with him, a connection that went beyond sex. Like his dark seriousness could balance out her light frivolity. Like they could compliment each other perfectly if only he'd let it happen.

She could feel something inside her cracking open, her heart peeking through the fissure, wondering if it was safe to come out. *Oh, God, it's happening again.* No matter how hard she tried to protect herself, to guard her heart and be more cautious about letting strong feelings develop too soon, she was helpless to stop it.

Was she so starved for love, so pathetically needy, that she'd let herself believe a man like Derek would feel anything for her beyond lust? Why couldn't she just take what she could get and be happy with it, instead of getting carried away like she always did?

But it wasn't that simple. She arched her neck back, fog

misting her face, moaning at the feel of Derek's fingers stroking between her legs. She could feel the edge of desperation in his touch, the barely contained hunger that made his hands shake and his breath come fast.

What he felt for her went past mere sex. Alyssa was sure of it. She could feel it in him, the deep emotion and old pain he kept hidden behind his cool mask. But whatever she made him feel, he didn't like it, didn't like the threat to his control.

She tilted his face up to her, covering his mouth with hers. She poured everything into that kiss, trying to tell him without words that he was safe with her, safe to let go, safe to let the truth come out.

He sucked her tongue into his mouth and fumbled along the deck until his hand closed over the foil packet of the condom. His hands disappeared beneath the frothing surface of the water for a moment, and then he lifted her over him. Their mouths stayed fused as she slid down his thick length. She spread her knees wide and rocked her hips forward to take all of him until he was so deep she could feel him at the base of her spine.

He thrust up against her as though he couldn't get deep enough. Hot, bubbling water surged and splashed around them, closing around them, fusing them together until Alyssa couldn't tell where her body ended and Derek's body began.

Derek was suffocating, but he couldn't make himself release her mouth. The heat of the water boiled around him, surrounding him in steam. His heart pounded in ferocious need and outright panic.

Something was happening to him, with her. He couldn't get enough of her. Her taste, her smell, her hot, sweet pussy gripping his cock, kneading him from the inside out like a wet little fist. Fierce need exploded within him. He gripped her hips, holding her still so he could thrust up into her, holding himself as deep as he could go. He couldn't get close enough, couldn't get deep enough.

With Alyssa, nothing was ever enough.

He couldn't breathe, the heat of the hot tub suffocating him, pounding in his head until he was afraid he would pass out. He turned and lifted Alyssa so she was out of the tub, her butt resting on the padded bench that surrounded it. He knelt on the underwater bench, breathing a little easier now that his body wasn't submerged in one-hundred-twenty-degree water.

Derek didn't break his rhythm as he pushed Alyssa gently back onto the deck. She tried to pull him down with her, but he stayed braced above her, needing to put even that small bit of distance between them.

It was all too close, too much. The twisty feeling in his chest was back, pulling at his gut. He looked down at her, moaning and writhing under him, her hips pumping against his as she eagerly met every thrust. Steam rose from her body in the cool air until she looked like some mythic seductress who had emerged from the sea to drive him insane. Her gorgeous tits with their candy-pink nipples bounced with every thrust, and his cock gleamed with her juice as he slid in and out.

Her gaze locked on his, the green depths hiding nothing. Everything was there for him to read, the heat, the need. The tenderness. The trust.

Then her lids fluttered closed, and her hands tightened on his hips as she urged him faster, harder, harsh cries echoing up to the gray sky as her tight sheath clenched and shuddered around him.

Derek closed his eyes. Watching her come was like staring at the sun. Too intense for him to look at. But the image was there, burned into his brain, bringing his own orgasm down on him with the force of a collapsing building.

She pulled him down on top of her, her warm palms chasing away the chill of the air.

"Derek," she sighed his name, "you make me feel so good." She found his mouth with hers, kissing him so sweetly he wanted to melt into her and never come back up for air.

But the contentment lasted for maybe a breath, chased away by the alarm bells clanging and banging their way into his consciousness. Reminding him that he didn't get involved for a reason. He'd seen what happened when a man let a woman crawl too deep inside him, let himself be stupid enough to let his cock and his heart overrule his head.

He'd already made enough mistakes when it came to Alyssa. Danny was right. He was letting her get to him, letting her hot body and poor-little-rich-girl routine cloud his judgment, and taking this all way too personally. Alyssa and the strong pull she had on him were nothing but a test of his resolve, of his professionalism, of the vow he'd made a long time ago to never let anything as stupid as emotion influence his decisions.

She was a test he wasn't about to fail.

Derek pulled away and got out of the tub without a word, ignoring her soft protest. He grabbed a towel from a plastic bin next to the tub and tucked it around his waist.

"Why do you always do this?" Alyssa's voice chased him into the living room. She'd draped a towel over herself like a blanket. Her hair was wild, her eyelids heavy, her cheeks pink in a postorgasmic flush.

"Do what?" he asked, deliberately turning his back on her. He was afraid if he kept staring at her he'd forget all his self-recriminations.

"Pull away after sex." Her bare feet thudded on the floor as she marched over to him.

"I don't know what you're talking about," he lied.

"Bullshit." She poked a slender finger into his chest. "Last night you rolled off me and bolted like the feds were after you." *Thump.* Her fingertip met his pec. "And now you can't

even give me so much as a 'Thanks, that was nice' before
you scatter like a roach." *Thump.*

He grabbed her wrist. "You said you wanted to fuck.
You didn't give me any rules about what came next."

She studied him for a moment, and then something like
understanding flowed into her eyes.

Which made him nervous as hell.

But not as nervous as the sympathy that immediately followed.

"I understand it's hard for you to let people in, Derek."
Her smile was soft and way too inviting. "I can only imagine how much your mom leaving messed you up."

Hell, no, she wasn't going to go there.

She flattened her palm against his chest, stroking, soothing
him. "It's not the end of the world to let yourself care about
someone, Derek." Her voice, her hand stroking him were so
hypnotic he almost wanted to believe her. "And it's not the
end of the world to let someone care about you."

He could see the warmth, the emotion in her eyes as she
reached out to him, offering comfort he didn't want and
didn't need, asking him to give it right back to her. She was
crossing the line, building this up into something more than
sex. Setting herself up to get hurt when she realized he could
never open up his heart to her the way she was trying to
open up to him.

He knew exactly what she wanted, as well as he knew he
wasn't the man to give it to her.

The sooner she realized that, the better off she'd be.

Alyssa jumped as Derek's hand locked over her wrist, halting
the progress of her hand over his chest. His mouth, which
had started to soften, pulled into a thin, tight line as his eyes
went dark and cold as chips of black ice.

"Don't try to climb into my head, Alyssa. It's not a place
I want to share with you or any other woman."

His words sent a chill through her as he yanked her hard against him and covered her mouth with his. She moaned, struggling as the pressure ground her lips against her teeth, threatening to bruise her. "Stop," she gasped, trying to yank out of his hold. "What's wrong with you?"

His hand stayed locked around her wrist. "Nothing. This is what you wanted, right? Me treating you like any other woman?"

"Do you turn Neanderthal with all the women you sleep with, or just the ones who want to talk to you?"

"That's the thing," he said, reaching out his hand and yanking off her towel before she could stop him. "I don't talk. I don't cuddle." He flicked off his own towel. He was already hard again, his cock thick and red and angry looking as it thrust out at her. "I don't share my feelings." He grabbed her hips and ground himself crudely against her naked stomach.

And as the smooth, hot tip of him glided over her skin, God help her, but she felt a bolt of desire between her thighs so fierce it bordered on pain.

"I fuck," he said. "And you like the way I do it. Don't kid yourself into thinking it's anything more than that."

He bent his head to hers. When she tried to turn away, he fisted his hand in her hair, holding her in place for his kiss. His tongue swept into her mouth, sending heat searing through her. She'd crossed a line, and now he was trying to put her in her place. But even that realization couldn't stop her body's response. Arousal flooded between her legs, embarrassing in its intensity. Angry at her own loss of control, she closed her teeth over his bottom lip, hard enough to draw blood.

Derek yanked his head back, his eyes narrowed into dark slits as he glared down at her.

"You're acting like a jerk," she choked out.

His hand slid between her thighs, cupping her sex. His

thumb insinuated itself between her pussy lips, grazing against her clit.

She wanted to die of humiliation when she felt a surge of wetness coat his hand.

"But you still want me," he said.

"You're an asshole," she said, feeling her throat tighten and tears pierce the backs of her eyes as her hips rocked against his probing fingers. What was wrong with him? What was wrong with her?

Her only answer was a moan as first one thick finger and then two slid up inside her. She should have been exhausted, wrung out from before, but she was already primed. As wet as he was rock hard against her.

She moaned again, this time in protest as he pulled his hand from between her thighs and pushed her backward onto the couch. He hooked her knees over his shoulders and buried his mouth between her legs, licking and sucking, taunting her with deep thrusts and slight flicks of his tongue.

She could feel her orgasm building, shaming her even as she strove for it, arching against his face, begging him wordlessly for firmer pressure. Just like he had last night, he kept it just out of reach, teasing her, exerting his control.

Last night she had loved it, loved the way he seemed to revel in her response and get off every little twitch of her skin.

Now in the cold light of day she felt manipulated and easy and ashamed at her lack of control over her body's response.

But no less needy as his mouth hovered over her, the hot kiss of his breath coasting over her sensitive flesh.

"Tell me how much you want me," he whispered.

She clamped her lips together, felt a tear leak from the corner of her eyelid.

His tongue dipped into her, penetrating her, but not nearly

hard and deep enough. Her whole body jumped and shuddered.

"Come on, Alyssa. You wanted to fuck. Tell me to fuck you."

She squeezed her eyes shut. "Fuck me." The words slipped past her lips, and she hated herself.

She heard the rip and crumple of the foil packet and kept her eyes closed as he caught her by the hips, urging her to kneel on the floor in front of the couch. Big hands gripped her hips as he fitted himself against her. Alyssa gasped, her back arching as the thick head penetrated her. He was on her, over her, feeling even bigger inside her as he fucked her from behind.

What was wrong with her that she could get so turned on when he treated her like a piece of meat? Like a blow-up doll, nothing more than a warm place to stick his dick?

Okay, that wasn't totally true, she was forced to admit as he slid one hand around and cupped her sex, stroking her clit in time to his slow, deliberate thrusts. He took everything he'd learned about her body, what she liked, and used it, swiveling his hips at the end of each thrust so he bumped the bundle of nerves deep inside her. Whipping her up into a frenzy until she was nothing but a puddle of helpless need, slamming her hips against him, moaning as she braced herself against the couch so she could get more leverage as she rode his thick shaft.

Keening sounds emerged from her throat as she strained for orgasm, growing louder and louder as Derek stroked her clit. Finally she broke, release thundering through her, stars exploding behind her closed eyes. He held himself deep inside her, rocking his hips into her until the last pulse fluttered through her.

He whispered her name and kissed her shoulder. Then he gripped her hips and rode to his own orgasm, pounding into her in bone-jarring thrusts that left her feeling more than a little battered. He came with a curse, almost as though he was angry. At her for making him come so hard. At himself for giving into the attraction he obviously hated to feel. Stupid. So stupid. Thinking he would respond to her clumsy attempts to get him to open up. Now she was the one exposed. Ripped open, all of her parts scattered for the entire world to see.

Alyssa hadn't been conscious of the chance she was taking with Derek until it was too late. Hadn't even realized what she'd wanted from him until she was in too deep to stop herself. She didn't want to admit it to herself, but now she couldn't deny the feeble hope she'd fostered that Derek would see her, the real her, and find someone worth knowing, beyond the sex. Someone worth sharing himself with.

Someone she could trust with herself.

But now as she lay under him, her skin going cold as his heart pounded against her back, she was reminded of the lesson a smarter girl would have learned by now. A girl in Alyssa Miles's position couldn't trust anyone.

This time Derek wasn't the one to pull away and duck for cover. As soon as her breathing slowed down Alyssa scrambled from underneath him. She clutched her towel to her like a shield as she streaked down the hall. Seconds later he heard a door slam and the shower running.

The look in her eyes was like a spear in his chest. He rose from his knees and sank down onto the couch. He felt wasted, weak, and about a hundred years old. He bent his head to his hands and caught sight of his penis. Still half hard, sheathed in the condom.

His lips pulled back in distaste. The offender, the enemy. This whole fucked-up fiasco was the damn thing's fault. He laughed humorlessly. Okay, he couldn't really blame his dick, but he wanted someone—something—else to take the fall for what had just happened.

What the fuck was wrong with him? Taking her like that. He hadn't hurt her, not physically anyway. Then he remembered the faint finger marks he'd left on her hips and felt a little sick.

She'd called him a Neanderthal. He wasn't even sure he'd evolved to caveman status. Sure, he made sure she got off, and hard, but he'd made her feel like shit about it. Bile rose in the back of his throat as he thought of the things he'd said, the way he'd used her body's response against her, all so she'd understand he'd never be open to anything more than no-strings sex.

The look on her face, her eyes big green pools of devastation, flashed in his brain. Mission accomplished. His hand clenched into a fist, and he wanted to punch a wall. And her skin, always so warm, glowing with heat against his, had gone cold. Like her body had shut down, her temperature dropping a good five degrees after the sexual haze had lifted and reality set in.

He heard the shower turn off, and his chest went tight with the need to escape. He didn't know what the hell to say to her. The effect she had on him was like nothing he'd ever dealt with before, and for the first time in his life he couldn't put his finger on the most rational, civilized way to deal with the situation.

Grab your car keys and run.

Yeah, he couldn't do that either, since he was on Van Weldt's clock and supposed to be looking out for her. Taking a man's money to fuck his niece and make her feel like shit about it.

Nice.

Derek pulled a towel around himself as guilt settled in his gut, mingling with the self-disgust until he felt like he'd swallowed a cannon ball. He waited until he heard the bathroom door open and the bedroom door close before he went down the hall to the bathroom. The small room was thick with fog and the scent of Alyssa's shampoo. The fresh, fruity scent curled around his insides and made him want to burst into her room and . . . what? Beg her forgiveness? Tell her he was sorry, but he wanted her more than any other woman he'd ever met, and his puny little brain didn't know how to process it?

He shoved the urge away. No way was he opening that can of worms. No way was he going to compound stupid with stupid.

He stood under the scalding hot spray, hot enough to melt off the top layer of skin, trying to get the feel and scent of her off of him. He got dressed in the bedroom, and when he emerged several minutes later, Alyssa was waiting in the living room.

She was dressed in the same sweater and cargo pants she'd worn the day before, her damp hair pulled back in a messy braid. A black backpack rested near her feet.

"You can call my uncle now." Her voice was tired and lifeless.

"I promised you until tomorrow," Derek replied, wondering why he was arguing.

She looked at him then, her green eyes wide and steady as they stared into his. Gone were the curiosity, the expectation, the anticipation that he hadn't even realized were there until they were gone. "Like you said, I can't play make-believe forever. I have to face reality eventually, so I might as well get it over with."

Her small shoulders set in a tight line under her sweater as she grabbed her backpack handle and slung it over her shoulder. He opened his mouth to protest and then stopped himself. Another day alone with her would be a complete and utter cluster fuck. He'd already shown himself to be capable of anything when it came to her. He already felt torn up inside. He didn't want to stick around to see how much worse he could make it.

"One thing, though. Please don't tell anyone exactly where we are. I know I can never really hide, but I need to know this place will stay secret." Alyssa's look was urgent, pleading.

"Of course," he said.

Her lips pulled into a small smile. He tried not to notice that they were still red and puffy from kissing. "And I trust you not to tell anyone what went on here."

She shouldn't trust him as far as she could throw him, not after what he'd done. But she could trust him in this. No way in hell was anyone ever going to know that he'd completely lost his mind over Alyssa Miles.

Derek flicked open his cell phone and walked down the hall to pack his overnight bag. Van Weldt answered on the first ring.

"Ah, you finally deign to call me. I trust you have news."

Derek felt his hackles raise at the man's clipped, condescending voice, but kept his tone smooth and professional. "Yes, sir. I apologize for not returning your calls yesterday, but I wanted to be sure I had information before I bothered you."

"Returning my calls would hardly have been a bother. Your evasiveness borders on unprofessionalism."

Derek had a sudden vision of himself kneeling on the floor as he took Alyssa from behind. Unprofessional. The guy had no idea. "You'll be happy to know I found her, sir. We'll be back in the city in a few hours."

"Good. I'm sure I don't have to tell you, but don't let any photographers or members of the press see you. I can only imagine the shape she's in."

"She's perfectly fine, sir," Derek said, unable to keep the edge from his voice as he sprang to her defense. "All she wanted was a break from the scrutiny for a few days."

"Scrutiny is her reality, Mr. Taggart, and given recent events, the reality of our family. Alyssa will learn to deal with it properly, or she will face the consequences."

The connection broke, and Derek glared at his phone. His thumb hovered over the redial button as he struggled with the urge to call Van Weldt back and tell him to go fuck himself, that he was taking Alyssa and keeping her away from the prying eyes of press and family that would drive any sane person to numb herself out with drugs.

He flipped his phone closed and slipped it into his pocket. Alyssa, her crazy life, and her possible drug habit weren't his problem. Doing his job and getting Gemini's reputation back on track was.

But as he watched Alyssa climb into the passenger seat of his Audi like she was a prisoner being shipped off to death row, he remembered the real fear in her eyes as she'd tried to convince him someone was slipping her the drugs. Was he an idiot for wanting to believe her when the most logical explanation stared him in the face? Dread settled in as he realized he couldn't brush her off so easily. He had to stay close, even if it meant his own doom.

Chapter 12

ALYSSA STARED OUT the window of the Audi as coastal cliffs and fog gave way to the mist-enshrouded forests that lined highway 128. When Derek had suggested—okay, insisted—that she ride home with him and leave her car for one of the other Gemini guys to retrieve, she hadn't argued. Wasted and wrung out, she hadn't been able to summon the energy.

Now she wished she'd tried a little harder. Only fifteen minutes into the two-and-a-half-hour journey, and she wanted to climb the walls. He filled the car with his size and presence. The heat and tension pulsed off him in palpable waves. The scent of him—fresh soap, cedar, and musk—permeated the interior.

And after everything that had happened, she still had to fight to keep from leaning over the gearshift and burying her face in his neck and taking a long, deep inhale of warm skin. After the way he'd made her feel—cheap, stupid, used—she still wanted to curl up against him and trust him to keep her safe. Some sick, twisted part of her couldn't stop wanting him, couldn't stop wishing he would pull her close and protect her from a world she was starting to think was out to get her.

She shoved away the irrational yearnings and paranoid

delusions and shifted as far from Derek as the car would allow. Head pressed against the glass of the passenger window, she listened while Derek called his brother to let him know they were on their way back to the city.

"She decided she wanted to get back sooner."

Alyssa almost laughed at the simplistic explanation. She'd decided, all right. After Derek had turned her inside out and shown how little regard he had for her or anything happening between them.

The rest of his side of the conversation consisted of terse responses before he hung up.

"They couldn't find any information about the anonymous calls you've been receiving, but Toni's going to dig a little deeper."

Alyssa nodded. Great. She'd have to change her number yet again.

Derek didn't say anything else as he cranked up the stereo. The harsh, angst-ridden sound of Nine Inch Nails thundered through the car. It settled in Alyssa's shoulders and spread to the back of her neck until her head was pounding. She closed her eyes, embraced the pain as it distracted her from the overwhelming presence of the man beside her and her irrational, futile, masochistic attraction to him.

By the time they got to her place she was physically and mentally drained. There were a handful of photographers loitering out front, so Derek took her up through the side entrance.

"You don't need to come up," Alyssa said. "In fact, you probably don't need to come around at all, since I'll be, like, under house arrest for a while." She tried to laugh, but the sound came out all weird and rusty. God, she didn't want to deal with her uncle, didn't want to worry about how she was going to deal with her mother's expenses in the coming months.

Derek didn't respond, waiting silently as she unlocked the

door. His phone rang as the door swung open, and he scowled at whomever the caller was. "We just got into the city," he said, each syllable snapping with irritation. "I'll be at the office in—"

His voice cut short, and Alyssa froze, one foot over the threshold as his face went white.

"No shit," he said, his stomach dropping to the soles of his feet. "They really think it could be her?"

"I don't know," Ethan's voice was tight. "There were two bodies, and from what they can tell so far, it's possible one of them could be her."

"But how—"

Ethan cut him off. "Look, just get to Dad's house. De Luca is here, and he can tell us everything he knows."

The line went dead. Derek spent several seconds staring at it like it was an alien life-form.

"Derek?" Alyssa's hand curled around his forearm. "What's wrong?"

He struggled to focus on her face, her eyes dark with concern. "There was a landslide outside of La Honda last week. It uncovered two bodies that had been buried up there. The heavy rains over the past month had washed away a chunk of the hillside, in an open space preserve, taking a vacant cabin with it."

Understanding dawned across her face, and her skin went even paler. "Is one of them your mother?"

"We don't know yet." He struggled to keep his tone steady, keep himself from blowing into a million pieces. "But that's where she was last seen, where we found her car."

Her grip on his arm tightened. "It could be a coincidence."

"Or it could be her." He'd considered the possibility she was dead a thousand times in the past eighteen years. Yet that didn't ease the punched-in-the-stomach feeling.

"Derek, I'm so sorry." Her eyes damp, she reached her

hand up and cupped his face. He closed his eyes and leaned into her touch, letting her warmth and concern flow into his skin. She stood up on tiptoe and kissed him, and shameless, selfish, undeserving bastard that he was, he took it. Held her to him and kissed her hard, sucking in every drop of warmth she offered in an effort to stave off the cold taking root in his gut.

He wanted to stay there, follow her up to her bedroom, bury himself in her heat until he forgot the last twenty-four hours. But he was a realist, and he knew that wasn't an option.

He took a last, lingering taste and buried his face in her hair. "God, you are so sweet," he whispered and pulled away before it was too late. "I have to go. I'll get in touch with your uncle."

She nodded and swiped away a tear with her thumb. She was crying for him—the realization hit him like a knife in the chest. She looked small and alone, watching him go. "I'll have someone cover for me, okay? In the meantime, you be careful. Anything weird happens, you call me."

As he flew down highway 280 on the way to his father's house, he couldn't get the image of Alyssa's wide green eyes out of his head.

Derek, I'm so sorry. The warmth of her hand against his cheek. Pouring all her heartfelt sympathy into a kiss that had filled him with heat and light even as it had scraped him raw with guilt.

After the way he'd treated her, gone out of his way to cheapen what they had, made it clear to her he was using her only for sex, she had still opened up her soft heart and tried to comfort him.

That he wanted her so much—and not just for sex— should have been enough to make him glad for an excuse to get away from her.

About fifteen minutes after Derek had left Alyssa's, Danny

had called to tell him Harold Van Weldt had canceled his contract with Gemini Securities.

Seemed he was concerned about Derek's unprofessional behavior and questioned his priorities when it came to keeping Alyssa in line and out of the public eye.

With everything else going on, Danny hadn't given him the ass chewing he so richly deserved, but Derek didn't kid himself that it wasn't coming.

But even knowing he'd fucked up big-time, knowing he'd let down his brothers, his company, himself, for Christ's sake, he didn't feel one speck of the relief he knew he should.

All he could think about was that Alyssa was alone, unprotected, and she was convinced someone was out to get her.

He pushed his worry aside. Harold would keep her close to home, probably hire another security firm to keep an eye on her. As long as she was careful, she should be okay. But as he thought of her strained, pale face, her eyes tormented, begging him to believe her, he couldn't get past the gut feeling that when he'd left her that afternoon he'd thrown her to the lions.

He arrived at his father's house in only thirty-five minutes instead of the usual fifty it took from San Francisco. Ethan and Danny were already there, along with their father who sat stone cold and silent on the worn sofa in the study.

"What do we know?" Derek asked. That's all he wanted. Just the facts. He couldn't start thinking about the ramifications yet. What it would really mean if the body was that of Anne Taggart. What would happen to all of them—especially their father—if they finally had a body and could stop chasing after her ghost.

"We don't know much more than I told you on the phone," Ethan said. "Two bodies were found near La Honda. Initial analysis of the remains showed one of them could be the right age, height, all that stuff. Hank called Dad."

Hank de Luca was a friend of their father's from the San Mateo County Sheriff's Office. He'd been involved in the initial investigation of Anne Taggart's mysterious disappearance eighteen years before. Though the case had been left cold more than a decade ago, Hank had continued to work with Joe Taggart in an unofficial capacity, helping Joe out however he could with his ongoing quest to find out what had happened after his wife walked out the door that long-ago morning in May.

Danny regarded Derek with cool gray eyes as he handed over a copy of the coroner's report. Danny's mouth was tight, his jaw hard, and not only from the news of the body.

"That's all the information we have so far," Ethan said. "The bodies are badly decomposed. There's no way to identify her." Derek scanned the report.

Just the bare facts. A pitiful handful of words to describe a life. A life that might have been his mother's. His throat went tight, and he thrust the thought away. No reason to get emotional about it before they even knew anything. "How long before we know if it's her?"

Derek saw his father's shoulders stiffen and instantly regretted his harsh tone.

"At least a few weeks," Danny replied, his voice uncharacteristically soft as he regarded their father. "In her," he paused, keeping a careful eye on his father's face, "condition, we're looking at dental records and DNA matching."

All requiring lab tests that would take several weeks if not months.

Danny reached across the couch and gripped his father's shoulder. "Come on, Dad, let's go get a cup of coffee."

Joe nodded wordlessly and rose from the couch, looking past his sons as if he didn't really see them. Derek's stomach clenched at how old his father suddenly looked. His shoulders were still broad, his tall body still strong, but he'd lost the ramrod-stiff posture, the air of unquestionable authority he'd developed over a decade in the military and successful career in finance. Now he looked weary, his face carved in deep lines.

"I really hope that's not Mom," Derek said to Ethan as his father and Danny disappeared down the hall.

"As fucked up as it is," Ethan said with a humorless laugh, "I kind of hope it is. At least we'll know."

Derek nodded. "I hear you. But I'm afraid it might kill him," he said, nodding in the direction of the kitchen. He sank into a leather club chair and leaned his head into his hands. "What a fucking week."

He raised his head and was pinned by Ethan's piercing, laser-blue stare. Derek forced himself not to squirm as he met his brother's gaze head-on. As much as he appreciated his close relationship with his brothers, especially his twin, sometimes he hated the way Ethan was able to dig inside his head whether he wanted him to or not. Of course, Derek did the same to Ethan, so he supposed that made them even.

"What?" he said, filling his mind with images of lead curtains, brick walls, anything to mentally block Ethan out and keep him from asking questions Derek couldn't begin to answer.

"Was it worth it?" Ethan said, his eyes narrowing as his mouth pulled into a knowing smirk.

"Was what worth it?" Derek raised his eyebrows, striving for deadpan.

"Come on, Derek, don't play dumb. We all know you didn't spend the last twenty-four hours building sand castles and looking for seashells."

Derek remained silent. He and his brothers were close, but he'd spent the last thirty-two years sparring with them verbally and physically. The best strategy was not to engage.

"Toni's always leaving those celebrity rags laying around. Alyssa has an interesting past."

Try as he might to fight it, Derek couldn't stop the in-stinctive narrowing of his eyes, the clenching of his fists.

Ethan knew he'd hit pay dirt and didn't miss a beat. "Ac-cording to that guy who took those awesome pictures of her, she was the worst lay in Hollywood." Ethan shook his head and made a chiding sound. "Hardly worth losing an important client over."

Derek's blood boiled in his brain, his vision clouding until his vision was filled with a red haze. Every muscle and sinew in his body tightened, his fists clenched, prepared to pop his brother square in his smug, smirking face.

He closed his eyes, blocked out Ethan's shit-eating grin, took a deep breath, and pulled himself back from the edge.

Barely.

"I'm not going to talk about her," Derek bit out. "But I don't want you saying shit about her. She's a nice girl." God, what a weak-assed description for one of the sexiest, big hearted, sweetest women he'd ever met. But no way was he going there, not even with his brother.

"So you're saying she's not a drug-addicted mess with well-documented shitty taste in men?"

Unbidden, the memory of Alyssa, her eyes bright with unshed tears as she'd scrambled to get out from underneath him, stabbed into his brain, and shame bubbled through his veins like acid. "The shitty taste in men is right." Derek was no better than the rest, another in a line of men who used her and hurt her.

As to the other . . . he still wasn't sure. Which was fucked because he had the facts, the data in black and white. Lab results didn't lie, and with her lifestyle, there was no reason to believe her wild claims. Still, his gut told him different.

Yeah, and last time you listened to your gut when it came to a woman, twelve people were blown into hamburger.

"I'm not saying she doesn't have problems," Derek said

finally. "But as of today, they're not my problems to deal with."

And considering the uncontrollable emotions Alyssa brought out of him, they were both a hell of a lot better off because of it.

After Derek left, the rest of the afternoon and the next day passed in a blur. Her uncle called to chew her out and inform her he'd fired Derek. She swallowed around a lump of guilt, only half listening as Harold told her that under no circumstances was she to speak to the press.

Physically and emotionally exhausted, Alyssa planted herself on the couch and watched Andy busy herself around the apartment. She was grateful for her assistant's quiet, competent presence as she kept the apartment from becoming oppressively, depressingly empty.

What was Derek doing right now? Was he okay? Was he mad at her for getting him fired? Or too preoccupied by his mother to care about her?

She didn't think she'd ever forget the look on his face after that phone call. The devastation in his eyes, pouring in like thunderheads. The way his tan skin blanched, his stubble stark against his jaw. The way he'd pulled her close and kissed her like a dying man.

He needed her.

Right. Needed her like he needed a hole in the head.

But she hadn't imagined the ferocity of his grip as he'd held her to him.

She was reaching for her cell phone before she snapped herself out of it. He had bigger things to worry about right now. He didn't need her calling, trying to get him to talk about his feelings.

She yawned and settled back into the couch and flicked on the TV. She was reading a magazine, only half paying attention to the images flickering on the flat screen, when she heard her name blaring through her living room.

There was a time when Alyssa had lived and died by entertainment news shows, obsessively recording each and every one, watching to see if she'd made it on that evening's edition.

Now they made her cringe. But she couldn't help but look at her image filling the fifty-two inch screen. A knot formed at the base of her neck when she realized it was from the party three nights ago, right as she was being led away from the podium. A hand—Derek's hand, she knew, though he was out of the frame—gripped her arm as her knees visibly buckled. Her cheeks were hectic pink, the rest of her face stark white, a gleam of cold sweat glistening on her skin.

"Another starlet headed for a meltdown?" the hostess asked, her voice full of false concern. "Celebrity party girl Alyssa Miles was on the way to revamping her image in the last several months after becoming the spokesmodel for the Van Weldt's 'Diamonds for All' campaign."

Another image flashed, this one from the last ad campaign. Alyssa had her back to the camera, naked except for a line of diamond butterflies marching down her spine.

"But since her father's death, Alyssa's been spiraling out of control." The producers helpfully played video footage of Alyssa slumped in the corner of a nightclub from the AIDs benefit two weeks ago. The night Alyssa was convinced she'd come down with food poisoning.

As she thought of the toxicology report from the other day, she wasn't sure at all.

"In the last two days, Alyssa seems to have disappeared entirely, missing scheduled appointments and appearances. Her reps won't comment, but sources close to her speculate that after a stint two years ago for an addiction to cocaine, old problems may have come back to haunt her."

Alyssa jumped as a hand reached out and snatched the remote from her hand and clicked the TV off. "You shouldn't be watching that," Andy scolded, sounding like a sixty-year-old grandma instead of a recent college graduate.

"I might as well know what they're saying about me," Alyssa said.

"Bull," Andy said as she came around the couch to take a seat beside Alyssa. "You need to ignore everything. You need to lie low and get some rest until this all blows over." She patted Alyssa's leg reassuringly. "Here, drink this."

Alyssa took the steaming mug and gave it a cautious sniff.

"It's chamomile. It will help you sleep."

Her night was restless, full of waking dreams. She worried about Derek, haunted by visions of his harsh face white with barely disguised devastation. Demons chased her, watching her every move, poisoning her.

The next morning her brain was cloudy, unfocused, and no matter how much coffee she drank, she couldn't shake off the fatigue that had settled into her bones.

She planted herself on the couch and checked her cell phone. A rush of adrenaline pierced through the exhaustion when she saw the first text.

I no the truth. We need 2 talk.

It was the fourth message in two days, in addition to the two hang-up calls. She wondered if anyone at Gemini had found any more information about the caller. Then again, they had more important things to worry about right now than finding out who was prank-calling a woman who wasn't even their responsibility anymore.

Kimberly had called. "I'm worried, Alyssa. Just call me to let me know you're okay. Whatever you're going through, I'm here for you."

Trite words, but Alyssa appreciated them all the same.

She skipped to the next voice mail. From Louis. He'd heard she was back and said it was urgent that he see her.

She made a mental note to tell Andy to get her a new cell-phone number.

She scrolled through the rest of her messages, vaguely listening as Andy fielded calls, offering endless rounds of "No comment" to whomever was on the other line.

Her phone rang, the shrill ringtone piercing the air. UN-KNOWN CALLER flashed on the display. The events of the last few days caught up with her in a sudden rush. The drugging. Derek. The new wave of unflattering press coverage.

And now some asshole had gotten hold of her phone number and wouldn't stop fucking with her. "What do you want?" she snapped, ignoring Andy's startled look from her seat at the kitchen table.

"You're a hard woman to get ahold of. I've been trying to run you down for days. Guess the curiosity finally got the better of you."

The voice was deep and male; a faint east-coast accent threaded through.

"Who is this?"

"Are you alone?"

Her gaze flicked to Andy, who had turned her attention back to her computer screen. "Why does that matter?"

"I read the interview in *Bella*."

Her sleep-deprived brain had a hard time following the jump in conversation.

"I know you have your suspicions."

Her brow furrowed as she tried to remember what he might be talking about .

Sometimes I dream there's someone else there, waiting to kill me, too.

Her blood ran cold. She pushed herself off the couch and walked over to the big bay window that looked out over the street. Was he out there? Watching her as they spoke? "What are you talking about?"

"Are you alone?"

"No."

"Then I'll call you later."

The connection abruptly dropped.

"Who was that?"

Alyssa jumped as Andy's voice came from right behind her, so close she could feel the other woman's breath on her hair.

"Just a wrong number."

"Kind of a long conversation for a wrong number." Andy's brown eyes were wide and inquisitive.

"It was nothing," Alyssa said, her voice sharp with annoyance. While she loved the way Andy effortlessly took care of everything, the lack of privacy sometimes grated on her.

Andy's phone rang, cutting off any further questions. "No, she's fine," Andy said. *It's your uncle,* she mouthed, rolling her eyes. "No, she hasn't gone anywhere."

Alyssa's irritation grew in force. Her uncle was still watching her, using Andy as a spy to report back to him. And Andy was playing along.

"You don't work for him, you know," Alyssa snapped when Andy hung up. "I still pay your salary."

"I know," Andy said, her brow knit in concern. "But I figure it's easier for me to tell him what he wants to hear than to make you deal with it, right?"

Alyssa immediately felt bad. Andy was just doing her job, and a damn good one, too. The phone rang again, this time Alyssa's landline. Andy hurried to answer it and brushed off the caller in record time.

"That was your mother," Andy said with a wave of her hand. "I know you don't want to deal with her."

Alyssa's irritation reared its head again. She knew she was lucky to have Andy, but sometimes the woman was almost too efficient, too nice. Her "I know exactly what you need better than you do yourself" attitude was great at the beginning but was starting to cloy. Andy was a full year her junior, but she acted like her mother.

Well, maybe, Alyssa conceded, not *her* mother specifically. But a mother, anyway.

"Can I get you anything to eat? I can run out to the crepe place if you want."

Alyssa shook her head, pushing away her annoyance at the same time. Andy was just being her helpful, hyperefficient self. It wasn't her fault Alyssa felt like crap and couldn't shake her bad mood.

She left Andy in the living room, crawled back into bed, and pulled the covers up over her face. She wanted to wake in a world where the last month hadn't happened. Her father would still be alive, she wouldn't be receiving cryptic anonymous calls from wackos claiming to have information about his death, and, maybe most importantly, she wouldn't be completely hung up on the most physically and emotionally hard man she'd ever met.

She slept hard and woke, disoriented, at the insistent ring of her phone. She squinted at the clock, shocked to see it was after eight PM. She'd been asleep for nearly nine hours.

The call went to voice mail. She picked up her phone and scrolled through the missed calls, her stomach twisting when her unknown caller showed up four times. The guy was messing with her, some nutjob, or, worse, a stalker, who wanted to get close to her. She should just dump her number and be done with it.

But when she emerged from the shower after fifteen minutes and heard her phone ring, she sprinted to catch the call. Heart pounding, she pressed the button to accept the call and lifted the phone to her ear.

"Are you alone?"

She pulled her thick terrycloth robe tight around her as

though afraid the man might be watching. "Yes. Now tell me what the hell this is all about."

"Not over the phone. Too easy for people to listen in."

She rolled her eyes. Why had she taken the call? "You know what? You can take your crackpot theories and big-brother paranoia and shove it up your butt. I'm getting rid of this number and finding out who you are, and if you come within a thousand feet of me I'll have you arrested."

"You know the truth, Alyssa, you said it yourself. You know someone else was there that night."

Her breath froze in her chest.

"You never pushed the police on it. The case was so cut and dry, you knew they'd never believe you, vapid, flighty, drugged-out party girl that you are."

She listened silently as he laid out her inner turmoil with eerie clarity.

"I believe you, Alyssa. But you need to show me you can trust me with the truth."

"And how can I do that?" she snapped, fully expecting him to prove her wack-job theory right and request a pair of shoes or underwear or something.

"Meeting me, for starters."

"Okay, fine. My assistant and I will meet you at the Starbucks on the corner of Larkin and Post tomorrow. Name a time." Perfect. The coffee shop was always crowded, Andy would be there as backup, and, as a bonus, the paparazzi camped outside her front door would tag along and catch him in the act if he tried anything crazy.

"Sorry. No can do. We need to fly under the radar, for your protection and mine. Meet me in one hour at Zed's, and come alone." He rattled off the address.

She flipped open her laptop, plugged the address into Google, looked at the result, and gave a sharp laugh. "You want me to go to that part of the city alone at night? Are you trying to get me raped and killed? And that's assuming

I can sneak out unnoticed. You may not have noticed, but I'm not the most inconspicuous person in the world."

"You'll be perfectly safe as long as you don't do anything stupid. As for sneaking away, I'm sure you'll manage. I'll see you in an hour."

The connection dropped.

CHAPTER 13

ALYSSA PULLED ON a pair of jeans, a bulky, nonde-
script sweater, and a pair of running shoes. She couldn't
believe she was even contemplating the meeting.

Don't do anything stupid. No shit. Going alone to one of
the seediest, worst neighborhoods in San Francisco to meet
with a man who'd somehow gotten hold of her cell-phone
number fit firmly in the stupid category.

Yet she couldn't stifle the voice that shouted, wailed, insisted
that she hear what this man had to say. The subconscious
whisper that haunted her dreams became a full-fledged roar,
demanding that she sit up and pay attention to what it had
been trying to tell her.

Andy jumped up from the couch when Alyssa came out
of the bedroom, looking almost guilty to be caught doing
nothing. She smoothed a nervous hand over her hair and regarded Alyssa with concern. "Are you feeling better? Can I
get you anything?" A frown knit her brow as she took in
Alyssa's attire. "Are you going somewhere?"

"I have to meet someone," Alyssa replied, making it clear
in her tone that she wasn't up for more questions.

Andy made a move toward her bedroom. "Just let me
grab some shoes, and I'll go with you."

Alyssa put a hand on her arm to stay her. "No. I have to go alone."

Andy's mouth pulled into a nervous smile. "What's going on here, Alyssa? You're kind of freaking me out."

Alyssa licked her lips, debating how much to tell her. Finally she replied, "Someone has been calling me, claiming he has information about my father's death. That's all I can say."

"You shouldn't be meeting him by yourself," Andy said, positioning herself between Alyssa and the door. "If he has information, you should make him go to the police."

Alyssa shook her head, grabbed Andy by the shoulders, and firmly moved her aside. "I want to talk to him first. I'll be back in an hour, okay? And if my uncle calls, don't say anything about this to him. Or to anyone else."

She darted out the side door before Andy could say anything. It was only after she'd slipped out the back, around the corner, and into the back of a cab that she thought maybe she should have told Andy where she was headed. Something along the lines of "If I don't come back tonight, look for my body at the intersection of Fifteenth and Church." She pulled out her phone to call but thought better of it.

Alyssa didn't doubt Andy's loyalty but knew she was worried about her like everyone else. She might call Harold or Richard, meaning well, and then Alyssa would really be up shit creek.

Anything weird happens, you call me. Derek's parting words echoed in her head. Anonymous calls from someone claiming to have information about her father's death certainly qualified.

And something about the way he had said it . . . Of everyone around her, he alone seemed to be willing to entertain the possibility that maybe, just maybe, she wasn't a druggie.

Too bad he was off God knew where dealing with his own problems. Her heart clenched at the memory of the pain in his dark eyes. Was his mother dead? After all these years, would the mystery of her disappearance be solved?

With everything he was going through, she didn't want to be another burden. But, really, how stupid was she, going off alone to this part of town to meet a man she'd never met? She needed to tell someone, in case the worst happened.

She'd still be dead from her own foolish impetuousness, but at least they'd know where to look for her killer.

Alyssa felt a mixture of relief and regret when the call went straight to voice mail. On the one hand, she secretly— okay, not so secretly—was psyched to have a valid excuse to call him and maybe find out how he was doing. On the other, she didn't want to hear the censure in his voice when she explained exactly what she was doing.

Richard answered on the first ring. He sounded breathless and irritated. Andy could hear a woman's voice murmuring in the background. Whoops. Looked like she'd interrupted Richard in the middle of getting a piece.

"What do you want?"

"You asked me to keep you informed," she replied. "Alyssa left here about five minutes ago, saying she had to go meet someone."

"Who was it?"

"I don't know, she wouldn't tell me. But whoever she's meeting claims to have information about Oscar's death."

Richard swore softly. "Did she say anything else?"

"No, but I have an address," she said, unable to banish the smugness from her voice. After Alyssa left, Andy had gone into her room and opened Alyssa's laptop. The screen was locked, but Alyssa had given Andy her password months ago and hadn't bothered to change it. One click through Alyssa's browser history, and Andy found the Google map pinpointing the bar's location.

"Where?" Richard said.

Andy breathed a sigh and picked a piece of lint from her navy cashmere sweater. "I'm going to need an extra deposit."

"You little bitch. Who do you think you're talking to—"

"Listen, Dick," she said. "I know it's been ages since you've been in school, but do you have any idea how much it costs to go to Brown these days? Not to mention, with the way Harold's cutting Alyssa's income left and right, I may soon find myself unemployed." She named a figure.

"That's ridiculous," Richard spluttered.

"How much do you think the *Enquirer* would pay for my story, Dick? Double that? Triple? I hear *OK! Magazine* pays well—"

"You'll have it tomorrow. Now give me the address."

Richard hung up on Andy, the knot in his stomach tightening as he dialed Louis's number. He hated dealing with him, had been convinced it was a bad idea from the very beginning, but as usual he was overruled. Richard existed to do whatever the Van Weldt family required of him, no questions asked, and dealing with Louis was no different.

They were playing a dangerous game with Abbassi, and he knew if Louis found out they'd been planning to kill Alyssa all along, there would be hell to pay. But after what Andy had told him, even Louis wouldn't be able to deny it was time to take care of Alyssa once and for all.

"We have a problem," Richard said as soon as Louis picked up. "We need to take care of her, and I know a way we can do it." He quickly explained the situation, as well as their plan, as though he'd only just come up with it.

"You know of a place to take her?" Louis asked.

Richard had the perfect place in mind. "It's totally isolated. No one will look for her there, especially if we tell the press she's in treatment."

"Fine," Louis said. "You bring her to me. I will take care of other arrangements."

Alyssa kept her head down, shoulders hunched as she slunk past the panhandler shoving an empty McDonald's cup in her face. Even if she wanted to, she couldn't give him any money, having spent all her cash on the cab. She rolled her eyes at her own stupidity. This part of San Francisco was not the kind of place a woman should be walking around alone, much less walking alone looking for an ATM.

Keeping a constant bead on her surroundings, Alyssa looked at the scrap of paper in her hand and checked the address once again. She cursed under her breath. She had the intersection right, but she'd been up and down the block twice now, on both sides of the street, and still hadn't located Zed's.

"What you lookin' for, beautiful?" a homeless guy called out to her from a doorway. He was stringy and filthy, his face half hidden by his scraggly beard.

She gave him a wide berth as she walked past. Other people looked her way. She was starting to attract attention. Sweat beaded and itched around the neckline of her sweater as her eyes darted around. Finally she spotted it, a cardboard sign no bigger than a standard eight-by-ten piece of paper, taped on the inside of a window of an otherwise innocuous building.

It didn't look so much like a bar as a crack den. Alyssa took a deep breath and braced herself as she opened the door.

The bar was full, even on a weeknight, the crowd an odd mix, ranging from people who'd scraped enough together from their McDonald's cups to buy a beer, to groups of slick yuppie types who'd ventured into the wild from their multimillion-dollar condos on the gentrified block around the corner.

One of the yuppies looked up to see who had walked in.

Alyssa dipped her head even farther, sending her hair spilling over her shoulder to hide her face, and prayed she went unrecognized.

Apparently the patrons hadn't gotten the memo about San Francisco's citywide smoking ban, because the air was so thick with tobacco smoke and worse she could barely see through it enough to make out features. Not that she had any clue who she was looking for. Her heart picked up speed, and she was struck once again by how colossally stupid this was. She'd fallen for this stupid cloak-and-dagger prank, and it was probably all some ploy to get her alone and vulnerable so some psycho could do whatever he wanted to her.

She started to reach in her pocket for her phone. A hand curled around her forearm, and she jumped about two feet off the ground.

"Did anyone see you? Does anyone know where you are?"

She shook her head.

The man's eyes darted over her shoulder and canvassed the dim room. "Head to the back. We can talk privately."

She swallowed hard, questioning her sanity even as she let him steer her to the back of the dark, smoky bar. Alyssa slid into one side of the small booth, and the man took his seat across from her.

"You came. I wasn't sure you would." His eyes were bloodshot behind the lenses of his glasses, darting around the room as he tried to see everything at once. He raised a hand to signal the cocktail waitress, and Alyssa didn't miss the telltale tremble.

A drunk. Or worse.

"Who are you?" she asked. "What do you want?" Convinced by the second she'd been snowed, she wanted to cut to the chase, find out what he thought he knew so she could get the hell out of there.

"Martin Fish. Thanks for meeting me. This is good. This is good," he repeated, nodding compulsively. The waitress came over and took his order for a triple shot of Johnnie Walker, neat.

"Let me guess, you're a fan?" Alyssa said.

"I'm a reporter."

She pushed herself up from the bench seat with a soft curse. "I'm out of here."

He lunged across the table and grabbed her arm, his grip so tight she could feel his fingernails even through the thick knit of her sweater. "Sit down. You want to hear what I have to say. And if you don't you're even stupider than I thought."

Veins stood out on his wiry forearm as his grip urged her to sit back down. Satisfied she wasn't going to bolt, he released her. Alyssa sank back and took a good look at Martin Fish.

Other than the rabid glint in his eyes, he was completely unremarkable looking. His hair was a dusty brown with a few threads of gray, swept back from a slightly receding hairline. His face was tanned dark, weathered as an old bomber jacket, and his eyes were deep set and dark behind round tortoiseshell glasses that had gone out of style about five years ago. His nose was wide, and a scraggly goatee framed thin lips and distracted from a slightly weak chin.

The waitress brought his drink. He sucked down half of it in one gulp, closing his eyes and sighing as if it were ambrosia.

"Why don't you tell me what I'm doing here, Martin? You said you have information about my father's death," she prompted.

"Do you like diamonds, Alyssa?" Martin asked, his eyebrow cocked, his lips pulling into an odd smile.

"Sure." Alyssa shrugged, not sure where this was going. Though in truth she was more of an emerald girl, ever since her father had given her a pendant for her twelfth birthday and claimed it was no match for her eyes. But she wasn't about to share all that with Martin Fish, whose vibe was growing weirder by the second. "Girl's best friend and all that."

"The ad campaign has been very successful, hasn't it? Everyone loves a pretty girl draped in diamonds." His eyes roamed over her, as if he could see through her clothes. Alyssa's skin crawled, and she cursed herself for turning down Andy's offer to accompany her. "Do you know where those diamonds come from? Do you care where they were before they touched your naked skin?" Martin prodded.

This was such a mistake. She needed to get out of here.

Then she remembered the dreams. The drugs in her system.

Alyssa couldn't leave, not if there was even a slim chance he had any information about her father's death. She stared him dead in his crazy eyes and recited, word for word, the verbiage on the card that accompanied every piece of diamond jewelry sold by the Van Weldts. "While it is difficult, if not impossible, to trace the origin of our stones, we guarantee that all our diamonds are legally obtained from sanctioned mines that enforce humane mining practices, pay their workers fairly, and make the safety of their employees the utmost priority."

"How PC," Martin said, his thin lips stretching into a smile that left his eyes cold. "Too bad it's a load of bullshit."

"What are you talking about? My father would never sell conflict diamonds." Not only because it was unethical. As much as Alyssa had loved her father and wanted to believe in his integrity, she also knew what a hit her father's business had taken in the wake of the Leo DiCaprio movie.

The issue of blood diamonds wasn't a new one. It was an open secret that every year a certain amount of illegally mined diamonds were smuggled over the borders of civil-war-torn countries, and their proceeds were used to support the armies of the various factions. But after the success of the movie, the issue of blood diamonds was on everybody's radar, and now everyone wanted to make sure the diamonds they bought were from legitimate sources. Major diamond dealers—her father included—did whatever they could to assure their customers their diamonds were from "clean" sources. "My father would never risk the company's image that way," Alyssa insisted.

Martin's lips peeled back from his teeth in a disgusted sneer. "People will do anything for money."

Alyssa shook her head. "He knew everything about the business. He only bought diamonds from reputable cutting operations."

"Like Louis Abbassi?"

"Yes," she said cautiously as she waited for the trap to spring.

"How well do you know Louis?"

Not as well as he'd like to know me. "We're friendly," she said cautiously. "As were he and my father before he died."

"What if I were to tell you that Louis Abbassi is helping to arm some of the most brutal warlords in southern Africa?" Martin said, cocking his head as he waited for her reply.

Alyssa shook her head. "That's ridiculous. Louis is a businessman. His mines are all sanctioned—"

She jumped when Martin's palm slammed onto the table. "You want to believe that, don't you? Want to ignore the fact that Abbassi's planes are moving more than rice and bandages in and out of the jungle." His face grew flushed, lines deepening as his expression radiated contempt. "You have no clue what goes on in the world. Just want to sit here on your useless, privileged ass, and you don't give a fuck that girls are raped and children are forced into combat."

Alyssa shook her head. "Of course I care, but Louis isn't—"

"You know why they're called blood diamonds, don't you?"

"Of course," Alyssa replied, "but my family would have nothing—"

He leaned over the table and lowered his voice to a bone-chilling whisper. "Let me spell it out for you. Louis gets guns to local warlords in exchange for mining rights and uses his cutting operation in South Africa to get them into the distribution chain."

"That's ridiculous. Louis has certificates for all his stones—"

"Really? Do the certificates mention that he sometimes pays for the stones in Kalashnikovs?"

Alyssa shook her head. This was insane. *He* was insane. A ranting conspiracy theorist with a grudge against Louis and the Van Weldts. "So tell me what this all has to do with my father's death," she said. "Don't tell me—Louis drove my stepmother to commit murder suicide."

Martin's face grew somber, and for a moment he looked almost sane. "I talked to your father a couple weeks before he died. He got very defensive when I prodded him on Louis and kicked me out of his office. But I think after that he went back for a closer look at Louis's operation."

"And you think my father found out, and Louis had him killed before he could tell anyone. Is that it?"

Martin nodded, fingering his scraggly goatee. "It's a little more complicated, but that's it in a nutshell."

"More complicated, how?" Tension wrapped cold tentacles around the base of her neck, coiling and tightening until a headache took root. Alyssa brought her hands up to rub at her temples.

"Someone made the deal with Abbassi, someone with as much authority as your father." Martin's already deep-set eyes went squintier behind his glasses. "I guarantee who-ever that was had a pretty good idea Abbassi wasn't completely legit."

Her gut clenched and twisted in concert with the pounding in her head. "Are you saying my uncle had my father and stepmother killed?"

Martin held his hands up, fingers spread. "It all fits, right?"

A harsh laugh erupted from her throat. "Maybe in crazytown this all fits. You can't prove any of this. You just come out spewing these wild accusations about my family. What's your problem with the Van Weldts, Martin? Did they screw you over? Sell you a piece of jewelry that still wasn't enough to convince some poor woman to sleep with you?"

His lips again pulled into a sneer. "You're so quick to jump to their defense. This family that wanted nothing to do with you until they figured out a way to use you."

The blood drained from her face as the blow hit home. "I'll sue you for libel before I let you destroy the company my father worked so hard to build."

"It's only libel if it's not true."

"Okay, fine," she said, clenching her teeth and crossing her arms. "If you're so convinced my stepmother didn't kill my dad before offing herself and that the Van Weldts are buying their diamonds from an arms dealer, why tell me? Why keep it secret? Why wouldn't you go to the police, or Interpol, or whoever it is that tracks down international arms dealers?"

An eager gleam glowed in Martin's eyes. "Because you're going to help make sure everyone knows the truth. Like you said, I need proof that someone in the company knew about Louis and wanted to keep it covered up. I know your father left you a significant stake in the company in his will. You have the kind of access I need."

She gave an involuntary snort. "You overestimate me," she said, remembering her uncle's disdain when Alyssa had suggested she be involved in the marketing strategy meeting. "I'm just the face in the ads. They don't let me mess around in the actual business. Besides, why in the world would I help you?"

"Are you kidding me? We live in a world where Britney Spears making a Starbucks run is headline news on CNN. No one cares about miners suffering in Africa or teenage girls getting raped." He paused, and for a moment real despair flashed across his face. It disappeared in an instant. "Stories like that are relegated to two columns in the back of the world-news section. Even if I do link the Van Weldts to Abbassi, without proof someone knew what was going on, it's a minor PR problem for the company. But if Alyssa Miles, the hottest celebutante since Paris Hilton, helps me find the proof and break the news, we've got the hottest story of the decade." His eyes glowed with a mercenary light. "We're talking about exclusives with the networks, a book deal; you could even play yourself in the movie. Don't try to tell me you don't want to be a part of that."

Alyssa swallowed hard against the nausea churning in her gut. "You think I would accuse my family of something as horrible as this just to get my face on the news?"

"It's a hell of a lot more dignified than leaking nude photos of yourself."

She reached out, grabbed his drink, and threw it in his face. "You're disgusting," she said and stood up. "And you're crazy. I don't believe any of this," she said, ignoring the doubts clamoring in her head. She was twenty-four years old, for Christ's sake. Too old to be this stupid and impulsive. "If you try to contact me again, I'll have you arrested for stalking."

She started to slide out of the booth. Martin was on her in a second, pinning her by the shoulders to the wooden backrest. His breath was hot on her face, stinking of whiskey. "We have to tell people. We have to make them see the truth." He released her as abruptly as he'd grabbed her. "Don't leave," he said as he pulled out a pen and paper and scribbled something down. He shoved the paper into her hand. "Go to this Web site and enter the log-in and password I've written down. You'll get a small taste of what I've seen. When you're done, call me at the Marina Motor Inn."

Alyssa stalked out, ignoring the quizzical stares and whispers of "Is that . . ." from the other patrons as she walked by.

Paranoid, delusional freak. Not that she was any better, thinking she was going to get answers from some weirdo calling out of the blue. She paused under a streetlight and squinted at the scrap of paper. www.FishBait.org. Login: mARfiSH669. Password: MAlaurRe85.

Fishbait. She shook her head. What a tool. It was probably like his own amateur porn or something equally freaky and disgusting. She crumpled the paper and shoved it in the front pocket of her jeans, calling herself an idiot as her angry strides ate up block after block.

But her initial fury faded, leaving room for the niggling doubts to creep in. What about the dreams? What about the drugs? Someone was slipping them to her, she had no doubt about that.

Was it all related? Was it possible she really had seen something that night but didn't really "know" it? And someone wanted to make sure she never found out for sure?

She trudged up the last hill to her house, skirting around the block so she could sneak in the back way. Dressed as she was, this time of night, even people who knew she lived around here didn't recognize her as the glammed-out creature from the tabloids.

Making sure no one was watching, she keyed in the security code for the back gate and walked quietly across the Victorian's small backyard. Maybe she should take a look at the Web site. Just to be sure.

She walked up the stairs to the living room and found

Andy perched on the edge of the couch as Anderson Cooper played on the TV. Andy jumped up and rushed over to Alyssa. "Are you okay? I was so worried."

"I'm fine," Alyssa said, rubbing the base of her skull in an attempt to ease the dull ache that had settled there. Ignoring Andy's questioning look, Alyssa went to her bedroom to find out once and for all what "secrets" Martin Fish so badly wanted to share.

She plopped down on her bed, computer in front of her, but before she could log on, Andy appeared in the doorway with a plate of food and a glass of sparkling water.

"You haven't eaten anything all day," Andy said, holding out a dish piled high with raw vegetables, pita, and hummus.

One of Alyssa's favorite snacks, but she knew there was no way she could fit any food on top of the knot in her belly. "Thanks. You can put it right there," she said, indicating the empty spot beside her.

"You really need to eat something," Andy said.

Annoyance tightened her shoulders as Alyssa realized Andy wasn't going anywhere until she ate something. She stifled the urge to tell Andy to back off, that she didn't need a keeper. Andy was just trying to look out for her and make sure she didn't starve herself on top of everything else that was going on.

She scooped up a blob of hummus with a pita triangle and took a bite, washing it down with several gulps of the sparkling water. "Thanks, Andy," she said around another mouthful of bread. "I don't know what I'd do without you."

She kept a smile pasted on her face and gave Andy a little wave as she backed out of the room. Thirsty from her long walk home, she finished the water, opened up her browser, and clicked on FishBait.org. She leaned up and dug around in her pocket for the scrap of paper.

Nothing.

She came up on her knees and dug more frantically. *Unbelievable.* In desperation, she stripped off her jeans and turned every pocket inside out and scoured her floor for a balled-up wad of paper.

She must have dropped it when she went to shove it in her pocket. She squeezed her eyes shut, trying to remember the log-in and password. She remembered the log-in was some form of Mfish and some numbers, but with random capitalizations and digits she couldn't for the life of her conjure up. Still, she spent almost half an hour trying various permutations, on the off chance her brain would cough up the right information, until her vision blurred and her head renewed its throbbing.

She needed an Advil. She stood up from the bed, startled when her legs didn't seem to work and she slid to the floor.

What was wrong with her? A steady gray fog overtook her brain, thick and soupy like the mist rolling into the Northern California coast. Her eyelids were lead weights, and she leaned her head back against her bed.

She was vaguely aware of her door opening, voices that sounded like they were talking to her underwater. She forced her eyes to focus, startled to see Richard Blaylock standing in her room, Andy beside him, arms folded as she stood next to him. Alyssa held up a hand that felt like it had an anvil attached to it. Neither made a move to help her.

"How much did you give her?" Richard's voice was deep and muffled.

"Enough to keep her out for several hours, just like you said," Andy replied.

It took several seconds for Alyssa's brain to process. When it finally did, the truth exploded in her brain, a white-hot, blinding flash of clarity.

"You bitch!" Her voice sounded echoey and distant. Her limbs were heavy, but she mustered every last bit of strength and launched herself at Andy. Taken by surprise, Andy tumbled over and backward, shrieking in pain when her cheek hit the corner of the bedside table. "Why?" was all Alyssa could push past her lips as her vision tunneled. The last thing she saw was Andy's look of utter contempt.

CHAPTER 14

MARTIN UNLOCKED THE door of his motel room, taking one last, frantic look behind him before he stepped inside. No one there. Just as there'd been no one as he'd taken a circuitous walking route back from Zed's.

He couldn't shake that dogged feeling, the prickly sense of being watched.

You're totally safe. No one saw her. And even if they did, no one knows what you were talking about. This wasn't the jungle hell of the Congo, where he had to worry about getting iced with a Kalashnikov if he looked at someone sideways.

He extracted his bottle of whiskey from a paper bag and opened it. He took a long swallow and reclined on the bed, not bothering to turn the lights on. Streetlight filtered through the blinds, striping the cheap nylon bedspread with yellow light.

He raised the bottle to his lips, trying to chase back the chill that had settled into his bones the second he'd arrived in San Francisco. His body couldn't stay warm in the damp cold, not after weeks in crushing heat and humidity.

He stared at the phone, willing it to ring. Alyssa had to be home by now, had plenty of time to look at his site and see the truth she wanted to deny. A sour feeling twisted in his gut as he thought of what she would see. She had to face the truth. They all did. She was the key. She would save them all.

Call. He'd told her to contact him. How could she not call after seeing the photos, the videos? A curl of unease unfurled in his belly.

He closed his eyes, gave into booze-fueled dreams of Alyssa, laughing, beckoning, her skin glittering with diamonds. She was joined by Marie Laure, diamond shackles around her legs and arms, crying tears of blood as she covered her swollen belly. He reached for them, knowing he had to warn them about something, but he couldn't run, couldn't catch them, couldn't tell them what to be afraid of. Alyssa's tears turned to screams as wounds opened all over her skin until her entire body was awash in thick, red blood. Marie Laure screamed at him, begging for help. Gunfire exploded once, twice. Marie Laure clutched her stomach and fell, her clawing hands bringing Alyssa down with her.

Martin jerked awake, assaulted by the stink of spilled whiskey and his own acrid sweat.

It wasn't gunshots, it was someone knocking at his door. *She was here.* His dream lingered, and he wasn't exactly sure where he was, he just knew Alyssa was waiting outside. He shoved up from the bed, wobbling a little as he stood and walked to the door.

He fumbled with the chain and turned the knob. The door exploded inward. Cartilage crunched, and his eyes filled with tears as he staggered back. Strong hands threw him facedown on the ground. His jaw hit the floor; his teeth bit nearly through his tongue. The metallic taste of blood flooded his mouth.

The dream fog disappeared, and he was acutely aware of everything. His heart pounding against his ribs. The stink of the man's sweat as he held Martin immobile with a knee in his spine. The sound of another man rummaging through his things, knocking over a chair, pulling the mattress from the bed.

Martin tried to struggle and got a sharp blow to the back of the head for his trouble. The knee in his back increased its pressure, and his attacker grabbed him by the hair, lifting Martin, arching his back until he thought his spine would snap.

His last thought was of Marie Laure as the cold bite of steel sliced into the skin of his throat.

"Looks like your girl is in trouble again."

Derek's eyes narrowed on Danny's face as he looked up from his paper and coffee. Danny sat down across from him, hard gray eyes glittering as he nodded over Derek's shoulder at the waitress serving the thin crowd of the small diner. Derek, Danny, Ethan, and their father had spent most of the afternoon and early evening the day before going over the crime scene where the woman's body had been found.

Ethan had gone home to Toni for the night and insisted their father, who had taken to long stretches of silence while staring off into space, accompany him.

Derek and Danny had elected to stay in the tiny mountain community's only lodgings, a small room over the diner where Derek was currently enjoying his fourth cup of tar-black coffee. The sun had broken over the mountains, spilling bright light across the damp parking lot, streaking across the diner's floor.

"Don't know what the fuck you're talking about," Derek replied curtly. Over the past twenty-four hours the tension between them had grown until they were circling each other, snarling and snapping like a couple of junkyard dogs. They'd put it aside to deal with this latest bombshell involving their mother's unsolved case. "But I think it's about time we had this out." Derek knew his brother was itching to tear him a new one. And as much as Derek knew he deserved it, facing the truth—that he'd let his dick do the thinking and lost them a major client—really sucked the big one. "You have something to say about the way I handled Alyssa Miles. Why don't you go ahead and say it."

The waitress came by and set a cup of coffee next to Danny, scurrying away when he gave her a smile that was closer to a snarl. "You lost us business—major business— over a piece of ass. And a messed-up piece of ass on top of it. Seriously, man, of all people, I'd think you would be able to avoid being sucked into that mess. You date PhDs for fuck's sake, not stupid, drugged-out sluts—"

Derek reached across the table and fisted his hand in his brother's collar. "Shut the fuck up right now. You don't say shit about her. You don't even know her—"

"Oh, and you do? While you're busy defending her, she's being hauled off to rehab, she's such a mess."

Derek's fingers uncurled from the neck of Danny's black T-shirt. A fist gripped his insides as a terrible sense of foreboding sent cold sweat trickling down his spine.

Danny's eyes were glittering slits as he used his massive forearm to knock aside Derek's hand. "It's all over the news. Didn't you catch CNN this morning? Hey, I think that's her right now." He gestured his chin over Derek's head. Derek turned to look at the small television mounted above the diner's counter.

He rushed across the small space, staring up at the screen. It showed Alyssa, her small frame nearly swallowed by the same bulky sweater she'd worn up at the beach house. Her legs were buckled under her as she was half supported, half carried by Richard Blaylock on one side and Andy on the other. Flashbulbs popped in her face, and her head fell back, her long, light brown hair obscuring half her pale face. "Can you turn it up?" he asked the waitress. She shot him and Danny a nervous look but grabbed the remote.

A female reporter's voice filled the room as the footage

continued to roll ". . . series of incidents, Alyssa Miles is off to a private rehab facility. Representatives for Miles refuse to disclose where she is going but want to assure her fans and supporters she will receive the treatment she needs. This will be the second stint in rehab for Miles, who attended the first time when she was just twenty-one."

Derek continued to stare, watching as Alyssa was loaded into the backseat of an SUV, his stomach churning as every instinct in his body screamed that this was not right.

Her enormous green eyes flooded his vision, pleading with him to believe her as she claimed she knew nothing about the drugs in her system. He hadn't wanted to believe her, afraid he was once again letting his emotions get in the way of his job.

Now that feeling that he'd thrown her to the lions was back with double the force.

Ignoring Danny, he stalked from the diner and flipped open his phone, determined to get to the truth of this. Outside the air was crisp and smelled like wood smoke and pine. He dialed Alyssa's number, cursing when his phone beeped alerting him there was no cell signal. Fucking boondocks had satellite TV but no cell coverage. He hadn't even noticed until now, he'd been so wrapped up in studying the crime scene.

Needles from the surrounding redwoods crunched under his soles as he circled the parking lot. Finally he got one faint bar and dialed again, but the connection dropped before he could get through. Before he could redial, his phone beeped, alerting him to a new voice mail. His blood ran cold when he heard Alyssa's voice, garbled, her words mostly unintelligible.

Anything weird happens you call me, he'd said.

"Dude, what's your problem?" Danny called as he jogged across the parking lot.

"Something's wrong," Derek said, hurrying in the direction of the hotel to retrieve his bag. "I have to go."

Danny stared at him in disbelief. "Are you fucking kidding me? You're not seriously so far gone after this girl—"

"This isn't right—they're going to do something to her, I can feel it."

Danny followed him up the outside stairs that led to their rooms. "You *feel* it? Are you shitting me? You don't *feel* anything. No one's going to do anything to her. They probably shipped her off to some spa for a couple weeks so she can get a couple massages and talk about her feelings. All another ploy for publicity."

Derek ignored him as he threw everything into his black duffel and zipped it up. He dug his fingers into his hair, pressing his palms into the sides of his skull as if that would contain the swirling mass of confusion. Danny was right. He didn't feel. He thought. He analyzed. But right now he couldn't focus, couldn't logic his way around any of this. The only thing he knew for sure was that he had to get to her, see for himself she was safe.

And if she was safe and snug in some four-star resort masquerading as a rehab facility, Derek would be the first one to have DICK FOR BRAINS tattooed across his forehead.

It took him ten minutes of driving down the twisty mountain road before he could get a clear signal and hear Alyssa's message in its entirety.

"Hey, it's me. Ummm, Alyssa, that is—no reason you should recognize my voice right off the bat." Derek's lips tightened in a grim smile. She had no idea that every detail about her, from her voice, to her scent, to the peachy sweet taste of her, was permanently seared into his memory. "So, remember how you told me to call you if anything weird happened? Well, my anonymous caller called again. This time I answered, and he said he had information about my father's death. So I'm going to meet him at Zed's in the Mission. Alone. Which I know is stupid, but he insisted, and I'm actually not supposed to be telling anyone, but I thought I should tell someone, in case anything, you know, happened. Which is really stupid, and I probably shouldn't be bothering you with everything you have going on, so feel free to ignore this message. And, ummm, I hope you're doing okay. My uncle told me he fired you. I know that's my fault, and I'm really sorry about that. But ummm, maybe you could call me sometime, just to let me know you're okay and everything." Her voice hitched, and the uncertainty in her tone curled up in his throat and settled there in a big lump. "I know you don't want to be, like, friends or anything, but it would be nice to hear from you sometime. Okay, bye."

He kept his eyes glued to the road as he hung up the phone and carefully placed it in the cup holder, focusing for the moment on not driving off the side of the road and pitching headlong into a ravine. His knuckles showed stark white as he gripped the steering wheel and tried to pull himself back from the brink.

The noise in his head was deafening as questions, fears, and guilt ricocheted off each other. Derek rolled his shoulders, admonished himself to calm down as he strove for the quiet calm he had always been able to summon at will. It was what had made him an elite sniper, able to wait in complete stillness as mosquitoes chewed his face in the jungles of Central America or the cold threatened to freeze his nuts off in the high mountains of Afghanistan. He had an uncommon, some would even say fucked up, ability to disengage, shut down all emotions, and deal with a situation with an analytic approach that would put Mr. Spock to shame.

But as hard as he tried, he couldn't get the gut-twisting, conscience-searing images of Alyssa out of his mind. Her big, sad eyes, her soft, warm hand as she offered him comfort. Her small body moving under his, taking everything from him even when he smacked her down for trying to get too close.

Under it all, rage was simmering, building until it filled his brain with a red haze. Someone was trying to hurt her, and for the first time in his life he really wanted to kill somebody. When he was in the military, taking out the enemy was a job, and he treated it as such. He took pride in his work, but he never—okay, rarely—let emotions come into play.

From the first time he'd met Alyssa, she'd brought out unwanted, unfamiliar protective instincts. It wasn't just her small stature—her soft, pampered, never-seen-a-hard-day's-work complexion. It was that damn openheartedness he'd tried to ignore, her willingness, after being screwed over so many times by so many people, to try again. To open herself up and offer love and affection, hoping it would be returned. It clawed at him, pulled at him, even as he'd tried to convince himself a needy, vulnerable woman was the last thing he needed.

He remembered the way her cold fingers had locked around his hand, her eyes wild in her drugged stupor. "Help me"—like he was her savior, her knight in shining armor. He didn't have it in him to be Alyssa's or any other woman's savior. A cold-blooded bastard like him would trample a hothouse flower like Alyssa under his big-booted heel.

But as his car ate up the miles between La Honda and Alyssa's house in the Marina, his blood was anything but cold. Like it or not, she'd crawled under his skin the first time he'd laid eyes on her. And the second he'd touched her, tasted her, he was gone. Over the cliff for a funny, frivolous, beautiful girl who didn't know how to do laundry but made his heart crack open a little more every time she smiled at him.

Realizing it didn't make it any better, and he still wasn't sure what the fuck he was going to do about it.

Right now he was sure of only one thing: someone was

trying to hurt her, and he would kill or die himself before he let anything happen to her.

Alyssa woke up in an unfamiliar room with a pounding headache and a mouth that tasted like she'd been chewing dirty socks. Her eyes were puffy and scratchy with grit. She blinked a few times, hoping when she opened her eyes she'd see the walls of her room instead of the cream wallpaper with its faded green and maroon grapevine design.

Where the hell am I?

Fear sprouted in her gut as she kick-started her brain and tried to put together the last several hours. She struggled to sit up in bed, wincing at an aching sting in her arm. Her eyes froze on the IV stuck in the inner crook of her elbow.

The fear sank its claws deeper. She reached instinctively with her left hand to pull out the IV. Fear became full-fledged panic when she realized her hands were secured to the bed by leather restraints.

Her chest heaved, and she tried to catch her breath to scream, but the sound died in her throat as the door opened and Richard Blaylock walked into the room, followed by Louis Abbassi and a tall, slender black woman wearing scrubs.

"Ah, I see you are awake," Louis said, smiling as if he were greeting her across the breakfast table.

"What's happening?" The words came out slurred, forced past a tongue that felt thick and dry. "Why am I here?" she tried again.

Richard pointedly avoided her gaze as the woman in scrubs—a nurse—came over to the bed, checked the IV, and injected something into the tube.

Everything came back in a flash. The meeting with Martin. Returning home. Drinking her water—the water only Andy could have dosed with something. Richard's blurry image before the rest of the night went dark.

"You had Andy drug me," she persisted, pushing every word through the thickening quicksand of her mind. "Why?"

Richard acted as if she hadn't spoken as Louis gave him a long, assessing look before turning his attention back to Alyssa.

Even in her fuzzy drugged state, she felt his stare on her like a thousand insects crawling over her skin.

"You sure she knows what she's doing?" Richard asked. "We don't want her dead yet."

Her head was slowly filling with cotton, but the "yet" registered loud and clear. Oh, God, what was happening? Through bleary eyes she saw the woman look at Louis and murmur something in a language she didn't recognize. Louis responded as he sat down on Alyssa's bed.

"Do not worry," Louis snapped at Richard.

"But you're sure you can cover up the IV marks," Richard persisted. "When it happens, it has to look like an overdose."

A black wave was closing in, threatening to suck her under. She fought it, knowing if she let it take her she would be lost.

"*If* it happens," Louis said sharply, "I will have the situation under control."

His fingers trailed down her cheek. Alyssa wanted to squirm away but couldn't make her body obey. "We can still work this out, Alyssa," he said in a voice that cut through the fog and sent a spear of dread to her very core. His hand slid down her neck, over her collarbone and came to rest over the curve of one breast. His head bent to her neck, and she felt the slimy heat of his lips against her skin.

Every cell recoiled in revulsion, and she managed to force a soft "no" from her throat.

Louis sat up, his mouth pulled into a cruel smile. "You will rethink your attitude, *chérie*, if you wish to keep your life." His fingers squeezed her breast, and she could feel them sinking into the tender flesh even though the drugs dulled the pain.

Louis's leering face hung above her. Richard's form was a blur over his shoulder. The black wave surged again, and this time Alyssa let it take her.

Louis gave Alyssa's small breast another squeeze, closing his eyes as his cock throbbed. She was exquisite as he'd known she'd be, her skin soft and tender under his hands. He could take her so easily, dismiss Catherine and Richard while he finally slaked his lust on Alyssa's body.

But he forced his hand to release its grip on her breast. He wanted her awake, her green eyes wide and aware as she felt his cock sinking into her small body, his fingers wrapped around her neck. He wanted her to look up at him, wide awake and knowing that he held her life in his hands.

Soon. I will have her soon.

But right now there were other matters to take care of.

He rose from the bed and met Richard's look of disdain.

"You have a problem, my friend?" Louis asked as he motioned Richard out of the room.

Richard lifted his too straight nose into the air. "I don't think it's good for our case if she turns up looking like she was raped before she died."

Louis's nostrils flared as he struggled to control his temper. He wanted nothing more than to reach out and snap Richard's neck, this man who made his living by acting the lap dog for others. Following orders, jumping to do their bidding. And now he dared try to tell Louis what to do. "As I said, when and if she dies, I will have the situation under control." He paused and pinned Richard with a stare that had weaker men squirming like a bug under a pin. Richard was no different. "But you did not believe that? Yes? Even after I told you I would deal with Alyssa if the need arose?"

Richard's bland blue eyes darted back and away. "We

wanted a backup plan. In case she remembered something else."

"She remembers nothing. She saw nothing," Louis hissed.

"She said in the interview—"

"She said she saw a raccoon!" Louis snapped. "No one took her seriously."

"Yes, because we made it look like she was spinning out of control! And after tonight, you should be thanking us for laying the groundwork for you."

Louis could smell the fear filming on Richard's skin. He should be scared. Louis wasn't one to tolerate being double-crossed. And while Richard's point was valid, especially after Alyssa's meeting with the reporter, Louis was no fool. He knew the actions against Alyssa had little to do with the cover-up of Oscar's murder and everything to do with personal vendetta. From the first time Louis had seen Alyssa, he had claimed her as his own. He would do what he wished with her, when he wished, and Richard and the others would pay for very nearly ruining his fun.

"Yes, perhaps you are right in that after all."

The relief on Richard's face was almost comical. "I thought you'd see it that way," he replied, arrogance dripping from every syllable. "Now, what are we going to do about Fish? Has he been"—he paused—"taken care of?"

Spineless, weak worm. Speaking in euphemisms because he didn't want to dirty his soft white hands with the realities of business. Louis nodded. When Richard had called earlier, Louis had sent Marius and Ivan to Zed's. Marius had followed Fish back to his hotel while Ivan had followed Alyssa home. "Marius, as always, is fast and discreet."

Richard swallowed hard and nodded. "Well, if we're finished here, we should get back to the city. We're scheduled to meet at four to discuss the production ramp-up for the holidays. You should probably sit in."

Louis nodded. He would deal with Richard and the others in due time, but for now he still needed them to move his latest inventory. "Yes, as always there is business to take care of."

"What are you doing here?" Andy jumped in surprise as Derek came up the stairs into the living room. Cheeks flushed, she moved in front of the couch as though to hide the over-size duffel filled with clothes and shoes. Andy looked at the bag and then back at him. "Alyssa wanted me to take some things to give to Goodwill."

She was lying so hard Derek could practically smell it, but he didn't give a shit if Andy was staging grand-theft wardrobe. "Where's Alyssa?"

"How did you even get in here? You don't work for the Van Weldts anymore," Andy countered, her chin tilted up in that know-it-all way of hers he'd come to recognize.

"I still have the security code. Now tell me where they took her, and I'll get out of your hair."

"I'm sorry, but I can't share that information with any-one outside the family." She turned back to the pile of clothes and the bag on the couch and busied herself folding a dress. "But rest assured, she's getting the help she needs."

Anger raged, firing his veins until sweat beaded on his brow. He slid out of his fleece jacket. "Somehow I doubt that."

Something in his tone made her look over her shoulder. She tried to hide it, but he saw the way her eyes locked on his chest, his arms straining the short sleeves of his T-shirt. "Really, Derek, I can't tell you anything more. You really need to go." The flush deepened in her cheeks, and her gaze skittered away.

So. There was an actual woman underneath Andy's robot-like facade.

Time to try a different tactic. What would Ethan, his

younger, much more charming twin, do in this situation? Derek pasted what he hoped was a sexy smile on his face. "Come on, Andy, you can tell me. I just want to make sure she's okay. She was spouting some crazy shit on the way back the other day."

"I can only imagine," Andy said, an involuntary smile on her lips. "With everything she's on, you wouldn't believe some of the things she comes up with."

He closed the distance between them until he was standing right next to her. He spotted a piece of flame-colored fabric and plucked it from the pile. His fingers tightened in the delicate silk when he recognized it as the dress Alyssa had worn the night they first met.

"Hey, you're crushing it," Andy scolded, placing her hand over his, letting it linger there for a few seconds.

Right. He needed to focus. "Sorry." He released the dress and looked over to see Andy watching him through her lashes. In contrast to the pile of designer crap she was looting, Andy was dressed in jeans and an oversize gray sweatshirt, giving her all the shape of a potato on legs. "Brown," he said, reading the front of her shirt. "That's where you went."

"I did," she replied, smiling with smug Ivy pride.

"I've always loved smart girls," Derek said, looking at her like her mouse-brown ponytail was the sexiest thing he'd ever seen.

"Really," she said, her eyes going wide, pupils enlarging with awareness and arousal. "You don't have it for Alyssa like every other man in the universe?"

You have no idea. "Sure, she's cute, but brains—that's what I find really sexy." He almost gagged, he was piling the BS so high, but Andy was buying it, if her nervous "oh" and rapidly beating pulse were any indication.

She turned to face him fully, and that's when he noticed

the purple mark staining her cheekbone. "What's this?" he asked. He brushed his fingers across her cheek, and her color deepened to tomato red.

"N—nothing," she said. "I ran into a door."

She was lying. He knew it like he knew his own name.

A phone rang from a giant leather purse on the couch.

"That's mine. I need to get it," Andy said almost apologetically.

She reached for it, and Derek grabbed it off the couch. "Here you go." She took the purse, and Derek registered her look of fear as the purse slipped from her shaking fingers. It fell to the ground, the contents spilling across the hardwood floor.

Derek watched in disbelief as a half dozen pill bottles went rolling across the floor. Andy dropped to her knees, her phone skittering away as she scrambled to retrieve the bottles.

He swooped in like a hawk, scooping up several labeled bottles of pills along with a vial of liquid.

"Give me those." Andy slapped and swiped at his hands, but Derek had no trouble shaking her off long enough to read the labels. OxyContin. Methadone. Ketamine. Two out of three substances that had shown up on Alyssa's drug test. All with prescriptions made out to an Alice Waters from an online pharmacy.

Derek held on to them all, including the liquid-filled vial he bet contained GHB or Rohypnol.

His blood went cold and then hot with rage. Andy had a veritable pharmacy in her bag, and she'd been pumping it all into Alyssa's unsuspecting body.

The bottles dropped, the plastic bouncing on the hardwood floor in a series of sharp cracks. The suave seducer disappeared in an instant as Derek grabbed Andy by the shoulders. "What the fuck is going on here? Why are you drugging her?"

Andy's brown eyes were wide with fear. "Th—they're hers. I hold them for her—"

He gave her a shake, struggling to keep his anger in check. He'd never intentionally hurt a woman, but all bets were off where Alyssa was concerned. "Tell me the truth, or I call the police."

She tried to struggle out of his hold. "I'll tell them you broke in."

His grip on her arms tightened. "A risk I'm willing to take. Now tell me where she is."

"I don't know!" she shouted.

"Do you realize what will happen to you if something happens to her? You'll be named an accessory to murder."

"No one's going to kill her," she scoffed.

"What makes you so sure?"

Andy's already pale face went pasty. "But why would they want to kill her?"

"Why would you want to drug her?" he countered.

"They paid me to. I needed the extra money. I didn't ask any questions."

He swallowed back his rage as he focused on what she was saying. He had to keep his cool, keep his eyes on the prize. Andy wasn't the mastermind here, she was merely an immature, spiteful girl who wanted to get back at her prettier, richer, famous friend. "Who? Who told you to drug her?"

Andy pressed her lips together and shifted her weight from foot to foot.

"You think they'll protect you? When this comes out, they're going to pin the hole thing on you. That is, if they let you live long enough to talk."

That hit home. "Richard," she whispered through lips gone gray.

"Richard Blaylock? The corporate counsel?" Derek pictured the man in his head, with his bland good looks and expensive suits. The man didn't look creative enough to come up with such a scheme. "Why?"

"I don't know," Andy said again, the pitch of her voice rising in panic. "I didn't ask. He told me he'd give me a bunch of money if I made sure she was fucked up at some of her appearances and then told me to leak to the press that she was using again. Maybe he wanted her uncle to kick her out of the business."

Derek shook his head to clear it as his brain spun. Blaylock had something to do with Oscar Van Weldt's death. That had to be it. Alyssa being drugged and de facto kidnapped by Blaylock right after she'd gone to meet her anonymous caller couldn't be a coincidence.

Everything he'd read about the Van Weldt family described Blaylock's close personal relationship with the family, particularly Oscar. He'd been the son Oscar had never had, his right-hand man. Oscar hired Blaylock straight out of law school, made his career.

Had the man paid him back by having him killed?

Derek wondered what Blaylock had done that was so bad he was willing to kill Oscar Van Weldt to cover it up.

Maybe Alyssa and her mysterious caller had the key. But at the moment he didn't really give a shit about Richard and his secrets. All he knew was Richard had hurt Alyssa, was probably going to kill her, and for that he'd have his balls in a blender. But only after Derek got her home safe.

"Tell me where they took her," Derek said, closing in on Andy.

"I told you I don't know," she said, taking several hasty steps back until her hips hit the arm of the sofa. She went tumbling over and landed in a tangle of arms and legs.

"Think," he said through clenched teeth. "Anything you can think of, any comment, no matter how innocuous."

He braced himself over her, so close he caught the stink

of her sweat, could see the pulse fluttering frantically in her neck. "Tell me everything you can remember."

She squeezed her eyes shut and pressed her fists to her temples. Derek swore softly. He was going to find Blaylock and beat the truth out of him.

"The Tahoe house," Andy said suddenly. "Before they left, Richard called someone and asked them if everything was ready at the Tahoe house."

The back of his neck tingled, and he knew he'd hit pay dirt. "Where is it?"

She shook her head. "I don't know exactly. I've never been there."

"I'll find it." He flipped open his cell phone and dialed Ethan's number. As he waited for the call to connect, he turned back to Andy. "I suggest you get out of town and don't look back."

Her throat bobbed as she swallowed. "Do you think Richard will hurt me?"

"I don't know. But if I ever catch you within one hundred feet of Alyssa, I will."

CHAPTER 15

ALYSSA WAS FLOATING. *I am a leaf on the water. A dandelion on the breeze. I am the air, and the air is me.* Wow. This was the best meditation session ever. For the first time she really felt out of her body.

Little by little she became aware of herself. The dryness of her lips. The heaviness of her limbs. The gritty feel of her eyes behind the closed lids. She forced her eyes open, and whatever peace she felt fled as her foggy brain took in her surroundings. Awareness teased her, hanging around edges. She didn't know where she was, but she remembered it was bad.

She rolled carefully to her side, caught a glimpse of a steel pole. Right. An IV line. The IV some woman came in and pumped drugs into every few hours. The last time she'd come in, Alyssa had tried to speak to her, tried to get her to call someone on her behalf. But the woman had muttered something in French and studiously avoided her gaze.

Now Alyssa forced her brain to focus. No one was going to help her. No one was going to come for her. She needed to find her own way out.

She tried to swing her legs over the side of the bed, but it was as though they were anchored to the bed. She was no longer restrained, but whatever they were giving her made her limbs so heavy she might as well have been paralyzed. Hot tears squeezed from the corners of her eyes. Why were they doing this to her? What had she ever done to Richard and Louis to bring them to this?

She had a vague memory of someone, something about her father. Right. She knew something about her father, the night he was killed. Or did she? She really didn't think so. But Richard and Louis must have thought otherwise. She had no idea what she knew, and trying to remember made her brain hurt.

She had to get out of there. But she couldn't do that if they kept her loaded with enough drugs to subdue a small elephant. She closed her eyes and focused all her energy into moving her right hand. It took an eternity, but finally her palm made it halfway across her rib cage. She rolled to her side to let gravity help her and was able to reach her left wrist.

Even in her blurry state she knew she had to do this carefully. Her clumsy fingers pulled at the tape holding the needle in a vein in her left wrist. She wondered briefly why it wasn't in her inner arm but brushed the thought aside, needing all her meager brain power if she was going to have a chance at pulling this off. She grasped the needle between fingers that had all the dexterity of two hot dogs and pulled very gently until the needle slipped from her skin.

She very carefully took the tape and placed it back over the needle. Light footsteps sounded outside the door. Alyssa hastily smoothed the tape and tucked her wrist close to her body. She closed her eyes and tried to even out her breathing. She heard the door open, the squeak of rubber-soled shoes on the room's hardwood floor.

The nurse—or whatever she was—adjusted the bag on the IV and straightened out the plastic tubing. Alyssa struggled to keep her breathing steady as she felt liquid drip onto the back of her hand, roll down onto the blanket beneath.

By some miracle, Louis's lackey didn't check the needle. Through cracked lids, Alyssa watched her pull a bottle and syringe from her pocket. She filled the syringe with the liquid and pumped it into the IV line.

Another surge of moisture ran down Alyssa's hand. The trill of a cell phone echoed through the room. The nurse answered, and though Alyssa couldn't understand, it sounded like she was trying to reassure someone. The universal tone of "yes, yes, everything is fine."

Alyssa wondered if it was Louis. Panic gripped her stomach at the thought. She wondered how close he was. When he would be back.

She breathed a sigh of relief as the nurse left. But relief quickly turned to frustration when she realized she could still barely move. Whatever they had given her needed more time to wear off before she could move. She'd managed to avoid one dose. It had to be enough to get her back on her feet long enough to make a break for it. With the wetness rapidly spreading on the blanket, her IV slip wouldn't go unnoticed next time.

If she could only move, she thought she had a decent chance of getting out of there. Though she'd heard a dead bolt slide after the nurse left, no one seemed to be watching her all that closely. Though the passage of time was a little vague, she didn't think the nurse was coming in more than every few hours or so, and she hadn't seen or heard anyone else.

Of course, there was always the possibility that Louis was there waiting, ready to pounce at any time.

The thought spurred her into action. Or, at least, attempted action, as she still couldn't make her legs and arms obey her demands to move. So she craned her head, studying the room, and tried to identify her best options for escape.

There were three windows in the room, none of them

barred. She had no idea what floor she was on. Louis's face flashed in her brain, and she vividly recalled his bruising grip on her breast, the nauseating slide of his hand up her thigh. As soon as she could move she was getting out of there, even if it meant risking a broken neck.

Derek kept his mouth shut, his gaze focused on the dusty skyline of downtown Reno as Ethan piloted the Cessna through its final descent into the Reno airport. Other than his steady communication with the tower, Ethan remained blessedly silent, as he'd been for the entirety of the forty-five-minute flight over the Sierra.

Once Andy had tipped him off about the Tahoe house, it had been a cakewalk to find the address of the Van Weldt family retreat on the northeast shore of Lake Tahoe. According to the building plans, the lodgelike home rested on three secluded acres behind heavy iron gates. The perfect place to hide away.

Or keep someone hidden.

Ethan taxied the plane to a private hangar while Derek checked his gear. In addition to the equipment he would need to disarm the estate's alarm system, he had his Sig Sauer .45 with two extra clips and a Taser capable of delivering a million volts fully charged and ready to go.

If the shit really hit, Derek would rely on the Sig, but he and Ethan had agreed they should do what they could to keep the body count low.

Ethan gave the plane a quick once-over and told the ground crew to turn it around as quickly as possible. "I'm not sure when we'll be back, but we need to be clear to go as soon as we get here."

Derek watched as Ethan checked the clip in his Beretta and slipped it into the shoulder holster he wore under his fleece jacket.

"You know where we're going, right?" Ethan asked as they climbed into the unremarkable sedan that awaited them at the hangar.

"Yep." Derek started the car and focused on following the highway as it changed from straightaway to curvy mountain road. Images kept trying to force their way into his head. He had no idea what he would find. Would she be hurt? Dead?

The very real possibility had been dogging him, twisting his guts in knots since he'd left her place. She could be dead, and he would bear no small blame. Because he hadn't believed her. He'd made his judgment, delivered his verdict. She was a needy, emotional mess, a woman he needed to avoid at all cost no matter how much something in him demanded he grab hold of her and never let go.

Christ. She could be dead already, and one of her last memories of him would be of him summoning every shred of meanness in him to push her away, all because he was too much of a goddamned coward to deal with how she made him feel.

"It's going to be fine," Ethan said, his laser-sharp blue eyes mirroring back Derek's dread. "You're going to find her, and she's going to be fine."

Derek nodded, not believing it for a second. He knew what Ethan was really saying, even if he didn't say it out loud. Derek had to believe Alyssa was fine if he wanted to stay sane, to keep his cool. He did what he always did before a mission. Took all that fear, all that anxiety, all the emotion that held no use for him, and shoved it out of his mind, out of his body. Boxed it up and buried it so deep even he didn't know where to find it.

After the longest thirty-minute drive Derek could ever remember, the heavy iron gates of the Van Weldt estate came into view. Gates shut tight—autumn leaves and pine needles littering the driveway—the place looked deserted. Not surprising, because from what he'd found out, the family used the place only from December to September. After that it was cleaned up and locked up tight for the fall.

A fact Blaylock had obviously counted on. He couldn't risk any surprise visitors popping in and finding Alyssa held captive.

Or dead.

Derek shoved the thought aside as he parked the car several hundred yards from the estate. He and Ethan set out at a swift clip. Late autumn air bit through his lungs, and the scent of pine rose as needles crunched underfoot. It was late afternoon, the brilliant blue mountain sky darkening as the temperature dropped.

Derek pulled a pair of binoculars out of his bag and scanned the front entrance. Two men stood out front, one next to the front door, one closer to the gate but still far enough back to be invisible from the road. He recognized the telltale bulge of shoulder holsters under both men's jackets.

Skirting the main gate, Derek and Ethan bushwhacked their way to the lake. The mansion held prime position on a small private beach. Only one man stood guard out there, a stocky guy of medium height; his gaze was hidden by aviator frames as he stared out at the lake and paced back and forth.

Careful not to pop so much as a pine needle under his foot, Derek made his way through the brush until he came to the edge where brush met sand. He waited for the guard to amble his way back to his position. When he came into reach, Derek reached out and snagged him one-handed. He pressed the Taser to the guy's neck and covered the guy's mouth to muffle his startled grunt. The guy seized as electricity coursed through his body. His eyes rolled back, and he slid to the ground, down for the count. They quickly bound and gagged him and dragged his still-twitching form into the bushes.

Derek had studied the floor plan on the plane and decided their best way in was through the mudroom off the kitchen. He quickly disarmed the alarm system, and the dead bolt slid free. They crept inside, keeping eyes peeled for any sign of Alyssa.

Or anyone else, for that matter. The interior of the house was silent, the only dim light from the fading sun outside.

The place seemed deserted.

Dread clenched at his gut as they moved silently through the empty kitchen, through a formal dining room, great room, and to the main entryway. Still nothing. No lights, no sound to indicate anyone was in the massive log home.

Then he heard it. Ethan's head snapped up, indicating he had, too. The low murmur of voices. A laugh track from a TV. It was coming from a hallway off the main entryway, the one that led to a separate wing. They inched down the hall, and the laugh track grew louder.

They followed the narrow staircase at the end of the hall and paused before passing the open doorway on the right. The TV was in there, blaring some lame sitcom. Over the noise, he heard a feminine giggle and a woman's scolding voice. A man laughed and murmured his reply.

In French.

Abbassi. A red haze filled Derek's vision, and he moved toward the door.

A strong hand wrapped around his forearm, and he met Ethan's warning stare.

Derek drew his gun slowly and held it up in front of him. But when he snuck a glance around the doorjamb, it wasn't Abbassi he saw, but a shorter, slighter guy with slicked-back blond hair. He sat on a love seat next to a woman, murmuring to her as he traced his fingers along her dark cheek and slid his hand along her slim thigh. The woman didn't seem to mind, laughing and playfully slapping at his hands while making no attempt to get away from him.

Derek would have left them to their flirting if two things hadn't tipped him off. One was the nurse's scrubs the woman wore.

The second was the Glock 9mm lying forgotten on the coffee table in front of the couple.

Derek pounced on the gun like a mountain lion, scooping it up before either had time to move. The man sprang to his feet, only to sit back heavily when faced with the barrel of his own gun.

"Where is she?"

The man sneered and spat and said something in French. Derek smashed the butt of the gun against his temple. The woman shrieked as he slumped, unconscious. The scream died in her throat as Derek pressed the barrel of the gun against her forehead. "Alyssa. Where is she?"

The woman threw up her hands and babbled The only word he could make out was *Abbassi.*

"Abbassi put you up to this?" he said as he motioned her up from the couch toward the door.

"Oui, Abbassi. Louis Abbassi." And she was rambling again, no doubt explaining how she was just an innocent bystander and had no guilt whatsoever. As she talked, her hand inched toward the walkie talkie clipped to her waistband. Like a striking snake, Derek snatched it off and tossed it to Ethan.

Derek cocked his gun. "Alyssa. Where is she?"

The woman spared a worried glance for her companion, who lay limp, a trickle of blood tracing down his cheek as Ethan secured his hands and feet with plastic flexicuffs.

Derek lifted the barrel to the center of the woman's forehead. "Where. Is. She?" She damn well understood the intent if not the words because she frantically gestured to the door and took a cautious step.

"Show me," Derek said. Ethan left the bound thug unconscious on the sofa and flanked the woman's right. She led them down the hallway and stopped in front of a door. Though the door was old and weathered, a shiny new dead bolt had been recently installed.

When she reached for her pocket, Derek stopped her with a dig of the gun into her ribs. She froze and lifted her hands while Ethan fished out a key ring. The dead bolt slid free with a soft thunk, and Ethan opened the door. Derek trained his Sig on the woman as he stepped inside, while Ethan stood watch outside in case the guards at the front heard the commotion and came in to investigate.

The room was dim, lit only by a single lamp on the dresser. Derek quickly took in every detail from the rumpled sheets on the twin bed to the IV pole and bag next to it. And no sign of Alyssa.

He whirled on the woman, grabbed a fistful of her scrubs, and slammed her up against the door. "Where the fuck is she?" He punctuated the question with another slam against the door. Her lips were moving, but he couldn't hear her through the rage roaring through his brain. Strong hands gripped his arms, and he registered Ethan's voice shouting his name.

"Derek! Derek! Calm down. I think she went out the window."

He looked across the room as Ethan's words registered. Jesus, he was fucked if he'd missed a big detail like a wide-open window with the cold autumn air blowing in.

He released the woman, who slid down the door in a daze, and sprinted to the window. He peered into the dusky light. His heart lodged somewhere in his throat as he made out the small crumpled figure several feet below. The house was built into a slope, and below the bedroom's window, a small deck jutted out. Below that was another ten or so feet to the ground.

"Alyssa!" He called her name, thought he saw her stir, but couldn't be sure. He swung his legs out the window and jumped, careful not to land on top of her. The deck shook when he landed, and she flinched at the impact, crying out in fear, her arms and legs flailing as she tried to scramble away.

"Alyssa," he said more softly and gathered her against him. Small hands shoved at his chest as she tried to twist away. "Alyssa, it's Derek." She was still out of it, her movements awkward and thick, but she finally registered his voice.

"Derek?" Her cold fingers came up to cup his face.

"Yeah. It's me. I'm here." He swallowed back his fear, his anger, everything. He could lose his shit later. Right now he had to get her out of there.

"What are you doing here?" she slurred as he pulled her tighter against him.

He winced as his arms came into contact with her icy limbs. She wore only a short-sleeved nightshirt, and her feet were bare. The temperature had dropped into the forties after the sun went down. He had no idea how long she'd been out there, but her legs and arms were like ice.

He unzipped his fleece jacket and wrapped it around her and then ran his hands over her cold body to check for any breaks. Other than the drugs, she seemed to be uninjured. He buried his face in her hair and took a long, bracing inhale.

"She okay?" Ethan called down.

"Yeah," Derek said, his voice thick and strained as it pushed past the baseball in his throat. "Take care of Nurse Ratched, and let's get Alyssa the fuck out of here."

"Already taken care of. But someone's trying to get her on the radio, so we need to get out of here before the two meatheads from the front come in to investigate."

Derek hoisted Alyssa in his arms and carried her through the house and met up with Ethan at the side door. They backtracked to the car from the beach and through the woods, Ethan scouting ahead in case anyone showed up unexpectedly.

Derek swallowed back his regret that Blaylock and Abbassi were nowhere to be seen. He relished the chance to tear them both to pieces for what they had planned to do to Alyssa.

"You'll have time for that later, man," Ethan said, hearing Derek's thoughts as clearly as his own. He squeezed Derek's shoulder as he placed Alyssa in the backseat of the sedan. "You got her out. That's the important thing."

Derek nodded. Alyssa curled up in the corner of the backseat and fell asleep, and he couldn't resist reaching out and smoothing her tangled hair back from her face. She was safe. That was all that mattered.

Abbassi's and Blaylock's faces flashed in his brain—Abbassi's smug and slick, Blaylock's bland and weak. He would get them. Soon. But first he needed to get Alyssa someplace safe and make sure she knew Derek would never, ever let anything happen to her again.

The plane was ready to go when they got to the airport. Alyssa roused when Derek lifted her out of the car and buckled her into one of the jet's leather seats.

"I can't believe you came for me," she said, a wide, blurry smile on her face. "I didn't think anyone cared." Her words were slow, slurred, as the drugs worked their way out of her system. "You came for me," she repeated.

His chest constricted, and his throat bubbled with crazy promises, but she fell asleep again before he could vow that he would always come for her; no matter what, he would never leave her alone. He leaned down and kissed her, ran his finger over the thick fringe of eyelashes resting on the high curve of her cheek.

He turned back to get settled in his seat for takeoff and caught Ethan's knowing stare. "You are so fucked, dude," Ethan said with a smirk and a shake of his head.

Derek didn't even bother to argue as he buckled himself

in. "Not as fucked as Abbassi and Blaylock are going to be when I get my hands on them. When we get back, we need to find out everything on both of them and that whole fuckin' family. I want to know what they're hiding that's so goddamn important it's worth killing for."

Andy grabbed another dress off a hanger and shoved it into the duffel bag. There was no way Alyssa's size-two dress would ever fit Andy's substantially larger frame, but Andy knew the dress, along with the other barely worn designer dresses and shoes in the suitcase, would make her a hefty chunk of change on eBay.

Though she already had a sizable sum in her online savings account, thanks to Richard's bonuses, she knew she needed to get every dime she could. She didn't have any doubt Derek Taggart would come after her if she didn't get the hell out of town, and fast.

She grabbed another pair of shoes, shoving away the pinch of guilt when she thought of Alyssa. She hoped Derek was wrong. Richard wouldn't really kill her, would he? She was uneasy not because she really cared about Alyssa—so the world would lose another brainless, useless celebrity who did nothing but take attention from people who really deserved it. No, Andy just didn't want to take any of the blame when a celebrity turned up dead.

She shook off the fear. Even if Alyssa was in serious danger, Derek would get to her in time.

But just in case, she was taking Derek's advice and getting the hell out of Dodge.

A door slammed somewhere in the house. Andy shoved the duffel into the corner of Alyssa's walk-in closet and froze as she heard heavy footsteps echo down the hall. The housekeeper was gone, and Andy wasn't expecting to hear from Richard until tomorrow.

She heard the murmur of low male voices, too low for her to make out the words. Uneasiness curled in her stomach and stung her throat with bile. Was it Derek?

Just remembering the hardness in his dark eyes was enough to make her heart pound with fear. He'd had murder in his eyes when he'd realized the truth about Alyssa. Thank God she'd been able to pull the information about the Tahoe house out of her ass, or she didn't want to think about what he might have done to her.

Fear curdled her insides as she wondered if maybe the Tahoe house was bogus, and now Derek was back to get his revenge.

As quietly as she could, she crept from the closet, intent on making it to the phone on Alyssa's dresser. Andy's own phone was in the living room on the coffee table, useless.

She stepped out of the closet, intent on reaching the phone. The door burst open, and Andy had time only to register wide shoulders filling the doorway before a hand clamped in her hair and slammed her head into the wall.

Her ears rang, and a mewling sound broke from her throat. She struggled to focus, saw a full mouth framed by a pointed goatee, slicked-black hair, and dark eyes that radiated pure evil.

"Louis," she gasped. "What—"

He slammed her head again, cutting her off. "You drugged her. I said she is not to be touched, but you drugged her."

Oh, God. She'd known he had a thing for Alyssa but had no idea it was this bad. "Richard," she gasped. "He told me to. He paid me."

His thin lips curled in a sneer. "He will be dealt with. After I deal with you."

His hand curled around her throat, and her eyes stretched wide in terror. "Please," she whispered, frantic, her voice thready from the increasing pressure of his hand. "Don't hurt me. I'll do whatever you want." She reached out her hand, awkwardly stroking his stomach through his suit jacket. "Anything." Anything to stay alive.

He laughed, an oily, snaky sound that sucked the hope from her soul. "I would not waste my time to fuck a cow like you."

Pressure built in her face, throbbing, until her eyes popped from their sockets. Gasping, choking, her tongue spasming in her mouth. Darkness.

CHAPTER 16

IT WAS PITCH dark when Derek pulled into the garage of the little two-bedroom house tucked off a winding road in the hills above Palo Alto. Up here there were no streetlights, no sidewalks, and the only light came from the half full moon streaming its light through the oak trees obscuring the little house from view. Once a summer retreat for a wealthy San Francisco family, the cottage had been retrofitted and remodeled to accommodate year-round living. Derek and his brothers had bought it a few years ago, partly as a real estate investment, but mostly to use as a safe house should any of their clients need a place to lie low. Ownership was through a dummy corporation that would be nearly impossible to trace back to the Taggarts, unless someone knew where to start.

He was banking on the fact that even when Blaylock and Abbassi found out Derek had Alyssa, they wouldn't have a fucking clue where to start looking.

He would have taken Alyssa there even if he hadn't gotten the alert from Gemini's security network that someone had tried to break into his house. Because Danny was still in La Honda, Derek had asked Alex to check it out after they landed at the airport. "Doesn't look like they touched much of anything," Alex said, "but there was a guy parked in

front of your complex. I called my buddy at the Palo Alto
PD and had him cited for loitering."

Derek had given Ethan a heads-up that Abbassi and Blaylock were already onto them. "Tell Toni to be careful,"
Derek said.

Ethan nodded. "I called Moreno before we left Reno and
told him to go keep an eye on her. She'll be fine." Despite
his brother's casual tone, Derek could see the lines of tension carving deep grooves in his face.

"Sorry to drag you into all this," Derek said.

Ethan gave him a tired half smile. "You did the same
when Toni was in trouble. Now you go take care of your
girl. I'll see you tomorrow."

Ethan's words echoed in his head as he tucked Alyssa
into the queen-size bed that dominated one of the small
bedrooms. She seemed to need sleep more than anything as
she came off of whatever they had given her. Whatever adrenaline rush had propelled her out of bed and out the window
was long spent. She'd slept through the entire plane ride
and drifted off in the car, and though she'd been with it
enough to drink some water and get to the bathroom on her
own, she hadn't raised a finger when he'd carried her to the
bed and tucked her between the sheets.

He left her to sleep and went to the living room to call
Danny, who had called half a dozen times since Derek had
lit out this morning.

"What's the latest?" Derek asked his brother as soon as
Danny answered.

"Why don't you tell me? Somehow I think your day's
been a lot more eventful than mine."

"So nothing, then?"

"Not since you left."

Derek bit back a curse. Hurry up and wait. "How's Dad
doing?"

"Holding on like the rest of us, trying to be patient until

we know for sure. From the way he sounded when I called, he's sharing an intimate evening with a bottle of Ketel One. Now, how 'bout you tell me what the fuck is going on. What's Ethan doing flying your ass over to Reno, and who the fuck is trying to break into your apartment?"

Derek told him what little he knew.

"Why the hell would they want to kidnap and drug her?" Danny asked.

"Got me. All I know is she was being guarded by people who spoke French and mentioned Abbassi by name. And Andy admitted Blaylock paid her to slip Alyssa the drugs. Alyssa knows something, but right now she's too out of it to tell me."

"Yeah, well, call me when you find out what it is," Danny said. He paused. "I hope she's worth it."

Derek thought of the woman asleep in the next room. Her long, light brown hair obscuring her small features. Dressed in the flimsy nightshirt, curled up in his fleece jacket big enough to wrap around her twice. A stabbing pain hit him in the chest, followed by a swelling sensation, like he was being squeezed tight from the inside until he almost couldn't breathe. "Yeah, she is," he managed to grind out before he hung up.

"Hey." A small, hoarse voice croaked from the doorway, and he turned to see Alyssa. She looked ragged and disheveled like a little match girl he'd pulled off the street.

His heart tripped over itself as he took in her pale face and green eyes. Strange impulses surged through him: the need to comfort and console, to strip her down and examine every inch of skin to prove to himself she wasn't hurt. He wanted to rush across the room, snatch her up in his lap, hold her tight, and promise her he'd take care of her and make sure nothing bad ever happened to her again.

But he sat there, paralyzed. *This was not him.* "How are you doing?" was all he managed to say.

She walked over on shaky legs. "Okay, I think. I'm still a little out of it."

She sat down on the couch next to him, and he immediately sprang to his feet. "Are you thirsty? Hungry? The fridge isn't really stocked, but I think I could rustle up a can of soup."

She nodded, watching him with still glazed eyes as he banged around the kitchen. She gulped down the glass of water he gave her and held it out for a refill.

"Where are we?" she asked as they waited for the can of soup to heat on the stovetop. She gave a soft little laugh. "For that matter, where were we?"

He tried for a reassuring smile, even as the thought of where she'd been and what could have happened made his blood bubble with murderous rage. "They took you to the family compound on Lake Tahoe. They had you hooked to an IV."

"Right, right." She nodded as if shaking the memories back in place. "I pulled the IV out sometime earlier."

He poured the soup into an oversize mug, and she accepted it with a grateful smile.

"That was smart, especially considering how messed up you were."

"They were going to kill me," she said softly. "Not right away, but I heard them talking about it. I knew I had to get out of there."

He wanted to ask her more about what she'd heard, why they'd taken her in the first place, but she'd turned her attention fully to the steaming mug. She spooned in a mouthful of the soup and then another and another in quick succession until the cup was drained. "Chicken and stars," she said, smiling in lazy satisfaction. "My favorite. It's been a while since I ate."

He nodded and refilled her mug. She was starving, exhausted, overwhelmed, and still working everything out of her system. Tomorrow would be soon enough to press her for answers.

She drained her second mug of soup as quickly as the first and then sat back in her chair and opened her mouth in a jaw-cracking yawn. "I couldn't figure out why I was so tired and out of it all the time," she said, almost as though to herself. "Now I know why the coffee Andy brought me never perked me up," she added with a little laugh.

Derek tried to muster up a smile of his own but couldn't. As much as he admired her humor in the face of such a messed-up situation, he didn't find anything funny about an innocent woman being drugged without her knowledge.

Especially a woman he'd realized he was ready to kill or die for to keep her safe.

He shoved the thought aside. He didn't have the energy to go head to head with the crazy, swirling mess of emotions Alyssa conjured inside him. "There's shampoo and stuff in the bathroom, if you want to take a shower," he said.

She nodded and wrinkled her nose. "Probably not a bad idea, I've been sweating and shivering in this gown for the past twenty-four hours."

Alyssa pushed back from the table, her movements slow and careful, but much, much steadier. Derek felt his tension ease a notch at the evidence of the drugs wearing off. He followed her down the short hallway and retrieved a couple towels from the linen closet. Then he rummaged through the dresser in the bedroom and pulled out a T-shirt and a pair of sweats from the stash of extras they kept in the house.

She took them with a little smile and started for the bathroom. He caught her wrist before she could close the door. "Call me if you need any help."

Her smile broadened, and a knowing glint appeared in her now clear eyes. "I'll let you know if there's anything I can't reach."

The words went straight to his dick as she shut the door in his face. Now that she was safe and well on her way back to normal, fear had loosened its grip on his libido. The driving desire and sexual heat that dogged him whenever he got within a few feet of her released in a flood. He heard the shower turn on and tortured himself with images of her naked under the hot spray, soap-slicked hands running over her sleek curves.

His fingers curled around the doorknob as he struggled not to bust in, tear his own clothes off, and join her in the tiny shower stall. His cock throbbed insistently behind the fly of his cargo pants. Now that she was safe, he wanted nothing so much as to run his hands and mouth over every square inch of her, drive himself inside her, lose himself in her incredible heat.

He forced his fingers to let go of the doorknob. After what she'd been through, the last thing she needed was for him to go after her like the Neanderthal she'd once called him. And after the way he'd treated her last time . . . The lump in his throat was joined by one in the pit of his stomach at the memory of his harsh words and harsher actions.

Sure, she was grateful to him for coming after her. But gratitude went only so far, and there was no way in hell she'd ever let him near her again.

He forced himself from his post at the door and retreated to the kitchen, rummaging through the cabinets, grunting in satisfaction when he found what he needed. Tequila wasn't his drink of choice, but it was the only hard liquor in the place, and Derek damn well needed something to take the edge off.

He slugged down two fingers and went to pour himself another drink, pausing when he heard the bathroom door open and close. Alyssa padded into the kitchen in bare feet, the rest of her swallowed up by the T-shirt and sweatpants. Her long hair spilled down her back, leaving dark wet spots on the shoulders and neckline of the green T-shirt. She should have looked ridiculous, clownlike. But all Derek could think about was all that warm, silky skin hidden under the sizes-too-big clothes.

He tossed back the second shot. "You should go get some rest."

She nodded, her eyes big and somber. "I just wanted to say thank you," she said softly and then gave a little laugh. "God, that's so inadequate for what you did—"

"It was no big deal," he started.

She marched over to him and smacked him across the chest. He flinched more out of surprise than pain. "Don't say that!" Her eyes went wet. "No one was coming for me! No one. I was set up by people I trusted. No one believed I was in trouble. And no one was going to come for me." Her hand reached out, shaking a little, and covered his. The warmth of her fingers penetrated his skin, sent a shot of heat straight through him. "You came for me." She strained up on her tiptoes and pressed a kiss to his jaw. "Thank you."

He couldn't stop himself from pulling her into his arms. "I'll always come for you."

Alyssa sniffed a little and slid her lips across his chin until they covered his mouth. It was a sweet kiss, a soft brush of her lips, given in gratitude, but Derek's body reacted like she'd shoved her tongue down his throat. He opened his lips over hers and swept his tongue inside her mouth, feeling something break open at the first taste.

He lifted her onto the kitchen counter so he could have better access to her lips, cheeks, throat. All the emotions she whipped up in him roared free and went pulsing through his blood. All the desire, the tenderness, the gut-deep need to hold her, taste her, take her, twisted and churned, and he couldn't have bottled them back up even if he'd wanted to.

He settled his hips between her legs, kissing her over and over, and he knew he was toast. He, the big tough warrior who thought nothing of blowing a man's head off if it was

what the mission required, had his ass handed to him by a
sweet little slip of a woman who couldn't have weighed
more than a buck ten.

As her lips parted under his, her tongue making greedy
forays into his mouth, he couldn't have cared less. With her
arms wrapped around his shoulders and the peachy-sweet
taste of her filling his mouth, he willingly released the reins
on his control and admitted total defeat.

He dragged the T-shirt up over her head, sucking in his
breath at the sight of her perfect little tits with their berry-
red nipples pulled into hard peaks.

"I will never get tired of seeing you naked," he murmured before bending his head to suck one hard tip into his
mouth. "You are so fucking beautiful you make me insane."

He pulled back to look at her and felt his insides ice over
when he saw the finger-shaped bruises on her right breast.
"Who did this?"

She looked down, startled by his harsh tone. "Louis," she
choked out.

A thousand horrifying possibilities raced through his
head. "Did he—" He couldn't force the word past his lips.

She shook her head. "He didn't rape me."

The breath he didn't realize he was holding whooshed
out of his chest. "I'm going to kill him," he said, his voice
icy with rage.

"I don't want to think about him right now," she murmured and leaned forward to kiss his neck. She tugged at
his shirt and ran her hands up his torso. "I'm safe with you
now. That's what matters."

She slid her hands under his shirt, and the hot glow of her
touch made him shake with the force of his mingled rage
and need.

"He'll never come near you again, I swear," he murmured against her cheek as he tugged his shirt over his

head. He pulled her close, a shudder of pure bliss running through him at the sensation of silky warm skin meeting hair-roughened muscles. For several seconds he just held her there, reveling in her soft heat and the rapid beat of her heart against his.

He took a deep breath and pressed a kiss to the crown of her head. He was raging, his cock rock hard with the need to sink inside Alyssa's body, but he forced himself to pull back, slow down.

She deserved better than a fast, hard screw on the kitchen counter. He wanted to give her more than that, needed to show her how much he wanted her, cared for her.

Fucking worshipped her.

He scooped her up and carried her to the bedroom, his mouth never leaving hers as he settled her against the pillows and came down over her. He savored her mouth with slow, openmouthed kisses, his tongue exploring every sweet corner. "Mmmm." The low sound of satisfaction vibrated up his throat. "So sweet," he murmured, tracing his tongue down the delicate line of her throat and then back up. "Sweet little peach."

She laughed at that, threading her fingers in his hair so she could pull his mouth up to hers. "I'm not that sweet."

He sucked her tongue softly between his lips, relishing the hot little sounds she made in the back of her throat. "It's true," he insisted, covering her breast with a soft squeeze. "Every time I kiss you, I taste sweet"—he captured her mouth again—"juicy"—he bent his head and sucked her nipple into his mouth—"peaches."

Alyssa moaned and arched against his lips, emitting a soft "ooh" when he drew on her with firmer pressure. "Must be my lip gloss," she protested weakly.

Derek gave her nipple one last lick and pushed up until they were nose to nose. "You're not wearing lip gloss," he said and traced her lips with the very tip of his tongue. "And you still taste like peaches." His palm coasted over her breasts, down the flat plane of her belly. He caught the waistband of the sweatpants and tugged, his fingers sliding low to cup her slick heat. "Everywhere."

She rocked her hips against his hand, and his eyes almost crossed at the silky hot feel of her.

"So juicy and delicious," he murmured as he traced a path of kisses down her chest and stomach. "You make me want to eat you up."

The light, teasing bedroom banter was new for him, but even more unfamiliar was the primitive need they concealed. He'd never felt this drive to claim a woman, consume her, mark every inch of her until there was no doubt she belonged to him.

He tugged the sweatpants off and ran his hands up the slim line of her legs. His mouth followed. He paused to set his teeth over the firm muscle of her calf, to lick the creamy smoothness of her inner thigh.

But even that sweet spot was nothing compared to the musky peach perfection of her pussy. Smooth and sweet and glistening with need, her sex lured him in like a hothouse flower unfurling petals in deepening shades of pink. The scent of her arousal rushed through him, hardening his cock another inch as he ground his hips against the sheets. But as much as he wanted to sink inside her, to feel the sweet stretch and slide of her taking him deep, he wanted her pleasure more. Wanted to show her with his hands and mouth how good he could make her feel.

How sorry he was for the other times he'd hurt her.

He wanted to tell her everything she needed to know with his body because he wasn't sure he'd ever be able to find the words.

Derek hooked her knees over his shoulders and stroked her open with a sweep of his thumbs. He licked his lips in anticipation and buried his mouth against her. His tongue traced firm circles around her clit, licked down her slit to thrust inside. A surge of wetness bathed his tongue, and he groaned, nearly coming in his pants.

He sucked her clit between his lips, drawing on the wet little berry until she was digging her fingers into the sheets and rocking her hips against his face. He focused on her pleasure, drawing on every memory of what she liked, how she wanted to be touched, to push her higher. He didn't want to tease or torment. This time he wanted to give her everything she wanted as many times as she needed.

Her hips rocked against his mouth, her fingers tightened in his hair. He sucked her harder, quickened the strokes of his tongue as her movements became more frantic. He pushed his middle finger inside her, pressing in and up until he found the little bundle of nerves. He groaned as a high "ah, ah" sound came from her throat.

Goddamn he loved that sound, he thought as her pussy pulsed around his fingers and her whole body shuddered in orgasm.

Loved it so much he was determined to hear it again.

And again.

"Derek," she said and flinched away when his tongue snaked out, gunning for fourths, "please. I can't anymore."

"Now, that sounded like a challenge," he said and flattened his palms against her inner thighs to keep her still.

"It wasn't," she said and tugged weakly at his hair. He reluctantly pushed up, letting her pull him up her body. He rolled to the side, resting on the pillow next to her as she regarded him with sleepy green eyes. Her entire body was flushed with satisfaction, glowing and radiating heat like she was lit from within.

He felt his lips curl into a smile.

"I'd tell you not to look so smug," she said around a yawn, "but that was . . . that was . . ." Her eyes drifted closed, and she was quiet so long he thought maybe she'd fallen asleep.

Then her eyelids fluttered open, and her mouth pulled into an answering smile. Her hand traced over the waistband of the cargo pants he still wore. He hissed in pleasure as she traced the hard ridge of his erection.

"I'm afraid I don't have enough energy to do much more than lie here," she said with an apologetic sigh.

His dick pulsed against her hand, greedy to feel the same hot yielding of flesh his fingers had just experienced. "Go to sleep, baby," he murmured.

"But you didn't . . ." Her palm was slack on his fly, her eyes already drifting closed.

He pressed a kiss to each eyelid and then to her soft pink mouth. "This time was all for you, all about making you feel good."

She let out a satisfied purr and nuzzled her face deeper into the pillow.

Almost immediately her breathing turned deep and even. Careful not to disturb her, Derek shucked his pants, sighing in relief as his cock sprang free from the heavy fabric to tent out the front of his boxers.

He gathered Alyssa close and pulled the sheets up over them, his dick throbbing as her smooth thigh slid in between his. Still, as much as his body ached for release, lying here, holding Alyssa, sleeping and sated from the orgasms he'd given her, was more satisfying than anything else he could ever remember.

He was so gone over this woman he was lucky he still knew his own name.

Gray dawn light filtered in through a crack in the drapes when Alyssa woke again. She'd slept hard, deep and dreamless, and for the first time in several days she didn't feel like she was swimming through layers of cotton as she struggled to wake up.

The drugs have worn off. With that realization came a flood of memories from the past two days. Helpless in the bed, strapped to an IV as they pumped drugs into her. Hopeless, certain no one knew what was happening, no one would come for her.

But Derek . . .

She closed her eyes and snuggled closer to the man sleeping beside her. He slept curled around her, his front to her back, his arm banded around her waist as though he was afraid she'd disappear. She'd never felt so safe. Like no one could get to her, no one could hurt her as long as he was close.

He came for me.

I'll always come for you.

The memory of his words rushed through her. She traced the back of his palms, his long, strong fingers. Heat flowed through her, emanating from her belly, pooling between her thighs, down her legs, tingling in her toes and fingertips. Something had changed in him. It was in the way he looked at her, the closed, hard look gone from his dark eyes.

And the way he touched her, like his whole world depended on making her feel good.

She arched back against him, her mouth curling in a smile when she felt the thick weight of his cock nudging against the curve of her ass. Poor man hadn't gotten off before, he'd been so busy with her.

Alyssa rolled to face him. She buried her face in his throat, inhaled his clean, musky scent. Her tongue flicked out to taste the salty skin. He mumbled and shifted onto his back.

She stripped back the covers, her body so hot she didn't notice the early morning chill. Her mouth went dry, and her pussy went wet as she took a moment to admire the mountain of tan skin and hard muscles sleeping in bed next to her. Her gaze ran greedily over him, from his dark, sun-streaked hair to his big feet, coming to rest on the enormous erection tenting out the front of his boxers.

Without hesitation she reached down and tugged at the waistband of his boxers until his cock sprang free, long and thick with a plump head that begged for her mouth to close over it.

She settled between his legs and gripped him at the base, holding him still for her kiss. Her lips closed over the thick, smooth head, her tongue tracing around the rim as she explored. Her mouth filled with his hot, salty taste, and she opened her lips wider to see how much of him she could take. She sucked him deep until he pressed against the back of her throat and then slid back again. A fresh wash of moisture bathed her sex as she felt him grow even bigger.

She sensed the instant he woke up, the hitch in his breathing, the new tension in his thigh muscles. She looked up to see him watching her with hot, dark eyes, a dimple creasing his cheek as his mouth pulled into a tight smile. "Hell of a wakeup call."

She let his cock slide free of her lips. "I aim to please." She kept her eyes locked on his as she ran her tongue up and down his shaft, swirled it against the head, and ran it over the slit at his tip.

His head fell back on the pillow, and a groan bellowed from his chest. The heavy weight of his hand stroked over her head; his fingers slipped through her hair. Every sinew in Derek's body was strung tight as he held himself still. The only movement came from the heaving of his rib cage as his breath sawed in and out, the clenching of his fingers in the sheets.

Alyssa had never gotten so turned on just from going down on a guy. But hearing Derek moan her name, feeling his cock twitch against her lips and tongue as she stroked and sucked, intensified the hot pulse between her thighs to a nearly painful pitch. She felt powerful, like she had a barely tamed animal under her spell. Like any minute he would lose control and go wild.

She wanted him wild.

She sucked him deeper, increasing the friction with her lips and her pumping fist as her other hand came up to cup the heavy weight of his balls. He shifted, spreading his legs wider as his moans grew louder.

His cock swelled in her mouth, rigid as steel. His balls tightened as his orgasm bore down.

"Fuck," he said. "Alyssa. I'm going to—if you don't want me to—" The words strangled in his throat as Alyssa sucked him as deep as she could and pumped him with her fist. Hot, thick spurts bathed her tongue as he groaned and shuddered, her name sounding like it was ripped from his chest as he yelled it up to the ceiling.

She didn't release him until the last pulse faded, kissing the tip of his slightly softened cock before she let him drag her up his body. He captured her mouth, sucking her tongue between her lips as his fingers threaded in her hair to keep her still.

"The things you do to me," he murmured. "I don't know what it is about you, but you rip me to pieces every single time."

That didn't sound very good. But Derek didn't seem to have a problem with it, pulling her close, devouring her mouth with the intensity of a man who had not come less than a minute ago.

He pulled her on top of him, and she felt his cock, rock hard, thick as a club, nudging against her belly. She drew back on a surprised gasp. "Aren't you supposed to, like, recover or something?"

He laughed and ground himself more firmly against her. "Not with you. See that? You make me defy the rules of human biology." A slightly disgruntled expression crossed his face. "And I don't know if you noticed, but I'm all about following the rules."

She couldn't help but laugh. This was a different side of Derek, teasing her, poking fun at himself. Like he was finally letting down the iron curtain he'd been so careful to keep between them.

She cautioned herself not to read too much into it.

Her breath hitched in concert with his when he slid his hands between her thighs and found her slick and ready.

"You're so wet, just from sucking my cock," he marveled as he took her mouth in a hot kiss. "My sweet, juicy little peach," he murmured, making her gasp as his fingers traced her damp slit. "So ready for me." He buried his head against her neck and stroked the tip of his cock against her belly. "And I'll never get enough of you."

Alyssa tried to tell herself it was nothing, meaningless sex talk. But that didn't stop the twisting, falling sensation, like she'd just been heaved off a cliff into open space.

And she could only pray Derek would be there to catch her when she landed.

CHAPTER 17

THE LOOK IN Alyssa's eyes made Derek's chest ache like he'd been punched. Open, trusting, looking up at him like there was no greater joy in the world than being here with him right now.

It was scarier than being trapped on low ground on an open mountainside in enemy territory.

The only thing scarier was the certainty that her look mirrored his own. The instinct to shut it down, block it off, reared inside him.

Only to be swatted down as she cupped his face in her hands and pulled him close, kissing him so hot and sweet he felt like she wanted to consume him even as she offered up everything of herself, his for the taking.

He sank onto the bed, rolling to his side and pulling her flush against him. He reached down and hooked her knee over his hip. His cock nestled, ramrod hard against the smooth skin of her belly. He kissed her, sucking her tongue into his mouth, tasting himself on her. He was glad he'd already come, or that would have been enough to set him off like a Roman candle.

He wrapped one arm around her back, cupping her face in his other hand. He couldn't get enough of her mouth, her skin, her taste, and this time he didn't even try to pretend he didn't want her to the point of obsession.

He kissed his way down her neck, over the curve of her shoulder, over the baby-soft skin of her inner arm. He explored every inch of her, skimming his lips over her palm, sucking her fingers into his mouth.

He licked and nibbled his way over her legs, knees, and thighs, urging her to roll over. She squirmed and sighed as he ran his open mouth up the backs of her legs to the soft curve of her ass. Derek gave her left buttock a gentle nip, laughing at her little squeal.

Then, higher up on the curve of her hip he saw the dark, smudgelike marks on her skin. Bruises. In the shape of fingertips.

His laughter choked in his throat, and everything in him froze. He'd been horrified, homicidal when he saw the marks Abbassi had left on her breast.

But Abbassi hadn't done this.

Derek squeezed his eyes shut, trying to force away the memory of the last time he'd been with Alyssa. But he vividly remembered pulling her to her knees, holding her hips in a too tight grip as he took her, hating her in that moment for making him lose control.

He ran shaking fingers over the mark, hating himself now.

Alyssa's muscles tightened, channeling his tension. "What's wrong? That's a weird place for my bikini waxer to have missed a spot."

She wiggled her ass enticingly, and Derek swallowed hard, not sure whether he wanted to laugh or cry at her attempt at humor. Fuck, he didn't deserve to be in the same room with her, much less naked in bed with her, touching every last inch of her like he had a right to.

"Derek?" she said again, this time pushing up on her elbows to peek over her shoulder, a hint of worry in her wide eyes.

He shook his head, the bitter words sticking in his throat, choking him. "I'm sorry," he finally managed.

She twisted until she was mostly on her back and could look up at him. "What for?" she asked, her arched brown brows pulling into a vee over the bridge of her nose.

"Last time I saw you—was with you . . ." He paused. Christ, he sucked at this. "The way I talked to you, the things I did to you—"

"Like you said, not like I didn't like it," she said, color blooming in her cheeks as she ran a hand down his chest.

He leaned down and kissed her. "Don't let me off the hook," he whispered, groaning when her tongue licked inside his mouth. "I don't deserve it."

"You saved my life yesterday," she said, kissing him harder. "As far as I'm concerned, that goes a long way in making up for any past infractions." She curled her hands over his shoulders and gave him a little push. "I'm ready to call it even in exchange for your body."

Derek felt hot pressure in the backs of his eyes, humbled by her willingness to forgive him so easily.

He pasted a grin on his face as he rolled to his back and spread his arms wide, willing to take whatever punishment she wanted to dish out. She climbed him like a mountain, straddling his hips, her small hands planted on his chest like a conquering warrior queen.

"Give me all you've got. I can take it."

She rocked her hips, rubbing her slick core against the hard muscles of his stomach. "Brace yourself, baby, cause I'm going to rock your world."

Alyssa looked down at Derek's grinning face, the dimples carving deep grooves in his cheeks, and thought for a moment that her heart might explode. She ran her hands over his chest, feeling every nerve come alive as his gaze raked over her, palpable as a touch. She'd never had sex like this,

going from sweet and sultry to funny and raunchy and back
again in a split second.

He was so different from before, the way he touched her,
the way he looked at her. The urgency was still there, in the
slight tremor of his hand as they did slow sweeps over her
breasts, hips, and back, in the way his dark eyes simmered
behind his thick lashes. But there was none of the restraint,
none of the anger from before.

No warnings to stay out of his head. No attempts to pretend this was nothing more than a cold, casual fuck.

He was anything but cold, his cock surging against her
inner thigh, rock hard and firey hot. She hitched her hips
lower until he was nestled against her pussy. She leaned over
until her nipples brushed his lips and slid herself up and
down the rigid shaft. He sucked her nipple into his mouth
on a groan, not bothering to tease or pretend he didn't
know exactly what she wanted.

Her breath caught as he licked and suckled, letting her
rub against him, offering up his big body for her pleasure.
She ground against him, so close to coming she knew it
would take little more than one flick of his thumb over her
clit, one more hard pull of her nipple.

But she wanted him inside her, needed to feel the thick
stretch and slide as she slid down his cock.

"Please tell me you have a condom somewhere in this
house," she panted, arching into his palm as he covered one
breast.

"Toiletry kit," he said, his voice muffled by her breast.
"In my gym bag—sitting on the couch."

"Don't move," she said and pushed herself off the bed.

He let out a weak chuckle. "I don't think I have enough
blood in my legs to walk," he said, gesturing with a grin at
his cock, which stood straight, purple veins pulsing and engorged.

She could relate. Her legs were weak and rubbery as she

trotted across the room, but she retrieved the toiletry bag in record time and extracted three foil packets. She tossed two on the nightstand and tore open the third. She smoothed the latex over him, licking her lips as the hard muscles of his abs rippled under his hair-dusted skin.

He was all brawny muscle, sinew, and bone, without an ounce of fat or an inch of softness. Shifting and straining under her like a barely tamed jungle cat. But his calloused hands were so gentle as he helped her balance over him, caressing her waist, cupping her ass as she fit his cock against the mouth of her sex. She sank down on him, so wet, so soft, so ready she took all of him in one smooth, downward slide.

"You are so fucking beautiful," he said, the last word dissolving into a groan as she slid up and down experimentally. She'd never been particularly fond of being on top, always paranoid about her performance. Was her rhythm working for him? Was she going too fast? Too slow?

But Derek was content to let her find her groove, groaning and whispering encouragement as she sank up and down, circling her hips so her clit bumped his pubic bone with every downstroke.

"That's it, baby," he said, cupping her ass as she took him so deep she could again feel him at the base of her spine. "Take me, take all of me." She spread her knees wide, ground herself against him, feeling the pleasure tighten and coil between her legs.

The room echoed with harsh groans, panting breaths, and the sound of sweat-slick skin meeting skin as she rode him hard. Derek lifted his hips off the bed, meeting her at every stroke, pulsing and pounding inside her as he pushed her to the edge. One big hand slid down her stomach and came to rest at the top of her mound. He burrowed the pad of his thumb between her pussy lips, stroking and circling her clit, and lifted his head to suck her nipple into his mouth. She tightened around him, her inner muscles clenching and rippling over the hard shaft of his cock.

It was too much, his hand and mouth on her, his cock buried so deep inside it was like he was trying to climb inside her body. The knot of pleasure pulled tighter, tighter before it finally snapped, sending pulses of release rippling through her. She ground her hips against him, holding him deep as she rode it out until she collapsed against him like a blissed-out rag doll.

Derek rolled her to her back and came down over her, cupping her face and covering her mouth. He rocked his hips against her, barely moving as he savored the last flutters of her orgasm. He licked into her mouth, tasting her moans, absorbing every detail of her pleasure. He reached down and hooked her knee over his hip. He'd never felt like this before, like he couldn't get close enough, couldn't get deep enough.

And this time instead of running from the need like a chicken-shit coward, he pulled her tighter, kissed her harder, fucked her deeper until he thought his head was going to explode from the pleasure. And still he staved off his release, never wanting to stop, never wanting to let her go, never wanting to leave the molten heat of her beautiful body.

But he couldn't hold off forever, not with her sliding her hot little hands down his back to cup his ass, wrapping her sleekly muscled legs around his hips to hug him close. He heard a low, animal keening, a sound of agonizing pain—or pleasure. He realized on some distant level it was him, but couldn't hold back his own deep, desperate groans as he surged inside her gloving warmth. His thigh muscles tensed, his balls went tight, and then he was blown into about a million pieces, every atom jerking and twitching in pleasure as he emptied himself inside her. She tightened around him, milking him in firm strokes that made his eyes cross and roll back in his head as she drained him of every last drop.

This woman is mine. The thought came out of nowhere, shot through his brain, took hold in his gut and wouldn't let go.

He collapsed down on the pillow beside her, waiting a few seconds to catch his breath before he got up to take off the condom. He poured them a glass of water to share and brought it back to bed. She drained it with a grateful smile and curled up against him, her head on his chest as she trailed her fingers along his skin.

He lay back and waited for the panic to set in, the need to flee that inevitably hit him after sex. Especially sex with her.

This time he was determined to beat it back, not about to do that to her again. But to his shock, as he searched his brain, all he found there was bone-deep contentment. The feeling that, even with all the shit they needed to deal with, there was nowhere in the world he needed to be, nothing he needed to be doing.

She nuzzled her face against his neck, sending an electric current through his nerve endings. His cock made a valiant attempt to rouse. Failed miserably. Derek felt a tired grin stretch his face.

Alyssa propped herself up on his chest and traced his lips with a soft fingertip. "I like it when you smile. You should do it more often."

He sucked her finger between his lips, swiped the tip with his tongue before releasing it. "You make me smile," he said and felt his face heat at how cheesy that sounded. But true, whether he liked it or not.

"I love you," she said.

His breath seized, his heart jerked, and he felt like he'd taken a round to the chest.

"Don't look so horrified," she said with a laugh. "It's not like I expect you to say it back."

"Oh. Good." He winced at the hurt that filled her eyes and tightened her mouth. "I didn't mean that like it sounded." He grimaced, scrambling for something to say. He sure as shit wasn't ready to say it back. Probably wouldn't be even if he did feel the same.

Which he didn't.

Did he?

No. Absolutely not. He cared about her. A lot. And liked her, too, way more than he ever would have expected. But he didn't do love. Not even with a surprisingly sweet celebrity heiress who made him grin like a fool and want her so much it tore his guts out.

"Don't worry." She smoothed her thumb over his frown and leaned down to kiss him. "I don't have any expectations. But with everything going on, I wanted to be sure to tell you. You know, in case anything happens."

Her words brought everything back into vicious focus, reminding him that for all they were enjoying the hell out of themselves and fucking like a couple minks, reality loomed, hard and cold, outside the bedroom doors. A reality where people wanted his woman dead.

"Nothing is going to happen." His tone was harsher than he intended, so he kissed her to soften the blow. But what was supposed to be a soft, comforting kiss turned into something hungry and claiming as everything in him rebelled at the thought of Blaylock or Abbassi or anyone else getting their hands on her again. His arms tightened around her so hard she gasped, but he couldn't make himself loosen his hold. "I'm not going to let anything happen to you." He couldn't remember the last time he'd promised anything to a woman, but this was a vow he intended to keep.

* * *

Alyssa fell back asleep quickly, snuggled in Derek's muscled embrace. She drifted in and out, smiling every time she woke up and still felt Derek's warm, solid presence beside her. Her body was tired and sore, and she was content to lie in bed with him for the next week or so. Having sex, making love, whatever you wanted to call how he used his hands and lips and cock to melt her into a sugary puddle of bliss.

Then this. Sleeping next to him, his arm curled around her like he didn't want to stop touching her, even in sleep. Unlike all the other times when he couldn't get away from her fast enough, now he couldn't get her close enough.

I love you. She didn't want to say it out loud again and have to see the tight, anxious look on his face. She didn't regret saying it—not at all. It was important for people to know they were loved. With no conditions and no expectations.

But she knew how this went. Even with no expectations on her side, she knew the more she said it the more she'd want to hear it back. Until not hearing it would eat at her like tiny vermin nibbling away until she got smaller and started wondering what was so wrong with her that no one could love her back.

She shoved the self-pity aside. Whether he said the words or not, she knew he cared for her, more than a lot of the guys who had professed to be in love with her. None of them would have questioned her family and risked their lives to come after her.

That had to count for something.

She dozed off again, waking to find his legs between hers as he slid into her from behind. He eased in slowly, plucking at her nipples, dipping his fingers in her folds to rub her clit till she was flooded with heat and slick with need. He fucked her slow and deep, making her come twice before he finally groaned against her neck and stiffened behind her.

When she woke again, bright afternoon sun streamed

through the drapes, cutting across the carpet and the bedspread to catch them directly in the face.

"I guess we better get up," Derek mumbled.

Alyssa sat up and swung her legs over the side of the bed, wincing at the pull of overused muscles and the slight ache between her thighs. As she headed for the bathroom she saw him grab his phone. She could hear the low rumble of him talking as she stepped under the spray.

The shower curtain whipped back just as she was rinsing her hair. She squealed in protest as Derek climbed inside, crowding her against the slick tile wall as he took up all the space.

"You're unbelievable," she said on a breathless giggle when she felt him, once again rock hard against her stomach. But she didn't resist when he pulled her on her tiptoes for his kiss and ran his soap-slicked hands all over her body.

She flinched a little when his hand slid between her thighs. Even the gentle touch was too much for her tender flesh.

"You're sore, aren't you, baby?" he murmured, easing up until his fingers barely hovered over her.

"A little," she said apologetically. "I think I've gotten more action in the last five days than I have in the last five years." She buried her face against his chest, not wanting to lose contact even if she couldn't have sex. "What are you doing?" she said when he knelt down in front of her.

He shot her a devilish grin, sexier than sin as the water ran down the hard lines of his face and even harder lines of his body. "I'm going to kiss you all better."

"You don't—" Her words locked in her throat as his lips and tongue slid over her in a touch that was as soothing as it was viciously arousing. "You don't have to—" she tried again, the protest lost in a moan as his tongue thrust deep.

"I want to," he said, the soft, sucking sounds of his lips bouncing off the tile and driving her insane. "I love going down on you, licking you, sucking you off. Tasting your

pussy is almost as good as fucking it." Another sucking caress. "Your hot peach juice running over my tongue. I want
to drink up every last drop."

He kept whispering to her between sucks and licks, hot,
filthy things that made her face flame and her body melt. If
it had been anyone else she would have been embarrassed and
turned off. But the way he touched her, the way he talked to
her, was different. Like something had finally busted free inside him until he couldn't hold himself back.

She threaded her fingers in his wet hair, pulled him closer,
needing him, wanting him, loving him as he took her over
the edge and sent her hurtling off into space.

When Alyssa came back to herself she urged him to his feet,
pulling his face up for her kiss. He stood under the spray, his
wide shoulders nearly spanning the width of the tub. Water
rippled over him, streaming down his torso, washing over
his jutting cock.

She closed her fist around him, squeezed him from root
to tip. He closed his hand over hers. "I'm fine. You don't
have to."

She ignored him and grabbed the bottle of hair condi-
tioner resting in the corner of the tub. She poured some into
her palm and slicked it over him, smiling in satisfaction as
every muscle tensed and he let out a rough curse.

"Show me," she said, pumping him in her fist. "Show me
how fast and how hard."

He covered her hand, his grip desperate, almost painful
as he showed her how he liked to be stroked. She kissed his
chest, flicking her tongue over his flat, dark nipples.

He let go of her hand, and she kept up the pace, squeezing and pumping as her other hand cupped and caressed his
balls. She watched, enthralled as the head got thicker and
darker, pearls of precome beading at the tip.

She looked up to find him watching her through slitted

eyes, his lips parted and swollen as his breath came in tearing pants. "Christ," he breathed. "Alyssa. Jesus."

She felt him throb, pumping like a heartbeat in her hand. Thick jets of come erupted over her hand. As he watched, shaking like a broken horse, she lifted her hand and delicately licked a thick, salty drop into her mouth.

He lifted her off her feet and pinned her to the wall so he could kiss her. She felt him fumble with the faucet. The water shut off, and he lifted her out of the tub, grabbing haphazardly at towels as he half dragged, half carried her into the hallway.

"You keep messing with me, little girl." He chuckled. "And you are going to get yourself in all kinds of trouble."

"Yeah, well, if you don't put some pants on, we're all going to be blinded by the whiteness of your ass."

They both froze as the deep male voice cut through Alyssa's sexual fog.

"Shit," Derek said, using his body to block her from view as he wrapped a towel first around her and then around himself. Satisfied she was covered, he moved so she had an unimpeded view of the two men and a woman standing in the living room of the safe house.

CHAPTER 18

THE WOMAN SPOKE first, offering Alyssa a tentative smile. "I'm Toni," she said, pretending Alyssa and Derek weren't soaking wet, naked, and about to do it in the hallway. But Toni's porcelain complexion wouldn't let her disguise her embarrassment. "Sorry we busted in at a bad time."

Alyssa decided to brazen it out, offering her hand to Toni, who was enviably tall and curvy with a striking Snow White–meets punk-rock-look. "Alyssa Miles. No worries. Not like most of the world hasn't already seen me naked."

Toni smiled and hefted the shopping bag slung over her arm. "Well, if you want to cover up, Derek asked me to bring you some clothes."

"Thanks." Alyssa reached out and stroked Derek's arm, touched by his thoughtfulness.

He nodded and moved away, his cheeks flushing deep red under the scrutiny of the two men. Heat flooded her own face as she met their inquisitive stares.

The first she recognized as Derek's brother Ethan. Though she'd been drifting in and out of consciousness the day before, Derek's twin had a face that was impossible to forget. And not only because it resembled Derek's so strongly.

With his dark hair, crystal-blue eyes and physique rivaled only by Derek and the other man, Ethan undoubtedly made an impression on every heterosexual female who got within ten feet of him. He flashed her a grin that might have melted her panties if she'd been wearing any and greeted her with a wave of his big, tanned hand. "Good to see you back on your feet."

The other man stood with his thumbs hooked in the waistband of his cargo pants. His black T-shirt stretched across about an acre of muscled chest, the sleeves struggling to accommodate the swell of biceps that were as big around as her waist. His speculative gray gaze flicked between her and Derek, who stood, arms folded across his naked chest. With his chiseled features and thick, dark hair, he had to be the third Taggart brother.

"Alyssa, this is my oldest brother, Danny," Derek said.

Danny's only greeting was a sharp nod before he pinned Derek with a steely stare. "How about you two get some clothes on so we can figure out what the fuck is going on here."

They retreated to the bedroom, the playful, sexy mood having evaporated.

"Sorry about the way they just showed up," Derek said as he pulled on his jeans. "When I talked to Ethan earlier I didn't think they'd get here this fast."

Alyssa pulled on the navy scoop-neck T-shirt and jeans Toni had brought, surprised they actually fit. "Yeah, you probably also didn't plan on taking a forty-five-minute shower," she teased and then felt her grin slip away as the realization of why they were here, the truth she had to face, sank in. People wanted her dead, and now they had to find out why. She shrugged. "I had to face reality sooner rather than later."

She moved to the door as he was pulling a T-shirt over his head. He caught her arm before she could leave the room. "Everything's going to be okay," he said and pulled her against his chest. "We're going to find out who's behind this and why, and everything is going to be fine." He cupped her face, tilting her head back as he bent his head for a kiss. Soft, warm, infinitely reassuring. "I promise I'll keep you safe until this whole thing is over."

"Then what?" she asked before she could stop herself.

His dark brows pulled together in a puzzled frown. "What do you mean?"

She licked her lips and cursed herself for bringing it up now. "Nothing. Never mind." She wasn't positive, but she thought she saw relief flash in his eyes. She pulled away from his hold and joined the others in the living room.

Danny had switched on the television and tuned it to a news station. He stood stone still, arms folded as he stared at the screen.

Toni sat at the kitchen table, her fingers tapping at the keyboard of her laptop. Ethan stood behind her, his hands resting on the back of her chair as he studied the screen. He pointed at something, and when he pulled his hand back he rested it on her shoulder, running his fingers along her neck in an unconsciously proprietary caress. Toni leaned into the touch without missing a beat.

Though they weren't overtly affectionate, it took only a few seconds for Alyssa to realize that despite the charming grin and appreciative look Ethan had offered her earlier, there was a deep current of affection and intimacy running between him and Toni.

Just then Derek walked into the kitchen and poured two cups of coffee. Without asking, he scooped two teaspoons of sugar in one and handed it to Alyssa.

"Did you find anything on Abbassi?" he asked as he rummaged through the bag of sandwiches the others had brought.

Alyssa's stomach roiled at the mere mention of his name, the memory of his hand closing brutally over her breast as she lay helpless all the more terrifying because it was so vague. Derek offered her half a crusty roll piled high with meat and cheese. Alyssa refused with a shudder, the coffee souring in her stomach.

"Not much," Toni said, and Alyssa moved closer to hear her over the noise from the television. "He's involved in everything from oil speculation to commercial real estate. And as far as I can tell, everything about Louis Abbassi and his diamond-cutting operation check out clean."

"The guy I met with the other night said Louis was dealing with warlords in Africa, transporting weapons for diamonds." Everyone turned to stare at her in surprise.

"Why didn't you tell me this?" Derek asked, and she felt her hackles rise at the irritation in his voice.

"Sorry," she snapped. "I guess I got distracted by the whole getting-drugged-and-kidnapped-and-drugged-some-more thing. It's taking a while for the last few days to come back into focus."

Derek's mouth immediately softened in apology. "Sorry," he said and caught her to him in a one-armed hug. He leaned in close and said, so only she could hear, "And it's not like we did a lot of talking when you were awake."

Alyssa gave a little laugh as he pulled away. When she looked up, she saw that everyone was still staring, but this time at Derek, as if he'd grown a horn out of the center of his forehead.

"What?" he said.

"Nothing," Toni said too quickly as she turned back to her computer screen.

Ethan and Danny looked at each other, back at Derek, then back at each other.

"You ever see that thing on *Wild Kingdom*?" Danny asked Ethan. "You know, where the gazelle adopted a lion?"

"Yeah." Ethan nodded. "I know exactly what you mean."

Alyssa didn't, but Derek must have, because he blasted his brothers with a glare and muttered, "Fuck off," before he released her. "Tell me everything you can remember," he said, turning back to her, "starting with your meeting with—what's his name?"

"Martin Fish," Alyssa replied. She sucked down the last of the coffee and poured another cup, hoping the caffeine would hone the fuzzy memories of the last few days. "He said he was a reporter—" Her words choked in her throat as her gaze caught on the TV screen, which showed a close-up of a man in his late forties with a long nose, shaggy hair, and bad glasses. The goatee was gone, but there was no mistaking the man. "That's him. What are they saying about him?"

Danny aimed the remote and cranked the volume. Alyssa's stomach knotted in dawning horror as she listened to the newscaster's voice-over.

"The body of a man found murdered in his room at the Marina Motor Inn yesterday has been identified as Martin Fish, a freelance journalist whose pieces on international politics have appeared in national publications. At this time police believe Mr. Fish interrupted a robbery of his room late Thursday. San Francisco police are urging anyone with information to call this number."

Alyssa felt the coffee mug slide from her numb fingers as the anchorwoman read the number. "Someone must have followed us," she said.

"Did you tell anyone besides me where you were going?" Derek asked.

"No." She shook her head. "Andy knew I was meeting someone. She must have called Louis or something." She pressed her fingertips against her eyes. She didn't want to break down here, not in front of three granite-hard men and one tough-as-nails woman. But it was hard not to lose it as the full force of her assistant's betrayal hit her. She was so stupid, falling for Andy's act. And she'd repaid Alyssa by drugging her and handing her over to people who wanted her dead.

"I don't think she knew about Louis," Derek said. "Richard's the one who put her up to drugging you. I don't think she realized what they planned."

Alyssa nodded. That softened the blow, barely. "When I met with Martin, he told me Louis's cutting business was a way to move the diamonds into the market."

"Blood diamonds," Toni murmured.

Alyssa nodded. "Because we entered into the agreement with Louis, the Van Weldts are his largest customer. If what Martin claims is true, we're running in a river of red."

"In your message you said he had information about your father," Derek said. "What about that?"

Alyssa dug her fingers into the base of her skull where a knot of tension had formed and was starting to throb. "He didn't have any proof. Only that he interviewed my father shortly before his death. He asked my father some questions about where Louis got his diamonds. My dad got upset, cut the interview short. But Martin thinks maybe Dad did a little digging. And someone—Louis, I guess, and Richard—wanted him to keep it quiet."

"But that's just a theory, right?" Danny said, running an impatient hand through his hair. "No proof."

Alyssa shook her head. "That's what I said. But he told me I needed to look at the evidence myself, see what was really happening, then see if I was as willing to cover for my family."

They all looked at her expectantly. "What was the evidence?" Ethan finally asked. "Photos? Documents? What?"

"It was a Web site," Alyssa said. "He wrote down an address and a password on a card and told me to look at it." She paused, closed her eyes, and dropped her head. "But I lost the card somewhere between the bar and my house," she said, not wanting to open her eyes, not wanting to see the disappointment in Derek's eyes as he realized she was, indeed, the brain-dead bimbo the press made her out to be.

"It's okay," he said, curving his hand around her neck,

his fingers honing in on the knot, rubbing until she was weak in the knees. "Try to visualize the card. Can you remember any of the information?"

Like a billboard, the URL popped into her head. "Fish-Bait. FishBait.org," she said, but her excitement faded immediately. "But it's password protected—"

"Not a problem." Toni gave her a dismissive wave and turned to her screen. "Give me ten minutes. Twenty, tops."

As Toni set herself to hacking into Fish's Web site, Derek gave Alyssa's shoulder a last squeeze and went to where Danny was standing in the cottage's small living room. "Any more news about"—he wasn't sure how to phrase it—"the bodies?"

"Nothing to help us out," Danny said, his mouth tight, unable to hide his anger no matter how hard he tried. "Everything's so wrecked from the landslide, it's going to be hard to find any evidence. The older female's teeth are so jacked up, dental records aren't going to help us any."

"Shit." Now they really were in for weeks, maybe months, of waiting for a DNA match.

Danny nodded. "Selfish bitch won't stop haunting us," he said, fury turning his eyes the sooty shade of storm clouds. "And the stupid old man keeps letting her do it." He turned his attention back to the television. But Derek knew he wasn't really watching. Behind Danny's unseeing gaze his brain was seething with nearly two decades of anger and resentment. At their mother who left them, and at their father who couldn't let go.

For all he tried to pretend he didn't give a shit that their depressed, alcoholic mother had run out on them, Danny had turned his grief into an impenetrable cynicism that didn't invite close relationships with anyone.

Derek understood too well. But he'd always secretly thought himself superior to both of his brothers because, unlike those two, who only *pretended* not to care, Derek really didn't care. Other than his family, he didn't allow himself to get emotionally invested in anything or anyone.

Or so he'd thought. Then Alyssa Miles had sauntered into his life and blown all that to fucking hell.

The cottage was suddenly too small, stifling, and he went outside to stand on the small redwood deck that stood a couple feet off the cottage's overgrown yard. He sucked in deep breaths, tasted the first bite of fall in the late afternoon air. Yeah, Alyssa had knocked everything askew. And in admitting he cared about her, he had to admit he cared about some other things, too.

"Hey." Her light footfalls sounded on the deck as she stepped out. Goose bumps rose on her arms, and her nipples puckered against the stretchy front of her shirt. He knew for a fact she wasn't wearing a bra. He let himself dwell on that, grateful for the distraction from too deep thoughts about losing his self-imposed identity as an iceman.

Well, not entirely an iceman, he thought as heat pooled low in his belly.

"You were talking about your mom, weren't you? You and Danny?"

Heat receded, replaced by old hurt he'd managed to keep at bay for the last eighteen years, but hadn't stopped nagging him since that morning at the beach house when Alyssa had poked and prodded and finally sent him over the edge. He'd fractured on landing, and now little bits kept oozing out, demanding to be pulled out and examined fully before tucked back away. "Yeah."

She slid her arms around his waist and tucked her head up under his chin. He stiffened reflexively, not wanting to have this conversation here and now. Or ever.

"It's okay if you don't want to talk about it," she said, squeezing him harder, her warmth seeping into his skin. Until he couldn't help but wrap his arms around her and bury his face in her hair.

He would have laughed if he weren't so afraid it would sound more like a sob. He'd never been with anyone like her, who offered herself up without reservation. He'd purposely avoided dating women who tried to have any sort of deep, emotional connection, who would ever openly profess their feelings without provocation.

It was like he'd told her: He didn't talk. He didn't share. He didn't let people in his head or his heart.

I love you. I wanted to be sure to tell you.

Somehow she'd wormed her way in there anyway.

He topped her by a foot and outweighed her by a hundred pounds, but right now her slim arms were the only things keeping him from blowing apart.

"They still don't know anything," he said, his hands tightening convulsively around her back. "We'll have to wait a while for the DNA tests to come in."

She nodded against his chest.

"Danny hopes it's her. Ethan does, too." He didn't want to talk about it but couldn't stem the flow. "I don't know what I want. I don't blame them, I guess. They want it to be done. To know once and for all."

"And you don't?"

He swallowed hard. "If it were just me, yeah. I'm sick of having to wonder what happened. I convinced myself she drank herself to death a long time ago. But now that we might know for sure . . ."

"Your father believes she's still alive, doesn't he?"

"Yeah, and that's why part of me hopes the body turns out to be someone else. Searching for her has taken over his whole life. I don't know what he'll do if we finally confirm she's dead."

"Maybe it will finally set him free. Give him closure, same as for you three."

Derek wanted that to be true. He wanted to believe his

father was capable of moving on. But never in a million years had he expected his father's life would stop when his mother left. Derek didn't hold much hope that he'd get a new lease on life if Anne Taggart turned up dead, even after all this time.

The sliding glass door slid open behind them, and Derek turned to see Ethan. "Toni's in."

Alyssa leaned over Toni's shoulder so she could get a closer look at the screen. At first look, FishBait.org was a news site, featuring articles by Martin and other journalists that covered war zones and natural and manmade disasters, seeming to focus on the harsh reality of life in forgotten parts of the world.

But Toni quickly found the password-protected section where Martin stored his notes, pictures, and any other materials related to his stories. Toni made an exasperated noise in her throat. "This is going to take days."

Alyssa scanned through the endless list of folders until her eyes locked on one labeled DFA.

"Try that one," she said, pointing to it on the screen.

"DFA. 'Diamonds for All.' That's the campaign tagline."

Toni shrugged and clicked it open, and Alyssa felt a tiny spurt of triumph when the folder opened to reveal a dozen subfolders with labels like OSCAR VW, ALYSSA M, and MINE CONDITIONS. She may not be a computer genius or a security expert, but she wasn't completely useless. "Click there," she said, indicating the mining conditions with her finger. She wanted to see for herself the deplorable conditions Fish accused them of supporting.

"Here, why don't you drive," Toni said, scooting her chair back so Alyssa could sit.

For a second Alyssa was afraid she'd pissed the other woman off with her backseat surfing. But while Toni's expression held a hint of impatience, there was no trace of irritation. "You know what you're looking for better than we do."

Alyssa sat down and clicked open a picture of an African man, his dark, weathered skin clinging to bones, covered in mud as he worked in the mines. The caption read NKUDA MINE, OUTSIDE MBUJI-MAYI, DEMOCRATIC REPUBLIC OF THE CONGO.

She swallowed hard. Alyssa knew some of the diamonds the Van Weldts sold came from mines all over Africa. She even knew some of them provided better working conditions than others. She'd accepted it as a fact of the business, swallowed it without ever questioning the morality. But she'd never seen conditions like those depicted in Fish's photographs. Men, women, children covered in mud, their bellies bloated with malnutrition, surrounded by armed guards who looked no older than teenagers.

One photo in particular made her heart ache like a giant bruise. It was of a girl, no more than fifteen or sixteen. Extraordinarily beautiful with her smooth skin, high forehead, full lips, and sculpted cheekbones. She was tall and slender. Except for her belly, which bulged in the late stages of pregnancy. The caption under it read, MARIE LAURE MWANDEKO. TAKEN FROM HER VILLAGE OUTSIDE BUKAVU. CHOSEN AS FIRST WIFE BY MEKEMBE.

"Isn't there an embargo on diamonds from the Congo?" Toni asked.

Alyssa nodded and clicked on a file marked VIDEOS. "But it's easy enough to sneak them over the border and pay someone to write false certificates of authenticity." Again, a widely known and accepted fact of the business, another thing she hadn't even had to ignore because she'd never really given it much thought.

Self-disgust burned bitter at the back of her throat, feeling very much the useless, ignorant party girl the press made her out to be. The girl, Marie Laure's, huge dark eyes haunted her. At sixteen Alyssa had been partying it up all over Los Angeles, Miami, the south of France, feeling sorry for herself at her parents' neglect. At the same age this girl had been kidnapped, raped, and would bear a child. Alyssa didn't know much about medical facilities in southern Africa, but she knew mother and child would be lucky if they survived the birth.

The first file video opened to show the interior of a tent. Four men sat around a table, huge machine guns propped within easy reach as they played cards and drank from sweating beer bottles. An argument broke out, and while Alyssa and the others couldn't understand the words, it was clear one man was accusing the other of cheating as he slammed his own cards down and made a grab for the other's hand.

Then the accuser picked up his beer bottle, smashed it on the corner of the table, and slashed the jagged edge across the other thug's face. A ragged tear opened in the man's cheek, soaking his face in blood as he stood and staggered from the table.

The table erupted in laughter, white teeth flashing in dark faces as the accuser tossed aside his broken bottle. He turned in the direction of the camera and shouted something. Most of it was unintelligible, but Alyssa understood one phrase: "Marie Laure."

The girl from the photo. Fish had hooked her up with a hidden camera. As she watched, the camera drew closer to the table. A slender arm and a hand holding a fresh bottle of beer appeared in the frame.

It took over an hour to go through all the video footage. By the time they were finished, Alyssa was sick to her stomach, hunched in her chair, her arms wrapped tightly around her waist. At some point Derek had brought her a soda, but even a sip of it made her want to vomit.

Fish hadn't been lying. Not only had the Van Weldts been selling illegal diamonds, they had gone into business with an arms dealer. There was Louis, clear as day, making a weapons exchange in front of Marie Laure's hidden camera.

But the horror came next, when Mekembe saw Marie Laure. The picture skewed, fell, until all they could see was the red dirt of the ground, hands, arms, fists, feet, flailing. The sound of cries, yelling, the meaty thump of fists meeting flesh.

That was the last video, dated three weeks ago. Right after Alyssa's father was killed.

"He's so brazen," Alyssa said, still struggling to accept the reality. "Why would he do this? How does he think he can get away with it?"

"In his mind, these two worlds will never cross. He has enough money, enough power; he doesn't think he'll ever get caught," Ethan said. "Classic megalomaniac."

"Thanks, Dr. Phil," Danny said. "So your father found out about Abbassi, and Blaylock and Abbassi had him offed before he could tell anyone Blaylock made a deal to sell Abbassi's blood diamonds through Van Weldt Jeweler."

Alyssa shook her head, her mouth pulling tight as the truth became brutally clear. "He has to be working with my uncle. Harold has always been in charge of dealing with suppliers. And even though Richard is involved in all the deals, he doesn't have the authority to do one on his own. Especially something as big as the exclusive agreement they signed with Louis." She shook her head; a cynical laugh exploded from her throat. "He was always going on about how I tarnished the family image. Meanwhile he was the one doing business with arms dealers."

"What about Kimberly?" Derek said. "Could she be involved?"

"No," Alyssa said with a vehement shake of her head.

"She worked with our dad on the retail side. She didn't do any business with the suppliers."

"But she works closely with Richard, and she and Abbassi looked pretty friendly at that fund-raiser," Derek prodded.

Everything in her rejected that possibility. "Kimberly wouldn't do that to me," she said, springing from her chair. "Ever since I moved up here, she's the only one who's been completely supportive. Even when my dad wanted to keep me pushed to the side of the business, she's the one who tried to get me more involved."

"She didn't believe you were being drugged," he snapped.

"Neither did you," Alyssa shot back, "and I gave you a second chance."

Danny, Ethan, and Toni watched, eyebrows raised, waiting to see how this would play out.

Alyssa took a deep breath, trying to rein in her temper, and held up her hands. "Trust me, Kimberly wouldn't involve herself in something like this. Forget about me—she was so close to our father. She wouldn't be involved in his murder. Not in a million years."

As they read through the rest of Martin Fish's documents, Alyssa felt a rage like nothing she'd ever felt in her life take root. Her uncle had known about this, or at least had a strong suspicion about Louis's diamond sources. Why else would he kill to keep this secret?

When stories about so-called blood diamonds had first hit the news nearly a decade ago, the industry had taken a hit. Many companies had suffered bad publicity, but they'd all recovered. Primarily by paying lip service, promising to adhere to regulations about certifying mines and diamonds.

Because it was almost impossible to prove that any jeweler had knowingly acquired or sold conflict diamonds, the scandal had blown over, and the industry had recovered.

But what Harold Van Weldt and Richard Blaylock had

done could never be glossed over. When this came out, it would destroy the business and family her uncle had been so eager to protect.

Alyssa didn't consider herself a vengeful person. But after what he'd done to her father and herself, she couldn't wait to deal the death blow to everything Harold Van Weldt held dear.

CHAPTER 19

"I DON'T KNOW what you expect me to do." Louis's fingers tightened around the phone. "You are supposed to be very smart. You will figure it out."

"Why should I figure it out? It's your men who let Taggart take her in the first place."

"And they have paid for their incompetence," he said, sparing a moment's regret for Catherine, Damon, Peter, and Andre, who now rested in the cold depths of Lake Tahoe. They had served him well, but they would serve as an example to others to never let down their guard, no matter how easy an assignment seemed or how isolated the location. "And now I am depending on you to get her back to me."

A scoffing laugh. "Taggart has her hidden somewhere. And even if we did know where she was, how am I supposed to get past him?"

"Kill him. I don't care."

"Right, I'm really going to get the drop on a former special-forces sniper."

"I grow tired of arguing. You will do as I ask."

"Or what?" The voice rose a notch as anxiety escalated to hysteria. "You'll tell? This is all going to come out. We're screwed any way you look at it, so I don't know what I have to lose anymore."

"You have your life," Louis said. "A life I should take for what you did to her, after I told you I wanted her unharmed." He could hear the swallow through the phone.

"It wasn't my idea—"

"Bullshit. I know you are the brains of this. The others would not have acted without you. Now, you find a way to get Alyssa to come to you, or you will find yourself as dead as your lover. If you are successful, I will give you everything you need to start a new life elsewhere."

"Everything?" Curious now, intrigued. Greedy.

"A new identity, an authentic passport, and fifteen million dollars in a numbered Swiss account."

"All for her?" Disbelief, disgust was evident in the reply.

Louis looked at the magazine on the table before him. It was open to an advertisement for Van Weldt's featuring Alyssa, naked but for sparkling jewels covering the tips of her breasts and the triangle between her thighs. Her skin was so smooth and creamy. He couldn't wait to mark it with his fingers and with his teeth. His hand twitched at the remembered feel of her tit under his hand. Next time would be so much better, with her fully awake, aware that she was in his control. That pleasing him was the only way to survive.

"I want her. And I will do whatever it takes to get what I want."

Danny cruised his jeep past Alyssa's Victorian as Derek scanned the sidewalk from the passenger seat. "There," Derek said. "Across the street."

"What?" Alyssa asked from the backseat. She peered through the window. "That guy in the trench coat?" A large, squarely built man stood across the street from her house, his bulk draped in a gray coat. With his blond crew cut and hard, angular features, he was a poster child for the Aryan nation.

"Yep," Derek said. "Ten to one that's one of Louis's boys."

"Not much for discretion, are they?" Danny said.

"I knew we should have left you with Ethan and Toni—" Derek started.

Alyssa cut him off before he could get wound up. "No way was I staying back at the house doing nothing when I can help you. Case closed."

Toni had easily hacked into the Van Weldt corporate computer network, but because it was after business hours, several computers were shut down and not connected to the network, including Richard's and Harold's. While Toni could access shared documents and e-mails archived on the corporate server, they needed to access deleted files on her uncle and Richard's hard drives if they wanted a complete picture.

Derek had been adamant that Alyssa stay back at the house while he and Danny went first to her house to retrieve her pass key to the Van Weldt office and then to the office to retrieve the computers.

Alyssa had been just as adamant that she go. "I can't remember where my pass key is, but if I can look at my stuff, I'll remember quicker. Trust me, it will be faster than having you search my room."

When their argument escalated, Danny cut it off with a short, "Shut up, both of you, and get in the car. This is better. I can keep a lookout and take care of anyone who comes along while you two retrieve the key and the computers."

Derek had looked like he wanted to punch Danny in the mouth, but instead he'd turned to Alyssa with a hard look. "You follow my lead and do exactly what I say." The only reason Alyssa hadn't snapped back was that he'd softened his harsh command by giving her a quick, hard kiss before opening the back door of the jeep so she could climb in.

Now they circled the block to make sure no one else was watching the house. But instead of turning right down her street, Danny took a left and drove a few blocks before stopping in front of a twenty-four-hour convenience store.

"Be right back," he said as he slammed the car into park and jogged inside.

Danny was back before Alyssa could voice her confusion. She recognized the bulge inside the brown paper bag.

"I think I have something in my liquor cabinet if you're that desperate for a drink," she said.

"Don't worry, sweetcheeks, I'm not going to get hammered—not now anyway. This is just for diversion."

"Did your brother really just call me sweetcheeks?" she asked Derek as the car pulled away from the curb.

"He's an asshole. Don't pay any attention to him."

Danny merely grunted and pulled the car up to the curb around the corner from her house, where Louis's thug wouldn't be able to see them.

"Give me a couple minutes," he said.

Alyssa watched in confusion as Danny got out of the car, cracked open the bottle, and poured the contents down the front of his T-shirt and canvas work coat. Whiskey fumes permeated the air as he took a couple steps down the sidewalk. Within a few yards, his gait changed from an athletic, predatory stride to that of a lumbering lush. If Alyssa hadn't known what he'd done, she never would have questioned that Danny had staggered his way here from one of the nearby bars.

Derek took her hand, and they followed several yards behind. His other hand slid back to rest along the waist of his cargo pants. Her stomach clutched when she saw the butt of a gun sticking out of his waistband. He rested his fingers against it, ready to move if the meathead didn't fall for Danny's act.

The blond guy stiffened as Danny approached, but he didn't acknowledge the big, stinking drunk weaving in his direction.

Not until Danny called out, "Hey, dude, do you know if thersh any cabsh around here?"

The man didn't answer.

"Yoo-hoo, buddy, talkin' t'you." Danny was now within a few yards of the guy. "I need a cab, man." He gave a convincingly drunk chuckle. "I'm so fucked up, man. Jus' started a new job. My buddy bought me shots. . . ." He paused, wavering directly in front of the thug. "Fuck, I don' even know where I am. What fuckin street—"

"Listen, friend, I can't help you," he said in a clipped accent, his words so low Alyssa could barely make them out.

"Hey, come on, dude, help me out." Danny staggered forward and gave the guy a sloppy pat on the shoulder.

"Fuck off, man." The guy slid his trench coat to the side.

"Whoa!" Danny jumped back and threw his hands up as if startled. "No need to get mean, here, dude." He staggered back and then righted himself as the thug took a menacing step forward.

Without warning Danny's fist flew out and caught the guy square in the face; then he landed a hard, martial-arts-looking jab into his chest. As the thug pitched forward, gasping, Danny reached in his coat and snatched the gun from his holster. A knee to the guy's crotch brought the thug's head down within easy striking range. Danny clipped him on the back of the head with the gun, and the thug was down for the count.

"Go on up," Danny said, barely breathing hard as he tucked the gun in his waistband and relieved the thug of his wallet, cell phone, and pager. "I'll take care of this clown. When he comes to, he won't be too eager to tell Louis he got rolled by a drunk."

"Wow, I've only seen that in the movies," Alyssa said.

Derek shot her a dirty look. "We're all trained to fight."

She patted his arm, purposely widening her eyes. "Oh,

honey, I'm sure you would have kicked his ass, too, given the chance."

Danny gave a half laugh, half grunt as he hoisted the thug over his shoulder in a fireman's carry. "That's right, sugardick, don't go getting all jealous." He shot Alyssa a grin. "But if you're ever looking for a real man . . ."

Derek flipped him the finger and tugged Alyssa across the street. "Let's find the pass key and get the hell out."

The house was silent as they went up the stairs to the living room. Alyssa breathed a sigh of relief that Andy was gone. She went into her bedroom and gasped. It looked like it had been tossed. Drawers hung open, clothes and shoes littered the floor.

"I think Andy did a little looting before she left," Derek said as he came up behind her. Sure enough, most of her dresser drawers were empty. And when she entered her walk-in closet, she saw a sea of empty hangers and shelves where rows of designer clothing and shoes used to be. "That bitch," she breathed. Andy had helped herself to tens, possibly hundreds of thousands of dollars' worth of her stuff. The final insult—

What was that smell?

Alyssa's nose wrinkled as she took another deep inhale. "What is that? That's awful." Her gaze locked on an oversize leather duffel bag in the corner of the closet. Everything went still, and suddenly she *knew*. Still, she took a step closer. She had to be sure.

"Alyssa, don't." Derek's voice was calm, too calm as he grabbed her arm.

She shook him off and lunged at the bag. She tugged the zipper down and choked on a scream at the sight that greeted her.

It was Andy, nearly unrecognizable with her mottled, swollen face. Her tongue stuck halfway out of her mouth, the whites of her eyes crimson with burst blood vessels. Nearly black bruises ringed her throat.

"Oh, my God, oh, my God, oh, my God." Everything seized inside Alyssa as she staggered back, would have fallen if Derek hadn't grabbed her by the shoulders. He steered her out of the closet, through her bedroom, and into the bathroom, barely making it before her meager dinner heaved into the toilet.

Derek held her hair as she retched and offered her a paper cup of water when the dry heaves finally passed. "I'm sorry," he said as he stroked her hair, his mouth pulling into a grimace. "I should have seen that coming."

She gulped the water, shaking her head as she took a seat on the closed toilet lid. "How could you have known she was murdered? I mean, she was murdered, right?" God, dumb question. People who died of natural causes didn't end up in duffel bags in the closet.

Derek nodded. "They'll do an autopsy, but it looks to me like she was strangled."

"Louis?"

"That would be my guess."

Alyssa nodded, bile searing her throat as her eyes burned with tears. "Poor Andy."

His dark eyes narrowed dangerously. "Poor Andy was slipping you drugs."

"I know." She sniffed. "But that doesn't mean she deserved that." She closed her eyes, but all she could see was Andy's frozen, grotesque stare.

"She helped Richard and Abbassi kidnap and drug you," Derek snapped. "Don't make excuses for her."

Alyssa nodded, though her stomach still roiled with a mixture of fear and confusion. "The police will want to talk to me." Oh, God, the press was going to have a field day with this. Her father's murder, her own drugging and kidnapping. She would be headline news for the next six months.

She shoved the thought aside. She couldn't worry about that now when she needed to focus on getting her uncle, Richard, and Louis caught and punished.

He nodded. "We'll call in an anonymous tip about the body. We can probably hold off talking to them for another day, but not more than that." He knelt on the floor in front of the toilet and pulled her to him. "It's going to be okay."

She nodded and stifled a sob against the thick fleece of his jacket. She had to hold it together. She couldn't fall apart on Derek, not yet. She pulled back, sniffed, and gave him a resolute nod. "Let's find that card so we can get the hell out of here."

"That's my girl."

Alyssa blocked everything out to focus on her search for her access card. Several times she cursed herself for not being organized, not being like—oh, God, Andy—and keeping track of things like keys, phone, ID, and office access card. But as soon as her gaze snagged on her small black clutch, she knew she'd find the key. She gave it and her phone to Derek while she packed a small bag of essentials.

Danny emerged from an alley as they exited the house. "Did you get the card?"

Derek nodded, and they started down the block to their car. While driving, Danny's expression turned grim as Derek told him what they'd found. He pulled over next to a telephone booth while Derek called in the anonymous tip. Alyssa closed her eyes and swallowed back bile. By tomorrow morning the dead body in Alyssa's house would be all over the news. Hopefully the cops would do as he recommended and look first and hardest at Louis Abbassi and Richard Blaylock.

From Alyssa's house it was a short drive to the Van Weldt

offices on Union Square. Derek and Danny slipped in through the alley entrance. In the time he'd worked with Alyssa, Derek had made himself familiar with every nuance of the Van Weldt security system, and she was impressed by how well he'd cataloged every flaw and vulnerability.

Alyssa's mouth pulled into an ironic smile. Harold had blown Derek off when Derek had offered to go through his list with their in-house security team and suggest improvements.

Now she was glad the bastard had refused Derek's offer to help. For Gemini men, sneaking into Harold Van Weldt's offices was child's play.

By the time they got back to the safe house, it was after two in the morning. Ethan and Toni were still up. Toni got to work running a decryption program on the hard drives. "We'll let these run overnight and get to them in the morning," Toni said, stifling a yawn. "And, Alyssa, I went ahead and changed the log-in and password on Fish's Web site if you want to get back in. The new log-in is *alyssa* all lowercase, and the password is *diamonds.*"

Alyssa muttered a thanks, numb and shell-shocked as the adrenaline rush wore off and the night's events started to take hold.

Toni and Ethan murmured their good nights and headed for the spare bedroom.

Alyssa felt an iron-hard arm wrap around her. "Come on, Alyssa. Let's get you to bed before you collapse," Derek said as he steered her down the hall.

She sat down on the bed and kicked off her shoes, feeling bone-deep exhausted. But her mind was racing with such violent images she knew she'd never relax.

She let Derek undress her like a child and tuck her under the covers. He turned out the lights, and she stared into the darkness, bombarded by visions of Andy, of her father and stepmother. Of Martin Fish, facedown on the floor as his blood puddled around him.

"Don't think about it," Derek said, his voice muffled in her hair as he slid into bed next to her and gathered her close.

She shuddered and buried her face against his chest. "I can't stop. I can't get their faces out of my head." He was silent, his calloused palm running up and down her back in a soothing, almost hypnotic pattern. "We have to make him pay for this. I don't want to spend the rest of my life looking over my shoulder, waiting for my uncle to shut me up."

Derek's hand stilled on her back, and she felt every sinew in his body go tight. "I will not let anything happen to you. I made the mistake of leaving you vulnerable before, and I will never do it again. If I have to shadow you every day for the rest of your life to keep you safe, I will do it. I promise you."

She didn't know why that made her feel even worse, like that was the only way to convince Derek to stay around. "Don't worry. I have enough money in my trust fund to hire a whole army of bodyguards if that's what it comes to. You'll be off the hook soon enough."

Derek's fingers clenched and released against the flesh of her hip. "I'm not talking about working as your hired bodyguard, and you know it," he said, his voice harsh.

"What are you talking about then?" She held her breath, grateful for the dark as everything in her world seem to ride on his answer.

"I . . ." he began, only to break off. "You . . ." he began again, only to stop again. "Fuck," he said finally. His fingers threaded in her hair. "I suck at this relationship. I'm not good about talking about how I feel." He paused. "I went a long time without feeling much of anything. I never let my feelings about anyone or anything get in the way of what I had to do. Except once. I made an emotional decision, didn't do the job I was supposed to do, and a lot of good people ended up dead."

Alyssa didn't press him for details, afraid if she interrupted he would cut himself off.

"After that I closed myself off even more. Ruthlessly killed any emotional response or impulse, shoved it back in the box so my brain could deal with life without interference or interruption. Then I met you." She could hear the rueful smile in his voice. "It was like getting hit with an EMP."

"Huh?"

He huffed a little laugh. "Electromagnetic pulse. It's a burst of energy that fries any electronic equipment within range so nothing works right anymore."

"That doesn't sound any better than getting ripped apart," she said, remembering his words from the day before.

"Guess I need to work on my metaphors. Point is, from the first second I saw you, you made me feel things I've never felt before. Things I convinced myself I never wanted to feel. I don't know what to call it yet, but all I know is I can't get enough of you."

"You know it's going to be bad, right? I mean, I'll do my best to keep a low profile from now on, but once all this gets out, the press are going to be everywhere. You, your brothers—everyone is going to be front-page news. Are you sure you want to deal with that?" Her hand fisted against his chest.

"I don't care how bad it gets. I want to be here for you, beside you, while we deal with this whole fucked-up mess. I'll never leave you alone."

She pushed herself up his body and found his mouth in the dark, drinking in his urgency, his intensity, letting it fill her, strengthen her, knowing she'd need everything she could get for the coming days. "That's the most romantic thing any man has ever said to me," she said between kisses.

He rolled her underneath him and slid deep inside. He barely moved, just held himself inside her as he kissed her mouth, her cheeks, her eyelids as his hands ran over every inch of skin he could reach. "You're mine," he whispered over and over. "Mine."

Alyssa wrapped herself around him, opening herself up, taking everything he had to give and giving it right back. She savored this last night of safety in their sanctuary. Tomorrow they would have to deal with the outside world and people who would kill to keep her from revealing their secrets.

But tonight it was just the two of them in the dark, and there was no question she belonged to him.

CHAPTER 20

"YOU'RE BEING RIDICULOUS," Alyssa said for the dozenth time as she and Derek drove from the secret cottage to San Francisco. "I need to call her and let her know I'm okay."

"No dice," Derek said and gunned his car down the steep, curving road that led to the freeway.

They had an appointment with Detective Reyes of the homicide department, the man who had been assigned to investigate Andy's murder. Reyes had left three messages on Alyssa's cell-phone voice mail before the mailbox got too full and started bouncing messages. When Alyssa had checked them earlier that morning, there had been over fifty new messages over the last few days. Her publicist had called several times with offers from magazines and TV shows that wanted an exclusive on her first postrehab interview.

Her mother had called half a dozen times, first to inquire about who would see that she received her monthly allowance from Alyssa. Then, after the news of Andy's murder hit the news, she left a tearful, almost incoherent plea for her to call and tell them what was going on.

"You cannot call her back, not until we talk to the police," Derek had said when Alyssa had started to dial her mother. "You know anything you tell her will be front-page news as soon as she hangs up. Right now no one knows where you are or exactly what you know, and I want to keep it that way."

She'd reluctantly caved on not calling her mother, but Alyssa still wanted to call Kimberly, who had left several messages, each more frantic than the last.

The first was from two days before, right after Derek had found Alyssa and taken her from the Tahoe house.

"I called the treatment center, and they said you've never even been a patient there. Now Richard isn't answering his phone, and Andy isn't either."

Later that day: "Alyssa, if you get this message, please call me back. I have no idea where you are, and Richard seems to have dropped off the face of the Earth. If you're in trouble, I'll help you, just please call me."

The last one was from earlier this morning. "Oh, my God, Alyssa, please call me. The police want to talk to you about Andy. I told them you couldn't have had anything to do with it, but I'm killing myself with worry that something has happened to you as well. Please call me so I know you're not dead in a ditch somewhere. I won't even tell the police you've called if that's what you want, but please. I love you, and I'm worried, so please call."

Alyssa had played the messages for Derek, but he wouldn't budge.

"What harm could come from calling her?" she asked again as the rolling hills along highway 280 flew by in a grass-covered blur. "It's not like she's going to tell the press—"

"But she could tell your uncle, or Richard if he calls her back."

"Not if I tell her not to," Alyssa said. "Besides, I think she deserves a little warning that the shit is about to hit the fan."

And how. Alyssa and Derek were headed to the police station armed with CD copies of all Martin Fish's files, along with copies of e-mails and additional files Derek and Toni had recovered from the Van Weldt network and the copied hard drives.

They'd discovered several files and e-mail exchanges documenting the deal Harold Van Weldt had made with Louis Abbassi. In exchange for an infusion of capital from Abbassi, Abbassi received a stake in the company and a guaranteed distribution channel for his stones. When the deal was inked, Harold was the decision maker, while Richard had dealt with logistics and paperwork.

But that wasn't enough to link Harold to Oscar's murder. The key to that had come from an e-mail exchange between Oscar and Richard that Toni had uncovered from the corporate network. "Dumbasses don't know that it doesn't matter if you delete it from your computer, it's still on the server," Toni had said with a shake of her head at their ignorance.

Oscar revealed to Richard that he'd conducted an investigation of Louis Abbassi and had discovered disturbing information not revealed when Harold had done his initial due diligence. Later, they had been discussing a termination agreement, in circumspect terms, never naming names as though worried the subject would find out about it. But it had involved a family member, as indicated by an e-mail from Richard: In a situation like this, where family is involved, there are inheritance issues to consider.

To which Oscar had replied: Monetary compensation for remaining shares will provide adequate legacy. Point is moot, as there is no issue to consider.

Uncle Harold had no children.

The day Oscar and Grace had been killed, Oscar wrote to Richard: We will alert the party tomorrow and execute the agreement this weekend. With luck, discretion will prevail, and any public scandal can be avoided. Will repay LA in full. He should not contest, as he will not want to damage his reputation further.

Disappointment had settled in Alyssa's belly as she read the exchange. Her father hadn't planned to alert the authorities to Louis's smuggling. He'd wanted to quietly fire Harold, sever the partnership with Louis, and sweep the entire matter under the rug.

But the Van Weldt Jeweler empire was Harold's life, and Alyssa wasn't surprised he hadn't been willing to go quietly off into so-called retirement. So when Richard had tipped him and Louis off about what was about to happen, they'd decided to kill Oscar to protect their secrets.

But it was another exchange, this one between Harold and Richard, dated two days after Oscar's death, that made Alyssa feel like an icy hand had run down her spine.

Oscar mentioned he was considering changing the will but had no idea he had executed changes to divide company shares between Kimberly and Alyssa. Small compensation— according to the terms of the trust, should anything happen to Alyssa, shares revert back to family and are not passed on to NOK.

Harold had made no secret of his horror that his brother's death had made Alyssa a major stockholder in the business.

"So killing you solves two problems," Derek had said tightly, a muscle throbbing in his jaw as his eyes scanned the screen. "You can't tell anybody about what you might have seen the night your father was killed, and he gets the shares back from the niece he hates."

They pulled up in front of the police station, and Derek parked his Audi. Before he got out of the car he reached over and covered Alyssa's hand.

"They're going to ask you some tough questions. Whatever you do, keep your cool, tell the truth, and try not to let them rattle you."

She nodded, her brow furrowing at the sudden note of gloom and doom in his voice. "I'll be fine. All we have to do is tell them the truth, give them the evidence, and this whole thing will be over with, right?"

"It might not be that easy. Are you sure you don't want to call an attorney? Anyone would kill to represent you. You could get the best."

He'd been badgering her about it all day. "I don't understand why you think I need an attorney when I haven't done anything wrong. I'll be fine, Derek. I've handled reporters who will make Detective Reyes look like a pussycat."

Derek watched Alyssa disappear into the private interrogation room with Detective Reyes, his gut clenching as she gave him a small smile over her shoulders.

A lamb marching into the lion's den.

He should have warned her, been more clear about what to expect. She thought she would just tell the detective the whole convoluted story, and that would be it. They would go arrest Harold Van Weldt, track down Richard Blaylock and Louis Abbassi, wherever they were hiding, and justice would be served.

But Derek hadn't had the heart to tell her that life wasn't like an episode of *Law & Order*. Criminals weren't arrested, prosecuted, and sentenced to life without parole in the space of an hour.

And a celebrity heiress with a reputation for drug use and heavy partying—no matter how undeserved—didn't make the best witness against one of San Francisco's richest, most powerful citizens.

Still, they couldn't hold the cops off any longer, not without starting to look like they had something to hide. And if they moved quickly enough the cops might be able to find evidence of Alyssa's captivity in the Tahoe house to back up their statements. Not that Derek was holding his breath on that count, as he was pretty sure Louis would have been in there with an extermination and cleanup crew after he discovered Alyssa was missing two days ago.

But Louis wasn't the one he was worried about right now. He was more afraid of what Harold Van Weldt was going to do to Alyssa when he found out they were going after him.

It was going to be a long, ugly battle, and Derek knew Harold would do everything he could to kill Alyssa's credibility. Her name would be dragged through the mud. Every mistake, every mishap in her past would be rehashed in the media, headline news on every station.

If Derek was going to stand by her through all this, he needed to prepare himself to be yanked squarely into that spotlight.

The notion stuck in his craw. Derek was by nature a private person. He'd built his career on staying to the shadows and going unnoticed. He didn't enjoy being the center of attention or answering a lot of questions about himself. He still vividly remembered the minor media circus that had happened when his mother had first gone missing. Reporters had camped out in front of their house. Waiting for him and his brothers to get out of school or finish football practice.

All the vultures circling, circling under the guise of concern. Waiting to pounce on anything negative he or his brothers might have to say about their mother, taking words out of context to use it as gasoline for the media fire.

Was he really ready to deal with that again?

He looked again at the Reyes's closed door. Even just thinking of Alyssa in there made his heart clutch.

For her, Derek might be able to stand another fifteen minutes of fame.

And he'd promised to stand by her. A promise he intended to keep, even if his heart hadn't been involved.

He actually sighed in relief when Detective Harris, Reyes's

partner, escorted him back to his desk to take his statement. Derek knew he was about to sizzle on the coals, but the questions served as a great distraction from where his mind had been wandering.

Alyssa sat across the table from Detective Reyes, feeling like she'd gone several rounds in a kickboxing ring. Not that she'd ever gotten any closer to a kickboxing ring than in a workout in her private gym with her trainer, but she imagined this must be what it felt like to get pummeled, over and over, with no end in sight.

"Let me go over this one more time," Reyes said, scratching the five-o'clock shadow that darkened his jawline. "You're convinced your uncle had your father killed to cover up the fact that he was knowingly selling conflict diamonds. Then he worked with Louis Abbassi, the diamond broker—"

"Diamond smuggler," Alyssa broke in, "and arms dealer, as you'll see on the CD I gave you."

"Right. Working with your uncle, they had you kidnapped, drugged, and were going to kill you by faking an overdose. Do I have all that straight?" He looked at her, eyebrows raised in a deceptively friendly manner. He would have been good-looking, with his thick, dark hair and thickly lashed, almost almond-shaped dark eyes. But he dressed like he'd pulled his clothes from the bottom of the Goodwill pile. That, combined with the condescending look on his face that said he doubted she had more than two brain cells to rub together, erased any good looks he might have otherwise possessed.

Alyssa blew out a frustrated breath and felt tension coil like a spring in the back of her neck. She wished Derek was with her but knew they wouldn't be interviewed together. "You're leaving out the part where Louis killed Martin Fish and my assistant, Andy," she said, her voice cracking on Andy's name. "I'm sure my uncle knew about that, too."

Reyes nodded. "We're looking into that. Unfortunately we've been unable to find Mr. Blaylock, but we have confirmation that Mr. Abbassi arrived in Namibia yesterday. We have reason to believe Blaylock was with him."

"Well, get them back," Alyssa protested.

Reyes shook his head regretfully. "Namibia has no extradition treaty with the US. And we'll do what we can to locate and apprehend Mr. Blaylock, but I can't promise the authorities will be cooperative. Not if Abbassi has as much influence as we believe."

Alyssa shook her head, feeling like she'd been punched again. "That's it? Three-people are dead, and you're giving up?"

"Like I said, we'll do everything we can to apprehend Blaylock. And if Abbassi reenters the United States, we'll get him. But because of extradition laws, our hands are tied."

"What about everything else? The illegal diamond mines? Selling guns to warlords in the Congo? Can't you get him for that?"

Reyes nodded. "After we review the evidence you provided, we'll turn a copy of it over to the FBI and Interpol. I wish we could be more helpful, but there's not a whole lot we can do."

Alyssa bit back a snotty retort as she recognized the sincere regret in the detective's eyes.

He stood from his chair and stretched. "I think that's it for now, Miss Miles."

She looked up, startled at the abrupt end to his interview. "I can go?"

"Yes. But I'm going to request that neither you nor Mr. Taggart leave town any time soon."

Alyssa stood up, feeling a muscle in her left butt cheek protest after spending so long on the hard surface of the folding chair. "What about my uncle? Are you going to arrest him?"

His lips pulled into a patronizing smile. "We can't arrest him for your father's murder, because it didn't happen in our jurisdiction. But if the Hillsborough police decide there's enough evidence to support it, they'll reopen the investigation. I have to tell you though, it doesn't look good."

"But he and Richard made the deal with Abbassi, and we have proof my father was going to have Harold fired. And he wanted to have me killed!" She tried but couldn't control the hysterical note that vibrated through her voice.

Reyes shook his head. "Even if your allegations are true and Blaylock and Louis conspired to kidnap and murder you, there's nothing to tie your uncle to their activities. As for your father's death, that isn't my case, but a few illegally obtained e-mails that never mentioned your uncle by name . . ." His look, though not unkind, wasn't encouraging. "I'm afraid you don't have much."

She dropped her gaze, her face heating with a mixture of anger and regret. Why hadn't she pushed harder, had more faith in what she saw or thought she saw moving through the shadows that night?

Now, unless they could find evidence Harold was involved in either her father's murder or the plot to kill her, he would continue his life as a free man.

He would get away with murder.

Alyssa strode from Reyes's office to the waiting area. Derek stood when he saw her.

"They're not going to do anything," she said as they hurried from the police station. "They're not even going to bring Harold in for questioning." She spit the last word out. "And Richard and Louis have already fled the country. They're going to get away with it. All of it."

Derek reached out, took her arm, and guided her to the car. "We'll find a way to nail your uncle," he said as he opened the passenger door so she could slide in. "And Homeland Security has Abbassi on their watch list. If he tries to get back in the country, they'll nail him. He won't be able to hurt you."

Alyssa shook her head. "I'm not going to let him off the hook. He can't just keep living his life like nothing happened."

Derek climbed into the driver's seat and slid his hand across the console. His hand rested on her jean-clad leg and gave her a comforting squeeze. "I don't like it any better than you do. But we're not going to stop digging. If your uncle's behind this, we'll find the proof."

"What do you mean, if?" she asked, whirling on Derek. "Are you like Reyes? Do you think I'm deluded, too?"

His mouth pulled into a hard, tight line. "I know you're upset and overwhelmed, so I'm going to forget you said that. After all I've been through for you lately, you should know how much I believe you."

"I'm sorry," she said, her voice high and tight with strain. "I just—I can't go on like this, always looking over my shoulder, wondering if he's going to come after me."

Fury bubbled up in her again. Her uncle, so devoted to maintaining the family image, the facade of propriety. Lashing out at her for her supposedly scandalous behavior.

And now that she knew the truth, the police wouldn't listen to her. No one took her seriously. She was just a stupid, useless trust-fund baby who had learned to manipulate the press and manufacture scandal to increase her fame.

Now it was time to put her skill to work for something important.

She knew exactly what she needed to do. If the police weren't willing to go after Harold Van Weldt, she was going to get him and get him good. Where it hurt most.

CHAPTER 21

"WHO ARE YOU calling?" Derek asked as he pulled away from the curb.

Alyssa ignored him as she dialed Kimberly's number. Everything that was about to happen was going to hurt her, too. And after all Kimberly had done for Alyssa, she owed it to her half sister not to blindside her with what she was about to do. Kimberly answered on the first ring. "Alyssa? Oh, my God, are you okay? I've been so worried."

"I'm fine," Alyssa said, turning away from Derek's warning glare.

"Where are you? Where have you been?"

"There's too much to go into right now. I'll explain everything when I see you. But, Kimberly, I just wanted to tell you . . . some stuff is going to come out."

"What kind of stuff?" Kimberly asked, her tone wary. "Is it about you and the drugs?"

"No, it's about—" She halted as Derek gave her leg a warning squeeze.

"Don't," he whispered through clenched teeth. "Don't tell her anything."

He was right. No matter how much she cared about Alyssa, Kimberly was loyal to Harold and loyal to the business. Alyssa didn't want her to tip him off and ruin her surprise.

"It's too much to go into over the phone. Can we get together later tonight?" Alyssa felt a twinge of guilt. If everything happened the way she hoped, the shit would hit the fan in a big way before she had a chance to talk to her sister in person. She could only hope her sister would forgive her, or at least understand why Alyssa did what she was about to do.

"I can't," Kimberly said, her voice clipped with tension. "I have to go to the Black-and-White Ball tonight. They're doing a special tribute to Daddy, and Uncle Harold is giving a speech."

Alyssa's stomach churned, and acid burned the back of her throat. After everything he'd done, Harold Van Weldt was going to stand up in front of hundreds of San Francisco's elite and pretend to honor her father.

"Perfect," Alyssa said, feeling her eyes narrow and her lips curl into a shrewd smile. "I'll see you there."

She hung up before Kimberly could respond and didn't pick up when her sister called right back.

Derek took his attention from the early evening city traffic to shoot her a suspicious look. "What's with that look? Where do you think you're going?"

"We're going to the Black-and-White Ball. And we're going to let everyone know the truth about where Harold Van Weldt gets all his diamonds."

Hundreds of heads swiveled in their direction as Alyssa strode into the main ballroom of the Ritz-Carlton, San Francisco, with Derek close on her heels. In her electric-blue satin mini dress, Alyssa stood out like a beacon amid a sea of black and white. They'd made a quick detour to Neiman's, where Alyssa had dropped an astounding amount of money on the dress, shoes, and makeup. She donned them all with the deliberation of a knight preparing himself for battle. Within minutes she'd morphed into the glamorous creature who drew attention like moths to a flame.

Derek stood out, too, the only guy not dressed in black tie. And Derek was willing to bet good money no one else in the room had a Sig Sauer .45 stashed under his jacket or a Randall Model 1 fighting knife strapped to his calf. Alyssa had given him a wide-eyed look when he pulled the weapons out of his trunk. He'd stashed them without a word and followed her closely through the parking garage, all the while keeping an eye out for anyone who looked remotely suspicious.

What she was about to do was a cluster fuck in the making, and he cursed himself for the hundredth time for being stupid enough to let her talk him into it.

"The hell you're going!" he'd said when she announced her plans to crash the charity ball. "You're not going to put yourself out in the open like that."

"What am I supposed to do? Spend the rest of my life hiding from him?"

"Let the police do their job. In the meantime, I'll protect you."

"We can't stay in the cottage forever. I have a life to get back to."

When Derek had continued to protest, she'd backed him into a corner. "Fine," she said, pulling out her phone. "I'll tell my publicist to schedule a press conference at the safe house, how about that? Or maybe we should have it at your place? It won't have the same impact as crashing the benefit, but I'll get the information out anyway."

"Just be patient."

"Screw being patient! I want people to listen to me, to hear the truth before he has time to put his own spin on it and totally discredit me."

Derek had relented, but the tension between them seethed and churned until it was like a living beast. He knew she had a complicated relationship with the press. Sometimes using it to her advantage, sometimes getting screwed. But no one could deny her attention-grabbing antics had made her a star.

She said she wanted to lower her profile. But that wasn't the case right now when the need to spin the situation in her favor outweighed her sense of self-preservation.

Her spine was ramrod straight as she made her way through the maze of tables.

A ripple of whispers started across the room as the guests took notice and turned their attention from Harold Van Weldt, standing at the podium at the front of the room.

Get in, let her do her thing, get her the fuck out.

They'd deal with the other shit later when hundreds of people and dozens of cameras weren't around.

As Harold began his speech, Alyssa approached the guy running the slide show that accompanied the speech. She whispered something and gave him a dazzling smile. The guy looked skeptical, but, still, he accepted the CD from Alyssa and loaded it into the computer.

Derek had to hand it to her. Even pissed off and scared for her life, Alyssa had something. A glow, a charisma that would make just about any man fall at her feet and do her bidding.

Except for her uncle, whose constipated frown told Derek he'd spotted her in the crowd. Still, Harold continued with his speech, singing his late brother's praises, not noticing when the PowerPoint presentation on the screen behind him was replaced by startling photos of bone-thin men, women, and children covered in the mud of a pit mine and teenage boys holding guns bigger than they were.

Murmurs and gasps filled the ballroom as the grainy video of Abbassi and Mekembe began to play. Finally Van Weldt got the clue something was up and looked behind him.

Alyssa and Derek were next to the podium now, close enough to see the sweat bead across Harold's lip and the vein pulse across his forehead. Kimberly Van Weldt stood just to the side, her garish red lipstick the only color in her chalk-white face.

Harold stepped back a few inches from the podium and covered the microphone with his hands. "What do you think you are doing?"

Derek moved out of the glare of the spotlight and scanned the crowd, his stomach clenching with dread. He didn't really expect her uncle to try anything on Alyssa, not there with this crowd, but he couldn't shake the feeling that Alyssa's public spectacle was about to go very wrong.

"I'm telling the truth, Harold," Alyssa said, leaning into the mic so her voice boomed across the crowd. "This is the truth about where the Van Weldt diamonds come from. Nine months ago, Harold Van Weldt and Richard Blaylock made a deal with Louis Abbassi—many of you already know him, but for those who don't, he's the dark-haired guy in the video—to buy diamonds exclusively from Louis's diamond-cutting facility. They didn't care where the diamonds were coming from, as long as Louis could save them money. They didn't care that the diamonds are being used to fund wars that kill children and hurt innocent people."

Derek had to admit it. She had a great sense of timing, pausing her tirade as the camera showed the first-person perspective of Marie Laure as she was beaten by her captor.

"Then my father found out the truth, but before he could do anything about it, Harold had him killed and framed my stepmother to make it look like a murder suicide."

Harold's face pulled into a mask of fury, burning beat red as his mouth opened wide in an angry black hole.

Alyssa barely caught a blur of movement before pain exploded in her cheekbone, radiating up and out until her entire head was filled with a dull roar. She stumbled on her high heels, landing in a heap on the dais.

"You little bitch! Do you have any idea what you're saying?" Harold Van Weldt stood over her. He looked like a rabid dog, his fine, aristocratic features unrecognizable as he screamed at her.

Then Harold was flying through the air before landing on a table surrounded by stupefied philanthropists. Alyssa saw Derek on top of him, his fist crunching against Harold's cheekbone. Three guards struggled to pull Derek off, who gave Harold one last backhand before he rose. "You come near her again and I'll beat you so hard you'll piss blood for the rest of your life."

Derek shook off the security guards and lifted Alyssa to her feet, ran his hands over her as all hell continued to break loose in the ballroom. Cameras flashed, the crowd rumbled, and the on-site security team struggled to control hundreds of guests trying to squeeze to the front of the room to get a better view of the scandal in progress.

Derek tipped her face up to his. "Open and close your mouth for me," he said, his voice tight and clipped. Okay, he was pissed. No surprise there. He'd been pissed since she'd backed him into a corner and forced him into bringing her there.

Tough shit for him. As far as she was concerned, a bruised cheekbone was worth the public crucifixion her uncle would suffer in the next several weeks. Still, she tried to make light of the situation, compelled to ease the tension that knotted Derek's shoulders and made the tendons stand out on his neck. "Wow. I didn't think Uncle Harold had that in him. Goes to show you even a little guy can pack a mean bitch slap."

A few guests standing nearby chuckled uncomfortably, but Derek's stone-cold visage didn't crack.

He grabbed her by the arm and pulled her aside, though there was no privacy to be had. Over his shoulder Alyssa saw someone pointing a cell phone at them, no doubt video-taping the exchange, while several other guests used their phones to document Harold being escorted out by the hotel's security staff, struggling and spitting like a deranged tomcat.

"You think this is fucking funny? That this is a fucking joke?"

Alyssa looked into Derek's dark eyes, feeling herself shrink at the fury simmering there. "It's not a joke—"

He gave her a rough shake. "He could have really hurt you." He shook his head. "I can't believe I was dumb enough to let you talk me into this stupid idea."

"It wasn't stupid. Now people will know the truth—"

"This isn't about the truth. This is about your need to spin things in your favor. You accuse Harold of being wrapped up in the family's image, but look at what you're doing. You're so concerned about getting the press on your side you don't care that you're putting your life at risk. It's called common sense, Alyssa, and you don't have a goddamn lick of it."

Alyssa wanted to cover her ears, run and cower in a corner as every word hit her like a blow. *Stupid. Pathological need for attention. No common sense. Stupid.*

"That's enough." She forced the words through numb lips. "That's enough."

"And the hell of it is, you got me to go along with it. I knew you were trouble the first time I looked at you, but it's like I drop IQ points just from being around you."

She shivered as goose bumps broke out on her bare arms. Her peripheral vision disappeared, and suddenly she wasn't aware of anything but Derek, his angry, disapproving face, his devastating words.

His words struck her like physical blows, stunning in their viciousness and unfairness. The urge to cower away fled in the face of rage, rage like nothing she'd ever known boiling up inside her. She was sick of trying to please people, only to get ground into the dust. Sick of loving and trusting people, only to have them screw her over.

She yanked her arm from his hold, drew her arm back, and

put all her weight behind the slap that caught him squarely in the cheek. He jerked his head back, and as flashbulbs popped, she could see the imprint of her small hand appear in his face.

"Who do you think you are to talk to me like that?" she said, paying no attention to the dangerous narrowing of his eyes. "You think I'm stupid? You're the one who didn't believe me, who thought I was making it all up until I was kidnapped and drugged. You're the one who was duped by Richard and my uncle until it was almost too late."

"Alyssa," he said, his voice a low, warning growl, "don't do this here."

She ignored him and swatted him across the chest with her handbag. "You're the one who's wasting his life pining after his mommy who left him, pushing away anyone who's idiot enough to try to get close to you because you're afraid they'll leave, too."

His face froze. "Don't go there," he said through lips that barely moved. "You don't want to go there."

"That's right," she said, her anger burning like acid in her throat. She was ashamed of herself for going for his jugular but was unable to stop herself. His knuckles showed white as his hands clenched into fists. "Push me away. Swat me down when you start to care too much. Well, don't worry." She planted her palms against his chest and gave him a shove. He didn't move an inch. "I'm done throwing myself at people who treat me like garbage. If you're too stupid to accept love when it's given to you, that's your loss."

She spun around and ran into another body. A slim arm wrapped around her shoulders.

"Are you okay, honey? Did he hurt you badly?"

Alyssa sighed with relief. Kimberly. She leaned into her sister for support.

"Alyssa!" Derek called out, but she let herself be swallowed by the crowd, steered away by her sister's firm arm across her back.

"I'm sorry, Kimberly," she said, suddenly awash in guilt. Derek was right. This had been a horrible idea, but she hadn't been able to see beyond her own need for vengeance to think about how this would spell disaster for Kimberly as well. Or, rather, she had considered it but had ultimately been too self-centered to care until it was too late. "I know this is going to make all kinds of problems for you and the business," Alyssa said as Kimberly somehow guided her through the crowd.

"Let's find someplace quiet to talk," said Kimberly, a slight tremor in her voice the only indication tonight's events were anything out of the ordinary.

She directed Alyssa to a door behind the dais and screen, and when they went through, Alyssa saw it was the entrance to a service hallway. A few waiters and a busboy walked by, barely sparing them a second glance.

The adrenaline was wearing off. Her entire face throbbed from Harold's blow, but the worst pain was from Derek's words, ricocheting through her body like shrapnel, tearing everything to shreds. He thought she was a vain, stupid, attention-addicted idiot.

What was wrong with her that she kept opening herself up to people who loved to smack her back down? Derek was right. She didn't have an iota of common sense.

No. She stiffened her spine. She was done being screwed over. Done being taken advantage of. Like she said to Derek, it was his loss.

She blinked back her tears and focused on her sister, trying to find the words to apologize to her. "I know I should have handled this differently," she said, avoiding Kimberly's gaze. As supportive as Kimberly was, Alyssa knew she'd see censure in her sister's eyes. "But I couldn't sit on the truth anymore. I had to let everyone know what had really happened."

"It's okay," Kimberly said. "It's good the truth is finally out there." Her voice was calm. Too calm.

Alyssa looked at Kimberly's face, and she knew.

She turned on her heel and started to run down the hall as fast as her spike heels would allow. Kimberly caught her by the hair and yanked. Alyssa screamed in anger and pain, hoping someone would hear. She wheeled on Kimberly and landed a closed-fist punch on the side of her sister's head, but Kimberly's grip didn't ease.

"Let me go, you crazy bitch!" Alyssa yelled, wondering where the hell the hotel staff had disappeared to. She hit Kimberly again, wincing as her knuckles connected with her sister's chin.

Kimberly grunted and raised her hand. Alyssa tried but couldn't block her as Kimberly landed a blow to her head with something hard—much harder than a fist.

Alyssa's knees gave way, her head ringing as she realized what Kimberly had hit her with.

A gun. Pointing directly at her face.

What the fuck was the matter with him? Derek had done it again. Let his anger get the best of him, let it take over so he said horrible, awful things he couldn't stop even as he saw the devastation washing over Alyssa's pale face. But when Van Weldt had hit her, when he'd seen her go down, rage like nothing he'd ever known had blown through him like a firestorm. It took every bit of control he possessed not to kill Van Weldt with his bare hands. As far as Derek was concerned, the guy was lucky to get off with a few bruises.

Then, when he'd seen the rapidly darkening mark on Alyssa's cheek, he couldn't hold it back. Anger was clawing him from the inside, demanding to be let out. And he let it out all over the woman he loved.

Sure, he was pissed at her, angry she'd taken such risks. But Derek knew exactly who was at fault. Himself. If he could have, he would have beaten his own ass to a pulp for being such an idiot. He had accused her of being stupid. But he was the one who had let her talk him into this against every shred of common sense he possessed.

She was right, he was the stupid one. He accused her of putting herself in danger, but he was the asshole who hadn't stayed close enough to stop Van Weldt from getting physical. He was the one who let down his guard, let her convince him her uncle wouldn't do anything really bad, not in front of this crowd.

And he supposed a smack in the face wasn't the end of the world, but any injury to her was too much in his book.

But instead of pulling her to safety, kissing her cheek, and getting her the hell out of there, he'd gone and creamed her.

His cheek stung from where she'd smacked him. He could have caught her hand, but he had taken the slap, knowing he deserved every blow, every angry word that had passed her lips.

. . . pining after his mommy who left him, pushing away anyone who's idiot enough to try to get close to you because you're afraid they'll leave, too.

She was right. And he needed to grow up and let it go, or he was never going to have a chance with Alyssa.

He scanned the crowd, forming his apology in his head. Should he first tell her he loved her to soften her up? His throat got tight with panic at the thought of admitting it out loud, but he had to do it sometime, and now was as good as any.

I'm done throwing myself at people who treat me like garbage.

Give me another chance, he thought as he stepped onto the dais for a better view. *I know I don't deserve it, but give me another chance, and I swear I'll treat you like a queen.* He cased the crowd, looking for Kimberly's tall figure and pale blond hair, easier to spot than Alyssa's much shorter profile.

He didn't see them.

It's fine, his rational analytical brain assured him. *She's with Kimberly. They probably found a quiet corner to tear me to shreds. And we've already determined Kimberly wasn't involved.*

The uneasy sensation he'd been nursing all night intensified, uncurling in his gut like a snake, slithering up his spine.

Had they really determined Kimberly wasn't involved? They hadn't found evidence that Kimberly was involved in the deal with Abbassi, but still. He'd taken Alyssa's word for it, believed in her fierce conviction that her sister would never want to hurt her.

Cold sweat filmed under his T-shirt. Had he done it again? Underestimated the enemy just because she was a woman and didn't look dangerous?

Derek scanned the crowd again, getting a little frantic when he didn't see them. He moved off the dais, oblivious to the questioning looks of the guests and staff as he ducked behind the screen where he thought he'd seen the two women go.

There was a door back there that led to a service hall. He looked up and down the hall, didn't see any sign of the two women. He was about to duck back in the ballroom when he saw a white-coated busboy carrying a tray full of glasses.

"Hey," he said. "Did you see two women back here? One tall, one short?"

"Si," the man replied in heavily accented English. "I think they go that way." He pointed down the hall.

Derek took off at a lope, dread building in his stomach as he pulled out his phone to call Alyssa. But before he could dial, his phone rang. He picked it up when he saw Toni's number on the display.

"What's up?" He'd come to the end of the hall the busboy had indicated. The only thing there was a service elevator.

"Is Alyssa with you? I need to talk to her."

The hairs on the back of Derek's neck rose at the urgency in Toni's tone. "She went with Kimberly."

Dead silence. Then a soft "Shit."

"What? What did you find?" He instinctively pressed the elevator button to the lobby level.

"You have to find her. I found a copy of the termination agreement Blaylock and Oscar were talking about. It wasn't for Harold, it was for Kimberly."

Oh, fuck.

"Exactly. And get this—Blaylock and Kimberly are having an affair. There are e-mails and IM logs. You should see the stuff she says about Alyssa."

He'd done it again. Overlooked the enemy when she was in plain sight.

Worse, he'd let his emotions get the best of him. In his anger at Alyssa, he'd dropped his guard, turned his back, lost focus long enough for the enemy to get the upper hand.

To take the woman he loved.

He hung up the cell phone and sprinted for the staircase. They'd been gone only a few minutes. He flew down ten flights of stairs and burst into the lobby, oblivious to the startled stares as he sprinted for the door. He ignored shouts from the valets as he ran down the ramp to the hotel parking garage. He was almost to the bottom when he heard the roar of an engine.

Big, German, and coming up fast. The lights hit him straight on, momentarily blinding him as they headed for him. Derek ducked and rolled, narrowly avoiding becoming a blood streak on the wall as the driver attempted to pin him.

Derek came to a stop just in time to register the license-plate number and Alyssa's terrified face in the rear window as the car sped off.

Derek. She wanted to hurl herself from the car, scream his name until he came after her. But hurling was out of the question because her hands were bound in front of her. And there was the matter of Kimberly's gun trained at her head. Screaming would only get her another knock on the head, and at this rate she was going to sustain serious brain damage before the night was through—if she didn't die first. If she wanted to get out of this, she needed to keep her wits about her.

She scooted as far as she could go across the leather backseat of the BMW and prayed that somehow, some way, Derek would find a way to get to her, especially because her purse, her cell phone, and, with it, Derek's tracking device were currently lying somewhere on the floor of the parking garage.

"Why?" Alyssa asked, unfreezing her tongue enough to ask the million-dollar question.

Kimberly made a scoffing noise and gave Alyssa a disbelieving look. "Are you kidding me? You've never been anything but Daddy's bastard and a family embarrassment."

"So you decided you needed to kill me?" Alyssa's tone was aggressive, impatient, but, hey, it looked like she wasn't going to make it through the night, and she'd be damned if she died without finding out why.

"I worked my ass off for the company," said Kimberly. "I did everything for the family. I brokered a deal to save the business. But who got the credit for saving the company? You! You and your skanky ad campaign with Van Weldt diamonds all over your twat."

"So that's why you killed Daddy? Because he gave me credit?"

The driver headed for the on ramp to the Bay Bridge, heading east toward Oakland.

"No, you idiot. I killed him because he was going to fire me. I got us enough capital to avoid bankruptcy, but when Daddy found out that Louis and the diamonds might not all be legitimate, instead of thanking me for saving the company, he decided to fire me."

"What did you expect him to do? You made a deal with a guy who turned out to be a diamond smuggler and an arms dealer." Kimberly's face pulled into a mask of rage, and Alyssa wondered if mouthing off was going to earn her another blow to the head. Or worse.

Kimberly visibly pulled herself together. "There was no proof we knew that when we made the deal. We could have easily spun it so we came out looking like the victim. But Daddy said I'd broken his trust. Like he's one to talk."

"What about your mother?"

"She was a mess. She was becoming more of a public embarrassment than you are." Kimberly was insane, a stone-cold sociopath without an ounce of regret or remorse. Kimberly's mouth pursed. "You're supposed to be dead, too," she said, her matter-of-fact tone more chilling than her earlier rage. "But not everyone was completely on board. Louis had something else in mind for you."

They came off the bridge, and the driver turned south on the highway.

"What do you mean?" But she already knew the answer to that question. A memory burbled to the surface. *We can still work this out, Alyssa,* he'd said, even as his hand squeezed her breast in a bruising grip as she lay there, helplessly strapped to the bed.

She shrugged. "I don't know, and at this point I don't care. All I know is, as much as I want you dead, Louis wants you alive. For now."

CHAPTER 22

*F*OCUS. ADRENALINE PUMPED through Derek's veins, bordering on panic as he wove through evening traffic. He took that energy and channeled it into razor-sharp focus, becoming the machine with no other goal than to take down his enemy and complete his mission. He accelerated and swerved, narrowly missing the bumper of the Prius in the lane next to him as he maneuvered his Audi to the on ramp of the Bay Bridge. He couldn't afford to think of Alyssa now, her terrified face in the car window.

The fact that he'd finally realized he loved her, and now it might be too late. . . .

He shoved all that out of his head, pushing it aside, put himself on autopilot.

It was the only way he could save her.

He checked his navigation system, which showed that according to Toni, the black Beemer hadn't made it across the bridge yet.

After Derek had picked himself off the floor of the parking garage and sprinted to his own car, he'd placed a quick call to Toni. Within minutes she'd hacked into the system of red lights and traffic cameras that monitored San Francisco and the Bay Area highways. With the license-plate number and general direction Derek provided, Toni by some miracle managed to pick up the car and sent its updated location to Derek's nav system.

"I should be able to get a visual soon," he told Toni, who had stayed on the line with him to give him verbal updates before sending the BMW's location. At this time of night, traffic was steady, but he wouldn't have any trouble picking the big sedan out of the throng. Then it was just a matter of keeping his distance and not letting himself get made.

And there they were. Several cars ahead. The BMW moved fast, steady, but not fast enough to attract attention.

He put Toni on hold so he could call the cops. They could pull the BMW over and end this right here and now.

The dispatcher picked up. "Nine-one-one operator. Please hold."

You've got to be fucking kidding me.

Alyssa shivered as Kimberly and the driver escorted her into what appeared to be an abandoned warehouse. The only sign of life was another dark sedan similar to the one she'd arrived in, parked in the wide driveway, and a faint light showing through the broken windows along the roofline of the warehouse.

Gravel crunched under her high heels, and she stumbled. With her hands tied she couldn't brace herself and took the impact on her bare knees. She cried out when a sharp piece of gravel stabbed into skin and bone.

"Shut up," Kimberly said as she jerked her back to her feet.

Across the street, a dark figure rounded the corner and shuffled past, a pile of old rags pushing a shopping cart.

Alyssa yelled at the top of her lungs. "Help me, please! I'm being kidnapped! Get the police!" Her cry was cut off by the butt of Kimberly's gun clipping her on the side of the head again.

Not that Kimberly needed to worry, Alyssa realized blearily.

The vagrant didn't so much as glance their way as he rattled his way down the block.

Kimberly and the driver opened the door and shoved her inside the dimly lit warehouse full of empty crates. Broken bottles and trash littered the floor, and it smelled like it might have been recently used as a bathroom.

And standing in the center, his dusky skin jaundiced by the yellow light, his lips pulled into a smile that was all the more frightening in its pure delight, was Louis Abbassi. He was flanked by two men carrying wicked-looking machine guns while another man joined the driver to stand by the door.

"Ah, you are here," he said, and Alyssa swallowed back bile at the glee in his tone. "It has been too long since I have seen you, beautiful Alyssa."

The way he drew out the *S*'s in her name reminded her of a slithering snake. "What do you want from me?"

He reached out to touch her cheek, and she couldn't keep herself from flinching. His smile fell at her response. Quick as a striking snake, he backhanded her across the cheek. Her ears rang, and her eyes filled with tears. *Now I'll have a bruise to match the other cheek,* she thought morbidly.

"You can taste pain or pleasure, *chérie*, but the more you shrink from me, the more determined I will be to break you." He ran his fingers down her throat, pressed meaningfully against her windpipe. Alyssa swallowed hard, her knees shaking as she thought of Andy, choked to death and left in Alyssa's closet. She forced herself to hold perfectly still as Louis ran his hand over her collarbone, down her chest, to cover one small breast.

She caught Kimberly's smirk out of the corner of her eye.

"I did what you asked," Kimberly said. "Now give me the passport and the account number, and I'll get out of here."

Louis nodded and gave Alyssa's nipple a rough squeeze. She struggled not to vomit.

Please, God, please let Derek be coming for me.
I will always come for you.

She clung to his words like a lifeline as Louis turned to Kimberly, who was standing, arms folded, toe tapping impatiently like she was waiting for a late train. Not like she had just cold-bloodedly handed over her half sister to a psychopathic killer.

"Yes," Louis said, turning from Kimberly to retrieve a briefcase resting on the floor. "You did as I asked, and now you will get what you deserve."

Unease replaced the smug impatience on Kimberly's face as Louis said something in a flat, clipped language she didn't recognize and nodded at the thug standing to his left.

The horrified realization on Kimberly's face matched Alyssa's own as, without a word, the man lifted his gun. There was nothing but a faint *pop,* and Kimberly's chest exploded. Her mouth opened in a silent scream as she staggered back several feet and then fell in a sprawl. Her eyes stared silently at the ceiling, and a trickle of blood ran out of the corner of her mouth.

Derek had parked his car several blocks away and crept to the warehouse where Kimberly had taken Alyssa. Now he stood just outside the door, his Sig raised, silent and still as he blended into the shadows.

He listened intently, his stomach boiling with sour bile as he listened to Louis. The sick fuck was obsessed with her. Derek had a feeling the whole deal with Van Weldt had been an elaborate way for Louis to get close to Alyssa.

Suddenly a woman was screaming loud, long wails. Every primal, male instinct in him bellowed at him to charge in there, gun blazing to protect what was his.

Alyssa. His woman.

Then he heard her sobbing. "You shot her. Oh, my God, you killed Kimberly."

Which meant Alyssa was still alive, and he needed to get a fucking grip.

He dug deep, summoning years of practice in shoving his emotions aside, all his military training. Following his emotions would get him killed, and Alyssa would still be in the hands of this sick fuck.

He drowned out the sobs that cut him like razors, forced himself to stay focused, to analyze the situation and come up with a strategy that would get them both out alive and unhurt.

He used the darkness to his advantage as he craned his head for a quick glance inside. The two thugs standing near the door didn't so much as feel the air stir. There were two more men inside with Louis, and then Louis himself.

Five men, all armed, against himself, armed with his Sig .45 and a wickedly sharp combat knife.

He cursed silently as he remembered his extra clip locked in his gun case in the trunk of his car.

Seven bullets.

Five men.

Good enough odds for him.

Someone was screaming loud and high like a siren wail. *Maybe it's the police. Maybe they're coming to save me.* Something hit her across the face, a big, open hand smacking her over and over. The siren wail stopped, and Alyssa realized it had been her screaming.

Suddenly everything became disjointed, disconnected, like her life had become a movie she was watching rather than living. She saw herself, hands to horrified mouth as she watched one of Louis's thugs drag Kimberly's body away.

She saw Louis draping his suit jacket over her shoulders and pulling her close in a sick attempt to offer comfort.

"You killed her," Alyssa finally choked out, coming back

to herself. "Why would you kill her? She was working with you, helping you."

"*Chérie*, you would be dead if she had her way. I could not let her live after she tried to harm you so. Don't you understand, I will do anything for you, even kill those who try to do you harm."

"You killed Andy, didn't you?" She already knew it was true but wanted to hear him admit it.

Louis's hand tightened painfully on her shoulder. "Vicious cow. She thought because that idiot Richard made her do it, she could get away with it." He pulled away slightly and tilted Alyssa's chin up to meet his gaze. "But I will not let anyone hurt you, you see?" His smile would have been tender if not for the half-crazed light in his eyes.

Christ, he really expected her to be grateful to him.

"You killed Richard, too?"

"Of course. After what he did to you, how could I not?" He shook his head. "And he tried to convince me it was all his idea, but I knew your cunt of a sister led him around by the balls." He nodded in the direction of the black smear of blood Kimberly's body had left on the concrete floor.

Nausea choked Alyssa. Louis had killed Kimberly, and Richard and Andy, too, all out of some twisted loyalty to her.

"But now you are safe, and we can finally be together."

Safe? Alyssa bit back a hysterical bubble of laughter.

"We would have been together much sooner if your would-be savior hadn't interfered," Louis continued, his mouth pulled tight in disgust.

Derek.

"Yes, Taggart."

Alyssa hadn't realized she'd spoken his name aloud.

Louis's eyes narrowed on her. "He has had you, hasn't he?"

She shook her head, eyes widening in panic as his fingers closed over her throat.

"Do not lie to me. I suspected it all along, and now I see the truth in your eyes. But now you are with me. You will forget about him, erase his touch from your memory, until all you know is me. I will drape you in diamonds, give you everything your heart desires. You will be happy with me, *chérie*, you will see." He smiled as his fingers loosened and slid across her throat in a mockery of a caress.

She struggled not to throw up. "You can't expect me to go willingly after what you've done—"

All hint of affection left his face. "Your mother is very ill, *oui?*"

Alyssa nodded and felt tears slip down her cheeks.

"You want her to live, do you not?"

Alyssa nodded again.

"Then you will do as I ask, in all things."

Alyssa closed her eyes, half wishing he would kill her. Death was preferable to what he had planned.

Derek slipped across the front of the warehouse. A cracked cinderblock lay in the driveway. Derek heaved it one-armed at the windshield of one of the black sedans.

The night exploded with the sound of shattering glass and the blare of the car alarm. Lights flashed, the horn honked, a siren wailed.

Derek crouched next to the car as two men rushed from the building, brandishing their guns.

He fired two quick shots at one, splintering his forearm and sending his gun flying. The other thug wheeled around and peppered the ground where Derek had been standing with machine-gun fire. Derek rolled around the other side of the car, popped up over the hood, and took out the thug with one shot to his gun arm and another to his kneecap.

The man fell, cursing and groaning. Derek ran past him, scooping up the machine gun the first one had dropped without breaking stride. He grabbed the other's Glock and tucked it into his waistband.

He could hear Louis bellowing inside the warehouse as Derek slipped inside the door. He let fly with a round of machine-gun fire pointed away from Louis, Alyssa, and Louis's two guards. Derek used the distraction to slip deeper into the shadows, ducking behind an abandoned crate.

Louis screamed in Afrikaans as his two men warily peered into the darkness, trying to get a bead on Derek's position. One of his men fired as Louis made a break for the door, half dragging, half carrying Alyssa in his wake.

Derek raised his gun, aiming for Louis's head.

A bullet sang past his ear, and he jerked back.

His shot went wide, slamming into the wall next to the doorway, but at least it halted Louis in his tracks. Alyssa took advantage of Louis's distraction and jerked from his hold, balled her bound hands into a fist, and brought them up hard against the bottom of his nose. She followed that with a stomp of her lethal heel into the top of Louis's foot. Louis staggered back, clutching his bleeding nose, and slipped his hold on her. But instead of running for the door as Derek hoped, Alyssa ran deeper into the warehouse, disappearing into the dark labyrinth of abandoned crates.

Louis took off after her. Machine-gun fire peppered the crate Derek was behind. He ducked down, felt wooden splinters embed themselves in his cheek. He popped back up, saw the barrel of the guard's Kalashnikov glint in the dim yellow light. He took aim, squeezed off two quick shots, and was gratified by the sound of a meaty thunk of a bullet hitting flesh, followed by the thud of a body hitting the floor.

He rolled and belly-crawled silently across the floor as bullets hit the crate he'd been behind just seconds before. He stopped and rolled up to his knee, squeezing off one shot to draw fire.

The other guard took the bait. Two more shots, and the guard was facedown on the floor with a bullet between his eyes.

Louis was nowhere to be seen, lost in the dark cavern of the warehouse.

So was Alyssa.

Derek held himself perfectly still, so quiet he couldn't even hear his own breath.

Nothing.

Then he heard it. A scuffle, a muffled, "No," and he saw Louis drag Alyssa into the pool of light. He had a Glock 9mm in his hand, and it was pointed directly at Alyssa's head.

"Drop your weapons and show yourself, Taggart."

"I know you don't want her dead," Derek replied from his hiding place. He set the machine gun down, creeping around the side of the crate. His Sig was empty, so he tucked it into his waistband, trading it for the Glock.

"It is not my preference," Louis said, lifting Alyssa up off the ground, holding her against his chest and blocking a head shot. "But if it comes down to a choice between her life and mine, I will not hesitate. Now come out where I can see you."

Derek didn't move.

Louis held up Alyssa's hand, grabbed her pinkie, and snapped the bone before Derek could react.

Alyssa's cry echoed through the warehouse, ricocheting through Derek like shrapnel.

"I may not want her dead, but I am happy to cause her pain. Perhaps you would like to watch me punish her for letting you touch her."

Derek's stomach roiled as Louis's fingers closed over the ring finger of Alyssa's right hand.

Alyssa slid down his body an inch, opening up a target. Derek raised the Glock, his thumb pausing over the safety.

He couldn't do it. If it had been his own Sig, which he'd fired thousands of times, he wouldn't have hesitated. He'd hit Abbassi with a double tap to the head and he'd be dead before he knew what hit him.

But he'd never fired the Glock before. Had no idea how it shot straight. If his trajectory was off, even a centimeter, he would hit Alyssa. He couldn't do it.

Derek stepped from behind the crate and held his hands up, letting the Glock slip from his grip to land on the floor with a thud.

Time for Plan B.

Derek didn't let his gaze linger too long on Alyssa, who cradled her wounded hand as she stood on shaky legs, her face sickly pale in the dim light, her eyes dilated with pain.

"Alyssa, I love you. It's going to be okay," he said, hoping his reassuring tone would penetrate.

"Yes, all will be well," Louis said with a serpent's smile. "Once I have dispatched Mr. Taggart, we will be on our way. Come closer, Mr. Taggart." He took his gun from Alyssa's head and aimed it at Derek.

"No." Everything in Alyssa froze. "Please, Louis." She yanked on his arm, the pain of her broken finger fading in her adrenaline-fueled panic. "Let's just go. I'll do anything you want, but please don't kill him."

Louis gave her a vicious shove and sent her sprawling.

She scrambled to her knees, wondering if she could make it to the gun Derek had dropped before Louis could shoot either of them.

"Now turn around," Louis said.

Keening sobs choked her. "I love you, too," she whispered, and she knew she was going to watch Derek die.

* * *

"Fuck you," Derek said. "If you want to kill me, look at my face while you do it." Everything came into sharp, vivid focus. The harsh sound of Alyssa's sobs, her sweet scent mingling with the sharper scents of fear, cordite, and spilled blood.

The cold blade of his knife pressing into his calf.

Louis's finger tightening on the trigger.

Derek jerked to the side just as the deafening boom echoed through the warehouse, hissed as the bullet dug a furrow through the right side of his rib cage.

Derek landed and rolled, unsheathing his knife and throwing it even before he stopped moving. The eight-inch blade buried itself to the hilt in Louis's upper right chest.

The last remnants of calm disappeared, lost in the killing rage that roared through Derek's veins. Derek sprang on Louis like a panther, grabbing Louis's gun hand and slamming it into the ground. Louis squeezed off a wild shot, and the gun went skidding across the floor. Derek eased up enough to grab the knife and yanked it out of Louis's chest.

Louis howled in pain, clutching at his chest. With one savage slice of Derek's arm, the howl turned into a death gurgle.

Derek smiled in savage satisfaction as the warm spray of Louis's blood arced into the air.

As quickly as it had overtaken him, the bloodlust was gone. Now his only thought was Alyssa, relief flooding him as he realized she was finally safe.

"It's over, baby," he said, pushing to his feet and turning toward her. "Now let's—"

His words froze in his chest, his relief turning to horror when he saw Alyssa lying in a crumpled heap, her thick, tawny hair sticky wet and black with blood.

CHAPTER 23

ALYSSA CRACKED HER gritty eyelids, wincing as white light stabbed her retinas and made her already throbbing head throb even more. God, this was even worse than her usual headaches, the pain not only pounding through her skull but stabbing and pulling at her scalp on the right side.

The pain in her head was joined by that of her hand, jolting up and down her arm to meet the pain in her head until the two joined forces somewhere in her neck.

She lifted her other pain-free hand to touch her head, jerking it away at the rough feel of bandages. Her eyes opened wider and darted around what looked like a hospital room.

Panic knotted her stomach as she remembered Kimberly and Louis. Maybe this wasn't a hospital. They could be holding her again. She felt woozy, like she'd taken something. And this time Derek . . .

Oh, God, Derek. She remembered him dropping his gun, coming out from behind the crate, and Louis aiming his gun at him.

Derek was dead, and it was all her fault. She'd been stupid enough to go off with Kimberly, gotten herself in trouble, and now she'd killed the man she loved. Sobs tore at her throat, and tears spilled from her eyes. The pain in her body was nothing compared to this.

"Hey, it's okay." A low voice, husky with sleep, curled around her. "It's okay, Alyssa, don't cry."

Derek. Was this a dream? A byproduct of the drug-fueled haze? She turned her head gingerly to the side, wincing as pain stabbed through her scalp.

"Easy," Derek whispered, "you don't want to put any pressure on this side." She felt a weight settle on the bed next to her, and then his face was leaning above hers. Lines of fatigue carved deep grooves in his cheeks, and his eyes were ringed with dark circles. But his lips were pulled into a smile, his dimples in full effect as his eyes glittered with what Alyssa would have guessed were tears had it been any man other then Derek.

Then, to her utter shock, a drop of moisture trickled from the corner of one dark eye. He immediately brushed it away with his thumb.

"Are you crying?"

"You scared the shit out of me," he said, not bothering to deny it.

"What happened? I thought he killed you." Fresh terror spilled through her when the memory of Derek standing in front of her, a gun aimed at his head, sprang into her head as sharp and real as if it were happening all over again.

He curled his fingers around her uninjured hand as he recounted his superheroics as matter-of-factly as if he were describing a game at golf. "His bullet grazed your scalp and knocked you out. We were so lucky—" He broke off and closed his eyes. "When I saw you lying there, I thought you were dead. I—" He broke off again and brought her hand to his lips.

He didn't need to finish. She knew exactly how he felt. "How bad is it?"

Derek swallowed audibly and forced a smile. "Well, you've got a few dozen stitches, a fucked-up haircut, and a broken pinkie, but overall you got off easy."

"He killed Kimberly," she said, still struggling to absorb the fact that her sister had been behind a plot to kill her. "And Richard, too."

Derek nodded. "They dragged Richard's body out of the bay last night."

Alyssa closed her eyes against the renewed throbbing of her head. So many people dead. Thank God Derek had come for her. "Thanks for saving my life," she said, wincing at how inadequate that sounded. "Again."

His eyes squeezed shut, and he was silent for several seconds as he pressed another kiss to her uninjured hand. "Anytime, babe," he finally said, his voice thick with tears.

She heard a thud outside the door, followed by muffled shouts. "What's that?"

He shot a glare at the door. "Probably another reporter who managed to sneak through. They've been trying to get in all day. You think your life was a media circus before, you better brace yourself."

His words, his annoyance brought back another painful moment. It hit her like a blow. Even though Derek had come to her rescue yet again, it didn't mean he wanted to be part of her life and the chaos that surrounded it. Sure, he'd said he loved her, but she couldn't bank on something he'd said when he'd thought he was about to get his brains blown out.

She started to slip her fingers from his, but he held tight. "I'm sorry," he said as if reading her thoughts. "I know I said things to you last night, god-awful things I didn't mean." He broke off and shook his head. "I was angry at myself, and I took it out on you. It wasn't fair, and you didn't deserve that. I should have known better than to let you put yourself in that situation."

"Derek, that was my choice. I forced you to let me go, remember?"

"I could have stopped you if I wanted to. I should have done a better job protecting you. And when Harold hit you, I flew off the handle. I'm sorry."

She flicked her eyes closed, unable to meet his gaze. "You're right though. I did want to make it a media event, and not just to get back at my uncle, but to finally get some press coverage that didn't depict me as a brainless idiot." She lifted her eyes back to him. "But that didn't give you the right to talk to me that way."

"I know," he said. "Believe me, if I could take it all back, I would. Please, Alyssa, I—" He broke off, cleared his throat, tightened his fingers around her hand. "I love you."

Hope swelled in her heart, and she wanted to believe him, wanted to believe that made everything okay. But her wounds were still too fresh; she'd taken too many blows from people who claimed to care about her, only to turn on her. "I wish I could believe you," she said, her head and hand starting to throb in concert, making it difficult to concentrate. "But it's like every time I feel like you're starting to care, you shove me away. And you know exactly what to say to hurt me."

"Alyssa." He closed his eyes and pressed his head against her hand. When he opened them again, they were dark with regret. "I love you. I meant it when I said it last night, and I mean it now. I've never said that to any woman, because I never felt it before. And honestly, it scares the living shit out of me. You're right. I don't let people in. What happened with my mom made me"—he paused, screwing up his face like he tasted something bitter—"afraid to feel anything or care about anyone too much."

"So what changed? How am I supposed to believe you've done this one-eighty?" Her heart hurt as much as her head, and she wanted to cry uncle already and throw herself into his arms. But she didn't want to make another mistake.

A smile quirked his lips even as his eyes filled up again. "I don't think I'll ever be ready for you, Alyssa Miles. You're a force of nature who came into my life and turned me inside out, and now all I can do is beg you to give me another chance."

"Really? You really want to be part of the media circus that is my life? It's not going to get any better. This is going to be a hot story for a long time, and they're going to dig up everything they can find about me and the people in my life. It's too late for you to avoid it completely, but if you get out now, it shouldn't get too bad for you."

A deep crease formed between his dark eyebrows. "I don't want out. I just want you." He slid off the bed and knelt on the floor. "See this, Alyssa. I'm begging you. In fact . . ." He stood up abruptly, walked across the room, and flung open the door. "Hey, you, get in here!" she heard him yell. "Moreno, let him go, get him in here."

Seconds later, a short, weasely looking guy with a camera ducked in the room, his eyes lighting on Alyssa like he'd won the lottery.

Alyssa groaned when she recognized Charlie Farris, his camera flashing as he shot another exclusive series of Alyssa-Miles-in-the-hospital shots.

"Take it all in, dude," Derek said, oblivious to the reporter and his history of photographing Alyssa. "You're about to get one hell of an exclusive."

He strode back over to the bed and resumed his kneeling position.

"I'm begging you," he repeated, "to give me another chance. I love you." His eyes were intense, focused. He pressed a kiss against the pad of her index finger. "I can't stop think-ing of you." He moved onto her middle finger, grazing the tip with his teeth. "I want to be with you all the time, have you next to me so I can reach out and touch you any time I want."

Alyssa swallowed hard and didn't respond. But a warm glow had taken root inside her and was unfurling like ribbons through her limbs.

"When I thought you were dead, I felt like my world had ended," Derek said, all teasing gone from his voice. He leaned over her and kissed her, first on the mouth and then on each cheek and the tip of her nose. "I love you, Alyssa." He lifted his head and smiled at her. "Now, I know I don't deserve it, but how about you forgive me for being such an asshole and tell me you love me back?"

She was silent for several long seconds as though seriously considering her decision. He swallowed hard, and despite his stoicism, she could see real fear lurking in his dark eyes.

"Forgive him," Farris said.

Derek rolled his eyes, stood up, and grabbed the guy by the collar. "Okay. That's enough. Take it to *People* magazine and run with it."

"Your welcome, Charlie!" Alyssa called as Derek shoved him out the door.

"You know him?" Derek asked, puzzled.

"Let's just say this will be the second time I made his career."

He came back to the bed and took hold of her hand. She tried not to gloat at the faint tremble in his fingers. He sank again to the floor. "I can see it now. Cover story of *Us Weekly*. ALYSSA MILES'S MYSTERY MAN BEGS HER NOT TO DUMP HIM ON HIS SORRY ASS." Deep grooves framed his tight lips despite his attempt at humor.

His gaze was unwavering as he waited for her answer, and she couldn't keep from reveling for a few more seconds in the fact that she had brought big, tough, impervious Derek Taggart to his knees.

Finally she let her smile break free and tugged her hand from his. She curved her fingers around his neck and wove them through the short, silky hair at his nape. "I love you back. And if you stay on your best behavior for the next fifty or so years, I'll think about forgiving you. Deal?"

His dimples creased his cheeks, and the love was evident in his face as he let the last piece of the wall around his heart fall away. "Deal."

Six weeks later . . .

Derek jumped up from the couch as soon as he heard the car pull into the driveway. He was out the door and on the driveway before the driver had unloaded Alyssa's suitcase. He opened her door himself, pulling her off her feet and into his arms before she even had a chance to get out of the limo.

He was being ridiculous, but didn't care. She'd been gone for two weeks in Africa. Right after she'd gotten out of the hospital, she'd worked with the United Nations High Commissioner for Refugees and, using the information in Martin Fish's notes, she'd located Marie Laure and her baby in a refugee camp in Kinshasa. Determined to help Marie Laure and victims of southern Africa's civil wars, Alyssa was working with UNHCR and UNICEF and made the trip to help the foundation bring the plight of the region's war refugees to the world's attention.

As Martin Fish had envisioned, with Alyssa's name attached, the world, or American media at least, took notice.

Derek had hated to let her go. Bad enough she'd barely escaped getting killed a few weeks before. Now her first trip away from him, she'd had to go to one of the most dangerous places on the globe. He could barely stand to let her out of his sight for a few hours, much less two weeks, but he knew how important the trip was, both to the foundation and to her.

Now, at least, he could get some sleep, something he'd done very little of in the time she'd been gone. He had nightmares about the night she'd been shot, but in the dreams more often than not, she didn't survive. He'd wake up in a cold sweat, heart pounding, convinced he was going to roll over and find her lying in a pool of her own blood. Only the sight of her, sound asleep on the pillow next to him, was enough to calm him down enough to fall back asleep. The nightmares, combined with the ongoing stress of not knowing if one of the bodies found in the mountains belonged to his mother, had made sleep a scarce commodity in the past two weeks.

This was new to him, needing someone. He still wasn't sure he liked it, but it was his reality, and he was working with it.

But he didn't begrudge Alyssa her time away. She needed this, maybe as much as he liked to think she needed him. After drifting aimlessly through life, Alyssa seemed to find purpose in using her celebrity to better the world.

She'd even made peace, of sorts, with her uncle Harold. At least, she'd apologized publicly for accusing him of murder. Though Harold hadn't been involved in the plot to kill Oscar Van Weldt or Alyssa Miles—that was all on Kimberly, Richard, and Abbassi—he wasn't entirely innocent. He'd willingly looked the other way when it came to Abbassi and to taking the man's money. And when the shit had hit the fan, he'd let Kimberly take the blame for setting up the deal. Anything to save the family business and his position in it.

Which of course backfired horribly. After the ensuing scandal, Van Weldt's retail sales dried up. After nearly seventy-five years in business, Harold Van Weldt was trying to find a buyer for the business. So far there had been no takers, as other jewelers were quick to disassociate themselves from the stain of contraband diamonds.

Alyssa, however, was still in the jewelry business and was busy developing a line of jewelry made only with gemstones and precious metals that came from environmentally sound sources with good working conditions for the miners. The first line wouldn't be out until later next year, but they already had thousands of buyers on the waiting list.

"Two weeks is too long," he grumbled, barely even noticing the sound of shutters snapping and shouts of "Alyssa, look over here!" coming from the other side of their gate. He'd gotten used to the paparazzi tailing them in the weeks since the Van Weldt blood-diamond scandal—as the press had dubbed it—had exploded in the media.

He'd gotten used to a lot of other things, too, like waking up with his morning erection nestled up against the sweet curve of her ass and looking over the *Marketplace* section of the *Journal* to see her thumbs flying over her BlackBerry keypad as she shot off e-mails to her manager, her publicist, or her contacts at the UNHCR and UNICEF.

Derek could put up with a few pictures if it meant he got all the other stuff. He turned Alyssa so her back was to the cameras and grabbed her ass so they'd have something good to shoot. As he kissed her, he could see the headline: PASSIONATE REUNION FOR HEIRESS AND BODYGUARD BOY TOY.

Danny and Ethan would have a ball giving him all kinds of hell, but he didn't care. He'd put up with a lot of shit to have it this good.

He let her down long enough to slip the driver a tip and grab her bag to take it to the door of the house they'd moved into right after Alyssa got out of the hospital. She couldn't go back to the Victorian for obvious reasons, and though it was secure, Derek's place wasn't private enough. So they'd moved into this three-bedroom ranch house, the key selling point that it was surrounded by a fifteen-foot wall and an iron gate sturdy enough to keep out unwanted visitors.

He closed and locked the door and followed her into the kitchen. "I missed you," he said, kissing her hard as he ran his hands over every inch of her, assuring himself she was okay. She'd texted or called him several times a day to let him know she was safe, sent pictures of herself grinning as she held Marie Laure's sleeping son in her arms, but he still needed to reassure himself she was here, in his arms, safe.

"I can feel how much you missed me," she said, cradling his erection between her thighs as he lifted her onto the kitchen table. She ran her hand down his side, coasted it over his hip, pausing at the bulge in his pocket. "What's that?"

His hand froze on her back for a split second. "Nothing."

She frowned and eyed him with mock suspicion and dug her fingers into his pocket.

He tried to squirm away, but it was too late, she'd already extracted the black velvet box from the front pocket of his jeans. He'd picked it up earlier that morning and had meant to put it away.

Alyssa's head cocked to the side, and she raised one eyebrow. "Is this . . . ?"

"I was going to wait to give it to you later."

"When later?" Her pink lips quirked to the side, and with her new short haircut, she looked like a mischievous elf.

"I don't know." He scrambled for words, wishing he had some slick comeback at the ready. "A special occasion." *When I was sure what your answer would be.*

Yeah, he knew she loved him because she told him all the time and showed him in dozens of little ways he would have never imagined he would have appreciated, but that didn't mean he was ready to bet the farm and let his ass hang out to be kicked.

She handed the box back, straightened her shoulders, and looked at him expectantly.

"You know, this isn't exactly how I expected this to go."

"I bet you never expected you'd be living with me and buying me jewelry either," she said. She looked pointedly at the box and smiled up at him.

He felt his mouth pull into an answering smile. He could feel the warmth radiating from her, his own private sun.

He knew damn well what her answer would be.

Derek flicked the box open. She gasped, her eyes widening when she saw the two-karat square-cut emerald set in a platinum band.

"It's gorgeous," she breathed.

"Yeah, I figured a diamond would be inappropriate. And besides, this matches your eyes."

Her eyes were wet with tears when they lifted to his, and he felt an answering tightness in his throat. *For fuck's sake. For thirty-two years you're the iceman, and now she's got you crying like a girl.*

Derek wished he'd had more time to prepare himself, to plan some elaborate speech that would tell her how she made him feel, how she'd brought him to life, how much he worshipped the ground under the soles of her size-six feet.

But right now, with her staring him in the face, her heart in her eyes, all he could choke out was, "I love you. Please marry me."

She hurled herself at him, squealing and crying as her arms and legs wrapped around him and pulled him close.

"I'll take that as a yes?"

"Yes"—both a sob and a laugh. She covered his face in kisses as he carried her down the hall.

"Good. Now let's seal the deal and make it official."

He had them naked in seconds, ignoring her protest that she was grubby from the plane. "We'll shower after," he said, his breath speeding up like it always did at the sight of her, naked and hot for him on their bed.

Their bed. Where they would sleep and make love and make their babies when the time was right.

He closed his eyes to cover the burn of tears as he fit himself against her, slid into the slick heat of her body.

She arched to take him deep, having no shame about her own emotions as tears leaked from her eyes and her breath came in little sobs. He barely got inside her before she came, shaking around him.

He was right behind her, coming with a speed and intensity that would have been embarrassing if she hadn't been even quicker on the trigger.

"I love you so much," Alyssa whispered. "You have no idea how much." She stroked his back, holding him on top of her, inside her, when he would have rolled aside. "You're never going to leave me, are you? Promise you won't stop loving me." He could still see it, the fear of rejection, the fear she'd given her love to someone who was going to use it all up and throw it back in her face.

Derek understood. And he would make it his mission to wipe that fear from her eyes, even if it took the rest of his life. "I promise. I've got you now, and I'm never going to let you go."